The Ultimate Dragon

MATTHEW WOLVERINE'S SCOTLAND

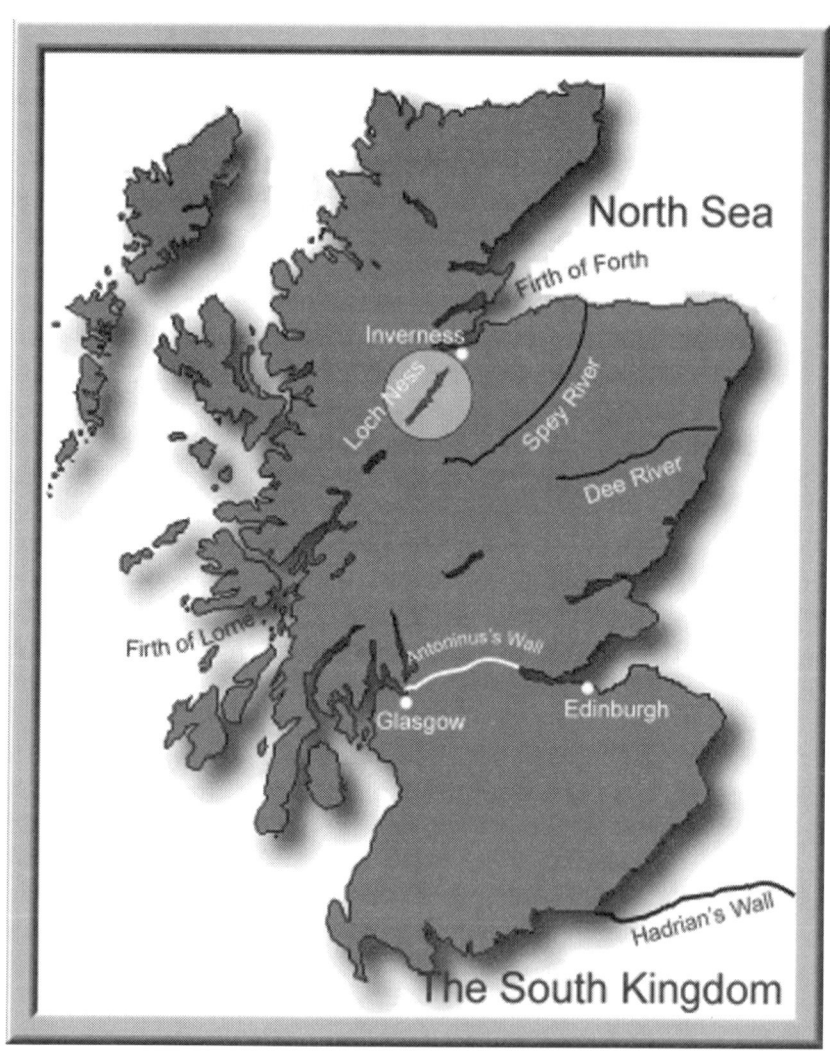

1st edition to Amanda
Sweet dreams always!
6/9/02

THE ULTIMATE DRAGON

a novel by
Daniel N. Jason

Daniel N Jason

TimeDancer Press
Houston, Texas

The Ultimate Dragon
© 2001 by Daniel N. Jason
All rights reserved
TimeDancer Press
ISBN 0-9659470-2-5

No part of this work may be reproduced or distributed by any means without the express written permission of the publisher.

This is a work of fiction. While some similarities may exist between characters, events, and locations within the story and actual persons, places, and circumstances, the reader is advised that extensive liberties were taken during the creative process, and these similarities are purely coincidental. To those who might take issue with any similarities or incongruities herein, the publisher suggests that they get a grip.

Printed with the assistance of Brockton Publishing Company.

Chis Book is Dedicated to . . .

*. . . the Scotland of myth and history —
    may God bless you as you make your way
        on your long march to freedom*

and . . .

*the soldiers through the centuries
    who have fought for freedom —
        may humanity someday outgrow the need for war*

and, most of all . . .

*the God who created
    a world of mysteries and possibilities —
        a world in which strange and wonderful creatures
            swim in deep waters,
                love turns up in the most unlikely times and places,
                    and evidence of grace is everywhere.*

ACKNOWLEDGMENTS

I would like to thank . . .

My beloved granddad, David McRoberts, who taught me Scottish honor and love for the clan.

First Cavalry Vietnam, for teaching me to survive under any circumstances.

Kathy Lewis, who listened to all my complaining and gave me sympathy.

Casanova, my Golden Retriever puppy, who inspired the wolf pup scenes, and who relieves me of all those unnecessary pairs of shoes.

UltraFuel™ by Twinlab® for helping me run faster marathons.

Leo Fortuno and Elie Chevli for the spellbinding cover design for this book.

My God, for giving me a vibrant imagination . . . endurance to reach any goal . . . and dyslexia.

*The ultimate dragon
is within you...*
    Joseph Campbell

*The dragon is fierce when raised,
and so must we be,
lest the dragon
control our lives.*
    Daniel Jason

Reproach has broken my heart, and I am so sick. And I looked for sympathy, but there was none. And for comforters, but found none.

— Psalm 69:20

Chapter 1

Matthew stared out the window, only half listening as the speaker's words droned in his ears. To himself he thought, *This jerk is so full of his own self-importance, he has no idea what's about to happen to him.* The jerk in question had made the unfortunate mistake of allowing his ego to guide him in his negotiations, and he was about to learn that, with Matthew Wolverine, such sloppiness meant death, at least where business was concerned.

Matthew was certain of the outcome of this latest deal; he had sat across too many negotiating tables with this same kind of blowhard. He could predict the man's words almost as if he had a script in front of him. His mind wandered to the voice-mail message his wife had left this morning. "Hi, Matt. It's Cate, of course. Rachel is looking forward to you coming to her birthday party at 3 P.M. and I have a real surprise for you tonight. Don't you dare be late this time. She still hasn't forgiven you for missing her last birthday, and the one before that, so you'd better be here for this one."

Imagining Cate's smiling face, Matthew thought of the surprise he would have for *her.* With this deal finished, and their portfolio fattened to the tune of seven million dollars, he would take her on the trip they had so often talked about. She had always wanted the two of them to see Paris together, but the constant pressure of keeping up with his empire had repeatedly pushed the trip a little beyond their grasp. He had always felt that he had almost enough, yet was driven incessantly to acquire just a little more. Well, beginning today, that would no longer be the case. As the voice on the other end of the table continued to drone on, Matthew thought, *Another ten minutes, and we're finished, even if the idiot doesn't know it.*

And then, Matthew could return to the beautiful woman who had married him twenty years before, and to the daughter who had heard too many excuses, celebrated too many birthdays without her

1

father around. A quick flight to Houston, a thirty-minute ride home, and he would give them the news that would dissolve their anger — and, of course, he would find out what Cate's big surprise was.

Then he heard the words he'd been waiting for. "Yes, Matthew, I think we've got a winner here. I'll sign the contract." Matthew's heart raced. All he had to do now was forward the contract to legal, with his notes attached, and Meridien Steel would be his. The images of his wife and daughter faded as he tasted that familiar rush of adrenaline. It was kill time! Not so intense as the feeling he remembered from so many lifetimes ago, in the jungles and villages of his own private hell, but not so different, either. Even now, his mouth went dry with the metallic taste, and he felt his heart pounding intensely. Ecstasy and anguish came in waves, interwoven with the rush that he hated, yet lived for. God, he needed a drink.

Two quick scotches later, he left for the limo that waited to take him to the airport. Sitting smugly enmeshed in his own thoughts, he was startled by the annoying chirp of his cell phone. Only two people had this number: Cate, and his secretary, Claire. He didn't want to spoil the surprise; he wanted to see his wife's face when he told her, so he was relieved when the caller ID showed him it was Claire calling.

"Yeah, Claire. What's up? I just finished the Meridien deal, and I'm on my way to the airport now. Gotta get home ASAP; hell, she's probably mad as a wet hen already. I was supposed to be back hours ago for some surprise."

There was silence on the other end of the line — unusual for Claire, who was normally like a machine gun with her information. "Matthew, I wanted to catch you before you saw the news on TV. It's Caitlin and Rachel. There's… there's been an accident. I guess they lost control of the car in the rain. No, I don't know where they were headed… they were on I-10, heading west, just this side of Katy. I'm so sorry, Matthew. They were both killed instantly."

Matthew sat, silenced by Claire's words. It wasn't real; it was happening to someone else. It wasn't so much that he was denying the reality of the situation as that it simply wasn't sinking in. He hung up without saying anything. The ride to the airport, as well as the flight to Houston, passed in a haze. Matthew tried to focus on the details of the Meridien deal, but his thoughts were constantly overtaken by images of Caitlin and Rachel, lifeless in Cate's Volvo. Even the double scotch the attendant brought him failed to blur those images.

Daniel N. Jason

Picking up his car at the long-term lot, he navigated the freeways he knew so well, yet they felt different, foreign this evening. The city, fresh-washed by the storm, still seemed clean and new. Houston's familiar skyline, with its muted shades of dusty rose and sea green and slate blue, greeted him as he neared his exit. He usually felt a surge of excitement at that sight — this view of Houston had always put him in mind of Oz and Valhalla and Shangri-La all in one — but tonight there was a pall over the city.

As Matthew pulled into his own driveway, he was struck by the darkness; there were no lights twinkling in the windows to greet him. Once inside, the eeriness was even more oppressive. Some part of his being registered the streamers hanging from the walls and chandelier...the bright blue "Happy Birthday" signs tacked to every wall...and everywhere, seeping from the very pores of his home, the silence. It was a silence such as this house had never known. The house had always been filled with sounds, from the rambunctiousness surrounding the presence of a pre-adolescent girl, and from the sexual tension between two dynamic adults, who, despite the fact that their marriage was teetering on the brink of disaster, were still very much in love.

But on this night...no sounds at all, except for the grandfather clock ominously ticking away in the shadowed hall outside his and Cate's bedroom.

Even the supple leather of his favorite chair seemed strange to Matthew tonight. The envelope on the chair-side table caught his eye. "Must be a bill Cate forgot to file," he mumbled. But on the front, there was one word: *Matthew*. Perhaps the envelope held the answers, or even the key to unlock this dream in which he was imprisoned. He opened the envelope and began reading.

Matthew,
Well, it's happened again. Rachel is upstairs, crying her eyes out. She says she hates you, and right now, I can't honestly give her any reason not to. You PROMISED you'd be here for her party, and once again, you broke your promise.

Matthew, you know I love you. I wouldn't have stuck around all these years, spent so many anniversaries alone, if I didn't. But I've come to realize that sometimes, love just isn't enough. Not for me, not for Rachel, and apparently not for you, either. You kept telling us that you were doing everything for us, building a future for our family. But you never could seem to understand that the "future" you were building would be filled with memories of disappointment. We didn't need all the damned

3

money you were trying to make. We needed YOU, and you were just never around.

The saddest part about all this is the surprise I had for you. You see, I'm 21 weeks pregnant. I didn't want to tell you until now, because I wanted to wait until Rachel's birthday and surprise both of you. I went to see Dr. Withers this afternoon, and he did an ultrasound that showed that it's a boy. You've wanted a son for so long. Well, your wish has come true, and you aren't even around to know it.

I sat here and had to face some hard facts. As much as you say you love me and Rachel, you're never here for us. We both have more bitter memories of you than happy ones, and I had to ask myself if those were the kind of memories I wanted our son to grow up with. I want him to be a happy child. I want him to learn to trust. And I want Rachel to learn that trust, as well. You haven't seen the cynicism that she's built up. I have, and I don't want our son to grow up that way. And, damn it, I want to learn to trust again, too.

I don't know what it will take to make you happy, Matt, but apparently it's not me, it's not a family. I honestly don't know what I want to do, but for now, I'm going to Mom's in Columbus. Please don't call me or come out. I need some time to think, and I don't want you making it more difficult for me, or for Rachel. I'll call you when I get there, to let you know we made it okay, but I really don't want to get into anything just now. If you really love us, you'll give us this time. Maybe you'll take some time to think about what's really important to you, as well. Maybe you'll even give yourself a chance to get rid of all those ghosts that haunt you. I want you, I want all of us, to be happy, Matthew. And with the way things have been for a long time, happiness seems like an unreachable goal.

Please don't be angry with me. This is the only way I can think of to begin to fix things. If we're lucky, and we all try real hard, maybe we can find some kind of 'happily ever after' that all four of us (our son included) can share. Keep us in your prayers. I will be praying for all of us.

Cate

Matthew read the letter over and over, trying to hear Cate's words as he read. He eventually lost count of how many times, and of how many scotches he downed as he read. Finally, after God only knew how many hours, the letter slipped from his hands, and he passed out in his chair. His last conscious thought was to wonder why he could never shed tears, even now. Mercifully, then, there was blackness, and temporary release from his waking nightmare.

Daniel N. Jason

* * *

The next few days brought an endless stream of visits from the people who had known and loved Cate. So many of them knew little things about her, intimate things, and yet most of these people were strangers to Matthew. How could she have so many people close to her that he wasn't even aware of? Had he really been that separated from her life? Mechanically he embraced the flow of strangers, and of family that he hardly knew. Strange how they all seemed to know that Cate was pregnant. He asked one of Cate's friends how she knew. She responded with an incredulous, "Because she was starting to show." There were no outward accusations from these friends, but Matthew could see the condemnation in their eyes.

A lovely but simple memorial service was held at a little church near Columbus, a small town west of Houston. Not one of Matthew's business associates showed up, not even the ones who had known Cate and had been frequent guests at Cate's and Matthew's dinner parties. "They must be off cutting deals," he thought. Yet he felt no outrage, no hurt at their absence, only numbness. And no tears would come.

Not even music could release his emotions, neither when the soloist sang "How Great Thou Art" during the church service, nor when the bagpipe band played "Amazing Grace" and "Abide With Me" at the graveside. Watching his daughter's small casket being lowered into the ground shattered something in Matthew, but even then he could not summon tears. He left the funeral without speaking to anyone.

It was a glorious spring day, but he scarcely noticed. At this time of year the bluebonnets would normally have been in full bloom in the fields around the little town. Cate had always loved bluebonnets, the state flower of Texas, and Matthew liked them too. But this had not been a good year for the wildflowers — the temperature and rainfall had been all wrong — and the fields, instead of being overrun with stunning sapphire blossoms, bore only a smattering of pale blue. It was as if the very earth had lost its heart for yielding beauty.

Back at the home of his mother-in-law, Glenna, Matthew found Glenna waiting for him. Now the conversation he most dreaded was right before him.

"Matthew, I know what was in Caitlin's mind and heart that night. She loved you so much, and she wanted to shock you into giving her and Rachel what they needed so badly. I'm certain she'd not have gone if she had known what would happen. But that doesn't matter now, not really. First, there are decisions to be made, and things that must be done.

5

"You know that it was Caitlin's wish that, when she died, she would be cremated, and her ashes scattered to the winds on Carn Mhic." Matthew recognized the name of a hill in the Scottish Highlands, where Cate had been born and had spent her early childhood.

In her soft Scottish brogue Glenna continued, "I've marked this map of Scotland, and written directions how to get there from Glasgow. This is so very important; the Carn was her special place when she was a child. I can't make the trip; I don't think my heart would take it, so it's up to you. Will you do this for her?"

It was obvious that there would be no arguing with the old woman, even if he hadn't agreed with her, and hadn't known full well what Cate had wanted. Matthew had failed his wife in life, but he would keep to her wishes in death. "Of course I'll go, I'll leave on Saturday. I'll have my secretary reserve my flight right away."

Glenna continued, her voice more gentle now. "I know what Caitlin wanted, but she never considered the possibility of having to make this kind of decision about Rachel. I don't think I could bear not being able to visit her grave, and even if she and her mother are laid to rest in different parts of the world, they'll still be together in spirit. I'm relieved you chose to bury Rachel someplace close by. That way, you can visit her grave, too, if you wish."

Despite her gentle voice, Matthew felt the judgment in Glenna's words. She had known her daughter's frustration for a long time, and probably blamed Matthew for Caitlin's death, at least to some extent. And why shouldn't she? If he'd been a better husband… He quickly brushed aside these thoughts, answering, "Yes, I thought it fitting to take her to that little cemetery near your church. She always loved the forests around here."

That night Matthew drove back to Houston, still numb but focused now upon the tasks before him. In his absence, Claire would coordinate with the folks at legal, and the Meridien deal would be closed without his further participation. Wandering through the house, he found every available excuse for not going through Cate's things. There were letters to be written to people he'd never heard of, yet who were expecting responses from Cate. How would he tell these distant strangers that she was gone? What should he share with them, when he had no clue as to what they had known of his wife? He put these tasks off; they would have to wait until his return from Scotland. He found he couldn't even bring himself to open her desk drawer, because then he would have to face the minutiae of his wife's mind in those days and weeks before.

The grandfather clock in the hall chimed the late hour, reverberating through the otherwise silent house, and still no tears came from Matthew Wolverine.

* * *

Houston Intercontinental Airport was unusually busy for a Saturday morning. Matthew was accustomed to being part of the crush of businessmen catching a redeye flight, but this was different. The other passengers awaiting international flights seemed more jovial, more relaxed than did his usual fellow travelers. The place seemed overrun with Scotsmen and people who were obviously of Scottish ancestry — unusual, really, even for a flight to Scotland — and they all seemed to be celebrating something. Standing in line to check his luggage, Matthew asked a red-faced gentleman in front of him, "What's all the hubbub about?"

"Ha'n't ye read the headlines, m'boy?" the man roared, trying to be heard over the noise of the crowd. He was only partially successful, but Matthew got the gist of it: "…latest election in Scotland… overwhelming… one step closer to true independence!" Then the man, apparently spotting a friend up ahead, pushed his way through the crowd and was gone.

Matthew remembered reading about a referendum in Scotland a couple of years before. Sometime back in 1997, if his memory served him, the Scots had voted overwhelmingly to form their own legislature. Subsequent elections and referenda had brought them ever closer to their centuries-long dream of independence from Britain. Cate had always kept up with these things more than he did, although Matthew, too, was of Scottish ancestry. Whatever this latest development was had apparently sent the Scots over the edge into nonstop party mode.

As he settled into the couch in the first-class lounge, Matthew ordered his typical scotch without even thinking about it. *Here's to the Scots*, he thought when it arrived. *Long may they… WE… be free.* He lifted the glass as if making a toast, and then he lowered it. He held it in his hand, weighing it, eyeing the bronze-colored liquid, and then put it down on the table. For some reason, he had no desire for a drink right now, even as he thought to himself how badly he needed one.

He sat in silence, observing the other passengers who were awaiting the same flight. His emptiness was touched only by a feeling of anger at these people, bitterness and resentment for the lives they enjoyed. Especially those audacious Scotsmen; how could they be so raucous and joyful in the presence of Matthew Wolverine, whose entire world had caved in?

For all the money he had amassed, for all the power he wielded, he realized that he had nothing worth as much as the most fleeting of smiles that crossed the faces of these strangers, and he hated them for it.

After an hour or so, the boarding call came for his flight, and Matthew settled gratefully into the relative seclusion of his first-class seat. Refusing an offered drink – a first for him – he settled in to study the map and directions Glenna had given him. He half-watched the movies being played until he fell into a restless sleep, fitful, but unavoidable. It was the first real sleep he had known since that first night.

*** * * ***

The airport in Glasgow was, to outward appearances, marginally different from dozens of others Matthew had seen, yet it was filled with the same energy he knew so well. He could read the faces of the passengers, tell their life story from the little things about them. Students, arriving on exchange programs, beaming with the excitement reserved for the young. Business men and women, in a hurry to handle critical details…fools, caught up in the same meaningless trivia he had lived for so long. Lovers, flying into each other's arms after an eternity apart, or sadly parting, seeking separate chapters of their lives. And the whole place was awash in manic waves of celebration that made the fuss at the Houston airport seem like a Quaker meeting by comparison. Joy resonated through the Glasgow airport, spilling out into the cities and villages and the green distant hills. From out on the streets came the sound of horns honking and people screaming loud cheers of freedom. Cops were everywhere, supposedly to contain the rapturous mobs, but they seemed to be in every bit as much of a partying mood as the civilians. There was no escaping the sense of jubilation. From every corner the cry came, like a hymn, like an anthem: "Scotland… is… free!"

But Matthew could not share in this joy. Like a condemned man, he felt as if he would never be free again.

*** * * ***

The rental car was nice enough — a new Jaguar. He'd have to get used to the right-hand steering wheel; no matter how many times he used such an arrangement, it always seemed completely alien to him. At least now, it was no more foreign than anything else he was experiencing. Traffic in Glasgow was hectic, so Matthew was relieved to leave the city as he headed north into the Highlands. The ever-present rain made the narrow roads more difficult to navigate, but he actually found himself enjoying the drive.

After a time, he began winding through low mountain forests in an area that, were it not for the road itself, he would think no other humans had ever visited. As he rounded a curve, the Jag sputtered twice, and promptly died. "Damn! I thought things like this were all in the past." He remembered the MG he had driven as a student in college, and its propensity for simply quitting for no apparent reason, only to spring to life again, hours later. He tried all the old tricks he had used so long ago to urge dead cars to life, but to no avail.

Finally, he gave up, and got out to search for a farmhouse, or anyplace else that might have a phone. "Better take this knapsack with me," he thought. It would be too tempting a target for any thieves who might come upon his crippled car. He was not so concerned about his personal gear as about the urn which held Cate's ashes. And it wouldn't do for him to have to explain the theft of his .44. The authorities weren't too forgiving about smuggling firearms into the country. He had checked his knapsack in Houston, but hadn't declared the weapon once he arrived in Scotland, and he knew the Scottish authorities could have been a real problem if he'd gotten caught. In fact, it was a miracle he hadn't been stopped at the Glasgow airport. Then again, those Scots were all so intoxicated on freedom right now that he probably could have smuggled a bull elephant into the country.

He thought about the pistol, and couldn't stop the thought that came next. *If all else fails, there is still a way out of this hell.* He forced his thoughts away from that dismal track. If there was one thing Matthew Wolverine was not, and had never been, it was suicidal. Suicide was a mark of despair, and he was beyond despair; he just felt numb. Truth to tell, he didn't care much, one way or the other, if he lived or died. All he knew right now was that he had to push on at least long enough to make good on his promise to Glenna and Cate. After that, well…

* * *

Matthew had been walking in the wet darkness for less than a mile when he spotted the old church. It looked as if it was sorely in need of repair, but to him, it was a beautiful sight. As he drew nearer, he saw that it was not just in need of repair; it was abandoned, its massive wooden door ajar, hanging precariously on one rusted hinge. "Well, at least I can get out of this rain for awhile. Probably won't hurt to spend the night here, and maybe I'll see something promising in the daylight."

As he passed through the tattered doorway, he felt something he couldn't quite describe. Was it warm in these ruins, or was he just shielded from the wind? He dug for the small flashlight in his pack, found his laser pointer instead, and chuckled at its uselessness. Finding the flashlight, he switched it on, scanning the massive hall for any sign of recent occupation. There was none. Then, at the front of the room, his eyes caught what seemed to be a faint glow. As he drew nearer, he saw a massive stone cross, smooth and polished, in contrast with the rubble elsewhere in the church. He felt somehow drawn to it, telling himself he was curious about this perfect object standing amid the ruins.

When he finally reached the cross, he suddenly felt the rush of feelings he had avoided these last few days — the desperation, the loneliness, and the remorse he had not allowed himself to feel. He knelt on the ground, studied the beautiful design that had been carved into the stone, and wondered at the strange symbol in the center of the cross. It was shaped somewhat like a dinosaur head, or maybe that Loch Ness creature in those fuzzy photos he'd seen in the tabloids. But he quickly forgot these thoughts and found himself, for the first time in years, talking to a God he had long ignored — asking for answers, begging for release from the pain that now filled him. He laid his head against the stone cross, marveling at its softness and warmth, where it should have been cold and hard. And, for the first time in long memory, Matthew Wolverine wept, with the passion and abandon he had never known. "God, I wish Cate could see me now. I wish she could have known the love I feel for her. I wish…"

His words dissolved into sobs, his thoughts into pure sadness. Without thinking the words, he wished for death to take his pain away, and allow him a moment more with his wife and daughter. As if nourished by his tears, the stone of the cross grew even warmer and softer, until it felt like a gentle hand, caressing the head of a weeping child. Then he noticed a subtle glow, and saw that a light was coming from the cross. The light grew steadily brighter as its caress seemed to envelop Matthew.

And then he felt as if his body was moving into the cross… *through* the cross, as if through a doorway, and into a distant light that was brighter than any he had ever seen. Intuitively he realized the darkness that had covered his heart could not go through the portal with him. That darkness was gone, replaced by peace and something that felt strangely like joy. *I've heard about this sort of thing,* he thought, but at once the thought dissolved, and then all thought dissolved, leaving him only with the capacity to feel. Along with the sense of immense peace came something else: the thrill of flying. After a moment of disorientation Matthew gave himself up to the sheer unadulterated exhilaration of flight, his body tingling as he jetted through space. This was like skydiving, but he was moving horizontally, not vertically. He stretched his arms, becoming a flying cross himself, to increase the speed and his enjoyment. If he was dying, well so be it. Surely this light, this peace, this joy meant that God had forgiven him.

Without warning his flight accelerated, the feeling of exhilaration giving way to nausea. Matthew closed his eyes against the waves of sickness, but to no avail. Then he landed hard on his back in… grass. Grass? What the…? With his eyes still closed, Matthew clutched a hand full of the stuff and wondered why Heaven had grass. If he even *was* in Heaven.

That was the last thought he had before he passed out cold.

The Ultimate Dragon

CHAPTER 2

Matthew awakened to the sound of songbirds. Opening his eyes, he squinted before the glare of new morning sunlight. He was surprised to find himself right outside the old church where he'd sought shelter the night before, and even more surprised to find the doorway intact, the heavy door flung wide, yet hanging solidly on both its heavy iron hinges. The church itself was immaculate. He wondered how someone could have stolen in during the night and repaired the ancient place without waking him. There wasn't even a speck of dust to be seen. The only thing unchanged was the massive cross itself, whose soft glow and odd-looking dinosaur-head symbol he could see within the shadowy depths of the church. He stood, expecting to feel stiff and heavy, but found that he was as limber as a twenty-year old, and, strangely, he felt little of the sadness of the night before.

Then he thought about last night. Boy, that was some hallucination he'd had — well, it couldn't have been real, could it? — because here he was! Maybe someone had sneaked some sort of drug in that drink he'd had while waiting for his rental car. Strange, though, that he didn't have any sort of a hangover…

He began to walk, trying to find his car, and was stunned at what met his eyes. Roses bloomed everywhere, and shrubs now lined the path to… the ROAD! Where was the paved road he had walked upon? All he saw before him now was a well trodden path through the forest. What had happened? Where was he, and how had he gotten there? Amid the incredible beauty of this place, Matthew was filled with only panic and confusion. And then he heard a voice behind him.

"Who are you, stranger? You look strange to me, and I know every clan for miles around."

Matthew wheeled around, and was struck with the image of a stout monk, short, yet proud looking. He was clothed in the kind of cassock Matthew had only seen in movies and old paintings. The monk smiled, revealing several gaps where teeth had once been.

13

It took Matthew a moment to realize that the monk had spoken to him not in English, but in Gaelic. Matthew had a working knowledge of Gaelic, both the Irish and Scottish varieties, partly due to Cate's influence, and partly because he had a native love of languages. Learning languages had long been a hobby of sorts for him. Besides Gaelic, he had taught himself Spanish, Italian, German, French and…in another life, a life that gave him no pleasure to remember, he had picked up more than a passing acquaintance with Vietnamese.

So he decided to play along with the monk, although he knew that the people in these parts spoke English too. In his best Gaelic he replied, "My name is Matthew Wolverine, and I flew in from Houston just last night."

The smile quickly faded from the monk's face, replaced with a look of suspicion. "Flew, you say? And would you then have been a bird of an evening, and a man by day? And what is this 'Hewston' you speak of? Is it off to the south, beyond the mountain? You get stranger and stranger, and I'm not so sure I like the looks of you overmuch, the closer I look."

Matthew stumbled over his words, unsure of what to say, and completely confused by this genial monk's sudden turn. He wondered if there was really anyone so isolated as to not have heard of Houston. And what was all this talk about being a bird?

As Matthew stood there grasping for the right Gaelic phrase, a look of terror and then wonder passed over the monk's face, and he made the sign of the cross. He looked to the sky and muttered, "Father in Heaven, it must be a sign of the End Times! The new Millennium is at hand; can Our Lord be far behind?" He looked at Matthew. "And you, Stranger, would you be a herald of the Second Coming, or would you be a messenger of the Prince of Darkness?"

Inwardly Matthew groaned. Even in this isolated place, millennial fever had apparently made its mark. He was sick to death of hearing about it — not just that ridiculous flap over the Y2K bug, but all of the news media reports about fanatical millennial groups — the "End-Timers" and their ilk — converging in Jerusalem and Rome and other spots throughout the world. Judging from the evidence before him, even the Scottish Highlands weren't immune. Sheesh.

Matthew held up his hands and said, "I am neither the Lord of Light nor the Prince of Darkness. I am just a tourist." The monk stared at him blankly.

Then he thought it might be wise to appeal to the man's religious bent, so he said, "But I am a man of faith nonetheless." As he said those words, he realized with a start that they were true. There was something about that experience last night that had pierced him to his very core.

He was still fairly convinced it was a hallucination, but he could not get it out of his mind.

He reached then into his pack and brought out the urn with Cate's ashes. He would explain his mission, and the monk would have to understand. "I just flew over to release my wife's ashes, according to her desires. My car broke down about a mile up the road, and I started walking to find a phone. This abandoned church is the first place I found."

Apparently, the monk wasn't comforted by Matthew's explanation. "First of all, stranger, I've been up and back on the road this morning for quite a long piece, and saw no carriage or tracks, and no horses running loose, either. And all this talk about flying, and wife-burning, it's not sitting too well. And what's that you've got pinned to your tunic there?"

Matthew tried to explain. "To begin with, there wouldn't be any horses, because I came by car. Secondly, don't any of the people around here ever fly? It's not that far to the airport, after all. And, to answer your question, this is a laser pointer in my pocket. I use it for presentations. Surely, you've seen one before."

At that, Matthew pulled the pointer from his pocket, pointed it at the monk's hand, and pressed the button. The monk recoiled when he saw the red dot on his hand, as if it were a snake.

"Begone with you, demon. You carry the eye of the devil in your hand. I've no doubt you flew here last eve, probably on a bat's wings. And don't be bringing that vessel closer to me, for I know now that it holds a demon as well. Now take yourself from this place, and bother no other folk in your passing. I command you in the name of God, begone!"

Then the monk pulled a short, broad sword from beneath his cassock, and raised it toward Matthew, who grabbed his knapsack and ran back up the path. "Lord, get me away from this nut. Just let me find the Jag where I left it. With any luck, it'll start right up, and I can tend to my business and go home."

Even as he reached the path, Matthew realized that more was amiss than a mysteriously repaired ruin and a crazy old monk. First of all, there was the path, where the road had been. It wound through the forest the same as he remembered, but was now merely a set of well-worn ruts, as if cut by the narrow wheels of a cart. And it seemed that the trees were different as well. Where was that huge old oak he'd seen when he first came on the grounds of the church? There wasn't even a stump to mark its place. Had someone carried him from the ruins in his sleep, without even waking him? Granted, he'd been exhausted, but…

And what about the cross? Surely there couldn't be two identical crosses, even in all of Scotland. That symbol in its center was so unusual. These thoughts filled his mind as he walked on. After several miles, he was stopped in his tracks by the sight of a mountain shaped like a goat's head. He had seen this very mountain the night before. So he was, indeed, in the same place. Yet so much had changed.

And everything was so quiet, so still.

The stillness was broken suddenly by an outcry in the distance. It sounded as if a fight was breaking out. Running forward, hoping to see something familiar – even if it was battle, Matthew came upon a group of about twenty men. They were standing in a circle, egging on two opponents engaged in an all-too-familiar sight: a fight to the death. Though these men were dressed like extras in an old movie, and not in the black pajamas of Viet Cong, the scene was the same. The two men were engaged in the crude parry and thrust of broadblade against shield, while the onlookers stood at the ready, waiting to finish the enemy, should their leader be felled.

As Matthew came closer, the larger man knocked the sword from his opponent's hand and moved in for the kill. The other man, bested, knelt on the ground before his enemy, and glared up at him with eyes steeled to death. Matthew knew that look: vanquished, yet not defeated, and facing certain death with an honor and dignity surpassing that of his enemy. Matthew knew instinctively that such bravery must be defended, and not allowed to die at the hands of a leering coward whose only superiority was in his size. He rushed forward, yelling at the top of his lungs.

The victor turned his attention to Matthew, who, though much taller, was not nearly as broad as he. The warrior grinned as he raised his broadsword to strike Matthew down. Matthew wheeled to the side, the swordsman's blow falling wide, harmlessly to the ground. A swift strike from Matthew's foot found the man's throat, crushing his windpipe. As the stunned warrior fell to his knees, Matthew wrenched his sword from his hands, and, in an instant, swung the blade, severing the man's head. The fallen warrior's companions ran forward, but Matthew was prepared for the attack. He sprang to his feet, bracing himself for what he knew was to come. Perhaps this was how his anguish was to be eased: to be hewn by a fallen warrior's kinsmen, a world away from the life he knew.

Then, a shout arose from the circle: "Be still! This man has bested the finest among us. Is it not our law that he be allowed to live, and to lay claim to old Damian's property?" A hush fell over the clearing, followed by whispers that rose to more shouting.

These people were speaking Gaelic too, Matthew noticed. Maybe, in the spirit of celebrating Scottish independence, there was some stigma about speaking English in these parts. Well, if you asked Matthew, they were going a little bit too far with this independence-from-Britain thing.

But something told him he'd better continue to play along, even though his puzzlement was growing by the moment.

As he rose from his crouched stance, Matthew was finally getting the chance to think about what had been happening to him this morning. Why had a gentle – if somewhat crazy – old monk come after him, brandishing a *sword*? How on God's green earth had he gotten himself caught up in a fight to the death between men he had never seen before? And what was the story on this ragtag group of swordsmen, anyway? Were they members of some strange cult, or fugitives from a Renaissance Festival somewhere? Why else would they be dressed like that, and using swords? Hell, even the poorest street punk had a pistol nowadays, and these were no street punks. He wasn't sure what they were. Whatever they were, though, it was apparent they were bound to some code of honor, and that code had just saved Matthew's life. Thinking quickly, he decided to play out whatever his part might be in this strange gathering.

Bending down, he removed a dagger from the dead leader's belt and placed it in his own belt. Then he pulled the man's sword from his lifeless fingers and said, in clear strong Gaelic, "My name is Matthew Wolverine, and I honor this man, though I have vanquished him. I accept that which he bequeaths me in death, and ask that the hatred which put his hand to sword be allowed to die with him." Again, the circle of warriors grew silent.

Then one of the fallen man's kinsmen spoke up, addressing the group. "Damian was my cousin, and my friend, and I will mourn his death. But this feud was between him and Robert over there. Now, Damian's sword has passed to this Matthew, and it be his choice to carry on the fight or lay aside his sword. If he chooses to end it here, then we, too, must sheath our blades."

The man Robert then arose and came forward, as well. "But for this Matthew, my wife would be a widow this night, and my children without a father. True enough, the fight was between Damian and myself, for Damian committed a wrong against me that I will have to struggle long and hard to forgive. But I have no desire for my life to be ruled by hatred. Damian is dead now, and if Damian's clan can put the war aside, I can do naught but join them in this new peace. Let us unite our clans this day. It could very well be that Matthew Wolverine was sent to us from God, to help us make peace with each other and prepare for the End Times."

Oh, boy, there it is again, more Y2K nonsense, Matthew thought. But he stood up straight, folding his arms and looking as authoritative as he possibly could, considering that he had no earthly idea what he was doing here with these lunatics. He listened as Robert continued.

"Perchance, standing at each other's side instead of at each other's throat, we can finally be freed from the terror of the water that has haunted all of us since time beyond memory. I say that our clans be joined this day, kinsmen in a new clan. It shall be called Wolverine!"

At Robert's words, both clans raised their voices and swords, and proclaimed their allegiance to the new clan Wolverine. The strongest warriors from each side stepped forward, and laid their swords before Matthew. He smiled, touched each one as it was offered, and placed its hilt back in the warrior's hand. To a man, they thought this as strange as Matthew himself. Then he spoke.

"I am here, not to rule your clan, but to follow my own quest," Matthew began. "If it is your desire to follow my will, then join your clans in peace, not as followers of the strongest one, but as leaders in a shared wisdom. Let the strongest voice among you not be a man with the greatest might, but rather with the greatest heart. Our God has given us brains to use, not to offer up to another man. Use those brains, and be free. And for myself, let me but linger in your midst, and share your table as I seek my own destiny. In exchange, I will offer you what knowledge I have, and will teach you how to protect the freedom you embrace this day." He was really starting to get into this role-playing. All those years he had attended the Renaissance Festival — quaffing ale and eating turkey legs, and participating in mock jousts with those strange folk who were lifetime members of the Society for Creative Anachronisms — had paid off.

Well, maybe. He looked at the faces of the warriors, and saw not approval but confusion. It hit him again that this was not a game to them. This was real. A man had died here, and by Matthew's own hand — a man who had been their leader, and they desperately sought someone to take his place. They were mumbling amongst themselves, and he could tell they were unsure of how to react to the lofty speech he had just made. They obviously understood him, so it wasn't his Gaelic that confused them. It dawned on him then that they were befuddled not by his language, but by the ideas he had expressed. Apparently these men had never so much as considered the notion that they had free will.

So he decided to set aside his noble speech, and find some better way to fit into his new role. After all, leaders who weren't trusted didn't live very long. Matthew had learned that lesson very well in Vietnam. He began again.

"There are many things that I find bewildering in this place, and I would learn much from you, as well. I will lead you, then, if you will but help me to know your ways. You speak of some terror of the water. What is this terror of which you speak? And is that the water you speak of, there beyond these trees? What body of water would that be?"

Robert looked upon Matthew as one would look upon any fool, asking a stupid question. "Are you daft, man? Even children know that is Loch Ness. And even the most wee ones know that the terror is the Loch Ness Monster."

Matthew registered the information but did not respond to it. Instead he returned Robert's stare, anger quickening in his aquamarine eyes, his features hardening. "If not for me, you would have died a slow death by the hand of your enemy. You will give me the respect I deserve, or you will die by my hand now."

Robert was stunned by Matthew's sudden turn, and found himself shaking. Brave man though he was, to face death twice within an hour unnerved him. His faltering hand reached toward Matthew as he said, "I am Robert Roybridge, friend of Matthew Wolverine, and I beg your forgiveness for my rash words."

The threat in Matthew's eyes was instantly replaced with the warmth of his broad Texas smile. Robert's shoulders relaxed as Matthew took his hand. "Robert, we shall be close friends."

"Praise be to Our Lord," said Robert. Then he turned around to the others and declared, "Now let it be known among all men here, that this hour, this day, in this Year of Our Lord 999, Robert Roybridge seals his friendship with Matthew Wolverine."

Matthew stopped him short. "What year did you say it is, Robert?"

Robert's eyes narrowed once more, and his brow tightened. Was Matthew Wolverine testing him? "It is 999 Anno Domini."

"You mean 1999, of course."

Robert looked at him, utterly appalled. "Begging your pardon, Matthew, and with all due respect, but the year is Nine-hundred and ninety-nine, Anno Domini."

Matthew dug for more information. "You use *Anno Domini*, so this means you have accepted the Christ, does it not?"

Robert's suspicions grew. Was this Matthew Wolverine a pagan Viking? Even in his doubt, however, Robert was unwilling to arouse the stranger's anger again, and he answered a simple, "Aye. Many of us have accepted Him, myself among them. And many believe that the Christ will come to earth again in the new millennium that is but months away."

Matthew hefted the weight of his new broadsword as he walked toward the water. 999? Well, that would explain the way these people were dressed, and the way they spoke, and the way they thought, but...

But it just didn't make sense. Or did it? There *was* the matter of that ancient church being new again, and the paved road being nothing but a well-worn path. Not to mention the complete absence of his Jaguar, or, for that matter, any other car... And then there was that monk. And these other nuts... well, in light of the information he'd just been given, they weren't that nutty, were they?

Hmmm. 999 A.D.

He began to ponder the bright side of this bizarre situation. First of all, this certainly wasn't Hell, and he didn't have the IRS or government laws or Y2K bugs to worry about. No sense in worrying about electrical power or phone service being interrupted, when these things were centuries away from existing. Of course, there was the Y1K problem — he remembered reading about the doomsayers and cultists of a thousand years ago — but that was just run-of-the-mill religious hysteria. That was something he could deal with. He could even use it to his advantage.

But still... this was all just too weird. He realized, however, that the mystery of how — or why — he had been transported one thousand years into the past was something he would have to contemplate later. There were more immediate problems that had to be solved. For example, how could he convince these warriors to bond to his commands? What did they feel was worth dying for? Matthew ruled out, for the time being, the idea of offering them liberty and freedom. Their response had shown him that they weren't ready for such strange concepts. But...a belief in a God...yes, that would bind them to him. So Matthew thrust his sword into the ground and continued walking toward the water's edge. He turned to face his new warriors. "My God protects me. The leader I killed served a lesser god, and his god did not protect him because I serve a stronger God. All that follow me must accept my God!"

At once, an expression of shock and terror formed on each warrior's face. Matthew wondered what he had said that had frightened them so. Maybe he had gone a little overboard with the fear-of-God spiel.

But this was not the problem, as he soon found out. A few of the warriors began to point high above Matthew's head, and then they dropped, cringing, to the ground. The sound of water, sloshing behind him, startled him. Why hadn't he heard this before? He slowly turned to confront a massive wall of gray flesh with two enormous flippers on each side. Matthew's stomach tightened as his gaze traveled up a long neck to a huge head filled with jagged teeth. The head moved slowly down toward Matthew's face, stopping only inches from his nose.

And there he was, face to face with the terror of Loch Ness.

CHAPTER 3

Matthew's military mind raced to formulate an attack plan. It was obvious that the monster was too close to outrun. It was too big to attack with just a dagger. All that was left was to talk to it. *If you can't defeat your enemy, convince him that he is your friend.* Matthew remembered Cate's stories of Loch Ness, and prayed that the stories were true. He faced the huge creature, and began to speak in a clear voice, loud enough for the clansmen to hear: "If you are truly the guardian of the Loch, then in 579 AD, Saint Columba ordered you not to hurt humans. Do you remember that?"

The creature's mouth gradually opened wider, and Matthew's heart stopped for a second. Inches from his face was a huge mouth, ringed with sharp, serrated teeth. Matthew clutched the hilt of his dagger for comfort, knowing that such a weapon would be useless against this creature. He imagined being shredded by those teeth, and almost laughed at the irony. "What a rotten way to die: as a dinosaur's dinner. There's not a snowball's chance in hell I'm going to get out of this situation." The realization steeled Matthew. He had faced imminent death many times before, had learned to embrace its inevitability calmly when there was no real alternative.

A gurgling sound began to rise from the back of the creature's throat. Matthew sensed that this was supposed to entice him, to beckon him to climb into the gaping mouth. And so, with no escape possible, Matthew pressed his left hand down on the monster's tongue. It lowered its head, and suddenly Matthew spotted something, deep within the creature's throat.

"So that's what you want," he chuckled to himself. Matthew slid inside, hoping that the monster would not instinctively clamp its huge mouth shut. A few of the warriors observing the scene fainted dead away. Robert began slowly moving towards his horse.

It was a tight fit in the monster's mouth, and Matthew braced his feet on the row of huge teeth. Reaching back as far as he could, he grabbed

21

the fishbone imbedded in the beast's gums and pulled with all his might. But the bone, set deep in the tissue, held fast. The monster let out a deafening roar, then jerked its head to full height. Matthew's brain pounded with the sheer power of the roar, and he wondered if the creature might involuntarily swallow him whole. Regaining his focus, Matthew grabbed his dagger, and with a side thrust, plunged it into the beast's abscessed gum and sliced toward the fishbone. He then seized the fishbone and pulled with every ounce of his hardened muscle and his will, finally wrenching it free.

The monster thundered in agony, flinging its head to the ground. It flung Matthew out of its mouth, and his back slammed into the ground. The fishbone bounced several times, coming to rest at Robert's feet. Matthew, stunned by the force of his fall, lay spread-eagled on the ground, his vision blurred, and his hands cupping his ears. The creature's roar echoed inside his head, and he felt as if his head would explode. The monster bellowed even louder above him, its tongue gyrating wildly, blood sloshing from its open mouth. Then, it grew suddenly quiet, and lowered its head to softly nuzzle Matthew's chest.

Matthew looked into those coal-black eyes and whispered, "Well, if you're going to eat me, just make it fast. Start with my head, because your bellowing is tearing up my brain." Instead, the monster started licking him with its two-foot tongue, starting with his midsection, and moving up to his face. After a few minutes of this, Matthew fairly reeked with the aroma of half-digested fish. The smell began to nauseate him, and he rose, stripping off his clothes down to his shorts. Ordering a warrior to get his knapsack, Matthew grabbed a bar of hotel soap out of it and waded behind the monster to wash off the noxious smell. As Matthew splashed water on his arms and chest, the monster grew curious, and turned to see what this man was doing. Its flipper unintentionally smacked Matthew square on his butt, plunging him headlong into the icy water. Matthew hated cold water, and resurfaced madder then a wet cat. He screamed — though with less profanity than a cat.

"How could you be so clumsy? Watch your flippers. I could have been killed!"

The monster started into the water, its tongue coming out to give Matthew another kiss. Matthew splashed backwards into deeper water. The creature lunged playfully into the water, its wake carrying Matthew farther out. Then it submerged, instantly coming up under Matthew before streaking towards the middle of the loch. Matthew turned on the monster's back, grabbing its skin and holding on for dear life. It was like riding a twenty-ton water jet. The powerful strokes of the monster's fins cut through the water with lightning speed. Looking back toward the ever-more-distant shore, Matthew felt the onset of hypothermia as his strength and will both began to falter. He imagined himself losing his grip and sliding into a watery grave. Well, at least he would be with his wife and daughter.

The monster sensed the loosening of the man's grip, and reversed its path, gliding swiftly back toward the shore. Upon reaching the shore, it whirled, gently sliding Matthew off its back, down its flipper, and rolling him onto the damp sand. Robert and the other warriors could do nothing but stand, frozen as trolls turned to stone by the morning sun, with their mouths agape.

Robert approached Matthew's prone, shivering body in reverence. Kneeling beside him, he covered him with his own cloak. "Matthew Wolverine, you have bested the strongest warrior among us, and beckoned us follow you. You even spoke of a God who is stronger than the one served by Damian McWrath. You be strange, there's no denying it. But now you have tamed the lake monster, and even rode upon her back. If the monster herself submits, so shall we all. And now that you have tamed her, so you must name her."

Still violently shaking from the cold, Matthew pulled a heating towel from his knapsack. After allowing the warmth to restore his composure, he spoke. He felt like Adam, ordained with the power to name the animals. It was a power not to be taken lightly. "From this day, her name shall be Alanna," he declared. He had always liked that name. "Come here, monster," he said gently. The creature rose up out of the water, just as if she understood every word he had said, and Matthew grabbed her head and looked into her right eye. "You will be called Alanna, which means 'fair and beautiful.' Do you agree?" Alanna's tongue slithered from her mouth, gently touching Matthew's face.

"Meets with your approval, and I smell like fish again," he said wryly. "That's just great. Well, you go back into the water now. We will meet again, Alanna." Alanna turned aside, slid silently back into the water and submerged.

✦ ✦ ✦

As Matthew dressed, his warriors began lining up. Robert remained close by his side. Now it was time to address his troops.

"You have seen the power of my God. Do you all accept my God above all other gods, or will you die here upon this shore?"

Out of the corner of his eye, Matthew saw Robert unsheathe his sword as three warriors who remained unconvinced rushed them. Robert's blade found its mark in the chest of the first assailant, but Matthew lashed out with well-placed kicks, killing the other two. He silently cursed his body for its brutal response to the attack, hating the reconnaissance training that had taught him to react instantaneously to any attack, without conscious thought. His body had a mind of its own, and only one goal: survival. Matthew would have to overcome that mindless response if he was to gain the loyalty of these men, rather than their fear.

Matthew scratched his head and looked at Robert. "Why did those men attack us?"

Robert's face glowed with hatred as he replied, "They worship the dragons. The dragons are their god."

Dragons? Matthew thought he understood the Gaelic word Robert had used, but couldn't be sure. "Describe these 'dragons'," Matthew said. Robert described huge, fearsome flying reptilian creatures, fire-breathing monsters that were cunning and crafty to boot — more demon than beast, to hear him tell it. In a word, *dragons*.

Ever since he was a child, Matthew had believed it was possible that dragons had really existed at one time. There was even something in the Bible about that, if his memory served him right. Well, if Robert was correct, and he had no reason to doubt him, there were dragons in Scotland now. And no one was safe from them.

Matthew glared at his remaining warriors and declared, "Those that will accept my God may remain, but those who still choose to serve another god — be it dragons or otherwise — are free to leave." Robert moved silently away from Matthew's side, grouping his warriors together. Robert still didn't trust these warriors, who had been so ready to draw his blood a few moments before. He knew it would be wise to prepare for another battle, which might come at any time Damian's clan saw weakness. It was Robert's feeling that, although this Matthew Wolverine was a great warrior, he obviously knew little of the power of the dragons, and needed protection so that he would live long enough to learn.

The warriors huddled into a large circle to talk among themselves. Some gestured toward their dead leader, while others pointed to the loch. In the end, they reasoned that the God of Matthew Wolverine had subdued the monster, and must therefore be stronger than a dragon. And so they came before him, swearing their allegiance to him, and kneeling to accept his God.

* * *

After the warriors had accepted Matthew's God, Robert summoned horses for their trip to Matthew's new castle. Matthew shook his head in disbelief and disgust at the sight of these horses. His own steed was little more than a small fur-ball on hooves. Its mane was matted, its body caked with mud, and it smelled to high heaven. The horse didn't seem to think too much of Matthew, either. It took one look at his enormous frame and, as if thinking, "No way am I breaking my back carrying that giant," it reared back, sending the warrior holding its reins flying. The warrior made the mistake of hanging on to the reins, and the horse dragged him thirty feet until the man, perhaps through divine revelation, decided to let go. The horse galloped to the top of the nearest hill and turned to whinny at Matthew.

Matthew shook his fist and shouted, "Same to you, horse! Don't come back, or I'll serve you up for dinner."

Robert chuckled and licked his lips. "Well, Matthew, at least I know you have good taste in food. Mmm, just thinking about roasted horse makes my mouth water. Don't worry. I will catch that horse someday and we will enjoy feasting on him."

Matthew was jolted by the impact of Robert's words. He thought, *Texans haven't eaten horses in about a hundred years, and then only when facing starvation.* His curiosity aroused, Matthew asked Robert, "What else do you eat?"

Robert tightened his forehead as he contemplated this question. "It depends on how cold the winter gets. A really cold winter, we eat cats, wolves, and rats, but I don't like rats. Boars, horses, sheep, and cows are more to my liking. But if we're to eat this night, we'd best be setting out for your castle. It is north of here, on the other side of the loch. And since we've no horse for you to ride, it will be slow going."

Matthew had the warriors bear the bodies of the leader and the three fallen warriors as they walked to his castle. He reasoned that, should he meet opposition at his castle, the sight of their dead leader's head, thrown over the wall, might tip the scales in his favor. Matthew again was saddened at the cold reasoning his of mind. His military expertise permeated his thoughts and actions. His recon training had taken so well that his mind automatically figured out the most effective course of action, without allowing him the luxury of even thinking about it. Now, after the swirl of battle and the threat of death had passed, he had time to think about – and be affected by – all that he had done. He turned to Robert and asked him, "That dead leader, Damian … why were you fighting him?"

Robert spit, as if to cast a bitter taste from his mouth as he replied, "May the Devil hold Damian McWrath close in his bosom. He ravished my daughter, and so I had to kill her. It was the hardest act I ever had to do. My wife stood there crying and wringing her hands. I loved my daughter, but Damian was pure evil. Any father in the Highlands would rather see his daughter dead than have her live after being sullied by Damian, with the risk that she might bear his offspring. When Damian ravished a girl, he brought shame not only to her, but to her entire family."

Matthew listened in stunned silence as Robert continued, his tone now as matter-of-fact as if he were talking about the effect of the weather on the crops. "No female could even think of Damian McWrath without also thinking of the icy fingers of Death encircling her throat, squeezing the life out of her. Every girl and woman knew that he was a constant danger. No girl above the age of ten, and no woman of childbearing age, was safe from him. I will say this, Matthew, many a lassie will sleep better tonight knowing he is dead — would that you could have shown up in time to save my sweet Ciara — but today you made some powerful enemies, and they will seek revenge. But when they come for you, I, and all the men of my clan, will fight at your side."

Matthew was still more or less in the frame of mind that it would be easier on him if he could just give up the struggle and join his wife and child in death. He was so tired, all of a sudden. But then, seeing as how he was one thousand years back in the past now, Cate and Rachel hadn't even been born yet, had they? Well, of course, in Eternity there was no linear time, but even so... Anyway, the point was moot. He knew that this man beside him would give his own life to prevent Matthew Wolverine's death. In order to achieve the everlasting peace that only death could offer, he would have to overcome not only his training and instinct, but the unwavering allegiance of Robert Roybridge.

Robert studied Matthew, deep in thought, and observed his features. Matthew's blonde hair, aquamarine eyes, and enormous height were more the traits of a Viking than a Scot. Viking raids were frequent, even as far south as Loch Ness. Personally, Robert felt that the Vikings' well-known hatred of the dragons and dragon worshippers was their one redeeming quality. Maybe Matthew Wolverine *was* a Viking. Robert decided he had better find out before he blurted out his disdain for Vikings. "Matthew," he asked, tying to sound nonchalant, "are you a Viking?"

Snapping out of his contemplation, Matthew replied, "A Viking? No, I'm a *Texan*." Even to Matthew, that word sounded odd in the midst of the Gaelic words.

Robert frowned and shook his head. "What is a 'Texan'?"

Matthew was tired; nothing had gone right this day, so he gave Robert the straight truth. "Texas is a land far to the west of Ireland. The world is round and Texas is on the other side."

Robert just nodded his head and looked at the ground. He moved a little farther from Matthew's side, thinking that Matthew was mad — but maybe only a little mad. Then he announced, "We approach your castle."

Daniel N. Jason

* * *

The wall around the castle was built of large, rough-hewn gray stones that rose to a height of twenty feet. As Matthew had expected, guards standing atop the wall issued a challenge. Matthew stepped boldly up to the gate, followed by four warriors carrying Damian's body and head. Matthew raised the head and flung it over the wall. "Your leader is dead, slain by my own hand. According to your law, I lay claim to all that was his, including this dwelling. Open these gates at once!"

It took a few moments for the people inside the castle to inspect the head. Then their murmur rose to a cheer inside the walls, and the gates swung wide. Matthew and Robert, followed by the warriors, entered the castle.

The first thing Matthew noticed about the people of the castle was how small they were; not a one of them was more than five feet tall. They were very lean and filthy, and garbed in rags equally as grubby. Most stunning of all, however, were the expressions on their faces as they gathered around the head of their erstwhile leader. Far from being enraged at his death, they actually seemed to be enjoying the sight of the carrion-birds as they circled above, waiting for a chance to swoop down to feast upon the head. Not one of them made any effort to shoo the birds away; they simply stood there watching, fascinated.

Matthew looked around him. The castle was three stories high, built with smooth gray stones on the inside buildings, in sharp contrast to the crude outer walls. It was obvious to Matthew that these people, or at least the people who built the place before them, took some pride in their craft.

But there was no time now to contemplate the glories of ancient Scottish architecture. Looking at the people who surrounded him and lurked in the doorways, Matthew was reminded of the urgency of his mission. He shouted for all of the people to assemble out in the courtyard. In response, they simply stared at this strange-looking man, but made no move. So he shouted again, this time a little more forcefully. "You see what I have done to the greatest of you. Which of you defies my order now?" His threat shook them from their wondering, and all the people began, as one, to issue forth from the castle.

On Matthew's right, from the stables, the chief of the castle guard pulled three men, one woman, and two children, all bound together with heavy chains. The female child stumbled and fell. The guard continued to drag her a short distance, then stopped and began to lash her back until she rose. Laughing when he first halted in front of Matthew, the chief was confronted not with the pleasure and gratitude of his old master, but with Matthew's icy stare. The guard shifted and looked away uneasily. This man, obviously, was not at all like Damian.

Matthew looked the guard in the eyes and demanded to know, "Why are these people in chains?"

The guard's eyes narrowed as he snarled, "These are filthy Picts that Damian recently captured. They are slaves. Does one of them please you? It is said that the Picts are adept at giving many pleasures."

Matthew ignored the guard's crude words, and walked past him, toward the female child. Her face was smudged with dirt, but underneath, bruises covered her face and shoulders. "Who gave you these bruises?"

She glanced fearfully at the castle guard with whom Matthew had just had the verbal exchange. At that she began to shake, and was overtaken with uncontrollable sobbing.

Matthew tried a different approach. "Warrior, bring me some clean water and a clean cloth." When these items arrived, Matthew gently wiped away the dirt, and with a smile, asked her age.

She looked into his eyes and her body relaxed as she answered softly, "I am eleven summers, and I will be twelve soon."

Matthew noted that her black hair would be shiny if washed. She reminded Matthew so much of Rachel — a little shy, but with the gleam of strength visible in her emerald eyes, even beyond the bruises. Like Rachel's, this child's eyes were deep green pools that one could get lost in. Matthew stroked her hair, then lightly touched the chain around her neck, causing her to wince in pain. Pushing back her hair, he noticed blood on the chain. It had cut deeply into her neck.

Matthew's shoulders dropped as he fought back the twin demons of sadness and rage. Looking deeply into the eyes of this hurt child, Matthew swore to his beloved daughter, newly dead, yet nearly a thousand years from being born, that neither this girl, nor any like her, would suffer like this if he could help it. He bellowed, "In my lands, there is no slavery. Guards, remove these chains at once."

As Matthew spoke, the chief of the castle guard slinked behind him. "These are filthy Picts, and I won't have them in my castle without chains." Then, with dagger drawn, he rushed Matthew's back. Pushing the girl to his left, Matthew swung his left hand backward to block the dagger. The blow deflected, Matthew's foot lashed viciously into the guard's stomach. As the stunned man doubled over in pain, Matthew's right hand seized the dagger, arced it high, and plunged it into the guard's Adam's apple. Matthew could feel the quivering caress of the man's tissue as it reacted to the intrusion of the blade, and he wondered, for a brief instant, if the familiar sensation would ever leave his memory. The guard could do nothing but seize the hilt of the blade in his throat as he choked to death on his own blood. Matthew rose to tower over his vanquished enemy, coldly observing the death throes as the last few seconds of the man's life were played out.

The people in the castle had never seen such a large man move with such swiftness, more like a cat than a warrior. When the chief had attacked Matthew, they'd felt certain that this stranger, who had so boldly proclaimed himself their new leader, would die. Instead he had killed the guard in one smooth motion, as if engaged in a child's play rather than mortal combat. Realizing that crossing this new leader would be unwise, the people rushed forward to remove the prisoners' chains. Once the chains were removed, Matthew gently cleaned the dirt from the cuts on the girl's neck. A stab of pain pierced his heart, as memories of his dead daughter began to flood into his mind. *Oh, God, how he missed her.* It occurred to Matthew that this girl's father must be worried sick about her. With a broad smile, he gazed deep into her green eyes and proclaimed, "I will send you home, to your father."

The girl's face instantly changed, her eyes filled with terror, as she furiously searched the grounds for some means of escape. Finding none, she threw herself at Matthew's feet, shrieking, begging for her life. Confused by the girl's sudden change, Matthew knelt and raised the child to her feet. In her young eyes, he saw the terror of a trapped animal trying to escape. Bewildered, Matthew asked, "Would your father hurt you?"

The woman prisoner stepped forth and said, "Aye, she was ravished by Damian, so our father must kill her."

Matthew's gaze settled on the woman. "What is your name?"

With a defiant stare she spoke. "I am Brigit, and my sister's name is Kar, which means 'girl of virtue.' But she is anything but virtuous now."

The pieces of the puzzle fell into place, and Matthew's eyes saddened as he asked, "Brigit, were you ravished by Damian?"

Brigit's body visibly tightened. "No, he felt I was too old and he knew my strength. I have lived sixteen summers. Thus, I may return safely to my father, but if she returns, she dies. What man would take my sister as a daughter or wife? None. Whether by my father's hand or the teeth of wild beasts, her death will come, and quickly. I love you, Kar, but your fate is sealed."

Matthew looked at Robert, but Robert's eyes fell, to stare at the ground. Matthew remembered that Robert had killed his own daughter after Damian had ravished her, so in the mind of Robert, Kar was beyond hope. The girl looked up at Matthew to plead, through her tears, for his help, for her life. Memories of Rachel tore at Matthew's heart. What if this had been his own daughter, begging another man for her life? If that man turned his daughter away, what would Matthew do? He would hunt the man down and kill him, of course, because such a man did not deserve his own life, much less the power over another's. Matthew pushed Kar away, and, as their eyes met, he said to her, "Kar, I lost my daughter; and there is an emptiness inside me that only a daughter can fill. Will you fill that void and be my daughter?"

Kar's eyes bore deep into Matthew's, searching for deceit or trickery. Sensing none, her eyes flashed, filled with a joyous light. She smiled, and broke free of Matthew's hold. Tears of jubilation streamed down her dusty cheeks as she threw her skinny arms around Matthew. At the top of her lungs she screamed, "Aye!"

As he returned her embrace, the sorrow in Matthew's heart began to recede, soothed by the healing medicine of a daughter's love. How long ago it seemed that Cate and Rachel had been taken from him. Was it only a few days ago, that horrible day that would not come for a thousand years? And yet, he felt the pain begin to fade as he opened his heart to this little child.

To complete that healing – for both of them — Matthew decided to hold a ceremony. "Kar," he declared, "you are no longer the banished child of another. I shall rename you. Now kneel in front of me."

Very solemnly, Kar released Matthew from her embrace and knelt at his feet, sensing the sacredness of this ritual.

In a voice loud enough to be heard by all in the castle, Matthew proclaimed: "Today, I take this girl as my daughter. Any man who would treat her harshly shall feel my wrath. From this day forth, she shall be known as Raquelle Wolverine, daughter of Matthew Wolverine. She is to be treated with all the love and respect due the child of your leader. Arise, Raquelle Wolverine."

Raquelle rose to embrace her new father. Matthew turned, the child clinging close at his side, and spoke to Brigit. "Woman, I wish friendship with your father, and shall repay him for the past injustice of your slavery, and for the hurt done to this child. What in the castle will please him most?"

Brigit's eyes narrowed, thinking that surely he must have known that the Picts were traders of great renown. "In your stables is a sow with a new litter. My father loves pork, and there has been no pork on our table for more than two summers. Give him the sow with her litter."

Matthew, who was reviled by pork and the very mention of pigs, managed to hide his revulsion. This would be an easy trade.

Matthew asked her, "What is you father's name?"

Brigit's chin rose high with pride as she answered, "Kial, which means 'firebrand,' so beware, Matthew Wolverine. He's not a man to be trifled with."

Matthew smiled as he thought, *Good. A warrior. I can use his friendship*. "Tell Kial that I present him with this sow and her litter, that there may be friendship between us, and, if needed, that we may fight together as one. I will come in seven days with my daughter, Raquelle, to see him in his camp. I do not eat pork, so don't offend me by offering it to me. Tell your father that I send to him three fatted ewes, as well. Ask him to slaughter one, and to prepare a feast to celebrate our friendship. Go now, Brigit, and may my God protect you on your journey home."

Rubbing her neck where the chains had been, Brigit ordered the other Picts to gather the swine and ewes. They marched triumphantly through the front gate, their swine and sheep before them.

"Begging your pardon, my leader," Robert said to Matthew in a low voice, as the two men walked towards the gate. "Why is it that you do not eat pork?"

"It is a long story," Matthew began hesitantly, not sure if he felt at liberty yet to confide in Robert. Well, it probably wouldn't hurt to reveal a little bit of vulnerability, in measured doses, to this man who had, after all, sworn his allegiance. So he took the plunge. "When I was only six years of age, I was out hunting with my grandfather in the forest. Suddenly a Russian boar, larger than any beast I'd ever seen or could ever hope to see, ran out of the thicket and gave me such a fright that I dropped my rifle and ran."

"Your what?" asked Robert.

"My weapon," Matthew corrected himself. "As the boar was gaining on me, and just about to take a bite of me, my grandfather shot him… aimed his weapon and struck him. The boar lunged at me, pinning me to the ground. The grunts of the dying boar filled my brain as I lay sobbing, immobilized under that huge mass of flesh. To this day, I loathe the creatures and refuse to partake of their vile meat." He looked at Robert to gauge his reaction, but the other man merely nodded and said, "Well, then, I can assure you that as long as I have anything to do with it, there will never be pork served at a table where Matthew Wolverine breaks bread."

"Good man," Matthew said, clapping him on the shoulder.

Matthew watched as the procession passed out of the gates before them, and he wondered at the ravenous looks on the faces of the castle people. With all the livestock gathered up in the stables and pens, could these people actually be as starved as their expressions would indicate? He would have to look into it, but for now, he needed to attend to the disposal of the dead warriors.

Matthew called to one of his men who was larger than the rest, and obviously held some rank among the others: "Warrior, take five men and bear these bodies to that hill just before the forest. Drop them by the roadside at its peak, but do not bury them. Do you understand?"

The warrior nodded, grateful that his position had been declared by the new leader. He duly picked five men to assist him. Just as they started carrying the bodies out of the gates, a protest came from someone in the crowd: "No! You must bury them, or the dragons will come and see their dead worshippers and burn our castle in their rage."

Without thinking, Matthew drew his sword, expecting another attack. A tall, black-haired woman came forward and knelt at his feet, her waist-length raven hair cloaking her body. Matthew stared in amazement at this vision of shimmering blackness as she spoke.

"My lord, I am Shalee, niece of Damian. He killed his brother, my father, then sacrificed my mother to the dragons. The dragons love him, and will avenge Damian when they learn that he is dead. Please, bury him."

"No, this man and his warriors don't deserve a burial. They shall lie in the sun until the ants and carrion-birds pick the flesh from their bones. Dragons or no, Damian and his warriors will not be buried." Turning to Robert, Matthew asked, "Robert, if the dragons come, will you fight at my side?"

Robert swallowed hard as his shoulders sank. He thought to himself, *This Matthew Wolverine is determined to get himself inside a dragon's belly. Why does he seek death and drag me along? Well, he did save my life, so I owe him mine.* Robert's eyes met Matthew's as he said, "My sword is ever yours, lord, but let me return first to my castle to set my affairs in order. I will return in six days. Perhaps the Picts will help us slay the dragons." At that, Robert took his troops and, with some sadness, marched out of the gates toward his own castle. He thought to himself that there was more of a chance of the earth being round than of the Picts rallying forth to help slay a dragon.

It was going to be a long, hard battle, keeping Matthew Wolverine alive.

* * *

With the most pressing matters attended to, Matthew realized how exhausted he was. This had been, to put it mildly, a hard day, and all Matthew wanted now was a hot bath, a decent meal and a good night's sleep. He turned to the beautiful black-haired woman and asked, "Shalee, do you have means to heat water, and a tub for bathing?"

Shalee wondered at the notion of a man who actually *wanted* to bathe, thinking that there was no end to this Matthew Wolverine's strangeness. Without giving voice to these thoughts, she simply shook her head and pointed in the direction of Loch Ness. "Alas, there is only one place for bathing, my lord, and it is in the icy waters of the loch." She could not take her eyes from him as he turned and headed towards Loch Ness. An odd man indeed, this Matthew Wolverine…. the kind of man a woman had best stay away from, for there was sorrow in those strange blue-green eyes of his, and it was a sorrow that ran colder and deeper than the North Sea.

The Ultimate Dragon

Chapter 4

Raquelle was like a little puppy, clinging at Matthew's side for protection. Resigning himself to not being able to soak in a hot bath, Matthew had picked up his knapsack, and now he and Raquelle were on their way to the shore of Loch Ness. He had decided to tell the girl the truth about his situation, even though he doubted whether she could believe, much less fathom it. He was having a tough time comprehending what had happened himself. After further consideration, he decided to skip the time-travel part for now. Instead he began, "Raquelle, you gained life today as my daughter, but I want you also to realize that my heart is still filled with a pain that causes me to fight every battle with no care for my own life. I yearn to be rejoined with my dead family. Until my death allows me to be with them again, whether it be a week or a month or a year, you must learn all you can from me, so that you may survive after I die. Do you understand how precious our time together is?"

Raquelle lowered her head to study the ground as they walked, considering her new father's words. They walked for a few minutes, and she tilted her head up to look at her father and replied, "Aye, when you die, I die. So I must keep you alive for a very long time."

Matthew was struck by the poignancy of her simple statement, but said nothing. They reached the shore, and Matthew slipped off his knapsack. Interesting, he mused, that the knapsack had made the leap through the centuries with him. Maybe it was because the strap was so securely over his shoulder when he was leaning against the cross in that church. At any rate, he was glad to have it. To Raquelle he said, "A few weeks before my wife died, she packed some things in the bottom of this knapsack."

"Why?" Raquelle asked.

Matthew swallowed hard and looked out into the dark waters of the loch. "We were planning to go on a weekend trip with our little girl."

"A what?"

"A journey that lasted two days. But at the last minute, I had to cancel because I had business to attend to. I told my wife to keep the bag packed, because we were going to make the journey on the following weekend."

"And did you make that journey?" Raquelle asked.

"No, something else came up…"

"Were your wife and your little girl sad about that?"

"Yes, they were," Matthew replied quietly. "Anyway, I never even looked to see what my wife put in the sack, because I was in so much of a hurry when I was preparing for this trip. So let's see what she packed."

The first items Matthew came across were those he had packed. There was, of course, the urn, and next to it was Glenna's map. He took both urn and map out of the sack and laid them gently by his side, vowing to himself that somehow he would figure out how to get to Carn Mhic — or whatever it was called in this time — and keep his promise to Cate. Raquelle was gazing with great curiosity at the urn. "I will explain this soon," he assured her. "But I want to take everything else out first." Next he brought out his running shoes and shorts, his .44 Magnum and ammunition, his Bowie knife, and a few miscellaneous toiletry items, and laid them aside with the urn and the map.

And then, with a catch in his throat, he took out the new bathing suit he had bought on that last trip to Dallas. It was to have been a present for Rachel; he had no idea why he had packed it, but now he was glad he had. He handed the suit to Raquelle now. She studied it with great curiosity, wondering what use there was for such a garment. Matthew took out his own bathing suit and laid it on the beach. Digging deeper into the compartment at the bottom of the knapsack, he found the items Cate had packed: a Bible, a map of the world, a book on the ABC's, a couple of other children's books, a book on how things work, and another heating towel, which he placed now by his swim trunks.

As Matthew laid down one of the children's books, Raquelle picked it up to examine the photograph of a sheep on the cover. She tried to reach into the book to grab the tiny sheep. After several frustrating attempts, she asked Matthew, "How did you capture this animal? Have you stolen its spirit?"

Laughing gently, Matthew replied, "These are books that have pictures of animals, not their spirits."

Raquelle opened the book and pointed inside. "What are these strange markings beside the drawings?" she asked.

Matthew replied, "These are words that tell you about the animals. Can you read these words?"

Raquelle squinted hard; then she shook her head. "Are these markings important?"

Matthew stroked her hair and pulled her close. "Aye, reading is knowledge. This Bible here is the voice of our God; you must learn to read it to better hear His voice. You get your first reading lesson soon. Now put on that swimsuit when I turn my back."

Once they were both in their swimsuits, they waded into the water up to Raquelle's waist. She began to splash Matthew, and he responded in kind, resulting in a full-fledged water fight. They were laughing and splashing when the water about thirty feet from them began to bubble and churn. Raquelle panicked and cried, "It is the monster! Run, my father!" She latched on to Matthew's hand and pulled for all she was worth, attempting to drag him toward the safety of the shore. Matthew swooped her up in his arms and ran for the beach.

Just as they emerged from the water and onto the beach, they were pummeled by a rain of dozens of huge fish, landing on the beach all around them. One particularly large fish struck Matthew square in the middle of his back, knocking him and Raquelle to the ground. For a moment, Matthew and Raquelle lay motionless on the beach, stunned by the bizarre scene of fish flopping all around them. Then the water fairly exploded, and a monster sprang forth, almost crushing both of them as it landed on the sand beside them.

The monster issued a bellowing roar, and the fish flopped farther inland. Matthew's sword and dagger were far beyond his reach, but he steeled himself, prepared to die fighting to protect his new daughter. He and the child both rose to their feet, and Raquelle scurried behind him, her eyes wide with terror. Matthew stood as a wall to protect her. The monster stopped roaring to look at these two humans, standing so brazenly among its food. It tilted its head to the right and lowered its head toward them, eyes narrowed. Without warning, it flicked out its huge black tongue and gently laved it across Matthew's face. As Matthew got his fish bath, Raquelle screamed.

Smiling, Matthew reached out to rub under the monster's chin. "Is that you, Alanna?" Alanna looked into his eyes and gave him another lick. Then she noticed that some of the fish were escaping back into the water. She snagged the one closest to the water, and, biting off its head, she placed it to her left. She placed the next fish she killed in front of her, and the third, to her right. As she continued this process, it dawned on Matthew this was her dinner. He snatched his sword and told Raquelle, who by this time had stopped screaming, to hold the fish's tail. To Raquelle's credit, she seized the tail without hesitation, and was promptly slammed to the ground by the fish, which was at least twice her weight.

37

The Ultimate Dragon

She staggered, dazed, to her feet.

At that Matthew went berserk, filled with all the protectiveness of a father determined not to let another of his children die. He thrust his sword into the ground and grunted deeply as he released a karate punch to the fish's head. His shout of, "Hai!" was so loud, and his punch so violent, that it stunned the fish.

Matthew yelled to Raquelle to take his sword and cut off the fish's head. She tried to pull his sword out of the ground, but could not. She ran to Matthew's clothing, removed his dagger, and returned to the fish, plunging the blade deep into its eye. Matthew continued to stun more fish, and then still more until his hands hurt, and then he found a piece of driftwood and began clubbing them. Raquelle followed behind, killing the stunned fish. After killing over forty fish — Matthew had long since lost count — he and Raquelle fell, exhausted, on the beach. Alanna seemed to beam with pride. She let out a trumpet call of triumph, then turned and sloshed noisily back into the water.

Matthew, out of breath and red-faced from the exertion, rose to his feet, shouting, "What! After all our work, you're just going to leave these fish?" Alanna turned her head and flicked her left front flipper up in the air at Matthew. Matthew leaned over and whispered to Raquelle, "Well, I think I know that sign from Houston freeways, and it doesn't mean 'have a good day!' Who'd have imagined it — a monster with a sense of humor, much less an attitude!"

Alanna waded deeper into the water and smacked her left front flipper three times on the water's surface. About fifty feet out, two small heads emerged and began swimming toward the shore. Raquelle was up like a shot, racing toward the water. As the first baby, a miniature version of Alanna, emerged on shore, Raquelle threw her arms around its neck. The baby emitted a low warning growl and prepared to attack Raquelle. Matthew's heart was in his mouth, a plan of attack formulating, not in his conscious mind, but in the very muscles and tendons of his body.

Alanna swiftly moved between Matthew and her baby and lowered her head to within inches of her baby's face. She issued a resounding growl from deep within her chest, its threat clear as the sunlight reflecting off her exposed teeth. The baby, understanding its mother's reprimand, lowered its head, allowing the unaware Raquelle to continue with her hug.

The second baby emerged from the water with a hungry cry, and Matthew realized that neither baby could get to the piles of fish. He told Raquelle to help him drag some fish to the first baby. The baby rushed up on the beach and began gorging itself, eating the fish as hastily as possible. The second baby, angry that it hadn't gotten its turn at the meal, began to wail even more loudly than before. Matthew dragged some fish toward it, and it began to eat voraciously. As Matthew watched, he realized that these beasts were gorging themselves because they were starving. Without his and Raquelle's help, most of these fish would have escaped back into the water. Alanna looked at her feasting babies, then at Matthew, and placed a pile of large fish and a single smaller fish at Raquelle's feet.

Raquelle licked her lips and proclaimed, "Alanna says *thank ye'*, and wants us to have these fish. We feast tonight!" She burst into a huge smile and rubbed her stomach.

Alanna finished eating her pile of fish, and then, with her mouth open wide, made a deep gurgling sound. Matthew moved to her open mouth and removed some fish bones. Raquelle watched, fascinated, as her new father fearlessly approached this monster and confidently stuck his arm deep within her mouth. She thought, *This man has power over the monsters of Loch Ness!* To show her courage — which was bolstered by the feeling that, as his daughter, some of that power was conferred upon her — she stepped forward to help him.

Suddenly Alanna reared back, glaring toward Matthew's castle. Startled, Raquelle jumped nearly two feet into the air. Upon landing, she checked to see — with no little bit of surprise and relief — that she still had two hands attached to her arms. Matthew fetched his sword, once more preparing for battle. He looked in the direction of Alanna's gaze. From over the hill marched ten warriors that he had not seen before. Spotting the monsters, the warriors stopped short, their eyes wide, and their arms hanging limp at their sides.

Matthew shouted, "Who are you, and why have you come?"

Hesitantly, one of the warriors mumbled that they had only just returned to the castle, and that Shalee had sent them to fetch their new master. Looking more like a chastened schoolboy than a mighty warrior, the man asked Matthew if the monsters would hurt them.

Matthew flashed them a broad smile. "Come on down and take these fish — all but the little one — back to the castle and cook them for supper. The monsters won't hurt you, at least not until I bid them to do so."

The warriors kept a safe distance from the monsters, but they were all licking their lips, and more than a few stomachs were growling as they gathered the large fish. Anxiously anticipating the feast that would take place in the village tonight, they cinched their bounty to their backs and quickly departed. Matthew knew that the rumors would fly this night, of

39

the man who had tamed the monster of the loch — stories that would weave themselves into tales enough to occupy old wives and fascinated children for many generations to come.

* * *

Alanna's babies were so stuffed after their meal that they lay smiling on the beach, their fins splayed before them, and their heads down. Alanna had to prod them back into the water, whereupon all three creatures ducked beneath the surface and swam away.

Raquelle looked at Matthew, sniffed, and turned up her nose. "Father, you smell like a fish."

Matthew had to laugh. "Well, my daughter, you don't smell too much better yourself!" They waded into the water, and he suggested that they swim a short distance.

Raquelle shook her head. "Father, I am not a fish, and I cannot swim. Can you teach me?"

Matthew was struck by how much he enjoyed being needed again, and he wondered, not for the last time, why he had failed to realize that simple joy during his other life. He nodded to Raquelle, then they both plunged into the water. Matthew showed Raquelle a few basic swimming strokes, along with the correct way to breathe. A natural swimmer, she was soon diving under Matthew's legs.

Before long Alanna emerged again, popping her head above the water to see what all the splashing was about. Fearlessly, Raquelle swam toward her and climbed upon her head. Raquelle was on all fours, staring eyeball to eyeball with Alanna. Alanna slowly moved into deeper water, then flipped her huge head, sending Raquelle flying. Raquelle put her feet close together and, with her arms outstretched like a bird, sailed through the air. Then she brought her arms together and plunged straight into the water.

Fearing Raquelle might be hurt, Matthew quickly swam to where she'd entered the water. But she surfaced to his right, splashed him once, then turned to swim back to Alanna. Matthew caught her by the waist.

She was one big smile as she squealed, "Have Alanna do that again! Oh, please, father."

Worry lines etched upon his face, Matthew asked her, "Are you all right? This water is freezing."

Far from being hurt, Raquelle was chipper, her recent fear — and the cold — long forgotten. "I'm all right. I'm not cold."

Matthew shook his head and released her. *Even one thousand years in the past, the mystery of how a child can be blue and shivering, and still swear she is not cold, is alive and well.* "One quick ride on Alanna's back, and then we go in. It will be dark soon, and we have a feast to attend!"

As Matthew spoke, Alanna dove beneath the surface, coming up with Raquelle and Matthew on her back. They hung tightly to her skin as she jetted through the water. Matthew sensed that Raquelle was tiring and that they needed to get to the shore. As if reading his thoughts, Alanna immediately turned and headed for shore. Matthew wondered if Alanna really *could* read his thoughts. He determined that he would test this in a few minutes.

Matthew and Raquelle emerged on shore, both of them blue and shivering. Matthew got the heating towel and wrapped it around Raquelle's shoulders. Then he turned to Alanna and, pointing at a 45 degree angle in the sky, spoke the words in his mind: *Bring fish to this beach when the sun reaches there tomorrow, and we will share the catch*. Alanna looked in the man's eyes before turning to enter the water. Matthew had the strangest feeling that she had understood him and would, indeed, return with more fish tomorrow.

Raquelle's question drew him out of his thoughts.

"Father, this cloth is hot like fire, yet there is no flame within it. I am warm, yet not burnt. How does it work; is it magic?"

Matthew was impressed that this child was so inquisitive. He thought to himself, *That shows she is intelligent*. "It absorbs the water, converting it to steam. To be honest, I have no idea how it does it, but they are selling like hot cakes in the States."

Raquelle frowned. "What do you mean *selling like hot cakes* and what are the *States*?"

Matthew yawned. "I will explain that later. Now, I am cold and need the heating towel for myself, so let's get your hair dry." As Raquelle dried her hair and dressed, Matthew warmed himself with the towel. When he was finally dry, he pulled his clothes on over the trunks. The two of them, tired, yet refreshed, walked over to a large tree and sat down. They listened to the sound of the waves splashing on shore as the sun set. It was very relaxing.

Raquelle rested her head on Matthew's chest, secure in the knowledge that her father would protect her from all harm. Her eyes closed, and she snuggled deeper into Matthew's chest, to dream of her fearless ride on the monster.

The sight of this precious child, so trusting, began to melt away the sorrow in Matthew's heart. Raquelle's need to be loved, and her willingness to give her love, turned the ice of Matthew Wolverine's heart into harmless steam. He gently stroked her hair as she slept, and a thought began to form in his mind. *She trusts me, and she needs me. Maybe my life is*

41

worth living, after all. He thought of all the strange things that had happened since he left Houston. *I came back one thousand years, I've become lord of a castle... and I can apparently communicate mentally with the Loch Ness "monster." This is either one fine delusion, or it is the hand of God.*

At this point, Matthew was leaning towards the latter possibility.

Even while gripping this thought, however, Matthew's battle-trained mind perceived the presence of danger, and he vaulted to his feet, clutching his sword. The same warriors who had carried the fish back to the castle crested the hilltop less than ten feet away, approaching cautiously. Relieved, but not completely at ease, Matthew shouted, "Halt, what do you want?"

The warrior's voice quavered with fear. "Shalee sent us to bring you back, my lord. It is near nightfall, and we must hurry into the castle before the predators come out!"

Matthew laughed and shouted back, "I do my best fighting at night, but my daughter and I are hungry, so let us go back to the castle at once." The small fish, left on the beach by Alanna, still flopped about, unable to reach the water. Raquelle rubbed the sleep from her eyes, saw the fish, and ran to pick it up before dashing back to her father's side. She clung tightly to his hand for the walk back to the citadel.

Chapter 5

As the party neared the castle, the delicious aroma of roasting fish wafted out from the kitchens, beckoning them, and bidding them to quicken their pace. In all the commotion of the day, Matthew had given little thought to food, yet now, as the aroma of the cookfires reached him, he could think of little else. As they entered the castle, Matthew saw ten large fires, each with a large fish being slowly rotated over it. Looking at the assembled crowd, he saw in their faces the ravenous stares of those who had long been denied a decent meal, yet sensed their hunger would soon be sated. Shalee stepped forward to address Matthew, "My leader, we await your return to start our meal."

As she spoke, a large golden cat nuzzled at Matthew's feet, mewing loudly. Matthew had always loved big cats, so he picked it up and cuddled it to his chest. "My, my, what have we here? A female cat, and she has recently had kittens." He gently set the cat down and took the offered fish from Raquelle.

Raquelle cupped her hand and whispered into Matthew's ear, "Father, how do you know she has kittens?"

Smiling, Matthew whispered back, "She dropped some milk on me as I picked her up."

Matthew held the fish high above the cat's reach, asking, "Would the hungry cat like some nice fresh fish?" The cat licked her chops, her eyes nearly doubling in size, and her head moving up and down as Matthew raised and lowered the fish before her. It looked as if she were nodding.

Matthew was enjoying himself now. He continued, in a solemn voice, "If I feed you, you become my charge, and I will not be responsible for a stranger. Kneel and be renamed." Shalee caught Matthew's drift and seized the cat's shoulders, pushing it to the ground. The woman, obsessed with her own hunger, wanted this foolishness over quickly. The cat's tail swished wildly in anticipation. In her cat-mind, she reasoned that she could put up with a lot of lunacy for a two-pound fish. Matthew loudly proclaimed, "You shall forthwith be called Yellow Rose, defender of the castle against rats and other vermin. Be fruitful and multiply." As Shalee released Yellow Rose, Matthew looked into the cat's eyes and said, with a twinkle in his eyes, "Would Yellow Rose like this fish on a plate, or would the tinge of castle dirt be more to madam's liking?"

The cat had reached the end of her patience, and lunged for the fish. Sinking her teeth into it, she shook it violently, flaunting her prize before dragging it toward the stables. Out of the stable door streaked eight kittens, with one thought in mind: *Mom has food*. As the lead kitten reached Yellow Rose, she sent it flying with a swipe of her right paw, and the other kittens, effectively chastised, held back momentarily. The hungry kittens formed a gauntlet that Yellow Rose managed to navigate with some difficulty. Matthew saw the look of starvation in the kittens' eyes, and felt ashamed of his little joke. He called to the kittens, and reluctantly they turned, sensing a more generous benefactor than their starving mother. Yellow Rose saw her opportunity for escape, and dashed into the stable, a hair's-breadth ahead of her ravenous litter.

Matthew spoke, as if addressing the kittens, but the crowd understood that he was speaking to them. "I did not realize the extent of the hunger in this castle. A good leader must provide food for his people, and allow none, not even the smallest and weakest, to remain hungry while he himself is fed. Let all gather around the tables, and let the cooks serve up the fish. Tonight, we will eat, and eat well." Then he called to the cooks who were roasting the fish, "Cooks, I want each of you to tear off a bite of the fish and taste it to make sure it is properly done, then take the rest to the table. And make sure these kittens get some of the cooked fish too." Hearing Matthew's proclamation, and rightfully fearing the impending rush to eat, each cook tore off a generous handful of fish to wolf down, and, in accordance with the leader's command, they fed the starving kittens too.

As Matthew entered the dining hall with Shalee and Raquelle, he observed that the guards were all seated at the head of the table, the warriors sat at the lower end, and the women and children were relegated to standing behind the men. Matthew asked Shalee, "Why are the women and children standing?"

This was something that had always bothered Shalee, and she was amazed to hear a man questioning the practice, rather than simply taking his rightful place at the table. She explained, "This is the way it has always been done here. The women and children eat what is left after the men have had their fill. Often there is very little left, but we are thankful for what we get."

Matthew now understood why the kittens had acted as if they would have gladly killed Yellow Rose for her fish. Overcome with righteous indignation, he bellowed, "Everyone, get up from the table!" One castle guard objected, and Matthew threw him against the wall, whereupon the man crumpled to the floor, out cold. After that, the rest of the warriors and guards gave Matthew wide berth.

"In my castle," he said, "the wives and children eat with their husbands and fathers. A warrior's family shares in his glory and wealth. You men — all of you! — stand up now. Husbands, stand with your wives. As I assign your seats, take them with your families. Men without wives, and women without husbands, take your seats too as I assign them. Those will be your seats until further notice. My daughter, you will sit on my right, and you, Shalee, will sit on my left." He found himself looking into Shalee's amazing green eyes, and then quickly turned away to continue the seating assignments.

Pointing to four of the largest warriors, Matthew ordered, "You, you, you, and you are brave warriors. Have your families sit there beside you, and you show your skill with a sword by cutting these fish into slices the size of your finger." As they began cutting, Matthew assigned the rest of the seats. When all had found a place at his table, he said, "Now, before any food passes our lips, we must thank God for the meal." He looked at the hungry faces, and decided to make it mercifully brief. It was the thought that counted, after all. So he bowed his head and said, "Thank you, Lord. Let us eat."

There was an instantaneous blur of hands grabbing for the pieces of fish, as ravenous hunger overshadowed any concern for niceties such as manners. Raquelle and Shalee both grabbed the same piece, tearing it in half. Matthew took two pieces for himself. The people inhaled their food before Matthew could swallow four bites. Raquelle continued to gnaw at her fish bone. Seeing this, Matthew took his second fish steak, broke it in half, and gave one half to Raquelle and the other to Shalee. The people at the table were stunned by this act, and all conversation ceased.

Breaking the silence, a warrior at Matthew's right voiced his astonishment. "Never have I seen Damian share any food. Why do you share what you have taken? It is yours."

Matthew pondered for a moment how to convey the concept of sharing to starving people. "We are a family in this castle. The monster of the Loch, which I have named Alanna, chased fish onto the beach to feed her babies. Raquelle and I killed many of these fish for her, and she gave us ten of them for our reward. She shared with us what was hers. I bid my warriors carry the fish to the castle and share them with Shalee.

45

Shalee shared the fish with the cooks. The cooks roasted the fish to perfection and served it on this table. We eat tonight only because each person shared what was given to them. If we fail to share, as all these others have, we shall not survive. We are all part of a big circle, and if we are to live, the circle must go on, unbroken." Then Matthew sat down.

The people weighed their new leader's words, and for a long time, no one spoke. Then an older warrior spoke. "Is this part of what your God teaches?"

Matthew nodded, then asked who could eat more food. Every hand went up. Matthew promised that tomorrow evening his God would provide more food than they could eat. The table burst into a chorus of excited talk of tomorrow's feast, with many boasting of all the fish they would eat tomorrow. They were beginning to feel that this new leader, and his new God, were portents of a bright future.

* * *

After finishing their meal, Matthew, Shalee, and Raquelle left the table. Matthew asked Shalee to lead him to his chambers. They climbed a long flight of stairs, until they came to a large, untidy room. The floor was covered in dirt, and the blankets smelled of urine. Matthew shook his head. "Shalee, this will not do."

Shalee said, "But, my lord, this was my Uncle Damian's chamber. Why is it not suitable?"

Where should I begin? Matthew thought grimly, regretting that disinfectant spray was a few centuries out of his reach right now.

"Shalee, I think it is abundantly clear by now that I am not Damian McWrath. And where I come from we have an old saying: 'Cleanliness is next to Godliness.' A long time ago, we discovered that if we keep ourselves and our surroundings clean, we chase away a lot of sickness — not to mention a lot of bad smells."

Shalee nodded and smiled. The part about smells, she could certainly understand. She was really beginning to like this Matthew Wolverine. He was not bad looking, and he did smell nice. But even so… there was still something disturbing in his eyes, something she could not quite name, but she felt its power. She forced herself to focus on his words as Matthew continued, "I am accustomed to sleeping, eating, and living in cleanliness and not filth, and as long as I am in this castle that is the way it is going to be, not just for me, but for everyone. Tomorrow, have the other women clean this room from top to bottom. They will boil all bedding that is of cloth, and they will scrub all furs.

"And then when my room is done, they will start on Raquelle's room, and then your own. This must all be done before the sun sets tomorrow. In the morning have everyone bring their bedding and dirty clothing for boiling and cleaning. Hang this bedding and clothing over the castle walls; secure it with stones on top until it is dry. I want this done weekly from tomorrow forward. Any questions?"

Shalee was puzzled. "What is weekly, my leader?"

"The week is divided into seven days." He thought for a moment and remembered the Gaelic equivalents, but then decided to tell her the English words. "The days are Monday, Tuesday, Wednesday, Thursday, Friday, Saturday, and Sunday. We will call today Sunday. Tomorrow is Monday, and Monday shall be wash day. Every Monday, all shall wash their bedding and clothing. This will keep them from smelling and getting sick."

Raquelle came in the room just then, perking up when she heard this statement. "Father, are you saying that we get sick because of dirt?"

Matthew felt a new respect for his daughter. She was very sharp. "Aye, Raquelle, disease breeds in filth, and this castle is filthy. It must be clean to prevent disease. Now, Raquelle, I would like to see your room."

Raquelle hung her head in dejection. "I have no room, father. Damian took me in the stables, and that is where I sleep, with the pigs and horses and the big cat… with Yellow Rose and her kittens. Do you wish me to go there now?"

"Of course not, daughter!" Matthew said, his anger rising. Were Damian McWrath not already dead, Matthew would gladly kill him all over again, and then once more, for good measure. Matthew comforted Raquelle, holding her close to him and stroking her hair. "Shalee, please make a bed in the far corner of this room for my daughter," he said, and Shalee nodded and set to work.

When the bed was made, Matthew said to both of them, "I have something very important to tell you. When I am asleep, under no circumstances are you to touch me. I have been trained as a warrior, and I awaken as a warrior, fully ready to do battle, and may injure or even kill you before I am even fully conscious." Both nodded vigorously. They had seen him fight, and had no desire to be the targets of his rage.

Finally, with all sleeping arrangements made, Shalee went off to her room. As the night deepened and settled in, sleep came one by one to all within the castle walls. It was as if the castle itself were breathing a long, deep sigh of relief.

* * *

Some time after the middle of the night, Matthew began tossing violently in his tortured dreams. He sat up straight, his body covered in sweat, and bellowed at the top of his lungs, "Caitlin, don't leave. Don't

47

take my daughter. Look out! Turn the wheel! Turn the wheel!" His shouts brought Shalee into the room, the glow of the candle she carried illuminating her lovely face, but barely piercing the darkness. She moved toward Matthew's bed to comfort him, but Raquelle leapt out of her own bed, blocking the woman's way.

Shalee resisted, chiding the child. "We should comfort him."

Raquelle's voice was firm, adamant. "No, Shalee. I do not think he is awake. Remember what he told us. If you awaken him, he will hurt you, and he might kill you without knowing what he has done. We have to stay back. Now, go back to your bed, and I will watch over him." In the faint illumination of a single candle, Raquelle watched as her father tossed and turned. She wondered what horrors filled his dreams, this man who had so effectively banished her nightmares, yet could not conquer his own.

These thoughts, borne upon her growing love for her new father, filled her, offering her both comfort and concern, until, after a long while, she succumbed to her own exhaustion, and fell into a troubled sleep.

ChAPTER 6

Raquelle awakened to the sound of grunting, and for a moment thought she was back in the stables with the hogs. As she rubbed the sleep from her eyes, Shalee entered the room, and both of them stood gawking at Matthew. He was dressed only in running shorts, lying face-down on the floor with his legs together and his hands shoulder width apart, raising and lowering himself for no apparent reason. He looked up and saw their stunned faces. Without missing a beat, he said, "I am doing pushups. I do 200 pushups each day, as well as 300 sit-ups, and then I run ten miles before breakfast. I do this five days a week." Okay, maybe he was exaggerating a little, but not by much. In any case, these numbers failed to impress Shalee.

"Why do you do such things?" she asked bluntly, looking at him, not for the first time and not for the last, as if he were slightly off his rocker.

"It keeps my body strong and ready to do battle."

"Oh." Shalee was silent, and could not help wondering what other activities his body might be primed for. She blushed at the thought.

Matthew stood up and stretched his muscles. Nodding toward the door, he said, "Now I will go out and inspect the bodies of the unburied warriors."

As one, Shalee and Raquelle blurted out, "You are not dressed!"

Matthew said, "Don't worry about it. I always go out running in the morning without a shirt. I know it is cold, but my body will adapt." As he started for the door, Shalee grabbed his arm, pulling him back.

Her face was a mask of fear. "You may go out naked, if you choose, but you certainly can't go out unarmed. There are dragons about, and dragon worshippers as well. You'll be killed!" With Raquelle's help, Shalee dragged Matthew toward his bed, where his Bowie knife lay in its sheath, and they placed the knife in his hand. Shalee stared intently into his eyes. "Your life may depend on having this weapon."

Grinning, Matthew sarcastically replied, "Yes, Mom. Anything else, Mom?"

Shalee returned his sarcasm. "Aye, you need a shirt on, son."

With knife in hand, Matthew shook his head, laughing, and strode from the room. The castle people gaped as their half-naked leader ran out the front gate and headed straight for the field where the corpses had been lain. Reaching the woods, he was surprised to find all the bodies gone. The first thought that entered his mind was, *Dragons*. He quickly dismissed the thought. He remembered Robert Roybridge's vivid description, and Shalee's warning not thirty minutes before, but Matthew, in the clear light of a new day, after a good night's rest and a vigorous morning workout, was feeling just a little bit cocky. His rational, educated, late-twentieth-century self was coming back to the forefront, and he was beginning to think that maybe those dragons were a figment of the collective imagination. After all, these were fairly primitive people, and he had seen no hard evidence of the creatures' existence.

The forest opened suddenly to a large clearing, washed in sunlight so bright that Matthew paused to let his eyes adjust. After a few seconds, he spied a large wolf, dragging Damian's body. Taking cover behind a tree, Matthew watched as the wolf heaved the body toward a small cave. As the wolf neared the cave, a thunderous flapping sound passed overhead, startling Matthew and causing the wolf to drop its burden and wheel to face the new threat.

Looking up, Matthew froze at the sight of what appeared to be a dragon from a long-ago nightmare. It was real, all right, and every bit as fearsome as Robert had described. It looked like a huge winged serpent, with great horns protruding from its head, and a harsh, hissing screech tearing from its opened mouth. It touched down only a few feet from the wolf, and the wolf leapt backward, snarling.

Matthew thought, *Perhaps Shalee was right*. He wished that he had taken his .44, rather than just the knife. He watched in awe as the dragon sniffed at Damian's body, then raised its head, and issued a mournful cry. Matthew thanked God he was down wind of this monster.

The wolf made a charge then for Damian's body, but the dragon whirled with blinding speed, covered the body with its huge hind claws, and then it faced the wolf. The dragon's head started to sway back and forth, the motion progressing down its neck, until its entire body swayed in a hypnotic, undulating dance. Both Matthew and the wolf stood motionless, staring at the incredible sight. Then the dragon's skin began to change colors, from red to blue to yellow, like a moving rainbow. Both Matthew and the wolf, mesmerized by the changing colors of the dragon's skin, began swaying involuntarily in sync with the beast. Suddenly, the dragon's eyes narrowed, and from its gaping jaws spewed a ball of red flame, instantly consuming the startled wolf. The wolf loosed a tortured howl as it was engulfed in the flames, and then it fell silent to the ground, a quivering mound of smoldering fur. The sudden fire broke the spell, and Matthew unsheathed his knife as he dashed back behind the cover of the tree. Gathering his senses, he peeked out from behind the tree.

At the mouth of the cave, the heads of the frightened pups appeared, yelping for their dead mother. The dragon, concentrating upon devouring the roasted wolf, looked up only long enough to send a fireball in their direction. The pups turned tail, entering the cave just as the fireball hit. Their rumps singed, the pups yelped again, this time from pain. The wolf devoured, the dragon clutched Damian's body in its sword-like talons and leapt upward, winging away toward the north, shattering the morning with another shriek, its shadow casting fear on all creatures as it passed. After waiting a few moments to make certain the dragon was gone, Matthew left the cover of the tree and headed toward the cave. Finding the entrance too small to enter, he decided to return to the castle. He would have his warriors return later with him to broaden the cave's mouth. Now he had best be getting back to the castle, to breakfast. He had had more than enough excitement for one morning.

* * *

As Matthew crested the hill and approached the castle, he saw Shalee and Raquelle, standing outside the castle walls, wringing their hands. Fearing some new crisis, he quickened his pace and ran to them. Raquelle was weeping. "Father, we saw the dragon fly overhead with a body in its talons. We thought it was you."

Matthew sighed with relief. "No, it was only the headless body of Damian McWrath. Shalee, I apologize for not taking your warning seriously. But where I come from, we were taught that dragons exist only in fairy tales. Robert Roybridge told me about them yesterday, but I think a part of me still did not believe they exist. Robert told me too that there are many of them about. Is that true?"

Shalee nodded and said, "There are many lairs throughout all of Scotland, but the one that flew overhead has a nest close by. Each new moon, a young female is sacrificed to the dragon to appease it and keep its wrath from our walls."

Stunned by her matter-of-fact reply, Matthew asked, "So it really is true that people worship these dragons and sacrifice humans to them?"

Raquelle, as pragmatic as Shalee, responded, "Aye, father. Some, like Damian, worship them, but not us. We Picts only offer sacrifices because we fear their wrath. Lately, though, their appetite for our women has grown greater. We know that something must be done, but it is beyond our might or craft."

Matthew saw an opportunity in this situation. He knew that all the people would rally under a leader who could alleviate their fear of the dragons. The only problem was that it would be necessary to kill all of the dragons in Scotland. Matthew felt that his .44 Magnum could kill a dragon at close range, but he had only so many bullets, and no earthly means of getting more, unless he could find a way to commute back and forth between centuries. So the dragons would have to be killed by spears and lances. And the warriors would have to be shown that a dragon *could* be killed. Well, then, that would be his first priority. He had taught them to share. Now, he must teach them to kill something besides each other.

Raquelle broke into Matthew's thoughts with a tight hug, and led him to breakfast. And what a breakfast it was! The cooks, confident of their new leader's ability to provide food, had had the women gather eggs from every hen in the castle, and deliver them to the kitchen, where the precious morsels were set to fry in the pans. The aroma of fresh-baked loaves of coarse bread rose from the kitchens, and every heart in the castle was made lighter by the promise of a meal, grand beyond their dreams only a few short days before.

When Matthew arrived at the dining hall with Shalee and Raquelle, he found the people seated at the tables according to his directions of the night before. The food was laid before them, yet there was none of the chaos of the last meal. Instead, they waited patiently for Matthew to be seated. Then, one old woman came forth with a great tub of freshly churned butter, offering it up as if it were a chest filled with gold sovereigns. Indeed, the assembled diners were astonished, as butter had not been seen at their tables for time beyond memory.

"Damian always bid me hide the cows," the woman said. "It seems only fitting that his hoard now be shared." And with that, Matthew bowed his head, giving thanks to his God for providing their bounty. When he finally said his "Amen," the crowd echoed with a boisterous "Amen" in response, and the feeding frenzy began, this time in celebration, rather than in the ravenous desperation of the evening before. Silently Matthew added another prayer of thanks to God for giving him a reason to live again.

* * *

After a breakfast heartier than any of the people had ever seen, Matthew returned to his freshly cleaned chambers and gathered up the book on the ABC's to teach Raquelle. The other children gathered round, and Matthew invited them to join the class. He issued a challenge to them. "Any child who can learn the alphabet can go fishing with Alanna, the lake monster, and maybe she will grant you a ride on her back." The children plunged in, eager as cats at a cream-tasting contest. They were remarkably fast learners. By late morning, they had learned the basics, and had even picked up a little bit of modern English in the process. Finally Matthew said, "Let's head for the beach!" They flocked out behind him, boisterous as would be expected of children who, on their first day of school, are instructed in the wonders of recess.

At Matthew's instruction, the children watched intently, waiting for the waters to bubble and the fish to leap out, but the lake remained calm. After awhile, they began to grow antsy; they wanted to see the fish, and the friendly monster of the loch, now! Matthew ordered them to get on their knees and pray to his God for fish. He wondered if Alanna had misread his signal the day before, or if, indeed, he could really communicate with her, after all. He also wondered what he would do if he could not provide a feast for tonight. How credible would he be then to these people? So Matthew got down on his knees, and told God that the ball was in His court now. Matthew and the children prayed very hard for nearly fifteen minutes. Finally, his heart sinking in despair, Matthew stopped praying and rose to his feet, shouting to the heavens, "My God, you have answered my prayers thus far. I know that You will hear them now, and the prayers of these children, and bring forth the fish, and the mistress of the loch."

Suddenly, the waters began to bubble and churn, Then came a rain of fish, their bodies flying out of the water and landing on the beach. The children descended upon the fish like hungry wolves. Some fish, over three feet long, were not going to die without a fight. In the struggle, some little hands found their way inside the fishes' mouths, and were nipped. The screams of wounded children filled the air.

Alanna reared her head above the surface of the water to observe the pandemonium. In between checking the children's wounds, Raquelle furiously clubbed fish. From over the hill came Matthew's warriors, who had been summoned by Shalee to carry the fish. Hearing the screams, the warriors rushed forward to protect their children. Upon realizing that the little ones were not mortally wounded, the warriors and their children together began clubbing the thrashing fish.

Matthew shouted, "Stun the fish; don't kill them!" As the stunned fish were dragged into two equal piles, Alanna proceeded to sniff each pile; her eyes narrowed to inspect every individual fish as closely as a jeweler would scrutinize a finely cut diamond. Her own children had appeared, and were paying close attention to their mother's technique of choosing the best fish. She issued a deep growl, and they come forward to inspect the two seemingly equal piles. This process took about half an hour, and some warriors became impatient. Matthew silenced them, saying, "Alanna is teaching her children how to choose the best of the hunt, as you each do with your own children."

The warriors nodded and began to watch with fascination. They were gaining a deeper understanding of, and respect for, this monster that they had feared for so long, and they stared in silence as Alanna and her children began to gorge themselves on the right-hand pile. Matthew was certain that the babies had grown since the day before. And no wonder, seeing the way they ate. They consumed fish after fish after fish, beginning with the head, and champing noisily until the tail disappeared. The days of plenty may have arrived, but Alanna saw to it that her children did not waste any part of the fish.

Matthew decided to try to communicate with Alanna. He sent this thought to her: *As long as you drive fish to this beach, I will station warriors here to stun the fish and divide them into two piles. You may then choose the best pile for you and your babies, and the warriors will take the other.* Alanna looked at him, and he could have sworn he saw her nod slightly as she continued to bolt down a whole fish. It was a very active fish, and Matthew could see its wriggling outline as it descended Alanna's long neck. *These lake monsters have never eaten so well,* Matthew thought with satisfaction. Indeed, all three seemed to smile at Matthew between bites.

Matthew gave orders that the left-hand pile, which held about 75 large fish, was to be hauled back to the castle. "Fifty are to be prepared for the day's meals, and the rest will be sent to Robert's castle," he commanded. Matthew, Raquelle, and the children trailed the fish-bearing warriors back to the castle. As they drew near, Matthew was pleased to see that from every inch of castle wall hung bed wraps, furs, and clothing. The cleaning campaign was going as he had ordered. The women were now assembled on the castle walls, staring in awe as their warriors and children returned, heavily laden with fish.

Shalee had stationed herself at the front gate to meet the warriors as they entered. She was a natural organizer. Matthew entered the gate and saw that she was already making plans for the disposition of the fish. She gave orders for twenty fish to be roasted on the fires that were blazing to her left, and twenty to be cut up and placed in pots filled with vegetables simmering for fish stew. "The other ten fish will be delivered, one each, to ten of the farm families under Matthew Wolverine's authority," she said. "And when you deliver them, invite them to a feast that will be held three days hence. They should meet their new leader." Matthew nodded his approval.

Matthew and Raquelle were treated as conquering heroes by the women, who were now busily cutting up the fish. As the new leader and his daughter departed, the women resumed the chatter among themselves, and Matthew, straining his ears to hear what they said, was pleased. "We will all eat our fill again today." "Yes, that never happened in this castle until this new leader arrived." "Whatever God this new leader serves must be a providing God, and we should serve Him." "Pray this new God does not require human sacrifices!"

Matthew's smile was never bigger or brighter then the one he wore as he left the food preparation area. He had always had an overwhelming need to be admired for his ability to provide. His new subjects, sensing this need, poured on the praise. He knew some of them were "kissing up," but he also knew that beneath the sycophancy there was genuine appreciation. A rush of pride came over him, which he quickly reined in. *Remember*, he told himself, *you had plenty of help with all of this.* He gazed heavenward, then cast his eyes back to where Shalee labored with the food preparations, and finally he looked out beyond the castle gate, toward the loch where Alanna and her babies frolicked. No, this was definitely not a one-man show.

* * *

As Matthew and Raquelle made their way across the crowded square, there suddenly came, from the back of the crowd, the rhythmic clatter of two sticks being struck together. Almost instantly, the happy sound of a lyre, well played, joined in. Raquelle grabbed Matthew, and they began to dance — a joyous, whirling movement that soon infected the others in the square. The other warriors and their wives joined in, and even the guards upon the castle walls came down to share in the merrymaking. For the first time in many a year, or perhaps ever, laughter rang out from inside this castle. The military part of Matthew's mind screamed that the guards should be on the wall because now the castle had been left vulnerable to attack... but for once, he shushed that part of his mind, and decided he simply didn't care. These people needed to laugh and have fun, after all. It occurred to Matthew that he could not remember the last time he himself had really laughed — not just an amused chuckle, but a laugh that began in the tips of his toes and shook its way up to the very ends of his hair.

So Matthew threw himself into the spirit of the gathering. Before long, the only people who were not dancing were the cooks, but the spring in their steps and the rhythm of their stirring spoons was obviously borne of the same joy that all the others were feeling.

After nearly two hours, with only brief breaks to take a sip of cool water, Matthew stopped dancing, waved to the merrymakers and walked to the stables to lie back on a pile of straw and catch his breath. In a flash, Yellow Rose pounced upon his stomach. With both hands, Matthew lifted her up in the air. "So you want to dance, too." Matthew started gently shaking the cat from side to side, to the rhythm of the music which still filled the square. The cat tilted her eyes up to the sky, as if to say, "How humiliating." Seeing this expression, Matthew pulled her to his chest and started vigorously rubbing her back. "Oh, you are such a good cat, but I saw some monstrous rats in the castle that you need to be killing, so I didn't bring you any fish today." Yellow Rose's eyes narrowed to slits, and she growled what sounded unmistakably like X-rated feline profanity. Matthew was thankful that he couldn't read the cat's mind.

Raquelle entered the stable at that moment, a small fish in her hand. The cat did a double take, bounced on Matthew's stomach, and leapt toward Raquelle. A moment later, Yellow Rose was literally covered with hungry kittens, who climbed over her head to get to the fish. The cat took this in stride, and tore the fish apart so her kittens could easily eat it. Matthew pointed out to Raquelle what a good mother Yellow Rose was, to feed her kittens before herself. "Much different from yesterday," Raquelle countered. "But she was starving then."

Shalee entered the stable carrying two bowls of hot fish stew for Matthew and Raquelle. Matthew took the steaming bowl, reminded by the fragrant aroma that he was famished. As he savored the delicious stew, he leaned back, grinning as he considered what a great day this had turned out to be.

Shalee leaned close to Yellow Rose and whispered something in the cat's ear. Yellow Rose's head shot up, and she raced out the stable door with the speed of a striking rattlesnake. The kittens stopped eating and ran after their mother. Matthew, Raquelle, and Shalee sat on the straw, laughing at the cats' antics. After he finished his stew, Matthew asked Shalee what she had said to Yellow Rose.

Shalee's face lit up as she divulged her secret. "I told her that twenty fish had been skinned to make the stew, and that the fish skins and entrails were lying, unguarded, beside the cooks. But we've little room to laugh at the actions of a few hungry cats. Both of you did a fine job of wolfing down that stew, yourselves."

Matthew shot up like a cobra about to strike, and smacked his forehead. "Wolfing! The wolf pups! I forgot all about them. They must be starving in that cave. Shalee, get me ten large empty sacks, and put some fish entrails into another two sacks."

As Matthew watched the bags being filled, a stout warrior happened by. Matthew asked him his name. The warrior lowered his head and said, "My name is Kele, my leader."

"Kele, how many horses in my stables are suitable for riding?"

Kele held up one open hand.

Matthew liked this man, so he baited his hook. "That is five. Do you know that is five?"

Kele's head dropped lower, "No, my leader, I just know that there are as many riding horses as I have fingers on this hand."

Matthew dangled the bait in front of Kele. "I have need of a lieutenant to carry out my orders, but he must be able to read, write, and count. Do you wish to master these skills and become my lieutenant?" Matthew had used the American English term and pronunciation, *lieutenant*, because he did not recall the Gaelic equivalent.

Kele's eyes again fell. "What is a lew-tennet, leader?"

Laughing, Matthew explained that a lieutenant was an assistant, a right-hand man, and a leader among the other warriors. Kele grinned broadly, nodding his head vigorously. He knew that holding such a rank would mean his family would never go hungry.

Using his fingers to count as he said the numbers aloud, Matthew said, "Good man! Now saddle three horses and bring them to the front gate. Then pick ten warriors." He counted off on the fingers of both hands. "These warriors will go with us to capture some orphaned wolf pups I found earlier today. Make sure each warrior is armed, and has with him a rope as long as his arm."

Kele rushed off, eager to fulfill his first charge as a lew-tennet. Soon, Matthew and Raquelle led a band of warriors out from the castle gates, each carrying one empty sack, with Kele carrying the two sacks of fish entrails. After a short ride, the group approached the cave entrance. The pups cowered in the cave, howling at the men. Matthew had Kele lay the fish entrails five feet from the cave entrance. A hungry wolf pup rushed out, and Matthew snatched it up, put a rope around its neck, and then let it down to feed.

Raquelle nudged herself past her father to the cave entrance as another pup scurried for the food. As Raquelle scooped it up by the back of its neck, Kele tied a rope around its neck, and Raquelle set it down beside its littermate to feed on the fish. The four remaining pups saw their sisters gorging themselves on fresh fish, and they rushed out. As they did, the warriors grabbed each pup behind the neck, put a rope around it, then set it down to eat. The pups ate ravenously until, stomachs bulging, they plopped down upon the ground. Again Matthew thought of how hunger ruled both man and beast in this age, and he knew his next priority must be to fill his castle with stores of food to last the winter.

Raquelle picked up a pup and stroked it. "Father, look. This pup has gone to sleep in my hands." The other pups tried to get back into their cave, but the ropes prevented their escape. The exertion of the escape tired them, and they finally plopped down on the ground to sleep. Kele ordered his warriors to gently pick up the sleeping pups and bear them back to the castle.

On the way back to the castle, Matthew thought of how quickly this Kele, and the woman Shalee, had assumed the responsibilities and authority he had given them. Recalling how Shalee had ordered the distribution of the fish, it dawned on him that she could count. He wondered if she could read and write, as well. After they entered the castle, Raquelle took the wolves up to her and her father's chambers. Matthew took Shalee aside and asked, "I have seen you at work, and I see you can count. That pleases me. Can you read and write as well?"

Shalee beamed and said, "Aye, I can count. And I can read and write Norman, Latin, *and* Gaelic."

It intrigued Matthew that a peasant woman of this time period would be so well educated. "How did you learn?"

"My father, Lord bless him, had a kind heart. He would often give hospitality to strangers. A traveling Norman priest arrived one day, claiming God had called him to Scotland, and to our home in particular. He stayed with us for a long while, slept in our bed, and ate our food, but he wouldn't do any physical labor. To pay his keep, my father had him teach me my letters and mathematics. He was an educated man, and taught me more than my father expected."

"What happened to the priest?"

"Damian sacrificed him to the dragons, but the priest swore that his God would send another to destroy Damian, drive the dragons from Scotland, and unite Scotland under His God. He said it would happen before the new millennium. Damian often laughed at this prophecy, but I continued to pray for your coming. And now here you are."

Matthew's face turned bright red. He didn't want to get started on this Y1K stuff again. "Well, I don't know about prophecy, but since you can read and write, you shall be charged with teaching all in the castle to read, write, and count. This may have to be done at night for the warriors, but the women and children can learn during the day, after their chores. I have some books in my knapsack you can use. Now, these books are written in a language called English, which is what we speak where I come from."

"Oh, I have heard of English," Shalee said. "It is spoken by many in the kingdom to the south."

"Yes, that's true," Matthew replied, choosing his words carefully. "But the kind of English we spoke in the land where I come from is quite different from the language you know about. Some of the words will sound familiar, though." Shalee nodded, her eyes shining eagerly. "I like to learn new languages," she said.

"Well, that is something you and I have in common." Then Matthew became more serious. "Shalee, there is more to be done, for which I must rely upon you. Before our people can learn, they need to know that their bellies will always be full — not just today, but every day. I have a plan that I think will free the people from their worries, but I need your help with it."

"I will do anything you ask, my lord," she said, fixing him with her piercing green stare.

Matthew pushed away the thought that came unbidden into his mind, and began to share his ideas about the subject at hand. He asked Shalee what fowl could be kept in the castle, and what herbs and grains could be acquired by trading the daily fish that Alanna and her babies would provide.

"Oh, there are several kinds of fowl we can raise," she said enthusiastically. "Capons, geese, and ducks of many kinds will flourish here, and they will feed us well."

"Good," Matthew said. He told her that he wanted to trade the fish for fowl, and to cut the birds' wing feathers so they couldn't fly. The children were to gather grains to feed the fowl, so that the birds would never go hungry, and they were to provide straw or grass for nests inside the stable, that they would feel safe within the castle walls. He explained that the birds would lay more eggs if they were well-fed and secure. Shalee would use some of the eggs for cooking, but the healthiest birds would be allowed to hatch their eggs.

"Our neighbors must learn that we will have fish to trade, each day, when the sun is highest in the sky. In the beginning, let our neighbors drive hard bargains, and let them take many fish for the food they trade. Word will spread that their goods will buy many fish from Shalee at this castle. Before winter comes, this castle must be filled with food enough to last us two years." Shalee nodded her head in agreement, but thought to herself that Matthew was raving. She could not comprehend that much food, even in all of Scotland.

Matthew said, "All right, Shalee, that is all for now. Oh, except one more thing. Those wolf pups we caught need milk. Will you see that they have it?" Shalee nodded again, and as she went off to fetch the milk,

Matthew returned to his chambers and the wolves. As he entered, he found Raquelle by his bed, trying to get the frightened wolf pups to come out from their hiding place underneath it. This place had become their new den, and they were not coming out willingly. Matthew told Raquelle to go and fetch Yellow Rose, and to bring her, with her kittens, to his bedroom. Then he sat on the floor by the door and waited for her to return.

Shalee entered the room with a bucket of milk and six empty bowls, which Matthew filled with the milk and set upon the floor. Not too long afterwards, Raquelle came in, carrying Yellow Rose, with the kittens following close behind. She set the cat down in a corner, and the kittens immediately surrounded their mother, anxious to nurse. Raquelle took her place beside her father, behind the row of bowls. The kittens purred loudly as they nursed, and Yellow Rose purred more loudly than all of them together. It was more a soft roar than a purr, and the pups poked their noses out from under the bed to investigate. Smelling the fresh milk, the pups' hunger proved stronger than their fear, and they inched their way cautiously toward the bowls.

At that, Yellow Rose's head jerked up, and the pups froze. But after a few seconds, they began to creep, inch by inch, toward the bowls that held relief for their gnawing hunger. Finally one pup reached a bowl and began vigorously lapping. An inquisitive kitten broke away from its mother's tit and crept forward to get a better look at these strange creatures. Before the kitten could reach the lapping pup, it was sidetracked by the sweet smell emanating from one of the bowls of milk, and it struggled to peek over the edge of the bowl at the treasure inside.

One of the pups came over to give the kitten a helping paw to reach the milk, but the kitten arched her back and hissed at the intruder. A battle royal seemed about to begin when Shalee reached down and picked up the pup, nuzzling him against her neck. This pup, no longer wary, licked and nibbled playfully at Shalee's hand. Setting him down to drink, she lifted up the frightened kitten, gently stroking its soft fur, until its hissing was replaced with a contented purring. Now, these two natural enemies shared not only their hunger, but Shalee's scent, and, sniffing each other, they cast their fear aside, and started to drink together in peace. The rest of the animals, craving Shalee's attention, crowded at her feet, and she picked up and caressed each of them before setting them down to eat with their new brothers and sisters. Matthew watched in admiration. Shalee definitely had a way with animals.

He turned his attention from the sight of this beautiful woman and the tiny creatures, and told Raquelle to get some slender rope. When she returned with it, he proceeded to tie off each wolf's tail about an inch from their rump. The pups barely noticed.

An inquisitive Raquelle asked, "Father, why do you tie the wolves' tails?"

"Their tails will fall off in a week or two. The wolves under our control will be without tails. This is the way the people of our lands will know our tame wolves from wild ones, and will not slay them in the forests." Raquelle wondered for a moment at her new father's reason for marking the beasts, until she realized that he wanted, in yet another way, to proclaim his dominion to the people in the surrounding lands. She smiled to herself at the wisdom this man possessed, and knew that she, and all the people of the castle, would reap its rewards. Even the beasts, busily lapping at their meal, seemed to know that their lives had changed for the better.

The Ultimate Dragon

CHAPTER 7

That night, the castle was filled with joyous sounds, as the people shared, along with their feast, stories, laughter, and singing. The fish stew heated and filled their insides, and then the loaves of bread and great platters of roasted fish were served. Tonight, there was no mad rush to grab the food. Bowls and platters passed freely from person to person, with each taking generous portions, yet knowing there was more food still on the table. Matthew encouraged his warriors to share stories of their valiant deeds, and their strange tales of dragons kept Matthew, and the children, enchanted well into the night. The people's confidence grew as their bellies filled, just as Matthew had told Shalee it would.

During the meal, Matthew noticed that some women were taking fish in their hands and putting them under the table. He bent over to see what they were doing, and spied several kittens under the table, scoffing down the morsels of cooked fish. It pleased Matthew that the women now felt they had enough food to share with kittens. A land freed from the worry of hunger could become truly free.

At one point, a warrior began rattling two sticks together. *Not too great on the rhythm*, Matthew thought, but then the people began singing, and Matthew joined right in. They sang song after song, some of which seemed vaguely familiar to Matthew, until Raquelle grew sleepy, her head dropping on Matthew's shoulder. He lifted the child up, bade his people a fine good night, and headed for their chambers.

Shalee trailed at his side. She said, "This is the first time some of these people have known a full belly, and I shudder to think how ill their humor will be if their hunger returns. Do you believe the monsters of the loch will continue to feed us?"

Matthew adjusted his grip on Raquelle, and her arms moved up to encircle his neck. "Alanna is not a monster, but a friend. She feels hunger, as we do. She cares for her young, as we do. And she obviously responds to kindness, as well. It benefits her and her young to share the food with us. By working together, all have full bellies. You have served up a wonderful meal tonight, Shalee. My chambers are clean, and my people happy, all because you, and others here, have worked alongside each other. Do you not also feel gladdened by the fruits of your own efforts? I feel glad for all of these things, most of all that I have, once again, a daughter who loves me, and a chance to be deserving of that love. Life is good." They entered his chambers, and Matthew tucked Raquelle into her bed, tenderly kissing her forehead.

Shalee turned and walked through the doorway into her own bedroom. Matthew could not help but notice the grace of her movements as she walked, and he remembered the feel of smooth skin beneath his fingertips in that long-ago life he had once lived. His eyes never left her body as he whispered to himself, "Yeah, life is good. But boy, do I hate sleeping alone."

When morning's first light fell upon Matthew, he was already well into his exercise routine. He was up to 190 pushups, with only ten more to go. A wolf pup crept out from under his bed, darted right under Matthew's chest and tilted its head up toward his face. Head down, Matthew bellowed, "Will you get out of the way?"

The pup licked Matthew's face, yipped, then backed up. Matthew completed his set of pushups and rolled over to begin his sit-ups. The pup was not to be put off, and promptly deposited its rear end on Matthew's stomach. Now, every time Matthew rose, he received a lick on the face. The pup found this extremely amusing, and howled with delight. This, of course, drew the other pups out from under the bed and they formed a ring around Matthew. The pup on Matthew's stomach encouraged them, and soon all were on top of his stomach and chest. Matthew started roughhousing with the pups, and they howled with glee. Soon it became a free-for-all, with Raquelle waking and joining in. Howls and laughter echoed throughout the castle, waking the other children. They streamed into Matthew's chambers like hungry children who know that a chocolate bar awaits them in the next room. Children and wolf pups crawled over and under the bed, toppled the chairs, and, all the while, filled the chambers with the sound of their giggling and pretend-fierce growls. Complete pandemonium reigned, until exhausted pups and children started to drop to the floor, desperately trying to catch their breath between fits of howling, growling or laughter. The pups thought they had joined a gigantic wolf pack, and the children knew, perhaps for the first time in their short lives, what it meant to be children.

Matthew was quick to seize the enthusiasm of this moment. "Who wants to help take care of these pups?" All the children, including Raquelle, threw their hands up high in the air. "Raquelle, each day you will assign different children to brush, feed, and clean up after the wolves. Now, appoint them." Raquelle told the girls that they were to brush the pups that day, and the boys were to get them some milk and clean up after the pups ate.

This good nature carried over to breakfast. The castle was charged with optimism. The people had a new leader, a new God, an end to their hunger, and laughter. They had endured under Damian; they were living under Matthew. Smiling women served the food and joked with the warriors. The warriors boasted that they could slay dragons, and the women teased them, challenging them for proof.

Matthew called in the cooks then, and admonished them for being much too thin. "Cooks in my castle should set aside some of the best food for themselves, and eat abundantly and often," he commanded. "How can anyone tell you are good cooks if you are not well fed yourselves? I'll tell you what: in two full moons I will inspect your weight, and any cook who remains skinny will cease being a cook." The cooks nodded and cheered. Finally, a leader who understood that a cook's weight should rise in direct proportion to his skills! They could not wait for the fish today, so eager were they to carry out the new orders.

* * *

After breakfast, Matthew, Raquelle, and Kele, accompanied by twenty warriors, headed for the beach to await the fish driven by Alanna. Matthew and Raquelle separated themselves from the warriors, walking down the beach. Raquelle questioned her father, "Why did you tell the cooks to take the best food for themselves?"

"It is from my military experience, my daughter, which you must learn. In the military, cooks receive all the food, and they always take some of the best for themselves because they love to eat. They learn to cook delicious dishes for themselves. They eat tremendous amounts of their tasty food, and experiment in different ways to produce even better meals, and they grow big. The size of their body states to the world that they are excellent cooks. As they learn to prepare more delicious meals, they share these dishes with the rest of us.

"Now our cooks can take some of the best food with a clear conscience, knowing it is the leader's order that they gain weight. No warrior will dare challenge a cook for taking some of the best for himself, because I am the one who instituted this custom. In fact, warriors will brag on the size of our cooks. One look at our cooks, and anyone will swear they never missed a meal in their lives. It shows other clans that my followers always eat their fill."

Raquelle pondered her father's words as she watched the loch waters splash upon the shore. "Is that why you let Alanna pick from two piles?"

"Aye, she does most of the work in driving the fish to shore, so she has first choice. Is it my imagination, or do you think her babies have gained weight?"

Raquelle looked at the babies and replied, "You are right! They are gaining weight! You must name them when they come to feed today."

Matthew smiled and pulled Raquelle closer, but his pistol, strapped on his right leg, jabbed her and she pulled away. "What is that, a weapon? If it be a club, you'd do better with a bigger one."

"Aye, it is a very powerful weapon, more powerful than any club. It could kill a dragon at close range, so I carry it when I leave the castle. Come to my left side so I can hug you."

Raquelle switched sides, and they watched as Alanna and her babies drove the fish on shore. Over two hundred fish flopped on the wet sand, and the warriors quickly separated them into two piles. Matthew wanted to keep the fish alive as long as possible. Alanna picked the pile on the right, and she and her babies commenced eating. Matthew waited until the babies finished eating before he approached them. Drawing near the larger baby, he proclaimed in a loud voice, "You shall be called 'Eric.'"

Alanna's head snapped upward as if she had been slapped, and Matthew heard a stern voice…or something…but he heard it in his mind. The voice said, *Can't you tell a female from a male? You're as stupid as an eel. Boy children have a purple mark on their heads. Do you see such a mark on the head of this young one?*

Matthew's mouth dropped, and he shook his head. Could it be that Alanna was, indeed, speaking directly to his brain? Well, then, he would continue this experiment. He directed his thought to Alanna: *How are you able to talk to me?*

Alanna's huge face wrinkled into a contemplative scowl, and then Matthew picked up this thought: *Some humans we can communicate with, but most run away before we have the chance to give them our thoughts. I was in so much pain with that fish bone in my gums when we first met that I could not form words which you would understand. Besides, I didn't want to scare you by talking, at least not until that horrible bone was pulled from my mouth. Then, you up and call me a sea monster! We are not monsters; we are the lake guardians.*

With that, Alanna threw her head high in the air and turned around so abruptly that Matthew and Raquelle had to leap aside to avoid being crushed beneath the weight of her tail.

Matthew ordered Kele to dispatch eighteen warriors to each bear two fish to the castle, and then to return for the rest. "Inform Shalee that we have one hundred fish, and tell her to trade what she cannot use for food, according to the directions I gave her." Kele immediately dispatched the warriors, and he and the remaining two warriors lingered behind to guard the remaining pile of fish.

Matthew turned again to the largest baby, and pronounced that her name was to be "Elizabeth." And the other, the one with the purple mark on its head, he named "Eric." Alanna smiled and thought aloud — at least to Matthew, *Much better! Those names have a pleasant ring.*

* * *

As Alanna, Elizabeth, and Eric slipped back into the water to cool off, Matthew and Raquelle began walking along the beach. Raquelle asked Matthew if the names he gave to Alanna and her babies had a special meaning for him. "I have always liked the name 'Alanna'," he said, "and 'Elizabeth' will be the name of great queens of the south kingdom."

"What about 'Eric'?" asked Raquelle.

"He is named for Eric the Red, father to Leif Ericson, who will one day discover my homeland."

Raquelle asked, "Father, how do you know the future? Are you one of those blessed with the gift of prophecy?"

Well, here it was: the big question — not quite the question every father dreads, but one that this particular father had been mulling over since he had acquired his new daughter, wondering how, or if, he should tell her the entire truth. Matthew decided it would be best to just be honest with her. Whether she believed him or not was up to her. So he began, "No, I have no prophetic gifts. Raquelle, I can no more explain how it had happened than I can explain why there are dragons… but I, myself, have come from the future. To me, the things you think of as prophecies are ancient history."

She was quiet for a few moments, taking this in. Then she asked, "What part of the future did you come from?"

"From a thousand years hence…a thousand revolutions of the earth around the sun…yes, the earth goes around the sun; I will tell you more about that later. When I left my homeland, the year was one-thousand, nine-hundred and ninety-nine, Anno Domini. When I arrived in this place, it was nine-hundred and ninety-nine. When Robert Roybridge first told me the year, I thought he was mistaken. But I had to consider that the clothes people wore here, and the way they behaved, and the way they talked, were not consistent with the people and things of my time. At first I had thought the people were playing some kind of game, but when Robert told me the year I became convinced he was telling the truth, and that I had traveled back in time."

Raquelle's eyes were wide. "How did you get here from a thousand years in the future, Father?"

"That I cannot tell you either, because I don't really understand it myself. When I left my homeland in my time, I came to Scotland, and…"

Raquelle interrupted. "How big was the ship you sailed on?"

"Well… I didn't come on a ship. I came in a big flying machine…. a popular means of conveyance in my time. I will show you a picture in one of the books at the castle. Anyway, I came to Scotland…"

"In the big flying machine, right?"

"That's right. I came to Scotland to carry out my wife's final wishes. The first night I was here, I got caught in the rain when my car stalled…"

"Your what did what?"

"A car is… was… will be… another kind of conveyance. It had wheels, and could move without being pulled or pushed. At least that was the idea. But something went wrong with it, and it couldn't carry me any further. So I took my knapsack and got out of the car, and went walking up the road looking for help." Raquelle's eyes grew wider as he continued the tale, describing as best he could the experience in the old ruined church, and what had happened when he touched the massive stone cross.

Raquelle was silent and thoughtful after he had finished. Then she asked, somewhat timidly, "If that stone in this building you call a 'church' got you here, could it take you back?" Tears were forming in her eyes.

Matthew quickly comforted her. "I do not know, Raquelle, and to tell you the truth, I have no desire to go back. I had nothing left back there, whereas here I have a new daughter, a big castle to take care of, and people who need me. And I have befriended the lake guardians. So maybe I was sent here for a reason. I don't know what the reason is, but I do know that I will stay as long as I am needed."

He left it at that, not giving voice to the thought that part of him still longed to join his wife and daughter in death. Though the delights and distractions of his new life were many, when Matthew lay alone at night with his thoughts, he found himself fighting despair. In those dark hours of solitude, all of his lofty talk of purpose and a reason for living rang hollow. Whatever else Matthew Wolverine was — leader, father, provider of food — nothing could make him forget that he was a man out of time, in more ways than one.

As for Raquelle, she had no reason to believe that her father would lie to her. Even so, the story she'd just heard was stretching her limits.

She believed in dragons and loch guardians because she could see them, but her father's story of coming from the future… well, it would take some faith.

* * *

Alanna's pile of fish quivered in the sunshine as the live creatures squirmed to get back into the water. Normally, Alanna would never risk leaving food unattended, but now she was just too full to care. Alanna and her children relaxed in the loch for a short break, and then began to feast again. What a luxury this was! It was the first time in Elizabeth's and Eric's lives that they were full, and had yet more food awaiting them on shore.

At that moment, the keen eyes of two young dragons, flying high overhead, spotted the vibrating mass of fish. Swooping speedily down, they landed to feast upon this easy prey. Kele and his two warriors were taken by surprise, and drew back from the fish to defend themselves as an enraged Alanna charged from the water to protect her catch. The dragons shot balls of fire at Kele, then turned toward Alanna, leaving their backs to Matthew.

That was their mistake. From the sheath on his belt, Matthew drew his razor-sharp Bowie knife as he sprinted toward the dragons. Leaping upon the back of one of the young dragons, he threw his left arm around its neck, seized its scaly chin, and, with a single, deft stroke, sliced through the leathery skin at the base of the dragon's throat. The other dragon wheeled at the sound of its sibling's gurgling cry as it drowned in the gush of its own blood. Alanna quickly descended upon the second dragon's neck, clutching it in the viselike grip of her massive jaws. She dragged the struggling dragon across the sand, and dove under the water. After a few moments, the gurgling and thrashing beneath the surface was stilled, and the dragon was never again seen alive upon the earth or in the skies.

As Matthew leapt away from his dragon, Elizabeth and Eric burst upon the beach, biting at the dragon's tail. The bleeding dragon thrashed about in the throes of its death, but Elizabeth and Eric held fast, finally pulled the dying dragon into the loch and under the water.

Kele and his warriors bolted to Matthew's side, breathing a sigh of relief as they watched the dragons slide under the water to their death. Matthew looked to his warriors and asked, "Are any of you hurt?" Before any could answer, there arose a fierce, howling wind above their heads. All froze in terror as the screeching filled their ears and chased all thoughts save their own deaths from their minds.

Looking skyward, they saw a pair of dragons, much larger than the two they had just killed, swooping down upon them with the ferocity of a huge falcon dashing toward frightened mice. Matthew immediately knew that it is was the young dragons' parents dive-bombing them. His first reaction was to sprint toward Raquelle. His movement shook the other warriors from their terror, sending them dashing toward her, as well.

But the blazing rage of the dragons' fire burst harmlessly upon an empty spot on the beach, singeing the wet sand. Livid in their frustrated rage, the dragons slammed hard on the beach and turned to race after these impudent murderers of their young. In a thousand years, no human in Scotland had dared kill a dragon's young. Matthew scooped up a petrified Raquelle and, spying an opening in the cliff, headed for it. The opening was not very wide, barely large enough for him to pass through. Matthew pushed Raquelle into the darkness, with Kele close behind. The two warriors following them were no runners, and they lagged, gasping for breath, far behind the three. The dragons, thundering in their blind rage toward the fleeing humans, trampled the slow-moving ones. The dragons lingered over the fallen men for an instant, tearing through their flesh, then casting them aside. The warriors' screams filled the air as the dragons rushed toward the entrance of the cave.

Both dragons flung their fire toward this opening, just as the three humans entered. The fireballs missed their mark, bursting upon the rocks at the sides of the cave entrance. This blaze illuminated the interior of the cave enough for Matthew to spot a boulder near the back, and they rushed to hide behind it.

As the dragons reached the opening, the female plunged her head into the chasm and belched fire inside. The boulder deflected the flames over the top of the three crouched humans, licking harmlessly at the lichens growing on the moist surface of the cave walls. The female dragon withdrew her head, only to be replaced by her mate's, who sent his own larger flame across the tiny cavern. The dragons took turns spewing their inferno across the inside of the cave. Matthew realized that they were trapped by this endless sea of flames, and recalled another time, in a faraway jungle, when he and his men cowered in a cave as enemies fired upon them with flame throwers. In an instant, he remembered how he had survived that seemingly hopeless situation.

He began to methodically explore the back of the cave, using the illumination of each dragon's fire. After a few moments, he spotted a shadow in the back wall. He knew that it might be an entrance into another cave, or just a shadow, cast by jutting rocks. Even behind the boulder, the dragon's fire burned him, and he saw sweat pouring down Raquelle's face. He knew that she would not last must longer.

But time was on their side. The intervals between each dragon's fire blast were getting longer as they grew weary, and Matthew felt that Raquelle could make it to the potential safety of the shadow if she ran quickly. By the light of the next fireball, he showed Raquelle the shadow in the rear wall, and ordered her to run like the wind toward it when he touched her back. The dragon's fire subsided, and Matthew gave Raquelle the signal. She took off like a shot, and was almost to the shadow when the ground swallowed her up. Matthew screamed at her at the top of his lungs, but his only answer was the female dragon, again thrusting her body into the opening, her energy diminished, but not her rage. A huge stream of fire streamed over the boulder with a heat so intense that Matthew's and Kele's eyebrows started to singe.

Death sat just inside the cave's entrance, licking her chops, and awaiting the imminent pleasure of devouring Matthew Wolverine. In every battle, however, there is one moment when the enemy is vulnerable, and desperation offers the loser a fleeting chance to emerge the victor. Matthew drew his .44 Magnum, ready to seize that moment. The enraged female dragon drove her body so deep into the cave's entrance that all outside light was cut off, and she was stuck. Struggling wildly, she thrashed her head from side to side, roaring in frustration. In the pitch darkness, Matthew stepped out from behind the boulder and knelt. He raised his pistol and fired blindly in the general direction of the cave's entrance. His shot struck high, slamming into the dirt above the entrance, spraying the dragon's head with dirt.

The dragon had never heard such a terrifying noise, and, for the first time in her long and evil life, she experienced the fear she had always used to pierce the hearts of her enemies. Panicked, she intensified her savage thrashing. Matthew fired again, this time his bullet creasing the dragon's jaw and tearing out a large chunk of her scaly flesh. The dragon involuntarily coughed a small rivulet of the liquid fire, which dribbled down her chin and dripped upon her front claws. This time, the fire burned only the dragon's mouth and front feet as it illuminated the cave. That momentary flicker of light was all that Matthew needed. He took careful aim and fired again. His bullet slammed home, exploding the dragon's left eye and flinging her free from the cave.

The dragon flailed in agony in the dirt outside, desperately trying to extinguish the searing pain in her head, as well as the smoldering liquid that crackled upon her flesh. The male dragon, frightened by the thunder that had erupted within the cave, and seeing his mate's agony, was clutched with fear. He sprang into the air, and, with the screeching female following close behind, flew swiftly away north, toward the safety of the pair's own cave.

Matthew called again to Raquelle, but there was no answer, so he and Kele made their way, catlike, to the outside. Matthew ordered Kele to go in haste to the castle, and to return with lighted torches, rope, blankets, and a squad of warriors. Scanning the sky for another dragon attack, Matthew moved toward his wounded warriors.

As he reached his men, they saw him and began to moan loudly. Both their backs bore deep gashes, and Matthew knew that, unless their bleeding was stopped, they would both die. With cupped hands, Matthew brought water from the loch to cleanse their wounds. The warriors winced in pain as the water flowed through their lacerations. Then Matthew saw that the ground all around them was soaked with their blood, and he knew that nothing short of a miracle could save them.

Kele returned, followed by all but the youngest and frailest who lived in the castle, and proceeded to set lighted torches on the beach. Shalee and the women attended to the wounded, as Matthew, Kele, and the other warriors entered the cave. They proceeded past the boulder to the back of the cave, and found a ledge overhanging a shallow well, with a drop of only three feet.

And there they found Raquelle, lying on her back on what appeared to be soft white sand. Matthew leapt down to her side and reached under her to lift her up. He was startled by a searing pain where his right arm had touched the sand, and he quickly set Raquelle down. Inspecting his arm, he noticed a small scrape that was bleeding. His attempt to brush off the white sand covering his injured arm only increased the burning.

Matthew reasoned that if this were poison, he would die quickly. In the torchlight, however, he noticed that his bleeding had stopped. He smelled, then tasted the white sand, and discovered that it was not sand at all, but salt. "Raise your torches higher," Matthew ordered his warriors, "so that you can see the walls around me!" They did so, and the flickering torchlight revealed a vein of salt, running the length of the cave wall. Each warrior was ordered to grab one handful of salt and take it outside to the wounded men.

Matthew picked up Raquelle and placed her on the ledge, then climbed up and carried her out into the waning afternoon sunlight. After a few moments, her eyes fluttered open and she asked, "Father, are the dragons dead?"

Matthew clasped Raquelle to his chest, his eyes tearing with his deep relief. "You are safe; that is what matters to me. I wounded one of the dragons but they flew away. The two smaller dragons are all we killed." And, to himself, he thought, *And this daughter, praise God, is not lost to me.*

*　*　*

Shalee and the women laid cloth against the warriors' wounds to stop their bleeding, but the bandages quickly became soaked. Raquelle and Matthew moved to the stricken men's side. Matthew ordered the women to bring fresh water from the loch, and to pour the clean water into the warriors' wounds until all the dirt was purged. Then he ordered the warriors carrying salt to pour their salt into the wounds.

The stricken warriors moaned with the sharpness of the new pain, then passed into unconsciousness. To Shalee's amazement, as the salt mixed with the warriors' blood, the bleeding stopped. Matthew told the women to sew the men's wounds closed, just as they would sew a piece of cloth. Those not tending the wounded crowded around to see what magic their new leader was performing. Matthew noticed one boy intensely studying how the water removed the dirt, the salt stopped the bleeding, and the sewing closed the wounds. Matthew caught the boy's attention and beckoned him to a fallen warrior's side.

With a stern face, Matthew addressed the boy, "Do you know of any beehives close to the castle?"

All eyes were on the boy, and he reveled in the attention. "Aye, there are three large hives at the edge of the forest."

Matthew looked doggedly at the boy and pointed to the fallen warriors. "Then the lives of these warriors are in your hands."

The boy sputtered, "What? Why my hands?"

Matthew knew that issuing such a grave challenge would get people to move with lightning speed. "You know where the beehives are, and they contain honey. Take Kele with you, and have the other children fetch three large bowls from the castle and meet you at the beehives. Start a small fire under each beehive, using green wood, so that there is plenty of smoke. The bees will grow sleepy from the smoke and fall out of the hive. Now, the bees will not be dead, so set them aside carefully, so that you are not stung.

"Then you must reach in and pull the combs from the hive and wring the honey from them into the three bowls. Bring the bowls to the healing rooms in the castle, and pour the honey into the warriors' cuts. When you have covered the wounds with the honey, cover them with clean cloth. You are now their doctor, so go, and be quick about your task!"

Eager to fulfill his new responsibility, and to flaunt his newfound importance, the boy shouted orders to the other children to get the bowls and bring them to him at the hives, and then he sprinted away toward the forest. Kele grabbed three torches, and ran as fast as he could after the rapidly disappearing boy.

As Matthew prepared to leave the beach to return to his castle with the wounded, Alanna broke the surface of the water, spit two large, black lumps upon the beach, and submerged again. Raquelle was curious, and ran to see what the lumps were. When she came near enough to see, Raquelle stopped short in disgust and horror; they were the heads of the two young dragons. Alanna did not want their lifeless eyes to look out at her in her loch. Raquelle returned to Matthew's side, shouting excitedly about the grisly "gift" Alanna had given them. With a grim smile, Matthew ordered four warriors to retrieve the heads and carry them to the castle.

After returning to the castle, Matthew set the two heads in the courtyard next to a rat hole. The brazen rats swarmed from their hole, and began to devour the flesh from the inside out. Matthew's darker side smirked at the sight of his enemies lying upon the ground, reduced from being objects of terror to being nothing more than rat-carrion. Then, the litters bearing the wounded men passed by, and Matthew followed them into the houses of healing. Matthew tried to comfort the men as they were carried to their beds, praising them for their valor. Despite Matthew's "magic" and the women's tender care, the men's wounds were too severe, too much of their blood lost, and they both died before the morning came.

The next day, when news of the warriors' death reached Matthew, a deep cloud of depression settled over him. Shalee noticed his gloom, and asked him whence it came.

Matthew blurted out, "I am tired of death! My pregnant wife and daughter are dead, and I wish to join them. I didn't ask to come here. I don't want to be responsible for all these people, and I do not want the blood of those two warriors on my hands. In truth, at this moment, I just want to die."

Shalee had heard quite enough of this talk of death, and she leveled her full wrath upon Matthew. "All of this that you face… it is as if a baby had been left at your front gate. You did not ask for it or even want it, but it is there, nonetheless, and it is now your responsibility. If you do nothing, the baby dies. If *you* choose to die, then, like the baby, Raquelle, myself, the people of this castle, and the people of Robert Roybridge's castle, shall die as well! The dragon worshippers are powerful, and will not allow us to live after you die. Your God made you responsible for us. Do we all have to suffer death because you are sad?"

Matthew recoiled as if Shalee had just slapped his face. He would get no sympathy from this woman. Her harsh words carried truth in them, however, and it brought the whole situation into clear focus in his mind.

Just like in the military, Matthew thought, *I am responsible for other people's lives.* Aloud he said, "Shalee, you are right. I have no right to wallow in my own sadness now. I must bury my past and focus upon the living who need me. But, right or not, you are a hard, cold woman, with no sympathy in your bosom. Would that it were a softer place, where I might rest my weary head awhile, but it is like stone, bearing neither tears nor deceit. You would make a great drill instructor."

Shalee was taken aback by his harsh words, and it was her turn to flinch from their bite. All she could think to say was, "What is a drill, and what does its instructor teach it?"

"A drill instructor is like a master of the guards, who causes his men to weep, then shows only disdain for their weakness. What he teaches his men is to have hearts as hardened as his own."

Shalee felt stung, and was struck mute by Matthew's description of her. She thought to herself, *If only he were not so blinded by his pain, he would see what my heart, and my body, would rather speak to him.*

She turned and walked away from him without looking back.

The Ultimate Dragon

Chapter 8

Standing in the courtyard after Shalee had left, Matthew examined the two white dragon skulls, gleaming in the sunshine. Yellow Rose ran up to him just then, brushing against his leg. Matthew picked her up, scolding her. "You are doing a lousy job of killing those rats. Look at those dragon heads, picked clean last night while you slept. Your belly is too full. No more fish for you until I see some dead rats." Matthew placed her on top of one of the skulls, then he turned and walked away.

The cat skulked off the dragon's head, issuing low, vulgar meows at the indignity she had suffered. Just at that moment, a monstrous rat made the mistake of coming out of his hole. The rat was nearly as large as Yellow Rose, and showed no fear in confronting her. The cat's tail and back fur bristled straight up as she issued an angry shriek, her eyes flaring with hatred as she contemplated her attack. The rat stood upright, dancing on its hind legs and daring her to attack.

With lightning speed, Yellow Rose sprang upon the rat's neck and sank her fangs deep into its filthy flesh. Her back claws tore at its stomach as her fangs crushed down to suffocate the struggling rat. The rat attempted to scratch and claw at Yellow Rose's head, but she deflected its futile attempts with her front paws. After only a few seconds, the rat lay dead and twitching upon the floor. Still not satisfied, Yellow Rose tore its lifeless body into bloody pieces and scattered the tattered flesh in front of the rat's hole.

The kittens, having heard the shrieking, raced toward her, expecting a meal. Yellow Rose hissed loudly at them, causing them to stop short. Skidding to a halt, they looked at each other, wondering at their mother's hissing. Never had they heard their mother so angry. As Yellow Rose continued her scolding, the kittens' tails drooped, and they turned to slink back to the stable. There wasn't any food there, but at least there was nobody there hissing at them.

The Ultimate Dragon

Yellow Rose pushed the two dragon heads across the floor, set them directly in front of the hole, and hid behind them. She didn't have long to wait before another gigantic rat emerged to sniff the fresh blood and eat the remains of his comrade. Yellow Rose leapt from her hiding place, landing squarely on the rat's back, her claws digging deep into its flesh as her teeth crushed the rodent's neck. Too surprised even to defend itself, the rat died quickly.

Yellow Rose dragged this dead rat across the castle grounds to the stairway that led to Matthew's and Raquelle's chambers. She was struggling to get the rat up the stairway when a castle guard, ascending the stairs, tried to kick her out of the way. Like a disturbed rattlesnake, Yellow Rose struck at her antagonist's ankle, causing him to cry out in pain. Then Yellow Rose stood up on her hind legs, with front paws swinging like a boxer, and shrieked like a banshee at the guard. All the guard saw was a buzz saw with fur. He reasoned to himself that, since he had no crucial business to attend in his leader's chambers, anyway, he would leave the stairwell and go somewhere a bit less hazardous, like perhaps the kitchens.

Finally, Yellow Rose reached Matthew's chamber, and deposited the rat in the middle of the room. The pups scurried out from under the bed to feast on the rat's carcass. Yellow Rose immediately moved between the pups and their intended meal, giving them a look that stated, "If you even think about touching this rat, your corpse will keep it company." Each pup looked innocently up at the ceiling, as if there was something terribly interesting to see there, and then they let loose with low howls and turned to head back under the bed.

Anyone observing this scene would have understood what had transpired. The head female of this wolf pack had just established herself…and she was a cat.

* * *

As all this was going on, Matthew, Raquelle, and the children were swimming and playing on the beach. Once again, Alanna and her children drove fish upon the beach, and the guards took Matthew's share to the castle for meals and for trading. Shalee had tables built outside the castle walls to display the live fish. Warriors came from nearby castles to trade, as word of Matthew's bounty had spread quickly through the surrounding lands.

Shalee limited the fish trading on that day to twenty of the largest fish. As a courtesy, each warrior who came to trade was given a large bowl of fish stew and a loaf of new bread to eat as he inspected the fish. The trading began as announced, when the sun was highest in the sky, and it began in earnest! Before one hour had passed, all the fish were gone. Some warriors came late, and had to return to their castles empty-handed. However, they did take with them full stomachs and tales of huge fish, traded at bargain prices.

Shalee made it a point to thank each warrior for coming, and made sure that none left the castle hungry. She knew that those who had arrived too late to trade would return earlier the next day. Word spread to all the other villages that whether they came to trade or not, in the castle of Matthew Wolverine, all guests were welcomed and fed.

Just as Shalee was finishing with the trading, Matthew and the children returned. Matthew introduced himself to the warriors, and praised them for the fine fish they were taking back to their castles. He encouraged them to return the next day with their families, so their sons and daughters could observe and learn from their fathers' expert negotiating skills.

But some of the warriors were hesitant to make the journey again so soon, expressing fear of the dragons that dwelt in the area. This gave Matthew an idea. "Retrieve those two dragon skulls from their place beside the rat hole," he commanded to Kele, "and display them on the table." Kele was gone a long time, finally returning with two gleaming white dragons' skulls and two very bloody hands. Matthew asked him where the blood came from, and was answered with only a scowl from Kele and two words, "Yellow Rose."

Matthew ignored Kele's response, took the skulls from him, and held them high above his head. "When dragons attack my warriors, the dragons die. Let songs of the valor of my warriors be sung and re-sung in your castles. Now, God speed you to your homes." With this Matthew tossed the skulls on the table, and turned, with Raquelle at his side, to enter his castle.

"I wish to go visit the pups," Raquelle told her father, and she headed for their room.

A glowing Shalee approached Matthew just then, and took him by the hands to the tables, laden with all the food and goods she had acquired in her trading that day. "I made sure that all of the visiting warriors left full to bursting with fish stew and bread," she said. Matthew was very pleased, and told her that these warriors would come again the next day, this time with their families. He told her to be certain that they all left, again, with their hunger satisfied. "Also be sure that the visiting children have a good time playing with the castle children."

Shalee looked at him quizzically. Matthew explained, "It is all part of making our visitors feel welcome and safe in our castle. It's very important that we do that."

"Aye," Shalee said, nodding.

Matthew asked, "Have the extra fish been sent to the farmers on my lands?"

"Aye, it has been done and will continue to be done as long as I have responsibility. The cares of the castle are my duty, Matthew Wolverine, and as long as I am here you need not concern yourself with such matters."

Suddenly the air was pierced by Raquelle's scream, and Matthew charged, sword drawn, to his chambers, with Shalee close behind. Matthew and Shalee entered the room to find Raquelle standing frozen, mesmerized by a line of five monstrous dead rats in the center of the room.

Raquelle ran to Matthew, a look of fear and disgust in her eyes. "Father, look what someone did — placed these filthy rats in our chambers!"

Matthew and Shalee comforted Raquelle for a moment, then Matthew pushed her to arm's length, smiling. "These dead rats are a present from Yellow Rose. Since cats cannot thank us with words, they bring us their kill to show their appreciation. If Yellow Rose continues to bring us rats such as these, soon our castle will be rat-free. Now, we must all give her lots of affection, to let her know her how much we appreciate her wonderful gifts."

Raquelle wrinkled her nose, but she had calmed down considerably, and a smile stole across her face. Kele and the other warriors rushed into the room to investigate, having heard Raquelle's scream. As they came up behind Matthew and Shalee, Yellow Rose strutted from person to person to be stroked and praised. She lapped up all the affection like a bucket of cream, and her loud purring could be heard even by the warriors standing outside the chambers. Matthew ordered the warriors to take the dead rats by their tails and deposit them beside the courtyard rat hole, and then to wash their hands to avoid sickness. Yellow Rose gave the pups a look that seemed to say, *What are you waiting for — let's chow down on these rats!* The rats were scattered by the rat hole, and the kittens, pups, and Yellow Rose began their own royal feast.

* * *

Over the next few days, families from more of the nearby castles arrived to trade for fish. Some warriors came early with their families to see Alanna and her babies drive the fish to shore. The children learned to swim, and many of them got a chance, much to their delight, to ride on Alanna's back.

Over the weeks there had been much talk among the people of this miraculous occurrence: the tall golden-haired leader who had tamed the terror of the waters. Surely this was a sign of more miraculous things to come as the new millennium approached, many people were saying. Maybe this Matthew was the new Messiah, some said hopefully. Or maybe he was the Antichrist, others said, with fear in their voices.

Of course, Matthew did everything he could to curb such talk on either side of the argument. It helped that he had made Raquelle promise not to talk to others about his trip from the future; his daughter was, from what he could see, the soul of discretion. Even so, in the eyes of the people there were so many things about Matthew Wolverine that were strange and different — those odd books with pictures of objects such as flying machines, that weapon he called a "pistol," and that strange wand with the red light. And there was the fact that he seemed to know so much about matters far beyond the reach of mortal men. He had brought many welcome changes since his arrival, but there were those in his midst who harbored a profound distrust of this new leader.

* * *

Shalee began to include the visiting children in her reading classes after she finished with her trading. As the days passed, there grew a steady procession of people, coming and going from Matthew's castle, and the castle soon became the center of trade and learning in the Loch Ness area. Matthew blossomed with all the company, and encouraged many to stay the night in his castle. One morning Shalee sent word to all the farm families in the area, inviting them to a grand feast on the following Saturday. As word had spread of the hospitality offered at Matthew Wolverine's castle, all the families came.

During the second of many courses of the sumptuous feast, Matthew announced to his guests, "I can increase your crops fourfold, using fertilizer and iron plows."

A few of the guests crossed themselves, whispering something to themselves about loaves and fishes. But most interpreted his announcement as mere brag, amplified by too many glasses of mead. The majority of the doubters merely mumbled to those sitting close by, but a few were much louder in their disbelief, offering catcalls or outright laughter. Finally Matthew slammed his fist down on the table, bringing the hall to silence.

All eyes turned to this man, to see what he might do next. After all, it was not wise to anger a man who could kill the strongest among them with his bare hands, dispatch a dragon — baby though it might be — with his blade, and turn the demon of the Loch into a pet. Matthew bellowed at them: "Hold your tongues, and look at the food in front of you. Does any other castle in all of Scotland have so much food or such large cooks? Does anyone leave this castle hungry? You have seen for yourselves what has already been accomplished. If you will but trust me and my God, your crops shall increase.

"I ask you to take a week to think on this matter, and talk it over with your families. This night, however, let us celebrate with feast and dance, and you may all sleep in the safety of my castle. You may return to your farms after breakfast tomorrow."

This greatly pleased the guests, who were loath to set aside their merrymaking to take up such serious matters. The music played on, and all danced well into the night. Naturally, such celebration was hungry work, and the castle cooks were kept running until well after the minstrels were silent. Eventually, the well-fed and exhausted guests retired to the chambers that had been prepared for them, where most of them dreamt of grand parties and extravagant feasts.

* * *

Raquelle arose the next morning as Matthew was doing his pushups, and told him that she and the other children were going into the forest to pick some flowers.

"Take Kele along for protection," Matthew told her.

Raquelle said petulantly, "Thank you, father, but I do not need Kele to watch over me."

Matthew stopped his pushups, walked over, and sat down on Raquelle's bed. Weighing his words carefully, he said, "Shalee gave me good advice about taking a weapon for protection when I leave the castle. I resisted her, and it almost cost me my life. Now, after I rise in the morning, my pistol remains strapped to my side, along with my sword and dagger. That pistol saved our lives in the cave against the dragons. I learn from my mistakes, and if you are as smart as I think you are, you will learn from them as well, without having to make those same mistakes yourself. Take Kele for your protection."

Raquelle stiffened her neck and narrowed her eyes. "Father, among the Picts, a woman is married by the time she is twelve years old and must be able to protect herself in the woods. I do not need Kele to protect me, and I don't want to take him!"

Patience was not a virtue that Matthew possessed in any great quantity, and he barked in response, "Take Kele or don't go. That is an order."

Raquelle huffed and puffed as she rose from her bed, but finally nodded in acquiescence. She dressed and headed for the courtyard, where the other children awaited her. Matthew entered the courtyard to find the children wolfing down their breakfast, eager to get on their way. "I will go fetch Kele," he told Raquelle.

After a brief search, he found Kele, and ordered him to accompany the children into the woods to pick flowers. Raquelle and the children were moving to the gate by now, and she was hollering up for the guards to open it. The children were growing impatient waiting for Kele, who protested that he had not eaten, and that guarding children picking flowers was not a job for a warrior. Raquelle finally decided she had waited long enough for Kele, and led the children out the gate toward the forest. A scowling Kele reluctantly hurried after them.

Matthew had mixed emotions on his daughter's assertion of independence, but he also knew that always worrying about your child's safety was part of the job of fatherhood. He was still brooding when he went back to the dining hall and sat down at the table. Shalee brought him his breakfast, but he just sat there, gazing at it. Noticing his unrest, Shalee asked, "What disquiets you, my leader?"

Matthew lifted his gaze and stared deep into Shalee's emerald eyes. "I try to be a good father, but I do not have a lot of patience, and I fear I may be bullying my daughter. I am comfortable issuing commands to unquestioning warriors, but not to a young girl who wants to know, but cannot always understand, my reasoning. She shows signs of rebellion or independence, I can't tell which. If I come down on her too hard, I will crush her independent spirit. If I let her have her own way, I am afraid she will be hurt or killed. I am just not very good at this fatherhood business. I wasn't a good father for my first daughter; I was scarcely ever there for her. Now I am trying to do things right, but I still feel I am doing everything all wrong." Matthew's head dropped, his shoulders slumping forward.

Shalee moved behind Matthew to gently rub his shoulders. Her eyes glazed over as she remembered her own father. "Even though my father was not always gentle with me, I loved and respected him. He taught me right from wrong, and he lived his teachings, even to his death. I did not always follow his advice, but he never doubted that I loved him and respected him. Your daughter is becoming a woman, and she tests her wings. She will be twelve soon, and then she may marry. You must give her the freedom to make mistakes."

Sometimes a man just needs to unburden his worries on a woman. Shalee sat down at the table with Matthew, and before he knew it two hours had passed as he poured his heart out to her. This intimate talk relieved some of his concerns, and soon Shalee had him laughing with her.

The relief and joy of this interlude ended abruptly when Kele rushed into the room, his face drained of blood. He knelt on one knee and whispered, "My leader, Raquelle has been kidnapped by the dragon worshippers. It is my fault. I was watching the other children, and she got separated. Three of the evil ones grabbed her, and one shouted back at me, as he disappeared into the woods, that the daughter of Matthew Wolverine would be a sacrifice to their gods tonight." Then he cringed, as if waiting for the punishment that would surely come.

Matthew yanked Kele off his knees, straight up into the air, roaring, "There is no time for recriminations; we will stop this sacrifice. When and where is it to take place?"

Kele pointed straight up, his feet still dangling in the air as he choked out, "When the moon rises to its full height, then she will be lowered into the dragon's lair. I know where the sacrifice is to take place, but it is best that I show you, because it is hard to find." As long as he was useful, Kele thought, he would be permitted to live.

Matthew pressed Kele for information. "What will the dragon worshippers wear?"

Somewhat puzzled by this turn of questioning, Kele gulped and replied, "They all wear black robes with black hoods."

"Do they wear sashes, and if so, what color are these sashes?"

"Aye, there are sashes of different colors, depending, I think, upon the clan to which they belong. I am not sure about the significance of the colors."

"Do any of them wear white sashes?"

"None that I have ever seen."

Matthew set Kele on the ground and turned to Shalee, asking, "Do you have enough black cloth to make robes with hoods and white sashes for twenty warriors and myself?"

Shalee nodded and ran to assemble the women to sew the robes and sashes. Matthew turned to Kele and ordered, "I want you to assemble nineteen of your very best warriors now. Have them report to the courtyard with their daggers."

"Aye, my lord," Kele said, and dashed off to gather his men. When the warriors had all gathered together, Matthew began giving them quick lessons, demonstrated on Kele, on how to slit an enemy's throat quickly and quietly. These men were awkward, he saw, lacking the fluid mobility of twentieth-century warriors. Frustrated, Matthew nonetheless continued to teach them, for what other choice did he have?

Finally Shalee brought out the finished robes and sashes. Matthew put on a robe with a white sash and informed his warriors, "Any robe bearing a white sash is worn by one of our warriors. Kill all others! I will rescue Raquelle, but let us feed the entire legion of dragon worshippers to their gods. This night, the dragons shall enjoy one last grand feast, and then die a painful death in the morning."

With the thought of fighting dragons, a flash of fear passed across Kele's face. "My leader, can Robert Roybridge help us? I can send a message so he can meet us at the dragon's lair."

Matthew nodded. "An excellent idea, Lieutenant. Then send the same message to the Pict leader, Kial, that Matthew Wolverine kills dragons. State that this is our one chance to be free of the dragons, and to meet me at the dragon's lair at sunrise — but not before sunrise."

Kele's face revealed shock. "Why sunrise, my leader? By then, the battle will be over."

Matthew smirked as he replied, "The battle with the dragon worshippers may be over, but the battle with the dragons will begin at sunrise, and that is when I shall need Kial and Robert."

* * *

It was late afternoon when Matthew led twenty warriors out the castle gate and up the hill into the woods. The band moved quickly through the forest, and reached the dragon's lair just as the sun set. They donned their black robes as Matthew surveyed the terrain.

Matthew asked Kele, "How much do you know of the sacrifice ritual?"

Hatred exuded from Kele's face as he sputtered, "Damian made me watch as a high priest, cloaked in red, sacrificed my mother to the dragons. May the Devil hold him close to his bosom. Do you see that circle of guards, close to the forest? The females to be sacrificed are held there until high moon, then they are tied with ropes and lowered over the edge of that hill, into the dragon's lair. I can still hear my mother's screams." He was silent for a few moments and then said, with more rage than Matthew had ever heard in his voice, "Shall we attack at once?"

Matthew shook his head. There were hundreds of dragon worshippers, and he didn't want any to escape. "We will attack when I give the word. Tell me, Kele, on that plateau to the left of the dragon's lair, many men in black robes are kneeling on the ground. Are they praying?"

Kele spit his words out. "Aye, they pray to the dragons for good crops."

At once a plan snapped into Matthew's mind. "Kele, take fifteen of your men to that plateau. Pass the four guards at its foot, and ascend the plateau to quietly kill all who pray. Move their bodies forward to the edge of the plateau. Then send four warriors, each with five gold coins in his right hand, to the guards below. Have the warriors tell the guards they have found many gold coins in a crack in the ground, but these were all they could reach. When the guards rush to the plateau, kill them, and place their bodies with the others in a position that will make them look as if they are praying. I will take four warriors and eliminate the guards who watch over the female captives. Then I will lure the more amorous warriors into the forest to their deaths. If you hear men screaming, know we are discovered, and lead your warriors to our aid."

Matthew guided four warriors to some nearby torches, which they confiscated. Then, from downwind and with their hoods up, they proceeded straight to the guardians of the sacrifice. These guards became uneasy as the group approached, so Matthew called out, "The high priest decrees that no virgins are to be sacrificed tonight. You guards, take these wenches into yonder woods and insure they are virgins no longer. We shall stand guard so no one disturbs you."

The captain of the guards grew more suspicious, and challenged Matthew. "Who are you to give us such orders?"

Matthew let a deep chuckle rise from his stomach. "One who offers you joy, but since your men now drag the women off into the woods while we stand here chattering, there may be none left for you. Do you really want to talk with me as your men pleasure themselves?" It only took the captain a moment to ponder the situation, whereupon he scurried off after his men. Matthew and his men followed close behind, and slashed the guards' throats as they entered the woods. Two of the women began to scream, and Matthew removed his hood and grabbed the closest woman. "If you scream again, the dragons will taste your flesh tonight. You do as I say or die. Do you understand?" Frightened, the women nodded as Raquelle rushed forward to hug Matthew.

Raquelle bubbled, "I knew you would come, my father. I just knew it!" In the torchlight, Raquelle pulled back to look into her father's eyes, then recoiled. The coldness in Matthew's face pierced her heart, and with a shiver, she asked if he was really her father, or merely one of the evil priests, who cast a spell of deceit.

Ignoring her question, Matthew said, "It is time to kill, without mercy, all who serve the dragon. We dispatch them to hell. You women must help with this, and here is how you will do it. You will make the sounds of passionate lovemaking. Know, however, that if your cries are not loud and convincing, the dragons will slowly strip us all of our flesh tonight.

"Now, all females will disrobe to the waist. As the dragon worshippers approach, welcome them with open arms and hungry eyes. Radiate a come-hither smile. Be certain not to scream as my warriors kill them."

He ignored the gasps that came from several of the females present, including his daughter.

Coldly Matthew continued, "Warriors, make sure the torches are behind the women's heads, with enticing light bathing their bosoms. As you lead the dragon worshippers to the women, slow your pace a little, to let your victim get in front of you. When he falls upon the woman, seize his chin and the back of his head, twisting as I have taught you, until you hear his neck snap. Each of you shall pick one woman as your bait, and give your dagger to her. If my warrior doesn't kill his victim on the first snap, you must thrust your dagger through the enemy's heart.

"And remember, if one enemy screams, it insures that we will fill a dragon's belly tonight. Now get busy!"

The women, looking shocked, did nothing at first. Matthew said, "Of course, if you wish to have your flesh ripped off piece by piece, you may remain clothed."

The females took only a second more to look at each other, then they quickly disrobed as he had instructed. Matthew moved them into five small separate clearings in the woods, and the women lay down and began making loud sounds of ecstasy. As the sound of ravishment floated on the night breeze, it whispered of forbidden pleasures — a whisper that bored into the minds of these men who had been deprived too long. Matthew soon had his first inquiry. A small man approached in a frenzy, huffing, "This may be my first time here, but why do you guards get all the wenches? I should get a turn!"

Matthew oozed with feigned sympathy for the man. "Aye, but the high priest wants the big men satisfied first. To be fair to you, if you tell ten big men to come forward, but not all at once, then you can have two of these hot wenches. That is, if you are sure you could handle two of them at one time!" Matthew's words catapulted the little man into the main body of dragon worshippers, and they soon started coming in small bands for the women.

Matthew led the first few in, and disposed of them quickly, dragging their bodies into the woods. Matthew whispered in one woman's ear, "Repeat to the next victim, 'You are so large; come here quickly!' Then moan loudly as he descends upon you, and repeat 'Deeper! Deeper!' And do so until he is dead."

Even by torchlight, Matthew could see the sweat of excitement roll off the men's faces. Never had he seen men rush to their destruction with greater anticipation. A steady stream of lustful fellows arrived over the next two hours, till eventually the line dwindled to nothing.

Then Matthew ordered his men to put up their hoods as the red-robed high priest approached, followed close behind by six burly guards.

The high priest barked at Matthew, "Since you have satisfied your pleasure, bring the wenches forward to be sacrificed."

Matthew snickered. "Aye, but first let my men and me have one more go at them." Matthew turned toward the woman at the center, but the high priest's six guards pushed him to the ground and rushed past. They were on top of the woman before Matthew's warriors could stop them. Matthew leapt forward, grabbing a guard, and immediately snapped his neck. Matthew's warriors followed suit, but one guard, blinded with his lust, continued to wrestle with a woman until she plunged her dagger into his heart. Finally, with the high priest's guards dead, Matthew shouted for the women to clothe themselves and come forward.

The high priest remained motionless, his face frozen in a stare of disbelief. As Matthew and the clothed women emerged from the forest, the priest was roused from his stupor, and screamed that his enemies would suffer unspeakable deaths for this blasphemy. Behind Matthew, fifteen black-robed men appeared. Seeing them, the high priest gained new courage. "Kill these blasphemers!" he screamed at them. The fifteen warriors marched up, falling in behind Matthew, and the high priest fell silent. Only then did he notice the white sashes that bound their robes.

Matthew's tone made the situation crystal-clear to the priest. "My warriors and I have killed all of your dragon worshippers. Now, for that unspeakable death you so eloquently spoke of, and so richly deserve. Kele, have two warriors strip this man of his clothes and bind his hands. Have our other warriors drag all the slain dragon worshippers to the crest of the hill overlooking the entrance to the dragons' lair. Strip them of all clothes and weapons, and place their naked bodies perpendicular to the ridge, with their heads jutting over the edge. Stack them like wood, but leave a space of honor in the center, from which we shall lower the high priest."

In a short while, naked bodies lined the crest of the hill as the moon reached its zenith. Loud growls of hunger echoed from the dragons' cave. Matthew had a long rope tied to the high priest's waist, and slowly lowered the priest over the crest of the hill. He then handed the rope to Kele, and laid down on the crest to peer over the edge at the dangling priest, who was shaking and screaming for his life.

Matthew assured the high priest, "The dragons would not hurt one who has served them so faithfully!" At that the priest hurled curses toward the ledge, but as the dragons' footfalls drew nearer, his curses turned once again to pleas for mercy. Matthew wondered how many other sacrifices had pleaded in just this way.

As the dragons reached the dangling priest, their huge noses inhaled his aroma as they very gently rubbed their faces over his body. The high priest gleefully exclaimed, "You were right, of course! These dragons will not hurt me. I knew it all along!" The dragons lightly swung the high priest to and fro, like cats batting a cat toy, and then their tongues came out and they began to softly lick his body. He cooed to the beasts with words of adoration.

Matthew began to wonder whether the dragons knew that this was their high priest or if they always waited for words of praise from their sacrifices before they commenced eating. As he pondered his next move, an ear-piercing shrill echoed through the darkness. Matthew called for a torch, and when it was brought to him he stretched it out as far as he could over the crest of the hill.

Even his years in combat could not have prepared him for the image before him.

Blood was slowly dripping down the priest's side, as the dragons systematically embarked upon their feast, making delicate gashes in the screaming man's flesh, and tearing at it, little piece by little piece. For an hour, growls that sounded like evil laughter, answered by the priest's screams, filled the air, striking terror deep into the hearts of all who could hear. The dragons took great pleasure in prolonging their victim's agony as they enjoyed their feast.

Finally Matthew, who took no pleasure at all from any of this, ordered his warriors to push the naked bodies over the crest of the hill to block the cave's entrance. Before long, over 200 bodies sealed the chasm. The dragons would literally have to eat their way out.

It had been a long night, and Matthew looked forward to a joyful reunion with his daughter. Little did he know that when they reunited, Raquelle's reaction would be anything but joyous.

The Ultimate Dragon

Chapter 9

There was business to attend to before seeking out Raquelle. Matthew summoned Kele and commanded, "Choose two of your bravest warriors to stand guard, while the rest sleep. Tell them that when they cannot stay awake any longer, they are to awaken you so that you can assign their replacements." Kele hastened away to carry out these orders.

The robes of the dead dragon worshippers were piled high on the ground, spilling over the hill. "You warriors may sleep on top of these robes," Matthew said. He then called aside the four warriors who had helped him protect the women they had used as bait. He told them, "If you wish, you each may lie with one of these women for the night to keep warm, but you are not to mate with her unless you intend to take her for your wife."

"But, my lord…" one of the warriors began.

Matthew shushed him. "These are brave women, and they deserve our respect. They are to be sheltered from the cold, but I will not have them violated. Is that clear?"

To a man they said, "Yes, my lord."

At last Matthew set out to find Raquelle. He found her on the crest of the hill, spitting on the bodies of the dragon worshippers that blocked the dragons' lair. Matthew drew near, preparing for the flood of gratitude that would surely await him. He even had his speech all planned out — a modest acknowledgment of what he had risked, tempered by a declaration that he had had no choice in the matter; Raquelle was his daughter, and he would gladly risk all to save her.

He was not prepared for the young woman who turned on him with fire in her eyes as she screamed at him. "Father, why did you have me disrobe? I am your daughter! Those dragon worshippers and our warriors saw me!"

Matthew sat down at the edge of the precipice, his legs draping over the edge. He did not answer her, but gazed silently at the stars. Finally, Raquelle sat down an arm's length from him. Matthew took a deep breath, and then, sighing deeply, let it out. He said, "I am sorry that, at such a young age, you must be transformed." Matthew's hands clenched his face. More softly, he said, "You choose when your life must be surrendered so that others may be free."

Raquelle, even by the moonlight, could see her father in turmoil, and she moved closer. "What do you mean, I must be transformed? Transformed into what? And what do you mean about my life being surrendered?"

Matthew knew the die was cast. He could not stop the transformation. In fact, he must encourage it, or else there might never be a free Scotland. "Raquelle, freedom is never free. You must come to love freedom above your own life. This love of freedom transforms you. You begin to care for the group, and what is best for the group, above yourself. You seek the rugged path of that which is right and just above the easy path of that which is ultimately wrong. At some point, you are forced to kill to protect this freedom... and that killing transforms you too. You become more forceful, and your survival decisions become more clear, but more costly. People sense the aggression in you, and are frightened by it. Even your friends begin to avoid you.

"For my plan to succeed, you had to undress, to entice the dragon worshippers to their deaths. If I had charged in with only twenty warriors, the dragons would now be feasting on us, instead of our enemies. You feel humiliation, and for that, I am saddened. You hate me for the choice I made, but you are alive to hate me because my plan succeeded. The humiliation you suffer, as well as my own anguish for having caused it, are a small price to pay."

From inside the cave, Raquelle could hear bones crack as the dragons devoured the bodies of the dead, and the image made her shiver. She weighed the facts: her father had risked his life for her because he loved her. With only twenty warriors, he vanquished an enemy tenfold greater than his own. Yes, he had shamed her and the other four females. She wondered if the other women hated her father. But then she focused upon the pure truth in his words: BUT YOU ARE ALIVE! Raquelle wrapped her arms around her father and whispered, "I understand." The transformation complete, Matthew and Raquelle rose to ascend the hill of black robes. Then, beside their slumbering warriors, they fell, exhausted, into sleep.

* * *

Matthew and his troops awakened at dawn to the sound of dragon wings, flapping overhead. Four of the beasts were circling above them, and then they suddenly plummeted toward the cave entrance. Matthew and his troops scrambled to crest the hill overlooking the cave, and were confronted with the grisly spectacle of the four dragons, landing upon a lake of human blood that had formed during the night. The dragons, trapped inside the cave, had been gorging themselves on the flesh of the dead dragon worshippers.

The four dragons slurped noisily at the pools of blood, and moved hungrily toward the pile of human bodies clogging the entrance of the cave. Fierce growls echoed from deep within the cave, causing the marauders to hesitate for a brief moment. The dragons roared back, and, brazened by their lust for flesh, moved forward to feast on the human wall. From within the cave erupted a deafening roar, as one of the trapped dragons burst forth, sending human carcasses flying into the air in his wake. In an instant, he was on the trespasser, snagging the neck of one dragon with his teeth, while his front claws pushed two other dragons, momentarily off balance, to the ground.

His mate then emerged from the cave, pouncing upon the last standing dragon with such velocity that they tumbled, head over tail, across the pile of decaying flesh. Her hind claws found their way into the interloper's belly, releasing fountains of his blood to mix with the pools below them. Her front claws dug into his eyes, as the blindingly quick assault of her back claws shredded his neck until long ribbons of his flesh dangled from him. Her front claws slashed upward, severing his head. The dragon's headless body fell, twitching and oozing blood, at her feet. She then turned swiftly to help her mate, who had slain one dragon, and was being besieged by the others. From behind the two, she pounced upon one dragon's back, raking his tail with her back claws, while her front claws dug into his back.

This melee was in full swing as Robert and Kial emerged from the forest with their warriors. Matthew and his troops removed their black robes and stood to wave these fresh troops forward. In the time it took the reinforcements to move within spear-throwing range, the dragons from inside the cave finished off the last of the intruders. A few young warriors flung their spears too early, and they bounced harmlessly off the dragons' bodies. The female dragon abandoned her mate to escape into the air.

Matthew drew his pistol and fired at the female dragon just as she flicked her tail upward. He and his warriors looked up in time to see the tip of her tail rupture as the bullet tore at her flesh. She screeched with pain to her mate, then flew away toward the north. Her mate, however, was forced back to the cave entrance by another wave of spears. The male dragon lashed out with balls of fire that set a number of lead warriors ablaze. Matthew holstered his pistol and leapt from his perch atop the hill to land upon the dragon's head. The dragon flailed up and down like a bucking bronco, trying to dislodge this unwelcome rider.

Suddenly a spear lunged from the arm of the Pict warrior Kial, barely penetrating the beast's neck, but momentarily stopping the dragon's bucking. Matthew grasped the dragon's right ear with his left hand, then sank his teeth into the ear to stabilize himself. Swiftly drawing his pistol, he thrust it inside the dragon's ear as he fired. The dragon jerked backward, its head all but destroyed, then stiffened for a moment before spiraling, lifeless, toward the ground. The crash of the creature's body as it struck the ground drove the Pict warrior's spear all the way through the dragon's neck and out the other side, and sent Matthew tumbling off like a flat rock skipping over water.

Alas, it was not water on which he landed, but rock-hard ground. A bruised and dazed Matthew came to rest face down in a pool of dragon's blood. Stunned by the violent fall, and drained of strength from the exertion of the battle, he lay semiconscious in the sticky liquid. His lungs started to burn for air, and involuntarily his body gasped for breath, but took in great gulps of the dragon's blood instead.

Matthew's body convulsed, attempting to cough up the noxious liquid and fill his lungs with the oxygen they hungered for, but he only took in more blood. As he grew increasingly weak from his futile struggle to breathe, Matthew's mind began to resign itself to the fact that his enemy had won. Abandoning his efforts, he slipped into a sea of blackness, and knew no more.

CHAPTER 10

A huffing and puffing Robert Roybridge reached Matthew and flipped him onto his back. Robert was greeted by the sight of Matthew's face, dark blue beyond the smears of blood which covered it. "Matthew, are you alive?" Robert asked worriedly.

He did not wait for an answer, but hoisted Matthew off the ground and crashed his massive right fist into Matthew's stomach. Like a geyser, Matthew's mouth gushed dragon blood all over Robert. Matthew coughed, then held his stomach as he alternately vomited up more of the dragon's blood and gasped for air. Upon seeing Matthew's body again show signs of struggling for life, Robert set Matthew down on all fours. Raquelle ran up and, seeing her father spewing blood upon the ground, was filled with panic. She frantically began wiping blood off his face, screaming, "Father, you cannot die. Please, do not die!"

Through his coughs Matthew spit out, "I am not dead, but what of the dragons? Are they all dead?"

Raquelle smiled and replied, "All dead except for the female dragon that flew away north."

Matthew steadied himself on Raquelle's shoulder, "Raquelle, find my pistol. It abandoned me while I was in flight. Never, ever do I want to ride another dragon. I don't blame my .44 for jumping ship. That was worse than any bull any Texan ever rode."

Gently Raquelle removed her father's hand from her shoulder and then she sped off to search. In a few moments, she returned to his side. "I found it, father, and I wiped off the dragon blood. Here is your clean weapon."

Matthew was still on all fours as a man in furs strode toward them and halted. In a booming voice he said, "So, you are the great Matthew Wolverine that my daughter Brigit goes on about. Well, you may be able to ride that dragon, but it is my spear that brought him down."

95

Raquelle was quick to jump in angrily and defend her father's deed. "It was not you, but my father who killed this dragon. You may be leader of the Picts, but Matthew Wolverine killed this dragon!"

Raquelle was ready to come to blows, if necessary, with this brazen man who had once been her father and had abandoned her to the fate shared by all of Damian's victims. Matthew jumped to physically restrain Raquelle before he responded, "Kial, leader of the Picts, I am so pleased to meet you at last. You are indeed a great warrior. I am certain that the throw of your spear can kill any dragon. But let all examine the spear that killed *this* dragon."

The four walked to the dragon, which lay motionless, with Kial's spear sticking through its throat. Kial's warriors began to encircle them as Matthew exclaimed, "Look at this spear! It passes through the dragon's throat, and juts out the other side! Such a throw can only be done by a mighty arm. Is this your spear, Kial?"

It took a few moments, but as Matthew's words sank into Kial's brain, the latter's chest expanded with pride. "Aye, that is my spear." Kial turned to smile at all his warriors, and he pounded on his chest as he repeated, "My spear, my spear, my spear!"

Matthew loudly issued a challenge. "Is there a warrior here who can deny that this spear killed the dragon?" Matthew gently cupped his hand over Raquelle's mouth before he proceeded. "Let all who doubt look at this dragon's throat, and know that only Kial, leader of the Picts, a great and mighty dragon slayer, could make such a throw. Oh, if only the Pict warriors could carry this dragon back to their village, so the females and sons of your warriors could look upon it. They would see that their leader possesses heroic courage and mighty skill to slay this great and fierce dragon. And for many generations, songs would be sung of Kial's mighty throw. Know that this act shall never be forgotten, and that Matthew Wolverine will treasure the friendship of such a great warrior."

This said, Matthew turned to extend his right hand to Kial.

Kial studied Matthew as his mind drank in these praises. Then Kial gazed at the dragon's neck, which still held his spear. His eyes glazed over. "Brigit spoke of the great wisdom of Matthew Wolverine, how he has brought food and plenty to his castle, and will not abide slaves within any of his lands," Kial said. "But I wondered whether you were a truthful and honorable man. And now, by your own lips, in front of all warriors, you have acknowledged that it was my spear, and my spear alone, that passed through this dragon's throat. You acknowledge that I am a great warrior, and proclaim that my village must see this mighty dragon, slain by Kial, leader of the Picts. This will give courage to all future Pict warriors, letting them know that they too can slay dragons! The wisdom of Matthew Wolverine is great, but our friendship will be greater."

With that, Kial brushed Matthew's hand away, and locked him in a bear hug. Matthew hugged back, praying he had no broken ribs from the fall. Kial released Matthew, and ordered his warriors to carry his dragon back to their village. As Matthew, Raquelle, and Robert watched, Kial's warriors rolled the dragon on its side. A hundred of his warriors pressed their shoulders beside the dragon's belly, bracing themselves for the load, as still others hoisted the dragon upon their shoulders.

Weaving like an army of ants carrying a massive load back to their anthill, the men began their ponderous journey. One hundred warriors marched on each side of the warriors who bore the load, ready to replace them as they tired. Matthew was astounded that these men could carry such weight. He had expected them to attempt to carry the dragon, but never thought they would succeed. His one overriding thought was, *What valuable allies these stout men will be.*

As the proud warriors slowly marched away bearing their trophy, Kial turned again to Matthew. "When the sun rises two more times, then we shall have a feast of my victory at my camp. Matthew Wolverine and his warriors will be welcome among the Picts. A place of honor awaits you at my feast."

A broad smile showed Matthew's appreciation. "In two days, when the sun rises straight up in the sky, we will be in your village to celebrate your great victory over the dragon and his worshippers. As a present to you, we shall bring twenty large fish from Loch Ness." Kial nodded, then turned to walk after his warriors.

* * *

After Kial was gone, Matthew embraced Raquelle and Robert. Overwhelmed with warm feelings, he said, "Robert, thank you for my life. Raquelle, thank you for my life. We make a good team. Robert, how did you learn to punch the stomach to start someone breathing?"

Robert stoked his chin, remembering. "Two summers past, one of my warriors was devouring large bites of lamb and he started to choke. He stood up and ran around the campfire in panic. None of us knew what to do, but he tripped on a root and his stomach fell squarely on a stump. Out popped a large piece of meat, and he began to breathe. I figured that a blow to the stomach would release whatever stops your breath. I have used this since, and it worked every time."

Matthew continued to massage his sore stomach, thinking that now would be a good time to teach his friend the Heimlich maneuver. "Robert, I want to show you something. Turn around, and I will place my arms around you, with my right hand closed into a fist just below your ribs, and my left hand on top of my fist. I thrust upward…like this…and the food is dislodged. This works in the same way as your method, and I'm sure you'll agree that your stomach is not as sore as mine."

Robert's eyes lit up and he nodded enthusiastically. Then Raquelle, who had stood silent as long as she could, finally blurted out the question that was plaguing her: "Father, why didn't you claim the kill of that dragon you rode? The dragon's fall drove Kial's spear through its neck; it was not the strength of Kial's arm."

Robert joined in. "Aye, she is right, Matthew. I thought to speak up, as well, but I kept silent because I saw you cup Raquelle's mouth."

Matthew put a finger to his lips, silencing Robert as the other warriors drew near. Turning to Kele, he issued orders. "Kele, this cave entrance must be clear of all bodies, but first, sever each dragon's head and set the heads beside the cave entrance. Then remove the dragons' bodies by slicing them into large pieces that two warriors can easily carry. Haul these pieces downwind from us, one hundred paces into the woods.

"After all the dragons are removed into the woods, carry the human bodies and throw them on top of their gods. As your warriors cut and haul away bodies, have each warrior relate his account of his actions in this battle to you. I leave it to you to select only our bravest warriors to carry the dragon heads into our castle. In my army, the reward for bravery is honor and glory. Now, bring me three lighted torches so Robert, Raquelle, and I can explore the dragons' lair."

With torches in hand, Matthew, Raquelle, and Robert entered the cave. When he was finally sure that no one else could hear him, Matthew explained why he had conveyed the honor of the kill to Kial. "Raquelle, learn to build alliances as I do, or you will not survive. I appreciate your loyalty to me, but realize that you almost forced Kial to attack us over the credit for the killing of the dragon. I ask you to weigh the situation. Robert, you commanded how many warriors?"

Robert boasted, "I led thirty warriors to fight the dragons."

"Then our combined force would be fifty warriors against over 300 Pict warriors. Even if we had killed most of them, the ones that eluded us, and there will always be some that escape, would have insured a blood war with the Picts. By making Kial the slayer of the dragon, we showed our appreciation of his bravery, because he came and stood with us to fight the dragons.

"More important, we have gained an ally. Kial knows that his spear did not slay the dragon, and he knows that I have given to him an honor that I could rightfully claim for myself. He now feels beholden to a man who places the honor of an ally above his own. When he visits our castle,

Raquelle, you must always request at supper that Kial tell the story of the day on which Kial, leader of the Picts, became Kial the dragon slayer, as we shall all address him from this day forth. Raquelle, you must never tire of asking to hear that story, for he will never tire of telling it.

"I know he was your father, and I know that he abandoned you. But you must put that in the past. If you listen to my wisdom, he will become an ally and friend who would gladly lay down his life for you. Empires are built from such alliances. Remember that, like Robert, Kial came prepared to die for us when we sent an urgent call for his help." Raquelle nodded gravely as she considered his words, and Matthew turned then to Robert. "Robert, your warriors fought bravely, but can you trust each of them with your life?"

Robert beamed and replied, "Aye, I am like a father to them."

As the three strolled through the monstrous cavern, Matthew envisioned wintering livestock in here. There would be with ample room also for food storage and living quarters for the herdsmen. An opening on the right wall intrigued him, so they entered. The path beyond the opening fell sharply, and after about 100 feet, their nostrils were assailed by a putrid smell. It occurred to Matthew that this was the dragons' dunghill. For centuries, the beasts had used this section of the cave to relieve themselves.

Matthew became excited as their torches revealed a mountain of dragon dung, and he blurted out, "This is the best fertilizer in the world. By spreading this upon our farmers' fields, their crop yield will increase fourfold."

Raquelle held her nose and scoffed, "Father, are you saying we can use this on our crops? Who would eat food grown in this horrible mess, and where could we get warriors to transport it? The smell is making me sick."

Matthew pondered Raquelle's questions as they returned to the main cavern. He knew that he must find something the warriors deeply desired to get them to overlook the rank odor and transport this dung to his farmers. He envisioned huge crops and deep green grass, with vast herds of sheep and cows grazing and growing fat. But he knew that sharing these visions with the warriors would probably not provide the incentive they required. No matter how much faith they might have in him, faith is only so powerful in the shadow of a dragon dunghill.

In any case, Matthew knew that he must acquire sheep and cattle. "Robert, are there wild sheep and cattle roaming the surrounding country?"

Robert nodded and told of his herds of 150 sheep, 10 rams, and 20 cattle.

Matthew decided that a partnership was in order. "I can acquire wild lambs and calves from the Picts. Robert, our combined herds can use this cavern as shelter in the winter. As this fertilizer produces abundant grass, great herds of sheep and cattle can grow, with our herdsmen living in these caves. Robert, do we have a partnership on raising livestock?"

Robert extended his hand and joked, "Matthew, with you as my partner I will become richer than the king of the south kingdom. But are you not afraid that the Picts will steal our herds? I would not trust them."

Matthew formulated a plan as they walked. "I will do what I can to ensure that this won't be a problem. I will pay the Pict warriors and their children to find us live wild lambs and calves. Kial realizes that starvation in winter is his worst nightmare, but starvation will not happen as long as these herds are protected. In winter, when the game is scarce, the Picts may take from our herdsmen what they need to survive. And so they will come to protect our herds, because this is their reserve food supply. By sharing with the Picts, we bind their loyalty to us and strengthen our alliance."

The three continued to make their way through the damp chambers, and their explorations took them to a center cave at the back wall. This led them to a large underground lake, large enough to water thousands of head of livestock, Matthew noticed. The last cave on the left wall turned out to be the largest of the four caverns, and the dragons' sleeping quarters. Matthew, Raquelle, and Robert entered the cavern with torches held high overhead, and swords drawn in case there were more dragons.

Then they stopped short and gasped, but it was not dragons that made them gasp as they looked at the cavern walls, sparkling like fresh-cut diamonds in the flicker of the torches. Matthew told Robert and Raquelle to stay put for a moment, and he proceeded ahead, alone. In the center of the cavern was a huge pile of treasure: gold and silver necklaces, cups, armbands, plates, crude coins, large bars of silver, small bars of gold, large bars of iron, and iron shackles. There were swords that had hilts embedded with precious stones, there were daggers, there was even a pile of crude armor. Matthew, who had never before seen such a sight, froze in his tracks. Raquelle and Robert silently came to his side, planted their torches in the ground, and rushed headlong into the treasure trove. They scooped up armloads of treasure. Matthew still stood mesmerized, but finally blurted out, "I thought the legend of dragon treasure was just a myth. Do you think all dragon lairs hold such treasure?"

In unison, Robert and Raquelle roared, "Aye." Robert continued,

"The dragon worshippers extracted tribute from all the people throughout Scotland by the threat of sacrifice. Only the people's best treasure would do for a bribe. If the dragon worshippers were displeased, they came in the dead of night and carried the people off to sacrifice to their god."

Matthew slowly walked toward the pile of treasure as Raquelle piled necklaces around her neck until they reached above her mouth. Robert separated plain gold cups from those encrusted with precious stones. Matthew began to uncover swords and daggers, envisioning a proud Scottish army, marching into glory, brandishing these grand weapons. The three of them sifted dreamily through the mounds of treasure like children, loosed in a candy store where all the candy was free.

Raquelle laughingly began to barter with Robert, presenting him with two golden cups, set with precious stones. "I will trade you these for five gold necklaces."

Robert took up the jest, baiting back, "No, I want three cups. Just look at these beautiful necklaces." Robert put the necklaces over Raquelle's head and hugged her. Raquelle dropped the cups at his feet to return his hug. The laughter of the three echoed through the halls, and out through the mouth of the cave.

Surveying the vast treasure, Robert proclaimed, "God has richly blessed Scotland through you, Matthew Wolverine. I trust His leadership and yours. How can we best use this wealth?"

Matthew took but a moment to weigh his options. "Let each warrior take one silver armband from this pile. Show all warriors the dragons' dunghill, and tell them that when they remove all the dung and distribute it among the farmers, they can take another silver armband or necklace, plus a sword and dagger. The iron will be forged into plows for our farmers. All silver bars are God's, to be struck into coins." Robert's eyes glowed as Matthew continued.

"Robert, the jewel-encrusted gold cups in this pile are yours. Raquelle owns the necklaces she wears. The gold bars, we shall melt down and strike into coins. With the swords and daggers that are left, we shall equip a Scottish army, and the rest shall be mine. Robert, station two guards at the entrance to this cavern, and leave ten men here to rotate the guard and separate this treasure into piles of similar items."

Kele and all the warriors were drawn by the sound of laughter, and cautiously came into the cavern to report that all the bodies had been removed. The warriors were spellbound by the sight of the riches. Matthew had them dig through the pile until each warrior had found for himself a silver armband. Matthew laid out his offer to them, and all the warriors anxiously volunteered for the assignment.

The Ultimate Dragon

Then the warriors gathered the black robes, wrapping swords and daggers in them. Kele assigned warriors to bear the dragon heads as Matthew led them back to his castle. Matthew's troops laughed and sang, all the while trading tales of their exploits in the battle. And each of the four women walked close beside the warrior who had spent the night beside her.

* * *

Matthew had sent a runner ahead to herald the victory of four slain dragons and Raquelle's rescue. As a beaming Matthew and a joyous Raquelle led their troops into the castle, Shalee stood alone in the middle of the courtyard, her radiant smile catching Matthew's attention and overwhelming his soul.

Matthew's romantic side was touched by her reaction to his triumphant return. It did not matter that the whole castle was basking in her rapturous smile, because Matthew knew that it was meant for him and him alone. Her smile was liquid fire to Matthew, igniting his all-but-dead emotions with the sparks of a love he had thought forever lost to him. Fragments of blinding rapture streaked through him until even the military part of his being was ready to surrender to his deepest hope: that love was possible.

Shalee's smile brightened even more as Matthew drew near, and his heart almost burst from his chest. For a fleeting moment, the wounded and cynical part of Matthew's mind interjected its greatest fear: *Matthew, are you a fool?* Almost immediately, the thought was crushed by Matthew's ache to feel Shalee's body next to his, to caress her velvety black hair, and to taste her enticing lips and savor the luscious sweetness of her kiss. As he rushed forward to embrace Shalee, Raquelle flew past him, straight into Shalee's arms. Matthew caught up with them, enfolding both of them in his arms, his heart aching.

After a long hug, Raquelle pulled back, breaking Matthew's hold, and her words came out in a rush of childish enthusiasm. "Shalee, we slew many dragons! See, the warriors carry four heads, and we slew over 200 dragon worshippers. The Picts carried a whole dead dragon to their village, and father and I are invited to a feast at Kial's camp in two days. Come on, Shalee, I want to see if the wolf cubs missed me." Raquelle pulled Shalee's hand, and they turned to head for Raquelle's room. Raquelle pulled so forcefully that Shalee couldn't even look back.

Matthew was crushed. He chided himself for being so self-centered, and his warrior mind admonished him for letting his defenses down. Obviously, Shalee's smile had been meant for Raquelle. This was understandable; Shalee must have been worried sick about her. Matthew lowered his eyes and moved toward the warriors who bore the black robes with the weapons wrapped in them. He tried to focus as his warriors unpacked the weapons, and he was grateful for the distraction of presenting a sword and dagger to each as a reward for bravery in the battle.

Raquelle and Shalee surprised the pups, who were busily playing in Raquelle's room. The pups swarmed around Raquelle's feet, and she sat down to hold them. The pups licked her face and nuzzled her, trying to get as close as they could. "You really missed me, didn't you?"

Shalee stayed for awhile and watched them, then she smiled and turned to go. But Raquelle rushed to stop her, her youthful smile fading into a worried frown. "I need to talk to you. I had never seen the side of my father that emerged during the battle, a terrifying side that I never want to see again. Also, he spoke very strangely to me when the battle was over, and told me things that were truly frightening. I am going to be twelve summers soon, and I need to know about the working of men's minds before I marry."

Shalee swallowed hard and shook her head. Shalee had never been married, or even been with a man. Raquelle's words only served to remind her that she had turned twenty-one that winter, and was still not even betrothed, a fact which hurt her deeply. Shalee looked to the ground, and answered, "Raquelle, perhaps one of the married women could give you better advice."

Raquelle hardened her face. "No! You are the one I need to talk to. My father doesn't scare you. But he frightened me so badly during the rescue that I thought he was another man. He has a temper that can erupt like a dragon's fire. Why doesn't he scare you?"

Shalee cupped her face in her hand and rubbed her brow. "Here is what I know about men. Some men are cowards and some are brave. Some are tender and some are hard. If you pick a tender coward to marry, you will soon be a widow. If you pick a mean, brave man, you may not survive his beatings. My Uncle Damian was the worst of all men. He was cruel, evil, and, if the bruises and welts suffered by my poor aunt were any indication, he enjoyed giving beatings more than making love. I, and all the women who lived under his roof, received only beatings from him, and no tenderness.

"Then my prayers were answered, and Matthew came to kill Damian. I studied Matthew as he killed the head castle guard; he killed him so quickly, that when I challenged him about burying Damian's body, I feared he might kill me, as well. But instead, he merely ignored my advice. Then I saw him with you and Brigit; he showed compassion and tenderness, and I began to understand what type of man he really was.

"Haven't you noticed his tenderness, Raquelle? Even with the animals… he loves the animals and they love him. He can be so gentle and caring. His touch to me is always gentle, yet he is bigger and stronger than any man I know. When he loves something, whether it be his God, you, Alanna, or Yellow Rose, it is with his whole heart. When he heard you were kidnapped, he did not cringe in fear of the dragons, nor did he seek to punish Kele for letting it happen; instead, he immediately set out to rescue you. He does have a temper to him, I'll not deny that, and he can be bullheaded, but I feel safe with him, and I don't think he would ever intentionally hurt me. And he would never hurt you either."

Raquelle contemplated Shalee's observations. "Then should I look for a man like my father to marry?"

Shalee burst into laughter. "Silly girl! Where in all of Scotland would you find such a man?" Raquelle joined in the laughter, then returned to the business of playing with the pups as Shalee slipped out of the room.

* * *

Matthew concentrated on busying himself for the rest of that day and the next. There were many details that required his attention, if not the blind focus he devoted to them. He tried to fill himself with anticipation for Kial's feast. He tried anything and everything to keep his mind off the one thing that consumed him most: his embarrassment about Shalee. He could only pray that she had not seen the naked need on his face as he approached her when he emerged from the forest.

From now on, he vowed, it would be strictly business with her. Never again would he let his defenses down in the presence of this woman, or any other.

Chapter 11

It was high noon on the feast day when Matthew and Raquelle, accompanied by twenty warriors, arrived at the Pict camp, bearing their gift of large shiny fish from the loch. Kial and Brigit pushed through the crowd to greet them, Kial giving Matthew a powerful bear hug, and Brigit embracing Raquelle. As Brigit broke her embrace, her eyes fixed on the five gold necklaces Raquelle wore. "Did Matthew Wolverine give you such gifts?"

Raquelle's eyes twinkled, and she wore a mischievous smile as the two girls began walking away from the men. "Aye, he gave me more gold necklaces then you have fingers and toes, plus six wolf cubs. He cares for me, truly cares for me. I knew when the dragon worshippers came to sacrifice me, that he would rescue me, and he did. I love my life at the castle of Matthew Wolverine. We swim in the loch with Alanna and her two babies. Father and I even ride on Alanna's back!"

Brigit's mouth fell open. "You mean the loch monsters?"

Raquelle's tone became a bit more forceful, even scolding, as she informed Brigit, "She is no monster, but a good friend. She and her babies supply us with fish. The fish we bring to your feast, she provided. My father and the lake guardians speak with each other. I do not know how, but they do. He is a great warrior, and speaks much of his God and a Messiah that his God has sent. I don't understand this, but I know he loves me with all his heart, so I will worship whatever God he chooses."

Brigit's eyes began to twinkle as well. "Those necklaces shine like the sun. I would do anything to have one."

With that statement, Raquelle removed a necklace and placed it over Brigit's head. "I love you, my sister. Now, with the sun around your neck, your eyes glisten brighter. Every warrior shall want to be your partner when you dance tonight."

Brigit caressed the smoothness of the gold necklace as she studied Raquelle. "You have changed, Kar. Before Matthew Wolverine, you were so selfish."

Raquelle stiffened at being addressed by her old name. "My name is now Raquelle Wolverine, daughter of the leader Matthew Wolverine. The Kar you knew is dead. Now, where did my father and Kial go?"

Brigit pointed south. "They went downwind to look at the dragon Kial killed. Men get such a thrill out of showing off what they kill. Anyway, we need to talk about something really important. Will you wear green, blue, or red on your ears for the dance tonight?"

Raquelle's hands flew to her face. "Oh, I didn't tell my father about the colors." Indeed she had not, and she had best do so, she thought, lest Matthew get himself into an awkward situation with some of the ladies at the dance that night. Eligible females placed a dab of brightly-colored paint on their earlobes to communicate their status. Green meant a maiden was too young; blue, that she wished only to dance; and red, that she needed a man tonight, and if she pleased him enough, she would be his mate in the morning. Raquelle said to her sister, "I know I could never find a man to treat me as well as my father treats me, so I will wear blue. And you, Brigit?"

Brigit's eyes narrowed into the slits of a predator who spots its next meal. "Does Matthew Wolverine have a mate at the castle or in some far-off land?"

Raquelle frowned. "No, his mate died, and he still grieves for her, so he hasn't taken another."

A scheme formed in Brigit's mind. "Then I shall wear red, but don't tell your father the meaning of the painted ears. He is a great warrior, so when I dance with him, I wish to see who will stand up to him for my love. The man who is brave enough to stand up to Matthew Wolverine will be the man I choose for my mate. But I will need your help, she who once was my sister."

Raquelle nodded, adding matter-of-factly, "Aye, I will help you, but we will always be sisters, no matter what our names. Now, let us find our fathers."

* * *

Looking over the dead dragon, Matthew marveled that the Picts were able to carry it this far. He realized again just how determined a people they were, and how desperately he needed them as allies.

Kial was the first to see Brigit and Raquelle approaching, and he yelled, "Come here, my daughters!"

Brigit ran to Kial's side, but Raquelle hung back, bracing herself for what she knew she must say. Drawing herself up to her full height, she looked Kial in the eye and said steadily, "I am not your daughter anymore. I am Raquelle Wolverine, daughter of the leader Matthew Wolverine."

Kial's face contorted with rage at the girl's disrespect, and he stepped toward her, his arm raised to strike her for her insolence. Matthew placed himself between the two, his eyes locked with Kial's. "Do not presume to punish her, whom you have cast away. She is my daughter now! Know that if you move toward her, you shall die, and none shall hear your tale of slaying this dragon. The next leader of the Picts will lay claim to the honor of this kill, and who would dare challenge his claim? Do you want the song of Kial, the dragon slayer, sung this night, or not?"

Kial glared at Matthew as he tried to save face. "I will not give up that which is rightfully mine and return to my chambers empty-handed."

Matthew immediately understood the proud Kial's predicament. It was no use reminding the Pict again that he had, after all, cast his daughter out and had even been prepared to kill her. Matthew saw the opportunity to for a quick resolution, and took it. "Nor should you depart empty-handed. That was never my intention. Raquelle, take off three of your gold necklaces and put them in Kial's hand."

Raquelle removed the necklaces, and Kial eagerly took them. He was mesmerized as the gold, still warm with Raquelle's body heat, shimmered in the sun. As Kial delightedly hefted the weight of the necklaces, Matthew leaned toward him to plant some seeds in his mind. "With the feast tonight, and the prizes you hold in your hand, the women will fight to get to you. You are without a mate, are you not?"

Kial put the necklaces over his head and adjusted them around his neck. Then, with head held high, he strutted like a peacock in all his glory toward the camp. As he entered the camp, a ray of sunlight broke through the clouds to shine brightly upon him. The necklaces glowed with a warmth unique to highly polished gold; Kial felt the glow and bellowed out, "Kial is a great trader, as well as a brave slayer of dragons. Three gold necklaces for a daughter; what a trade! Come, women, see the sun taken from the sky." The women crowded around him to touch the loveliness around Kial's neck, their minds filled with images of this piece of the sun around their own necks.

Matthew and Raquelle hung back from this scene, and Raquelle, snuggled under Matthew's arm, whispered, "I thought us dead."

Matthew pressed her to his chest, and kissed the top of her head. "We make a good team, and we had the best help available. I knew our God would protect us."

Raquelle sheepishly looked up. "Father, you must tell me more of this God, because I definitely thought we were going to die." Then, knowing this was not the smoothest of transitions, she added, "Oh, before I forget — will you dance with Brigit at the festival tonight? It would mean a lot to me."

Matthew considered the bravery of his daughter, then looked around at all the beautiful women, dressed in furs and tight-fitting skins. Raquelle could hear his heart pounding fast and hard in his chest as he replied, "Aye, I really like the women with red painted ears. They stir something inside of me that I cannot quite explain."

A mischievous smile formed on Raquelle's face, and she gently patted his chest and whispered softly to his racing heart, "That is their intention."

* * *

The feast began at sunset, and all in attendance ate until they could eat no more. Then the females began to dance, whirling dreams of unspoken pleasures in the minds of all who watched them.

Brigit's seductive moves aroused Matthew's primeval lust. Before he realized it, Brigit had him dancing with her, her body lightly brushing his. With the grace of a ballerina, she grasped his right hand and twirled into him, her back against his chest, and her hair effortlessly touching his cheek. She grasped Matthew's left hand, holding it away from her body. With her head tilted back, her body swayed up and down against Matthew as her silky hair caressed first his left cheek, then his right. Matthew's face bristled with each caress of her velvety hair as his body leaned into hers. Brigit needed all her strength to keep Matthew's hands at arm's length, away from her body.

As their bodies touched, Brigit could sense Matthew's growing hunger for her. She slid her hands to the back of his, her thumbs pressed between his thumbs and forefingers, slowly guiding his fingertips to brush against her heaving body. As his hands moved to enfold her breasts, she breathed in as deeply as she could, then moved away from him. Matthew burned for her, his passion wresting control of his mind as she was transformed into the most sensual woman in the world. Filled with passion, Matthew resolved that, when the music stopped, he would sweep her up in his arms and race for the nearest hut, to ravish that sensuous body until morning.

As Brigit whirled away from him, their eyes met, and the firelight shone on her *take-me-now!* expression, escalating Matthew's ardor to white-hot. His body ached for her, his passion demanding that he obey her silent command, and take her now. He broke her hold on him, his right arm reaching out forcefully about her back. With his left arm behind her legs, he swept her body up, and her arms encircled his neck as she covered his mouth with a deep, passionate kiss.

As Matthew's tongue gently probed into her willing mouth, her body shuddered at this new sensation. Savagely, Brigit's hands grasped the back of his head, beckoning him deeper into the kiss. Encouraged by her enthusiastic response, Matthew's tongue became more demanding, gently guiding her tongue into his own mouth. This was Brigit's first French kiss, but she hungrily explored virgin ground. Her passion was unrestrained, her kisses driving deeper into Matthew's mouth, sending his lust to new heights. At that point, Matthew abandoned any thought of self-control, and took her hand and raced toward the nearest hut with one thought consuming his entire being: he must have her.

The scream of a Pict warrior pierced the night air as he threw himself upon Brigit and Matthew, knocking them to the ground. Matthew's passion instantly evaporated as his combat-trained mind snatched control. This warrior, it soon became apparent, desired Brigit for himself, and he fought like a demon. Matthew snapped both hands straight out from his shoulders, clapping them hard against the warrior's ears. The blow only stunned the fellow, so Matthew struck his neck with a powerful karate blow, then kicked his feet out from under him. As the man fell, Matthew grasped his right hand and twisted his arm behind him, planting his foot against the fallen man's neck. Brigit screamed, dropping to her knees, begging Matthew not to kill her warrior…and something in Matthew's mind caused him to hesitate. He screamed back at her, "Why should I not kill him? Do you love him?"

Sobbing, Brigit pled, "Aye, he is the one I hoped to make jealous by going with you. I want to be his mate."

The warrior moved, and Matthew's body tensed, his foot pressing harder upon his victim's neck. "You move again and I'll snap your neck," Matthew growled. His mind reeled with anger at being fooled by this woman, his rage building like a tidal wave. At that instant, he wanted to snap the warrior's neck as badly as he had wanted Brigit only moments before. He was tired of being a nice guy. This time, he wanted revenge. He slowly surveyed every curve of Brigit's body, and he ached inside for her.

Then, all at once, he felt compassion for the man he wanted to kill. How could he hate this warrior for feeling the same passion that had so filled him? Matthew asked the warrior if he would marry Brigit now. A part of him hoped that the man would reject the offer, so he could snap his neck. Instead, the man stated that he loved her, and would take her for his wife, if Matthew would but allow it. With some regret, Matthew released him, and the warrior stood, thanked Matthew for his life, and turned to Brigit.

The Ultimate Dragon

"Will you have me, woman, though I have been bested by this man who would have you, as well?"

Brigit ran to him, holding his bruised face in her hands, kissing his mouth with a passion that Matthew bitterly recalled being directed to him but a few moments earlier. But he duly summoned Kial, who stepped forward to perform a short ceremony. After that, the couple slipped into the nearby hut, and the sounds of their ecstasy poured out into the night.

* * *

The celebration resumed as quickly as it had been stilled, but Matthew removed himself from the company to sit by a small fire, his mood solemn. The warriors and females around the fire could feel his radiating frustration, and moved away before getting up to dance. The anger in Matthew's eyes bore into the fire, and even the flames seemed to withdraw from the heat of his glare.

Raquelle stopped dancing and moved toward her father. Her partner tried to hold her back, but was stopped short by her words, which slashed at him like sharp daggers, "Do you truly wish to be the object of my father's anger?" Even by firelight, Raquelle could see the terror that filled the boy's eyes, and he quickly faded into the night. As she walked to her father, her hands began to sweat, and her mouth felt dry. "Father, are you all right?"

In a gruff voice, Matthew asked Raquelle if she had been part of Brigit's little scheme.

Raquelle's voice trembled as she spoke. "Aye, father, and I am sorry. I love you both. Brigit wanted to see if her warrior would stand up to a great conqueror for her love, and he did. So you see, her plan worked."

Matthew's frustration was reflected in the sharpness of his voice. "Let us walk and talk in private." Once they were on their way, he continued, "Your plan almost cost that man his life. Men have needs that we sometimes allow to take control of us. This is called passion, or sexual desire. When we desire a woman, and we think she desires us, that passion grows until it seems that it cannot be denied." Raquelle gave him a puzzled look.

"I can see I am losing you on this train of thought," he said patiently, "so I will draw you a picture with words. Passion is like a panther. Yellow Rose is a big, strong cat, but think of a cat as big as I am, black as night, with the power to remove your head from your shoulders with a single blow. That would be a panther. This passion I have told you about, it is as strong as a panther, and we men have it inside us. We must keep it caged most of the time. But passion hates to be caged, and it always seeks to be free and to mate. A woman has the key to this cage, and if she opens it, that panther leaps out, and she stares into the fiery eyes of a beast that must be satisfied. The only satisfaction this beast knows is mating, making love.

"With my wife dead, I have not had the opportunity to satisfy the beast in a long time. My panther has gained colossal strength. Brigit is so sensuous that while we were dancing, I was barely able to force my panther back into his cage. When I was out there fighting the man who is now her husband, the panther was continually roaring, *Snap the warrior's neck, take Brigit, and SATISFY ME!!!*"

A visibly flustered Raquelle blurted out, "But Brigit wore red on her ears to release your passion. You sleep alone at our castle, and I know you are frustrated. I hear you calling for your dead mate. It is not good to sleep in frustration. You need a woman to relieve your tension. I wanted my sister to give you pleasure tonight and relieve your frustration. I was just trying to help you *and* Brigit. When I agreed to help her, I truly thought that none of the Pict warriors would be brave enough to stand up to you, and that you and my sister would end up together. The plan did not work out, and I am sorry." Tears welled up in Raquelle's eyes.

At that moment, all Matthew could see before him was a little girl who wanted to please him. With a gentle hug, he forgave his daughter, and they walked, hand in hand, back to the camp. Matthew realized again that he had someone who really loved him, and that she had driven out the last vestige of sadness from his heart. He slept that night with a joyful heart, but a still-frustrated body.

* * *

The next morning, Kial emerged from his chambers with a huge smile on his face and three very beautiful women at his side, all wearing his gold necklaces and radiant smiles. Matthew was reminded of his own frustration, and he sarcastically blurted out, "I'm sure glad someone got lucky last night."

To which the gloating, and obviously very satisfied, Kial blurted out, "Aye, three times!"

Matthew quickly changed the subject, telling Kial that he wanted to make a pact with him. "I will trade one large fish for one lamb or one calf from you or any of your clan." Kial's mood may have been softened by his amorous adventures the night before, but he was a sharp trader, and demanded five fish for one lamb or calf, and ten for a full grown sheep or cow. To which Matthew replied, "I want only lambs and calves. I will offer you two fish for one lamb or calf."

"Why do you not desire full-grown sheep or cows?" Kial asked.

Matthew responded, "I want my own herdsman to raise the lambs and cows. But these animals will provide food and clothing for both my clan and yours. If, in the winter, your people fear starvation, they may come and take from my herds for food. And if the winter grows too cold, you and your clan are welcome to stay in the warmth of my castle, and eat of my food."

Kial considered Matthew's offer, found it to be most generous, and agreed to accept two fish for every one lamb or calf. Kial, being the keen trader he was, could not leave well enough alone. "Why do you offer to allow my people to take from your herds?" He knew that Matthew was too wily to simply give away something so valuable. "What do you expect in return?"

With a smile and a single word, Matthew drove home his desire: "Friendship."

To have his friendship so valued by a man like Matthew greatly pleased Kial, who answered Matthew's words with a great hug. On that day, Kial pledged his friendship to the clan of Matthew Wolverine, and blessed both Matthew and Raquelle, the daughter they shared, as the two left the Pict camp.

It was a friendship sealed with the blood of dragons and their worshippers, and in the months to come, this friendship would brutally test every ounce of Kial's strength and mettle.

CHAPTER 12

Back at the castle, Matthew busied himself with the task of teaching his people not only the skills they needed in order to improve their lives, but the sense of self-pride that would make them want to improve themselves, as well. From the dragon's treasure, he took large silver shields, once the raiment of proud warriors in a wealthy kingdom, and he had the village smiths polish them until they reflected as clearly as fine mirrors. These mirrors, he placed in the treasure room, so that all who entered could see how they looked. As the people gazed upon themselves, they began to take pride in their appearance, and the sight of an unwashed face soon became a rarity in the castle. The mirrors in the treasure room were soon in constant demand.

For the next month, peace filled the air, and laughter rang often from within Matthew's castle. The Picts traded many of their lambs and calves for Matthew's fish, and began to grow fatter from the increasingly regular meals they were enjoying. The fear of hunger all but vanished from the lands under Matthew's control, and the fame of Matthew Wolverine and his God spread throughout Scotland. In castles and villages far and wide, people excitedly told stories of the grand tables of Matthew Wolverine, laden with fresh fish, succulent roasts of lamb and beef, game birds, great loaves of bread, and vegetables at every meal.

It was often said that there were no strangers at Matthew's castle, only friends he had yet to meet. Feelings of warmth and hospitality permeated the castle, and Shalee made certain that no guest ever left her table hungry. Game birds were kept in the courtyard, and the guest who told the best story at supper was given one as a prize. Every Saturday night, a dance was held in the castle courtyard. The Picts would come to join in the dances, and many of the warriors wound up married the following day.

According to Matthew's instructions, warriors spread the dragon dung upon the farmers' fields, and Matthew's smiths made iron plows for the farmers. Matthew then went to each farm, teaching the farmers how to use the plows to turn the fertilizer into the soil and prepare the land for planting. To the farmers' amazement, they saw their crop yields increase fourfold, just as Matthew had promised. And, also in keeping with the leader's promise, the warriors who spread the dung were allowed to choose silver and gold necklaces for their wives.

The silver and gold coins that Matthew struck were to be freely traded in his castle and Robert's. Each coin bore the inscription, in Gaelic: "For God and A Free Scotland." Much of the dragon treasure now resided in Matthew's castle, and Matthew encouraged the people of the castle to enter the treasure room, search through this treasure to find items they desired, and bring the desired treasure to him. Matthew would then inform them how much work they must do to attain the item. He told them that if the work was not completed within one year, the item would go back into the pile, so that another person could bargain for it. The desired item was tagged with the person's name and date, and then was placed in a separate room. Though two guards were always posted outside this room, a person wishing to see his or her item could enter the room at any time with no guard present.

Raquelle wondered about what she saw as her father's carelessness, and finally asked him about it. "Father why do you allow the people to search through the treasure piles without a guard present? We have always been a poor people, and the temptation to steal will be greater than most will be able to resist."

While Matthew was not normally a person who appreciated having his judgment questioned, he genuinely appreciated Raquelle's challenge. He felt proud that she had the wisdom to consider such things, and warmed by her willingness to risk his anger in order to protect him or his assets. "By allowing the people to search the treasure unguarded, it shows them that I trust them. The women, especially, love picking out beautiful items. They then encourage their men to finish my projects quickly, so they can wear their new treasures.

"Consequently, I get a hard-working warrior who will labor from dawn to dusk to please his wife. When he gets back to the castle, he is greeted by a wife who is very interested to hear how his project progresses, and how soon she will be able to wear her present. She is anxious to see him succeed, and does everything she can to let him know that his efforts are appreciated. Such teamwork builds strong marriages. Surely, you have seen how few family fights occur at night in my castle. All the people possess one goal: to complete my projects as soon as possible. What I am doing is promoting a desire to succeed and excel among my warriors. That is the essence of capitalism."

Raquelle asked him about this capitalism, and Matthew explained. "It is a system for the accumulation of wealth. By allowing the warriors and their families to possess gold and silver items, the wealth of Scotland is shared. If I take their men to war, they know that they will share in the wealth of victory. It is for this reason that, when a project is complete, we have a party. I am happy because the project is done quickly, the women wear gold and silver jewelry, and the men pick out another sword or dagger from our weapons room. This is true capitalism, where every participant gains wealth."

As Matthew shared his logic with her, Raquelle was reminded that her father was not only a good man, but a shrewd one, as well. No leader before him had ever realized that the best way to get what you wanted from your people was to see to it that they got what they wanted, as well. She was delighted at the notion that doing for others wasn't merely something one did out of kindness, but was also an act of cunning. The more she knew of Matthew Wolverine, the greater grew her respect for him. Little did she know that the respect he held for her was growing in like fashion.

* * *

The next day, Raquelle found her father inspecting a row of strange-looking boxes. Each wooden box was topped with three panes of glass, sandwiched on top of each other, with a one-inch space between each pane. Matthew explained that the glass panes let the sunlight warm the ground and kept the heat inside the box. Raquelle watched her father open the box, dig a hole, and plant what looked like grass or a small tree. Matthew picked one of the plants and chewed off its top leaves.

Raquelle was stunned when she saw this, and asked him, almost accusingly, "Father, you eat grass?"

Matthew looked up, and laughed when he saw the look on her face. "No, this is not grass, but parsley. Here, eat some. It's good for you, and if you eat enough, you will have no body odor. It also helps prevent mouth odor. That will definitely solve one problem here in the castle. Raquelle, when this parsley grows, have large bowls of it placed on the tables before our meals. I like parsley, and you must learn to like it as well, so that the others in the castle will follow our example. Also, tell the cooks to start seasoning with it. And now, I have something else I want to show you," he concluded.

They walked a short distance to a site where dozens of laborers scurried around a large doorless building with a giant stone cross inside. Matthew explained, "This is a church, somewhat like the one I found when I first came to Scotland, and it is almost complete. What do you think of it?"

Raquelle shrugged, obviously not very impressed. "Why is it built without doors? It gets very cold here in the winter."

Matthew sat down on the ground, and began to explain to her, "Any true believer who wishes to pray will find this building always open, just as our God is always open to hear our prayers. Prayer is between God and a man or woman, but it is a private matter. We assemble on the Sabbath to worship, and after our meeting, we feast together. But prayer is done at any time, day or night, as the person feels the need. No door will ever bar them from this cross, which is the symbol of God's willingness to be always here for us."

Raquelle nodded her head. "When you explain it, the reason becomes clear. Why could I not see this reason before?"

Matthew's eyes revealed the pride he felt for his daughter. "You have an inquisitive mind, child. That is how you learn so quickly. Just keep asking questions and you will start to see the answers for yourself. When I was your age I did not see these answers, but you do, and as you grow, you will see even more. One thing I hope you are always able to see is that I am very proud of you."

Raquelle beamed a smile at her father, and basked in the approving glow in his eyes.

* * *

This spell was broken as Kele rushed toward them. "My leader, a warning comes from Robert Roybridge. The dragon worshippers from the East Coast of Scotland on the North Sea send an army to attack us in five days!"

Matthew spit out, "Why can't these putrid beings leave us alone? Kele, send a runner to Kial to inform him of our coming battle. I need him and all of his warriors at my castle at sunrise in two days. Each warrior must have two large armfuls of arrows. Next, send Robert's runner back to bid Robert come at once. Then gather any liquid in our castle that will burn, and place it in large jars. Have all the farmers stop their work and come to the castle with any instrument that will cut dry grass. Now go!"

Raquelle's face drew tight with anxiety. "Father, what can I do?"

"Tell Shalee to have the women prepare provisions enough to feed five hundred warriors for ten days. Gather our sheep and cattle close to the castle. This will be our walking food supply. And have the cooks load their cookware into our wagons."

Within two hours, Robert arrived at Matthew's castle. Matthew hustled him inside to the meal tables, where Matthew had laid out a number of books. Inviting Robert to sit down, he opened one book to a map of Scotland, and pointed to where they were on the map.

As Robert examined this map, a perplexing look crept over his face. He swallowed hard and shook a little as he looked at Matthew in awe. "Only God and his angels looking down from heaven could draw such pictures. Matthew, are you an angel?"

A deep laugh filled the room, with Matthew holding his side as he repeated, "An angel!" Matthew placed his hand on Robert's shoulder to steady himself, and found he was laughing so hard that he had to wipe tears from his eyes. "Robert, I needed a good laugh. Thank you. No, I am not an angel, but a man who needs your help." He returned his attention to the book, pointing at a spot on the page. "We are here on the map, and our enemy is here. Now, show me, on this map, a place where there is a small valley that the enemy must pass through on their way to my castle. It must have a gently rising hill on the north, sloping gradually to the south, and a forest to the west where our cavalry can conceal their horses."

Robert pointed to a valley west of the Spey River, one day's march to the east.

"Good," Matthew said. "We will use an L-shape ambush." It was a trick he had learned from the Viet Cong.

"Explain this ambush," Robert said.

"The enemy will be marching west," Matthew replied, "so I will place Pict archers out of sight, just over the north hill. To the south, the dry grass will be cut to soak with a liquid that will burn quickly as fire approaches it. This fire will drive the enemy to flee up the hill, into the range of the waiting Pict archers."

"But what about the enemy scouts?" Robert asked, concerned.

"Oh, I assure you, they shall willingly enter the valley. In two days, I will lead a Pict army to your castle, Robert, and then on to the valley and victory."

Robert still had concerns about Matthew's plan, but he left to prepare his warriors. As Matthew emerged from the room, Raquelle ran toward him and he grabbed her up, lifting her high in the air.

Raquelle caught her father's enthusiasm. "I know you will win, my father. May the bones of our enemies be food for a thousand wolves. May their widows be many, crying tears to fill a loch, and may all their children starve." She gave her father a big hug.

"It seems I have created a little monster," Matthew said. "The idea is to vanquish our enemy, but not to rejoice in their suffering. Our God does not rejoice in the suffering of even the most wicked.

"In any case, I love you, my little monster. Come, and pray with me that our God will grant us strength and wisdom for swift victory." Then he had an idea. "Go and get Shalee and the wolves, and we will pray as a family."

Raquelle hastened to the kitchen, where she found Shalee fretting over which foods to take, what to cook it in, and who would cook the food. She was also trying to figure out if they needed to pack extra clothes. Raquelle interrupted the proceedings and said, "Shalee, my father wishes you to come and pray with us for strength and wisdom from his God. The wolves get to come, too!"

Shalee scowled at Raquelle. "I have too much work to do, and no time to pray. Tell Matthew that I remain here to complete the preparation for his march. You get the wolves and go to him." Raquelle had hoped that Shalee would help her get the wolves, because they did not always listen to her. But she hurried away to Matthew's chambers.

As she had feared, the wolves did not want to obey Raquelle, and hid under the bed. Raquelle pleaded with them, "Please, come out. Shalee won't come, you won't come, and I fear my father's temper. Please, come out." The wolves ignored her pleas, and then Matthew entered the room. The wolves rushed to his feet, and he petted each one. They then fell in behind him as they started for the prayer room, and Raquelle hurried to Matthew's side.

"Well, Raquelle, has Shalee agreed to meet us for prayer?" Raquelle moved away from her father as she timidly related Shalee's message that she was too busy to pray. She braced herself for his explosion of anger, but it did not come. Instead, Matthew led the group quietly to the foot of the cross that stood in his nearly-completed church, and he took her hand. Raquelle and her father held hands as Matthew prayed aloud to his God, and she began to feel warm and peaceful inside.

Matthew poured out his heart to his God, asking for courage, wisdom, and protection of his warriors in the coming battle. The wolves lay around the foot of the cross like statues, so still that Raquelle couldn't even tell if they were breathing. It was as if the powerful presence she felt had stilled them, as well.

After the prayer was done, Raquelle looked at her father, and noticed a new doggedness in his eyes, and it scared her. The wolves also sensed the change in Matthew, and their heads hung in submission as Matthew rose to walk to the castle. On reentering the castle, Matthew headed straight for Shalee.

Matthew spotted Shalee in the kitchen. As he moved toward her, he shouted orders to her. "Get the black cloaks we used to slay the dragon worshippers, and the high priest's red robe, and bring them to me at once."

Shalee brushed off his request. "Just as soon as I have gathered all the food for your march. I am nearly finished."

Shalee turned her back to Matthew and started to go, but Matthew grabbed her arm almost savagely, causing her to fall to the ground. With an ice-laden voice, Matthew asked if she preferred death to obedience. Shalee glared in defiance into Matthew's eyes, but her defiance faded as a vision of death emerged from the steel of his eyes, reaching out to seize her. Shalee started to shake with fear, sensing her life flowing into the bony fingers of his stare. She implored Matthew's forgiveness, and his awareness rose to encircle the impulse of death that flowed from him. He pulled that impulse, kicking and screaming, back into its depths. Matthew released Shalee, and she scurried to get the cloaks.

Raquelle witnessed her father's actions with great concern. Shalee had told her that Matthew would never hurt her, yet he had just threatened her with death! Why? Raquelle cautiously approached her father and asked him to talk in their chambers. Matthew was irritated by the distraction of her request, but said he would give her a few moments. When they reached the chambers, Raquelle kept her distance as she blurted out, "Why did you threaten Shalee with death? If you marry her, will you beat her? Was her disobedience really so bad?"

Matthew's response, though not brief, was to the point. "In a very short time, we go into battle. The comfort of a happy family is a luxury that must wait for another day. For now, we are, all of us, warriors in an army, preparing for war. An army operates by force and respect. I cannot allow Shalee, or even you, to question my orders.

"Rebellion is infectious, Raquelle. Shalee refused my request to pray, then brushed aside my order that she fetch the robes. Her rebellion would soon infect our whole army. By Shalee not coming to pray with us, the seeds of disobedience could well have been planted, and could soon blossom until, lacking the unified will to defeat our enemies, *we* would be defeated. Then, we would all die! It is as simple as that.

"I love Shalee, and do not wish to hurt her, but I cannot allow her rebellion to remain unchecked. This battle is not just for the people at our castle but for all of Scotland, for our God's victory over the dragons and their worshippers.

"To your second question: if I marry a woman, it will certainly not be so that I may beat her. It gives me no pleasure to inflict pain on another. A wife is to be cherished, protected with my life, and shown love through my actions. I would never beat Shalee. When you marry, if your husband ever beats you, know that the day I find out is the day he dies." Matthew rose and left Raquelle alone to ponder his words. A warrior's actions were so complicated. Love was complicated too, and Raquelle wished that it were simpler.

Before nightfall, word of the incident with Shalee spread to every corner of the castle. The next day, Matthew's commands were executed with such swiftness that it seemed the instant he voiced a command, it was fulfilled. This control impressed Raquelle, but she kept her distance from her father.

* * *

At sunrise the second day, Kial and his Pict warriors arrived outside Matthew's castle. As Matthew rode out of the castle, Kial sensed the change in him, and a healthy fear shot up his spine. The army was quick to detect that Matthew was in sole control. Wagons, with caged game birds, fell in behind the Pict warriors, and the sheep and cattle trailed in the rear. Shalee and Raquelle rode behind Matthew and Kial, but Matthew took no notice of them. He spent his time riding up and down the line of marching warriors, encouraging them by telling them that his God would deliver the enemy into their hands. When they reached Robert's castle, only Matthew entered.

Matthew asked Robert, "Have you melted the gold down into coins with the new inscription?"

Robert nodded and handed Matthew a coin. It bore the inscription, "For God and A Free Scotland," with a large cross and a small cross below it. Robert had had two thousand new coins loaded into his wagon for the trip.

"What will this coin be called?" Robert asked.

"Good question," Matthew said, mentally weighing the coin in his hand. "One ounce. Well, let me see... I've got it. We shall call it a Scottish Cross. Every warrior who survives shall receive a Scottish Cross. Now, did you prepare the fire powder as I instructed you, and does it work?"

Robert grabbed a handful of the powder, and threw it into a burning torch. It flashed brightly and created a massive cloud of smoke. Robert questioned the use of the powder, and Matthew answered his question with a question, asking, "What better way to disappear, than behind smoke?"

Robert knew full well that this war with the dragon worshippers was for Scotland's very survival. He knelt now on one knee before Matthew, swearing to die at his side, if need be. As he rose, Matthew noticed the resolve that radiated from his friend's eyes. They turned then and rode out of the castle to lead their troops to the valley.

***

Matthew had the farmers cut the grass on the south side of the valley, then ordered the warriors to pour oil and other liquids over the cut grass. Pict warriors dug small cooking pits at the beginning of the valley, and larger ones at the west end of the valley, close to the forest. Five wild boars were flushed from the forest, and were greeted by Death in the form of Pict arrows. Matthew ordered these boars dressed and cooked slowly on spits, to be ready by noon the next day. For the sake of a free Scotland, he was willing to suffer the foul odor of roasting pig flesh.

To the cooks he said, "At sunrise tomorrow, also prepare half the game birds, lambs, and sheep in the smaller pits. The smell of delicious meats and fowl cooking must fill the valley at high noon." The cooks nodded, then guards were posted, and the camp slept that night on the north side of the hill.

Shortly before the dawn, Shalee nudged Raquelle, whispering loudly, "Awaken! The sun is rising, and your father prepares his troops. After the flaming arrows fly over our heads, we can climb to the hilltop to watch the battle."

At that moment, the troops were donning the black robes of the dragon worshippers, while Matthew himself put on the red robe of the high priest. Then Matthew assembled the warriors for his pep talk. "If any Pict archer gives away our position, I will personally thrust daggers through his hands and feet, then slice open his belly to let him slowly bleed to death. Become as quiet as a cat stalking a mouse. Let there be no talking until you see a flaming arrow fly over your heads, then shoot your arrows as quickly as you can over this hilltop, until one armful of your arrows is gone. Our enemy will only see death raining from the sky. Terror will fill their hearts because they cannot see you.

"As you fire your arrows, my cavalry, with horses trailing long ropes of burning branches, will circle the enemy's south flank. Only then shall you rush to the top of the hill and pour your remaining arrows into the fleeing enemy. Any enemy left standing, you must drive back into the fire and throw their wounded into the fire, as well. All our enemy's numbers are to be consumed in the fire. Any questions?"

A muscular warrior spoke. "How will you divide the booty of these warriors?"

Matthew liked directness. "In this battle, half the swords and daggers will be given to Kial, and half to me. Kial will distribute his share of the booty among his warriors as he sees fit. Now, get in position."

***

Hours had passed, and the smell of succulent meat cooking was making Raquelle's mouth water to the point that she squirmed with hunger. "Shalee," she said, "it is almost noon. With the tantalizing smell of the meat filling my head, I crave food, and still the enemy does not come. Do you think they went another way?"

Shalee shook her head. "You must be patient and have faith in your father's plan. Eventually he will lure the enemy to our midst. That delicious smell will draw them out, for they can no more resist the aroma of roasting meat than you can. And when they emerge, they will see the fires tended by men in black robes, men whom they will think are dragon worshippers, their allies. The plan is brilliant. Wait a little longer, and you will see."

But Raquelle was bored and restless, and before Shalee could stop her, the girl had crawled up to the hilltop. Shalee came up close behind her, and they both peeked over the ridge. One of the enemy scouts appeared at the east end of the valley. By the forest west of the valley, black-robed figures extended their arms to heaven, looking for all the world like dragon worshippers in the throes of religious ecstasy, and the red-robed figure — who was, of course, Matthew in disguise — beckoned the enemy scout to join them.

The scout hesitated only a moment, then nodded toward the distant high priest and walked toward a roasting game bird. The scout ravenously devoured the succulent fowl, after which more scouts appeared. As soon as they spotted the high priest, they too moved swiftly toward the food. The remaining enemy scouts reached the first pit and attacked the food, gorging themselves on the roasted birds. More enemy warriors appeared then, and saw their scouts devouring these luscious game birds.

All at once there was a blinding flash, and the end of the valley was shrouded in thick black smoke. Shalee rubbed her eyes. "Raquelle, did you see that? What can it mean? The black robes all disappeared! Where did your father and his men go? Are they not going to fight for us?"

Raquelle chuckled. "Shalee, weren't you the one who was just lecturing me about having faith? My father did not share the details of his plan with me, but I am certain that this smoke was part of the plan. Look! See how the enemy army moves toward the roasting sheep and lambs? And more enemy warriors move toward the roast boar at the west end of the valley, just in front of the forest where father and his men disappeared. They run like ravenous wolves upon a fallen deer. It sounds like they are shouting praises to their god for this feast."

Shalee nodded. Then it was Raquelle's turn again to doubt. She said, "But I wonder, why is my father not firing the flaming arrow?"

Shalee grabbed Raquelle's shoulder and pointed straight up as a flaming arrow soared high overhead. The Pict archers then loosed their arrows so rapidly that each had launched at least five arrows into the air before that first arrow struck land. And then, as Matthew had predicted, the sky was raining needles of death upon the dragon worshippers, and the valley echoed with ear-piercing screams as the arrows sank deep into enemy flesh.

The screams were answered with the thunder of hooves as Matthew's cavalry emerged from a now-burning forest, dragging the flaming branches behind their horses. They charged in circles wide to the south of the enemy, setting all the oil-soaked grass into a roaring inferno. As Matthew's cavalry raced to circle behind them to close the trap, the enemy faced a wall of Pict arrows raining down on them from their right flank, and fire in front and to their left flank. The enemy warriors, maddened with fear, turned to race up the hill to escape the inferno that was quickly engulfing them. But Matthew's cavalry reached the east end of the valley before them, and turned to charge into the chaos of their ranks.

Kial urged his archers to the crest of the hill, and they poured shafts of death down the throats of their stampeding enemy. The enemy turned east to escape the arrows, but Matthew's cavalry now blocked their flight. Matthew held his cavalry in check as the Pict archers loosed the last of their arrows. Then Kial raised his sword in signal, and the Picts charged down the hill into the enemy. Faced with a legion of swords that flickered with the reflection of the fires, the maddened horde of dragon worshippers was driven, screaming, into the hungry inferno.

The shrieks of men burning alive, and the smell of their flesh as the flames licked it from their bones, were more than Raquelle could bear, and she burst into uncontrollable wailing. Shalee wrapped her arms around the sobbing girl and pulled her away from the hilltop. Raquelle clung tightly to Shalee's chest, trying to escape the death screams. As Shalee gently moved Raquelle farther from the crest of the hill, she softly stroked Raquelle's hair, whispering that the shrieks would end soon. After what seemed like forever, the silence of death replaced the screams, but Raquelle still shook in Shalee's arms.

* * *

Matthew led his cavalry to Robert Roybridge, and inquired about the casualties. Robert happily reported that none of his warriors had died, but two were slightly wounded. An ecstatic Kial shouted the Picts had suffered no casualties at all. Matthew was relieved, and went to look for Raquelle and Shalee. Kial pointed to a spot on the crest of the hill and told Matthew that they were there during the battle. Matthew turned his horse toward the hill, spurring the beast to a gallop. As he crested the hill, he spotted Shalee in the distance, holding a limp Raquelle in her arms…and his heart froze.

Matthew whipped his steed to a full run and, arriving beside the two young women, leapt from his saddle. Matthew grabbed Raquelle, clutching her to his chest in a crushing grip. The tears welled up in his eyes as he fought back the scream that was building in his chest, "No! Not another…" Then, he felt a faint movement in her seemingly lifeless body. Opening her eyes, Raquelle squeezed him, and his grip relaxed. "Raquelle, I thought you dead. Are you hurt?"

Raquelle looked away and whimpered, "My flesh is not wounded, but those screams were more than my heart could bear. I am sorry I am so weak in battle."

"I know what you mean," he replied gently. "Some nights, I just want to bury my head in a woman's arms and be comforted, to have the sounds of battle washed from my mind forever. But realize, child, that my ways of war are necessary for us to remain free, and you must gain strength to lead Scotland after I go."

Raquelle and Shalee burst out in unison, "You are leaving?"

A quizzical look crossed Matthew's face until he realized that they did not think in military terms. So he explained, "We all die, and only God knows the day. Raquelle, you must be ready to become leader when this happens. From now on I will explain my actions to you, and you must question me until you understand."

Raquelle and Shalee loudly released the breath they were holding, and, though her eyes were still red and swollen, Raquelle managed a smile. Then she asked, "Why did our enemy have to burn to death?"

Matthew escorted Raquelle and Shalee to the top of the hill to overlook the fresh battlefield. "There are three reasons. First, to show the enemy where they will spend eternity because they worship the dragons. Second, my troops' lives have been spared by the use of fire. The lives of our troops are precious, and we don't spill their blood without cause. Third, these bodies are great breeders of disease, and burning will stop this.

"Our enemies will soon find these burned bodies piled before their castle gates. This will send a message to them that if they do not surrender quickly, they too will die a horrible death."

Raquelle was silent for a moment. Then she asked, "What do we do now?"

"Tomorrow," Matthew replied, "we march east to claim the lands of these dead dragon worshippers."

Raquelle's ears perked up. "How much land will we control, father?"

Matthew swept his right hand from east to the west and said, "From Loch Ness to the east coast of Scotland. We will bathe in the North Sea and eventually launch ships to trade with Europe. All who serve our God in Scotland will eventually be under our control, and all who serve the dragons, we shall either kill or send below Hadrian's Wall. God willing, before I breathe my last, I will vanquish the dragons from Scotland."

"Father, what is Hadrian's Wall?"

"It is a wall that separates a free Scotland from the south kingdom. This wall was built by a Roman emperor — a leader — to keep the Picts out of the south kingdom. All land above Hadrian's Wall is Scotland. All lands below are part of the south kingdom, and we will have nothing to do with them if they leave us alone. Now, that is enough geography for today. Are you feeling better?"

Even as she was repulsed by what she had witnessed, Raquelle felt proud of her new understanding. "Aye, I now understand that your war tactics are necessary to protect our freedom. Soon I will be twelve summers, and I shall become more brave, to protect our warriors and the freedom of all Scots."

Matthew pulled Raquelle and Shalee close to him as they gazed upon the smoldering battlefield. "I hope you both understand what I do and why it must be done. Even more, I pray that, someday, such wars may be nothing but an ugly memory."

The Ultimate Dragon

CHAPTER 13

Matthew, Raquelle, and Shalee stood on the crest of the hill to savor the bittersweet moment of victory. Both Shalee and Raquelle leaned hard upon Matthew, and he basked in their embrace. Then Robert and Kial marched up the hill toward them, shattering the moment. Matthew sighed deeply, and reluctantly released his hold on Shalee. Turning to the two men, he shouted, "Robert, do you know which castles hold dragon worshippers?"

Robert's forehead knotted as he pondered. Then he replied, "Aye, but I haven't been in them. What is your plan?"

Leaving the question unanswered, Matthew said, "Kial, send out scouts until we spot an enemy's castle. Robert, have your men cut down a straight, thin tree, four times your height, and strip the bark to form a pole. Then cut and strip branches as round as your fist and the length of your arm. Tie these branches to the pole, so that they form a stepped cross, with the branches close enough to each other that a man can easily step from one to the next. We shall use this as a scaling ladder to climb over the enemy's walls."

When Kial returned, Matthew showed him how to make garrotes by cutting three thin strips of leather, as long as the distance from the tip of his longest finger to his elbow, braiding the strips together, and affixing a short, stout stick to each end. Kial and two warriors assembled their garrotes and gave them to Matthew. Nodding his approval, Matthew then ordered Kial and Robert to each provide their best warrior. "They will team up with Kele and me for the mission," he explained.

When the warriors arrived, Matthew showed Kele and them how to use the garrotes. First, he tied a wide band of thick leather around each of their necks, and one around his own, to protect them from injuring each other. Then he placed the cord of the garrote between the second and third fingers of each hand, and formed the garrote into a loop. Stepping behind Kele, he flipped the loop over Kele's head. When the loop was just below Kele's Adam's apple, Matthew gently pulled the handles apart. Kele instinctively grabbed his neck, and Matthew released his grip, and explained the procedure,

"When the cord is in place around your enemy's neck, you must snap your hands apart with all your strength. I pulled gently only to show you how it must be done. If you do this properly, your enemy's windpipe will be crushed, and he will die without crying out. The bands around your necks will protect you while you practice. Now, each of you practice the technique until it comes naturally to you." After they had all practiced using the garrotes, Matthew asked if they had any questions.

Robert's warrior wondered aloud, "What if the leather breaks?"

Matthew pointed to his own Bowie knife. "You each shall wear your dagger strapped to the outside of your right leg. In one swift motion, plunge your knife deep into the enemy's back and through his heart. Your other hand must clamp the enemy's mouth, pulling his head back, toward your right shoulder. It is messy, but he dies quickly and quietly."

Robert's warrior complained, "My dagger gets stuck in my kilt."

Kial's warrior agreed, "Aye, so does mine."

Matthew called for Shalee, and when she appeared he said, "Shalee, make four pairs of pants like mine for these warriors and myself."

Shalee examined the pants Matthew wore. "I will need your pants as a model," she said, matter-of-factly.

Matthew ordered Kele to bring him a kilt, silently vowing that, on the next expedition, they would bring some tents. He removed the pants and handed them to Shalee, who was staring intently and shamelessly at him. "My leader, what is that white cloth you wear?"

Matthew cleared his throat and said, "It is called jockey underwear, and it is made of cotton."

Kele tilted his head and asked, "Why do you wear it?"

Matthew became flustered. "It helps keep me warm. Let me get this kilt on." As he pulled up the kilt, Matthew sheepishly explained, "Okay, I wear it so my pants don't rub certain areas raw. Whew! That wind coming up my legs is sure cold. How do you people keep warm?"

Shalee quipped, "Why do you think we marry so young?" Then she left, to the roar of laughter from Matthew and Kele.

Matthew commented on Shalee's sense of humor and her helpfulness. Kele nodded, telling Matthew she would make him a fine wife.

Matthew agreed, but said that they had battles to win and lands to claim, and these must be his first priority. Then he would take the time to win her heart.

Daniel N. Jason

* * *

At that moment, Robert and another man came sprinting toward Matthew. Robert cried, "My leader, this scout has just returned with a report of a dragon worshipper's castle, just east of the Spey River."

Matthew interrogated the scout, scratching out a crude map in the dirt. "Let's say this rock is the castle. Describe the surrounding landscape."

The scout explained, "To the northwest there is a wooded hill, circled by a road, due east of the castle. Fields surround the rest of the castle. The road runs from the Spey River, straight to the castle's west gate, then through the castle and out the east gate."

Matthew queried the scout as to how he knew this was a dragon worshipper's castle. The scout looked sideways at Robert, wondering if the leader was feigning ignorance to test him. Robert shrugged, so the scout said, "It bears the symbol of a dragon's head on the gates, as do all dragon worshippers' castles.

Matthew made a mental note of this and asked the scout, "How tall are the walls?"

The scout answered, "They are thrice my height. And guards are posted at both the front and back gates." Pleased with the job the scout had done, Matthew rewarded him with a Scottish Cross.

The scout marveled at the coin. "It is so beautiful. It captures the sun. What do these marks say?"

Robert proudly stated, "For God and a Free Scotland."

This scout dropped to one knee before Matthew. "You are a good leader. I will serve both you and your God. My sword, and my life, are yours for the asking."

Matthew pulled his sword and tapped the scout on both shoulders, bestowing his first title. "Arise, Sir Scout," he said, "and tell me, what will you do with your Scottish Cross?"

The scout rose and considered the question carefully. "At Robert Roybridge's castle, I have a good wife, and I want to exchange this for a gift for her. But what could I get her?"

This was Matthew's opening to implant shrewd trading skills in this man. "To the south, I hear, they have beautiful doeskins and very soft furs. If you trade wisely, you can acquire two doeskins, some furs, and a new dagger for yourself. Can you be a wise trader?"

The scout's face brightened. "Aye, but how do I get south to trade?"

Matthew replied, "As we make our way east, not all dragon worshippers will be killed. Some will be captured and escorted to Hadrian's Wall, to be released into the south kingdom. You will be one of these escorts. Have you ever been to Hadrian's Wall?"

The scout nodded. "As a boy, my father took me there, but, my lord, that it is a half a moon's journey, and very dangerous. Who will protect us, what with fleeing dragon worshippers — and angry dragons — about?"

Matthew's face glowed. "The God you now serve will protect you. Go show the other warriors your Scottish Cross, Sir Scout."

Matthew and Robert were left alone, but Robert whispered, "You shouldn't have him show off that coin. The other warriors will want one, and then what shall we do?"

Matthew thought his plan was so obvious that he would not need to explain it to Robert. "Let us go among the warriors and see what they want." A crowd was gathered around the scout, listening to him tell of how he would trade this Scottish Cross for doeskins, soft furs, and a new dagger. He bragged to his comrades that he was a good trader, and swore allegiance to Matthew Wolverine and his God.

At this, Kele approached Matthew, seething with anger, not bothering to keep his voice down. "We fought for you and will die for you. Why are we not rewarded with Scottish Crosses, like this scout?"

Matthew put his hand to his chin to over-dramatize his consideration of Kele's statement. A crowd of warriors formed around him, impatiently awaiting his answer. Matthew's eyes narrowed, and with a somber face, he turned to the crowd and said, "Aye, you fought for me, and would die for me...but do you all accept my Messiah?"

This assembly of warriors looked at each other, then back to Matthew. Kele responded for the group, "If, when you say 'Messiah,' you are talking about your God, then we accept him."

With a stern face Matthew bid them kneel, to pledge their loyalty to the Messiah. One part of him found it rather distasteful that he was bribing people to accept his God, but his pragmatic side told him this was the most foolproof way to ensure the warriors' loyalty, and to spread his message of Scottish unity and freedom. In these coarse and violent times, there wasn't always room for subtlety.

With the loyalty pledges done, Robert, Shalee, and Raquelle distributed one Scottish Cross to each warrior. To all appearances, Matthew stood there, impassive, but inside, he was jumping for joy. All the Picts except Kial knelt. Kial approached, obviously deep in thought, then knelt with the others. To Matthew he said, "You have won the hearts of my men. We fought a battle and won victory without losing even one Pict warrior. You say your God is responsible for this. Such a God, I will serve. And I will serve you; I am yours to command."

All Matthew's doubts faded away. He now had a Scottish army willingly under his command. He smiled and said to Kial, "Arise, my brother.

After we capture the land between here and the North Sea, you will take the prisoners we capture and banish them into the south kingdom below Hadrian's Wall. Make it clear to them that if they return to Scottish soil, they will die.

"Take these bags of Scottish Crosses, and when you reach Hadrian's Wall, give one to each warrior who has accompanied you. The rest are yours. But you must not return to your camp with even one Scottish Cross among you or your men."

Kial was bewildered. "What will happen to these coins?"

Matthew sprinkled the seeds of astute Scottish trading into Kial's mind. "As you travel south with these prisoners, stop at every Pict settlement. Tell the story of your brave warriors and their fight against the dragons. Especially tell them how your spear went through the dragon's neck and you became Kial the dragon slayer. And tell them about your leader and friend, Matthew Wolverine, who worships the true God, leads the fight against the dragons, and vows that before he dies, Scotland will vanquish all dragons and even the knowledge of them, reducing them to naught but fodder for the tales that old wives tell small children.

"And then when you have convinced them, show them your Scottish Crosses, and invite them to come at any time of the year to trade at Loch Ness. Bid them bring their finest goods to Loch Ness and trade for Scottish Crosses, gold necklaces, silver armbands, swords, daggers, and the great fish that the lake guardians drive to shore. Tell them that as the dragons are being killed, their worshippers are being driven below Hadrian's Wall. Promise them that after you drop these prisoners below Hadrian's Wall, you will return to trade with them only for their best items.

"Kial, you must trade with the wisdom of a fox, and return with your warriors to your camp, loaded down with doeskins, soft furs, and the very best the other Pict clans have to trade. Do this, and your women will sing songs of the great and shrewd trader, Kial the dragon slayer. Have you the mettle for such a great trial?"

Kial's smile stretched from ear to ear. "Aye, my leader, you can count on me."

Solemnly, Matthew placed the bags of Scottish Crosses into Kial's waiting hands. "These Scottish Crosses I entrust to your care. You are a great chieftain of your clan. Call your clan together and tell them of the quest your leader asks you to undertake after we reach the North Sea. And know, all of you, that our God will go with you."

Kial turned to leave Matthew, his gait proud and joyful. He sang a Pict war song as he strode, patting the bags of gold. Matthew thought the coins would weigh him down, but they did not. In truth, he seemed buoyed by the treasure, rather than burdened by it.

Robert, however, looked as if he were about to develop an ulcer. "Matthew, why did you give away all that gold?"

Matthew shook his head. "Robert, I thought you, of all people, would see what that gold could accomplish. Kial acknowledges me as leader, and accepts our God. The Picts to the south will hear of a fighting leader who slays dragons and their worshippers, and whose lands are full of bounty for trading. This will bring them to Loch Ness to trade. The Scottish Crosses will be traded in the outermost parts of Scotland, carrying with them our message of God and a free Scotland. Loch Ness will become the greatest trading place in Scotland.

"Before long, the tales of the treasures traded at Loch Ness will inspire all Scots to be drawn there, bringing their finest goods. I will strengthen the clans by trading with them as if we were one clan. At Loch Ness, the traders who come will have no fear of being robbed or cheated, and Shalee will make sure no guest is hungry. These clans will want to join us, but I will let them know that they must first accept my God. If we must spend all the treasure from all the dragon lairs we conquer, it shall be worth it. Fair trade and faith are the keys to a free Scotland."

Robert still fretted. "Aye, but how will you feed all the people who will come to trade?"

"Our God will provide the food, with our help. You worry too much, Robert. Now get yourself some roasted game birds from Shalee, and enjoy our victory."

* * *

At sunrise, Matthew ordered three wagons to be filled with the bodies of dead dragon worshippers. To the scouts he said, "After the enemy castle is captured, the rest of these slain warriors will fill that castle." The camp readied itself, then began its march to the Spey River, the wagons following far behind the marching warriors. The crossing took over two hours, but Matthew pushed his troops to within two hills of the enemy's castle. Robert and Kial prepared a camp as Matthew, Kele, and the two warriors pushed ahead to recon the enemy's castle.

For the rest of the day, they watched the activities of the enemy guards. There were ten lax guards: two patrolling the front gate, two at the rear gate, and six meandering around the courtyard or just outside the castle. Their elite warriors had been burned to death in the recent battle, and these were the leftovers. Matthew figured this would be an easy kill, and that the night raid would afford him an opportunity to evaluate the two warriors provided by Robert and Kial. As soon as the sun set, Robert, accompanied by many warriors as well as Shalee and Raquelle, brought up Matthew's ladder.

Night fell with the recon warriors lying on their stomachs as Matthew tied the ladder to their backs. He told them to crawl behind him until they reached the castle's side wall. "I will then untie the ladder from your backs and put it against the wall," he explained. "Then, you are to climb up the ladder and garrote the guards. Kele and I will kill the guards at the front gate, and you two men will kill those at the rear gate. Then you will throw the bodies over the outside wall. Do you have any questions?"

Robert's warrior spoke. "Even with these pants, you provide nothing for our hands and knees, and we must crawl a long way over thorns and thistles." Matthew acknowledged his point, and had Robert acquire pieces of leather to be tied to each warrior's hands and knees.

Then Matthew checked the Bowie knife on his right thigh, and his .44 Magnum on his right calf. The pistol was loaded with all of his remaining bullets. Only as a last resort would he risk firing it.

At last, with the leather in place, they began to crawl. About halfway to the castle, Robert's warrior loudly complained about a thorn in his hand. Matthew stopped the column to crawl back to the warrior, and sharply whispered, "If I have to return, your tongue will be lying on the ground beside you!" Then Matthew again took the lead until the group reached the side wall of the castle.

Matthew untied the leather straps and gently placed the ladder against the wall. He quickly scaled the wall to peek over the top, then lowered himself to the platform on the wall's interior. And there he lay, dead silent, flat on the platform, until clouds passed across the moon, casting a deeper darkness upon the parapet. Finally he rose to signal the others to climb up. As the warriors scaled the wall and lay flat upon the bulwark, Matthew observed that one guard at each end slept standing up, while the other kept watch over the fields outside the castle. A smile crossed Matthew's face as he realized that the military hadn't changed over the centuries. His plan was working smoothly.

Kele and Matthew crawled within five feet of the guards at the front gate and waited for the other two warriors to make their kill. They watched in silence as these two rose, tossing their garrotes over the guards' necks as they had been taught. Then, with the quickness of a cat, Kele rose and flipped his noose around his victim's neck and snapped his hands apart. At the same time, Matthew dispatched the sleeping guard, turning his dream into a terrible, if brief, nightmare. Then he looked at Kele as both held dead weight in their hands and smiled.

At that moment they glanced to the rear gate to see Kial's warrior holding a dead guard. Unfortunately, Robert's warrior was not so successful. He bounced his garrote off the sleeping guard's head, then tried again, but missed, allowing the guard to jump free. Matthew, however, felt there was still a chance for one swift thrust with a dagger to save the situation, and he prayed that Robert's warrior was up to the task. Indeed, the warrior reached for his dagger, but fumbled, dropping it to the ground. The sound of metal upon stone rang out clear in the stillness of the night. Matthew's heart and spirit sank with the falling dagger.

As the shrieks of the castle guard, fighting like a cornered rat, filled the castle, Matthew yelled, "Kele, dump the body over the wall and jump with me to the ground to unbar the gate." The two dead bodies slammed into the ground as Kele and Matthew hit the ground and rolled. In a flash, Matthew and Kele jumped up and turned to hoist the bar holding the front gate closed. It normally took six castle guards, using all their strength, to lift the bar, but Kele and Matthew attacked it with vigor and hope. They struggled and prayed out loud as the bar started to move. Their back muscles quivered under the strain of lifting the massive bar, but inch by inch, it moved upward.

The other six castle guards rushed from inside the buildings, swords drawn. Seeing the intruders unbarring the gate, they raced toward Matthew and Kele. Sweat covered Matthew's face, and both he and Kele grunted from the exertion, but still the bar held fast. Matthew figured that they had about eight seconds before the other guards' swords would nail them to the wall. He screamed, "Kele, draw deep strength from within, for we throw this bar up and over our heads now!" From the depths of Matthew's being issued the karate cry *Hai!*... and they raised the bar over their heads, launching it toward their attackers. The bar sailed a whopping three feet, and slammed to the ground, causing a massive vibration around them.

Kele turned to half-heartedly fling his dagger into the guard, but it bounced off the guard's sword. And then Kele collapsed, his back against the gate. Powerless and now weaponless, his limp body slid to the ground to await the bite of cold steel. He hoped the end would be quick.

Matthew had to fight his muscles just to will them to draw his .44, and when he did he simply started pumping off one shot after another. His right arm sank with each shot, until what little strength remained in that arm deserted him, and he vaguely heard his pistol hit the ground. His legs gave way, causing him to stumble back against the gate beside Kele.

Matthew could see the pile of dead bodies lying in front of the gate's bar, but he was too fatigued to even smile. Then, one body began to rise, clutching a dagger in his right hand. The dagger rose in a slow arc, much like a cobra as it prepares to strike an immobilized bird. With a dying gasp, the castle guard thrust his dagger at Matthew. Matthew could only watch as the dead guard's chest hit his feet, and, in a blinding flash, he realized where the dagger would land. "God, not there!" The dagger hit Matthew's jeans, just missing his belt buckle. Then Matthew doubled over, filled with a searing pain.

Chapter 14

Kial's warrior rushed upon the pile of fallen enemy guards, slamming the now dead guard, who was still tightly gripping his dagger, headlong into the gate. Then he threw the lifeless body to his right, the sound of the crash reverberating throughout the castle. Kial's warrior reached for Matthew, and, with a trembling voice, he asked, "My leader, are you all right?"

Matthew, straining even to whisper, responded, "Yes, but help me get up and out of here."

Kial's warrior lifted Matthew over his right shoulder, then grabbed Kele's arm, and dragged him away from the gate. Robert's warriors pounded on the front gate and pushed their way inside. From his perch atop the warrior's shoulder, Matthew rasped out orders to have the castle secured, and again ordered Kial's warrior to get him outside. Robert ran forward, forcibly stopping Kial's warrior to address Matthew. "My leader, what is the matter with your voice? Are you hurt? Do you want me to check your wound?"

The pain was still so intense in Matthew's abdomen that he could only whisper, "Just get me out of here."

Kial's warrior fought through incoming warriors as Robert followed. Just as the warrior deposited Matthew upon a patch of clear ground, Shalee and Raquelle appeared, both of them visibly frightened.

Raquelle attempted to stabilize her father, who was doubled over from pain. "We heard the noise of your weapon, and we feared the worst. Are you hurt? Do you want Shalee and me to nurse your wound?"

In that moment, Matthew was grateful for the darkness, for he did not want the women to see what he feared was a mortal — not to mention wholly undignified — wound. In desperation, Matthew bellowed, "Everyone just turn your backs to me. I will inspect my own wound." Matthew was sweating bullets as he gingerly unbuckled his belt and unfastened his jeans. He cautiously lowered his zipper, reaching inside to inspect himself. When he removed his hand, he was overwhelmed with relief to find that there was no blood on his hand. He looked upward toward the heavens, thinking to himself, *Thank you, God, for well-made jeans and metal zippers! Thank you! Thank you! Thank you!*

Raquelle impatiently told him to turn around so that she could tend to him, and, in a much more confident voice, Matthew told her no. Matthew refastened everything, then turned to hug Raquelle, then Shalee, and even Kial's warrior.

The warrior drew back in shock, until Matthew whispered in his ear what had happened. With a hardy laugh, the warrior proclaimed that if he had experienced such a miraculous deliverance, he would even hug Kial. Matthew liked the man's sense of humor, and asked him his name. The warrior proudly proclaimed, "I am called Trace, which means 'battler.'"

"Trace, you are well named, and I thank my God for you. Go bring Kele to me, for I am concerned for my brave warrior's health. Shalee and Raquelle, thank you for your concern. Your caring is one of the greatest ingredients of true love."

Shalee forgot herself, and spoke from her heart. "Within your life is my life, and if you should die, I would join you."

Matthew reached over and locked his fingers between Shalee's. "I am gratified, Shalee, that our lives are thus intertwined."

* * *

Kial and his warriors appeared then, dragging the women and children out of the castle. "My leader, should I commence with killing them?"

Matthew released Shalee's hand to turn and look at the captives, then spit on the ground as he said to them, "Your dragon god didn't save your warriors or this castle, did he? Your army's charred bodies will fill this castle before we march forward to the North Sea. If you have treasure in the castle, go in and fetch it. You will divide it here, in front of me, into ten equal piles. You shall pick one pile to take with you, and the other nine, I shall keep."

A crow-faced woman challenged Matthew, "How do we know we can trust you? You might keep it all."

Matthew glared at her. "I can kill you now or you can recover the treasure. Choose."

Her face paled, and she started to shake. "No, my lord, we wish to live." She turned with the other women to reenter the castle. After a short while she staggered back, carrying a heavy load encased in a thick, black cloth. She quickly divided it into ten piles, putting the most precious gold and silver items in the first pile. Matthew inspected the piles, then ordered her to choose one pile to take with her. She selected the first pile, wrapping it in her cloth, then slinging the bundle over her shoulder. She slyly watched Matthew, expecting him to stop her, and was surprised when he made no move to do so.

Instead he merely issued a command. "Go east, and inform the dragon worshippers that my God's army is coming for them. After today, those that I spare will be allowed to take one-tenth of their wealth and be escorted below Hadrian's Wall into the south kingdom. If they want to live with all their wealth, they will need to get to a ship, and sail below Hadrian's Wall before my army finds them. They may live in the south kingdom and worship dragons, but if they set foot on Scottish soil, they die! Do you understand?"

She nodded with a crafty smile. "Aye, but the dragons will defeat you."

Matthew's face flared with anger. "All of you flee quickly, because we travel east at sunrise. If we overtake you, then Death will personally greet you." Women and children, with their treasure, scurried away from Matthew's warriors and disappeared into the night, heading east.

* * *

Matthew motioned Kele to his side. "Are you hurt in any way?"

Kele squirmed a bit, and nervously replied, "No, but when I saw the dagger descend upon you, I feared you dead or at least unmanned. Did our God protect your manhood?"

Matthew's eyes narrowed and his brow furrowed as he remembered the falling dagger and the excruciating pain. His voice became gruff. "Aye, our God protected the three of us, because Robert's warrior almost got us killed. Robert, I don't want to see that man again. Send him back to your castle, or below Hadrian's Wall. Just keep him away from me. Then post five guards until dawn. Now, let us all get some sleep."

It had been an exhausting day for everyone. A few minutes after all had lain down, the camp was filled with a chorus of loud snoring. All about him, Matthew knew that men were dreaming of their victory. His own body, though totally exhausted, was tense. He lay upon the ground, still as a mouse in a cat show, longing for the sleep that would not come, as the minutes ticked by like hours.

Then a twig snapped.

Matthew's eyes shot open, all his senses on alert. In the moonlight, he caught the glimmer of a dagger's tip coming toward him. Matthew's left hand flung off his furs as his right hand launched his Bowie knife, sending it to plunge deep into the neck of his would-be assassin, burying itself to the hilt. The noise of the assassin's struggling and choking to death awakened the others. Matthew commanded Robert to bring a torch.

Sprawled on the ground was the warrior who had failed them on the wall. Matthew lamented, "I may have been too harsh on him in front of you all, or he may have been in league with the dragons. In any case, drag his body to the front wall." Matthew removed his Bowie knife from the assassin's neck, thanked God for watching over him, and laid himself down again upon his pallet. He closed his eyes, and knew no more, sleeping like a child with no cares until the dawn.

As the first rays of sunlight fell gently upon Matthew's eyelids, Raquelle barked into her father's ear, "Father, are you going to sleep all day?"

Matthew jerked himself out of a pleasant sleep and pounded on the ground, fumbling for the snooze button on his clock radio. Instead, he hit the stony ground, and his eyes flew open. For a moment, he just gawked, uncomprehending, at the green grass and rolling hills. Like a sledgehammer crashing down, the realization hit him that this was not his beloved Texas, and he wasn't dreaming.

He shook his head hard. To his right, Shalee slowly rose, stretching, from her sleeping furs, and as her chest rose with her yawn, he drank in every curve of her body. She shook her head, then smoothed her hair back with her hands. The sun accented the blue tinge of her black hair as it shimmered in first light. Shalee sensed Matthew's admiration of her body, causing her to accentuate every sensual move. She gracefully cupped her hands behind her neck and inhaled deeply. Matthew felt a warm flush surge through his body; he needed her. And then Shalee turned toward him, giving him a beckoning look that melted him. All that existed in his mind at that moment was a sensuous woman who wanted him as badly as he wanted her. Forgetting the vow he had made about letting down his defenses to her, he rose to his feet, flung off his sleeping furs and moved toward her.

"That's right, father. You need to get up." So said Raquelle, who had her back to her father as she poked the fire.

There is nothing like having your daughter present when you decide to make love to a beautiful woman. Raquelle's voice was like ice water, painfully dousing Matthew's burning passion. His eyes told Shalee of his need for her, and of his regret that now was not the time. At that point he decided that he really needed a cold shower to cool the fiery embers, so that he would be able to focus on other things. To his daughter he said, "Raquelle, bring Robert and Kial to our campfire. The four of us will have a war council after I return from washing."

Matthew walked to a nearby stream, intending only to wash his face, but the thought of a clean body enticed him to plunge into the frigid water. Any Texan would swear that Scotland has a monopoly on freezing water, but right then, it didn't matter to Matthew, because he could almost see the dirt leave his body. It surprised him that the water didn't seem all that cold, and he figured his body must be acclimating to cold water.

In fact, lately he had found that he could swim longer with Alanna before getting numb. Alanna! He worried about her and her babies. The night before they left his castle, he had taken a short swim with her, and they had shared from their hearts. She was worried about the supply of fish, since her tunnel to the North Sea had been partially blocked. The fish could get in, but she was too big to get out. How could she teach her babies to defend themselves against the many-legged killer of the vast waters?

Matthew wasn't sure what she meant by the many-legged killer, but assured her that the castle guards would feed her with sheep if the fish were scarce. However, he explained, he did not know when he would return. All he could do was pledge that he would return to Alanna, because he loved her. At that she gave him another fish bath, which necessitated a second swim, then a ride on her back. He sure did miss her. What a bizarre twist of fate — having a pet that weighed several tons, that he could talk with, and that could answer back! No doubt about it: God had a sense of humor.

Then he was drawn back to reality. He began to really feel the cold seeping into his bones, and he thought, *Enough daydreaming; this freezing water is stealing my body heat.* Matthew wished he had asked Shalee to get his heating towel.

Emerging from the water, he found the heating towel lying on top of his clothes. He wondered if he had been so lost in thought that he didn't hear Shalee, or whether he was so accustomed to her footsteps that his brain sensed no danger. Matthew smiled as he recalled the delicious image of Shalee performing her slow stretch that morning, and he shouted, "Wherever you are, Shalee, thank you!" He then realized that if he was going to continue fantasizing about Shalee's body, the cold bath he had taken was a waste of time. He put Shalee from his mind, finished dressing, and returned to his campfire.

* * *

Kial, full of piss and vinegar after his night's sleep, awaited Matthew with fists clenched in anger. "Are you an idiot? Why didn't you kill those women and children last night? They are the enemy! You let them leave with treasure! And why do you allow your daughter to be present at a war council?"

Matthew liked Kial's personality. There was no hidden agenda; if he didn't like something, he told you straight out. "Kial, I will answer your last question first, then the others. My daughter will be a leader someday. She needs to learn from the wisdom and battle knowledge of Kial, the great dragon slayer. And the reason I released the women and children is to spread our message."

Robert butted in. "What? You converted those dragon worshippers to our God?"

Matthew shook his head. "No, our message is that if a dragon worshipper meets us in battle, he dies. If we capture him, then he keeps one-tenth of his treasure, but he will be transported below Hadrian's Wall. However, if he chooses to flee by ship before we arrive, he keeps all he takes with them. If most of the dragon worshippers choose to sail and settle below Hadrian's Wall, then we gain their land without the death of one of my warriors. My warriors' lives are precious to me. My goal is to see the scourge of the dragons and their worshippers removed from Scotland. If they take some wealth with them, good riddance. If the dragons follow their worshippers to the south kingdom, all the better."

Kial wondered aloud, "What will become of the treasure they left behind?"

Matthew pondered a few moments, and then answered, "You and Robert will separate all gold and silver nuggets and bars. Robert will turn these into coins. The coins and the weapons are mine. You, Kial, shall have claim to all silver armbands. Robert shall claim all silver necklaces. All the remaining treasure shall be divided three ways, for distribution among our warriors." Kial was greatly appeased by this arrangement, and begged Matthew's leave, so that he might turn to the task of looking for silver armbands. Robert commanded ten warriors to perform the task of separating the piles.

Raquelle took Matthew's hand and led him away from the others. Matthew could tell that she was weighing her words carefully. "A lot of wealth left with those dragon worshippers. Are our warriors' lives worth the loss of that much wealth?"

"Aye, that and more. That is the very reason these men will fight and die for us. They appreciate that their lives are precious in our sight, and that we will not carelessly waste them. Do you know, child, that your life is worth more to me then these nine piles of wealth?"

Raquelle's eyes twinkled. "Aye, I know this."

Matthew brought his point home with a harsh voice. "How do you know this?"

His tone let Raquelle know that her father considered this question very important, so she took her time to reflect upon her answer. "You did not value your own safety when I was captured by the dragon worshippers, but came to fight them and the dragons. Death was the likely consequence for all of us, but still you came. Your actions toward me show you love me and care for my life."

Ah, now she was truly beginning to understand. Matthew continued, "So do our warriors need to see our love through our actions. Kial and Robert will be questioned by their warriors about this runaway treasure. When our warriors learn this was done to spare their lives, we win their hearts. To be a good leader, you see, you cannot become too attached to wealth. The love of money is the root of all evil. The bonds of love and friendship between us and our allies must strengthen through the years, but wealth comes and goes. The love I receive from you and Shalee far outshines all the gold and silver I will ever acquire in Scotland."

Matthew expected a big hug from Raquelle, but instead she dropped to her knees, arms at her side and head lowered. Matthew asked what she was doing. Raquelle replied in a somber voice, "I am telling our God that, even if there are ten thousand other gods, yet I will serve only Him, because He gave me you as a father."

Matthew's face suddenly became very hot. He was proud of his daughter, but embarrassed by such praise. He turned away from Raquelle, only to see Shalee kneeling a short distance away as well. Shalee must have heard the conversation.

Continuing his slow turn, he glimpsed a returning scout. Moving toward the scout, Matthew called for Kele to get Robert and Kial. As he reached the man, Matthew inquired as to his luck at finding a good campsite for the night.

The scout pointed eastward. "Ten hills east, there is a valley with trees and a stream. It is only one-fourth of a day's march. After the warriors bring the burned bodies to fill this castle, it will be a good place to camp tonight."

Matthew responded, "Scout, lead ten of Robert's warriors, as well as Raquelle, Shalee, and the cooks to that valley to prepare food and fires for our arrival. When the sun reaches the second hour past midday, return to me to lead us to this valley." Without a word, the scout left to round up his party, and departed for the valley.

Kial strutted toward Matthew then, wearing ten silver armbands and dragging two bulging bags tied with ropes around his waist. "The enemy must have loved silver armbands! Both bags are full of them. Matthew, I will give you my future share of the wealth of the dragons we slay if you will give me all the silver armbands in the castles from here to the North Sea."

143

As a starving cat pouncing on a fat rat, Matthew leapt at this offer. "All wealth of the dragon lairs and their worshippers shall be mine, but I grant the exclusive right for all silver armbands we acquire on this campaign to Kial the dragon slayer, leader of the Picts. To Robert Roybridge, I bequeath all silver necklaces we acquire on this campaign. Is this agreeable to you all?"

Robert and Kial vigorously nodded their agreement, and the bargain was set.

Matthew's warriors helped Robert's and Kial's warriors move the dragon worshippers' bodies from the battlefield to the castle that was to serve as their tomb. Matthew was pleased to see all the warriors work together in harmony, knowing how critical it was for them to develop an *esprit de corps*. With Matthew in charge, the Scottish army was truly coming into being.

An unbroken column of burnt bodies lined both sides of the road, ending at the open castle gates. The inside of the castle was filled with the rest of the bodies, and the place was shrouded in a terrible smell. Matthew commanded all warriors to wash their hands, arms, and chest in the nearby stream. Many warriors grumbled, but they all obeyed. Matthew resolved that these warriors would learn to wash their hands and bodies after handling any dead thing, and that this would become a Scottish habit. He figured that he might as well try to kick as much sickness as he could out of Scotland, along with the dragons.

Some hours later, the scout returned to lead them to the food and blazing fires. Matthew was looking forward to a good night's sleep. The smell of roasting game birds perfumed the air, setting everyone's mouths to watering. Shalee soon had great pots of enticing soup bubbling joyously, their aromas mingling with that of the roasting birds.

Seeing Matthew approaching, she scooped up a bowl of hot soup for him. The soup was so hot that Matthew could only take small sips, but he could still tell that it was delicious. Matthew commanded Kial and Robert to have their warriors fetch their bowls and line up in front of the cauldrons of soup. The warriors loved the soup, returning for second and even third helpings.

Shalee picked three game birds from their spits and sat down with Raquelle and Matthew to feast. Juice was dripping down Matthew's chin as a compliment welled up in him. "Shalee, you do a magnificent job of feeding me and our troops, always with delicious food. This game bird is the most luscious I have ever eaten. Where did you get the seasonings?"

Shalee shyly admitted, "I know which herbs to pick, is all. And it warms my heart that you enjoy my feast. Genuine appreciation is something we all desire."

Matthew realized then how much she needed to be told that her work was appreciated. In that respect, she was no different from anyone else — himself, most notably. Matthew thrived on praise and appreciation; why shouldn't Shalee? He made a mental note to compliment her more frequently.

After the feast, Matthew commanded thirty warriors to stand guard around their camp. Tonight should be filled with peaceful and restful sleep. Raquelle and Shalee slept together at Matthew's right, with Robert and Kial only a few feet away.

Laying his weary head down upon a pillow of soft furs, Matthew went straight to sleep, entering a pleasant dream. He was riding on Alanna's back as they jetted through warm, light-blue water. Matthew snuggled deeper into his furs, his body drawing in their warmth as his mind drew in the pleasure of the dream. The ride became more exhilarating, as Matthew saw the city of Atlantis rise from the waters. It looked as he had always pictured it, a glorious city covered with a clear dome. The buildings had tall columns of marble, sculptured with beautiful images of statuesque women. The beauty of such life-like sculpture, made of stone, yet appearing soft as a maiden's skin, took Matthew's breath away.

And it seemed so very real...

He was at peace, flying through the water toward the city. Warm water splashed his arms and legs as he urged Alanna forward. She swam faster, and Matthew's stomach was filled with the butterflies he had experienced as a kid, clinging for life on an exciting amusement park ride. He hugged Alanna tighter as the butterflies furiously fluttered inside him.

Then from the waters in front of Atlantis, a dark mist formed and came rushing toward them. Alanna made a U-turn, and as they tried to outrun the mist, Matthew could feel the strain in Alanna's back muscles. He looked back, and saw that the black mist was almost upon them, and a bone-freezing chill seized his body. The dark mist enveloped them completely, just as an earsplitting scream rang in his ears.

Matthew sat up straight, his eyes wide open. He was no longer dreaming. And charging down upon him was a warrior, enveloped in flames.

The Ultimate Dragon

CHAPTER 15

Without even stopping to think, Matthew flipped his furs over the warrior and wrestled him to the ground. Just as the fire was extinguished, the air filled with more screams. Matthew drew his sword, and wheeled to see the source of the panic.

As Raquelle and Shalee scurried behind him, Kial and Robert appeared at his side, a burst of flames narrowly missing them. Across the campsite, the remaining soup in one of the cauldrons was being gobbled up by one dragon. The other spit fire at the panicked troops, while holding three live warriors squirming under its hind claws.

Matthew knew that he must counterattack, or lose many of his warriors. "Kial, have your warriors throw spears and shoot arrows at the dragons. Go! Robert, we will attack with swords and daggers from the dragon's rear. Now move!"

Kial reached his warriors and shouted orders to throw spears and shoot arrows at the dragons. His warriors ceased their panic and turned to obey their leader. Both dragons turned to face the onslaught, which was little more to them than wooden bee stings. As a burst of dragon fire lit up the night, Kial launched his spear with all his great strength.

The spear passed through the flames to drill deep into the dragon's chest. The dragon's death screech pierced the night, sending chills up Matthew's spine. Then, with one final cry, the beast collapsed on top of the three terrified warriors, who were still trapped in its hind claws.

Matthew and Robert attacked the other dragon from behind. Robert stabbed his dagger into its left wing, as Matthew buried his sword into the right wing. The dragon started to fly, hurling Robert to the ground, but Matthew's sword held fast in its flapping wing. The arc of the dragon's right wing launched Matthew from the ground, and he clung to its back as it rose into the sky.

Matthew crawled to the base of the dragon's neck, his left hand clutching madly to secure a firm hold. With his right hand, he swung his

Bowie knife up to hack at the thick, scaly neck. The dragon continued to climb, but couldn't angle its head down to attack this pest. As they rose together, Matthew's slashing began to take its toll, and the dragon's flight became increasingly lethargic. Then, the dragon just hung in midair, and Matthew quickly holstered his Bowie knife and held on for dear life.

After what seemed like hours, but was, in reality, only a few seconds, the dragon dropped like a meteor streaking toward the earth. As they hurtled down into darkness, Matthew could envision his head smashing into the stony ground. When they finally hit the ground, the crash of their impact was deafening, and after a blinding flash, Matthew knew only blackness.

* * *

Sunlight beamed down upon Matthew as Raquelle violently shook him. "Father, please be alive. Speak to me, father. Scotland's fight for freedom cannot end this way."

Matthew eyes slowly opened to the bright sunlight, but closed again immediately. He could only mumble, "Dead dragon?"

Though Matthew's eyes were closed, and his brain addled from the fierceness of the fall, he could tell that Raquelle was grinning at him. "Aye, my father. Kial's spear killed the first dragon, and you killed the second. When you rode off on the dragon's back, I was afraid. You had said you would never again ride a dragon, but you did. In all our history, there has never been told a tale of one who flew on a dragon's back — not even once, to say nothing of twice! Are all 'Texans' so daring?"

Matthew did not answer because at that moment he sensed a shadow moving across his face, and he opened his eyes…just enough to see Kial standing over him. Seeing that Matthew was not harmed, he teased him, "Your knife took longer to kill your dragon then my spear did to kill mine, but then I believe you just wanted to ride on the beast's back. You seem to like riding on big creatures' backs. Admit it; you delighted in riding the dragon, didn't you?"

Matthew's mind began to clear, and he had questions that needed answers. "How did this happen, and why did they attack us after dark?"

Robert's eyes cast down at the ground as he moved behind Kial, but Kial turned to glare at him. "It seems that Robert's scout failed to go over the crest of the hill to discover the entrance to a dragon's lair. We camped on top of it, and the smell of our food drew them to visit us. I lost five warriors. It would give me great pleasure to slit this scout's throat!"

A pall of anger washed over Matthew's face as he struggled to sit up, and then to stand. "Bring him to me." The scout arrived, saw the rage in Matthew's face, and lowered his head.

Matthew said, "Men died because of your failure to explore the area surrounding our camp. Now, think carefully, and answer truthfully: will this ever happen again?"

The scout looked up, met Matthew's icy stare, and then swallowed hard. "No, my leader. I ask you to spare my life, and I vow that I will scout true to the end of my days. Never will I overlook another dragon's lair."

Matthew weighed the value of this scout's life against the benefit, to the other scouts, of his death...and he chose to give him one more chance. "See that it doesn't happen again, or the end of your days will come sooner than you like. Tell the other scouts to spread the word to all the clans from here to the North Sea: either fight beside Matthew Wolverine and his God, or die with the dragon worshippers. Every Scot must choose one side or the other, and live or die according to their choice. Now go." Then he turned to Kial and said, "Kial, assemble my army."

When they were assembled, Matthew inspected them. What a motley group they were, standing before him in the bright sunlight. Pacing up the line and then down again, he addressed them. "Henceforth, you shall be known as Scottish warriors — not Picts, nor warriors of any clan, but Scottish warriors who fight and work as a team. You will learn the meaning of the term *esprit de corps*. It means 'spirit of a collective body.' No matter where you or your clan come from, when you join my army, you are Scottish warriors, pledged to aid and defend one another. Now carry these dragons back to the castle, and place one inside each gate with their backsides facing out. The Scottish warriors under Kial's command are experts at carrying dragons, and will show the rest of you the way of it. Kial is charged with carrying out my orders to dispose of the dragons."

Kial's chest swelled with pride as he ordered the warriors to roll the first dragon on its side. A line of warriors moved underneath the belly of the dragon, then other warriors rolled the dragon upon their backs. This was the dragon that Matthew had killed, and the base of its neck ripped away from its body. Without missing a beat, Kial ordered other warriors to carry the severed neck. Two rows of warriors marched on each side of the dragon, ready to relieve any warrior who grew weary. Matthew was pleased, but knew that even with such a muster of stout men, moving both dragons would take Kial most of the day.

Matthew questioned Robert about the location of the entrance to the lair, and Robert pointed to the northwest, only a short distance away. Matthew ordered the scouts to bring torches and enter the lair with Robert, Shalee, Raquelle, and himself. The scouts were reluctant, fearing there might be more dragons in the cave.

Raquelle detected this, and unsheathed her dagger as she stepped forward. "I, with my God, will protect you," she declared. She grabbed a torch and started into the cave. The scouts grinned and shook their heads at their fear, then drew their own weapons and followed her, bearing torches of their own.

The cavern had a large main chamber, and then divided off into three smaller chambers. Matthew ordered the scouts to explore those to the right and center, and he led Robert, Shalee, and Raquelle into the one on the left. They had only passed a short way into this chamber when the interior of the cavern exploded into a rainbow of colors in the light of their torches. A colossal pile of treasure reflected the brilliance of a great pile of gold, silver, and jewels upon the walls. This pile made that first one they had found look small by comparison. Shalee's eyes grew to the size of saucers as her mouth gaped open in wonder at the sight. Raquelle rushed to the pile and dove in, surfacing with two handfuls of gold necklaces.

Matthew dropped back to put his arm around Shalee's waist, urging her into the pile to pick some items for herself.

Her amazement was transparent. "You mean I may have some of this treasure for my own?"

Matthew nodded, and Shalee rushed into the pile to try on gold necklaces and rings. She settled on a brilliant gold necklace, adorned with small hanging gold bars with small gold balls on their ends. With the piece touching upon the alabaster of her skin, Matthew thought that she looked like Cleopatra incarnate. Even in torchlight, the gold radiated regal splendor on her skin, offset by the silken sheen of her black hair and her radiant smile. Matthew felt certain that no queen on earth had ever looked more lustrous, and he impulsively blurted out, "Shalee, you are the most beautiful woman in the world."

Even in the dim glow of the torches, all present could see the redness that flushed Shalee's face. After a long silence, Shalee smiled at Matthew, saying, "It pleases me that you find me so beautiful, my lord."

From somewhere in the treasure pile, a small voice piped up, "Aren't I beautiful too, father?"

"Raquelle, you have so many gold necklaces on that I can't even see your face, but you are still beautiful in my eyes." Raquelle removed a handful of necklaces to reveal a toothy grin.

A rustling of feet alerted Matthew then that his scouts had entered the cavern. The illumination of such wealth stopped them dead in their tracks. Matthew asked them what the other caverns contained.

A lead scout finally found his voice to respond, "The right one is filled with dragon dung, and the other has a small lake. Where did all this treasure come from?"

Matthew replied, "Dragon sacrifices. Scouts, set Kial's silver armbands and Robert's silver necklaces apart from this pile. I give this as a bonus to my commanders. The rest, ship back to Loch Ness. This treasure means no more hunger for your families, and it shall pave the path toward a free and united Scotland under our God. Now, get started separating the piles."

Robert, Shalee, and Matthew walked out of the caverns into the sunlight. Raquelle wanted more gold necklaces, so she stayed to supervise the scouts, and to retrieve and inspect all gold necklaces and place them in her pile. On this day, Raquelle became the official inspector of gold necklaces.

Even Matthew was amazed at these huge piles of dragon treasure, and wondered aloud, "Robert, how long have the dragons been extracting tribute?"

Robert took a few moments before replying, "They were extracting tribute long before our Messiah was crucified. The wealth of Scotland lies in their caves. You are the first warrior to stand up to them and win."

Shalee's necklace sparkled in the sunlight, and Matthew could recognize the intricate workmanship. He made a snap decision. "Shalee, you quickly found the most beautiful necklace in that pile of treasure. You have an eye for the exquisite. I want you and Raquelle to accompany this treasure back to our castle, and there to separate the most beautiful items, which you will store in my chambers. The treasure pieces that are of fine workmanship, you will trade. Trade wisely, and acquire property that will give us future increases in our wealth.

"The poorly made items, you will send in wagons to Robert's castle, to be melted and struck into Scottish Crosses. Robert's craftsmen are skilled, and will ensure that all Scottish Crosses are of precise weight and gold content. The Scottish Cross must become the currency of Scotland. I ask the two of you to shoulder a great responsibility. The more dragons we kill, the more dragon treasure shall flow to you. I trust you with all my wealth, and, indeed, with Scotland's destiny."

Shalee's face tightened. "Aren't you afraid the south kingdom will attack us for all this wealth, especially if we store it all at Loch Ness, with our warriors abroad?"

"Shalee, that is a chance I shall have to take. Before we can give concern to the security of our castle from foreign attack, the dragons and their worshippers must be driven from our lands. If the south kingdom attacks us, then we will be forced to turn aside from our task to defeat them. Now, I must go with Robert to see that our warriors have placed the dragons' backsides facing out from the castle gates. Have the cooks prepare the evening meal for our warriors' return, but take care no food is left in the cauldrons overnight."

Robert and Matthew slowly walked toward the captured enemy castle. Matthew explained to Robert that Robert's services were needed back at his own castle, to supervise the minting of the coins that would spread the message of a free Scotland under one God. "Shalee and Raquelle will accompany you," he said, "and they will return to my castle, where they will be under your protection until I return."

Robert nodded as they crested a hill and saw the first dragon's buttocks, jutting forth from the east castle gate. They walked to the other side to find Kial, supervising his warriors as they placed the second dragon into the west gate. Kial turned to see Matthew and Robert striding toward him. He came forward, proudly proclaiming, "Just as my leader ordered. A dragon's butt faces out both ends of the castle. But why place the dragons this way?"

Hoping to instill some military recon reasoning into Kial and Robert, Matthew explained, "Within a week, this castle will fill with scavengers and carrion beasts, all come to feed on the dragons and their worshippers. Scavengers are lazy, and will make this castle their new home. Travelers will pass by this enemy castle and survey the picked-clean bones of two slain dragons, as well as those of the slain dragon army sent to slaughter us. They will see that the castles of our enemies become the dens of loathsome creatures. I could not ask for a better proclamation of the dragons' defeat. The news of our victories will seep though Scotland. Fresh warriors will flock to Loch Ness to join my Scottish army."

Kial hesitated, then asked, "So, you expect more Picts to join your Scottish army because of one battle?"

Matthew chuckled and pointed at Kial's silver armbands. "Not because of one battle, but Picts will join in droves after they see the mass of silver armbands you display. Your expedition to deliver prisoners below Hadrian's Wall will be a marching recruitment to journey to Loch Ness and join our army. Our warriors fought bravely in the last battle, and I think they each deserve a silver armband. What do you think of the idea, Kial?"

The blood drained from Kial's face, and his feet gave way. He clutched Robert to steady himself. Robert was none too pleased about Kial hanging on him, but stabilized him, nonetheless. Finally, in an unsteady voice, Kial agreed to give each warrior one silver armband. And true to his word, after the warriors returned to camp for the evening meal, Kial began to distribute all the silver armbands from the dragon's treasure.

Unfortunately, he was only able to supply half of his warriors with armbands, telling each man that the bands were a gift from Matthew, before the supply was depleted. This angered the warriors who did not receive the reward, and their grumbling grew to shouting, until Matthew stepped forward and told them that their silver armbands were in dragons' lairs to the east, and would be theirs to claim soon enough. He challenged them, saying, "However, if you are not strong enough to slay these dragons, then are you worthy of such a distinction of courage from the Scottish army?"

This subdued the warriors' complaints, and instilled in them a new eagerness to march east at dawn. Matthew informed Shalee that she and Raquelle would accompany Robert to their castle and institute trade for lambs, sheep, cows, and anything they deemed valuable, using the new dragon treasure and Alanna's fish.

"But I wanted to see the North Sea!" Raquelle protested.

Matthew said, "You are needed at our castle to help Shalee with the trade. After all, who is better at inspecting gold necklaces than you? There will be other opportunities for you to see the North Sea." Reluctantly Raquelle nodded, then hugged her father.

The next morning, the parting was swift as Matthew marched his army toward the east. The scouts came upon five abandoned dragon caves, which caused some warriors to grow lax in their caution. The next three caves were not empty, however, and these careless warriors were the first to die. After three days, the army was close to the eastern coast of Scotland. Ten scouts led twenty warriors east, and came upon a ridge, just as four dragons emerged from a large cave.

From the ridge, they hurled their spears and shot their arrows. When the warriors ran out of weapons, they pushed enormous rocks down upon the dragons. Matthew was encouraged that he had instilled in his army the realization that they could, indeed, kill the dragons. After an hour's battle, four dead dragons lay in front of their cave. From the ridge of the hill, the scouts could see the shore of the North Sea. One scout returned to the main body of warriors to inform Matthew of the kill. Matthew dispatched 100 warriors to move the dead dragons to the beach.

The sky to the east began to darken with pitch-black clouds of a violent storm. Matthew urged his troops to a faster pace, hoping to beat the storm to the eastern caves. Suddenly, sheets of rain, with drops the size of marbles, began to fall, pelting the army unmercifully. The scout could not see two feet ahead of him, and soon lost his bearings. The army trudged behind him for two hours in the deluge, until the scout finally stumbled, quite by accident, upon the cave's entrance.

153

Matthew and his army entered, drenched and nursing welts from the driving rain. The main cavern was large, but was soon filled wall to wall with soaking, ill-tempered warriors. The smell of wet furs and unwashed men soon permeated the air, further adding to the men's foul mood. Matthew looked out from the cave's entrance at the torrent of rain, and thanked God he was not sailing on the North Sea, which raged before him, as if at war with the storm. Heaven help anyone so unlucky.

He turned as his army bedded down to the sound of the deluge, and found himself a side cave with soft dirt to make his bed. He fell asleep, imagining the warm bed of his castle, with Shalee close beside him, keeping him warm.

The next morning, the putrid smell of wet furs assailed Matthew's nose, and he coughed himself awake. Like a jackrabbit, he hopped over sleeping warriors to escape the cave into the pouring rain. The rain provided him with escape from the smell, but it was icy cold, and stung when it hit him. Matthew squared his fur over his shoulders and walked to the beach. Giant waves lashed the coast, detaching boulders to streak crashing on the beach. Matthew quickly returned to the safety of the offensive cave. He knew that this second day of close quarters was going to make the men, including himself, increasingly restless.

Back within the cave, Matthew sought out the treasure room, and once he found it, scaled to the very top of the pile with a blazing torch. His military training had taught him that restless troops could be distracted if they performed some task, so he created a project.

Matthew summoned his troops into the treasure room. As they entered the room carrying torches, they saw a rainbow of colors reflected upon the walls and ceiling. The sight of such a tremendous hoard of wealth stopped the warriors dead in their tracks. Matthew commanded them to keep moving, and they soon filled the room. He directed the married warriors who were without silver armbands to step to the front. These warriors were to separate the treasure into smaller piles of silver bars, gold bars, silver necklaces, gold necklaces, iron, weapons, and silver armbands. When they found a silver armband they liked, they were to keep it, and pass the other armbands back to the other warriors who were still without silver.

"The other warriors may then take a silver armband, but are to place the excess just outside the cavern," he said. "Any warrior may trade from the pile of silver armbands for a better one, but after every warrior has a silver armband, the pile of armbands remaining will belong to Kial. Now, start digging!"

The married warriors without silver armbands dug like starving dogs after giant soup bones. The pile began to tremble, and Matthew rolled down it and hit the ground. Next time, he decided, he would leave the pile before he ordered the men to start digging.

Threading through his warriors, Matthew checked on the rain. To his delight — and, it must be said, his amusement — it had stopped raining. He realized that it was too late to cancel the scavenger hunt he had set in motion, and he would probably face a grand mutiny if he tried, so he headed for the beach.

Before he left, Matthew turned and called to Kele, bidding him send five warriors who had already gotten their silver armbands to accompany him as he walked on the beach. Matthew raced ahead to the cliffs before the others caught up, and scanned the beach.

Suddenly he spotted the battered remains of a ship. Matthew immediately intensified his search, looking for survivors. He saw bodies further down shore from the ship's remains, and called to his warriors to hurry and follow him down the cliff to the beach. Matthew approached a large man with flaming red hair, sprawled face down only five feet from the water.

From behind, Kele shouted a warning, "My leader, these are Viking raiders! With your permission, I will slit their throats."

The large man with the red hair heard these strange voices, and tried to rise, but fell back to the ground. Matthew drew his Bowie knife and, towering over the man, planted his knee in the middle of the Viking's back. Matthew seized his red hair to raise his head, then positioned his blade against the man's throat, right above his Adam's apple. "If I want you dead, you are dead. Let me feed you to refresh your strength. Then we can fight, if you wish. Agreed?"

The Viking grunted deeply, which Matthew took for agreement. Kele helped Matthew lift the Viking; they placed the man's arms over their shoulders and started back for the cave. As Matthew passed his warriors, he commanded in a low growl, "Check the other Vikings for life, but do as I did, with your knife to their throat, first. We will feed these Vikings, and see if they will join us."

As Matthew and Kele carried the Viking into the cave, Matthew's warriors stopped separating the treasure to inspect the prisoner. The Viking was set upon the ground, and Matthew ordered that he be given some hot soup. Matthew offered him the bowl, and the Viking's eyes narrowed to slits. In broken Gaelic, he asked why Matthew hadn't killed them on the beach.

Matthew explained, "My God commanded, 'Do unto others as you would have them do unto you.' If I am ever shipwrecked, I hope you would feed me until I am well, then let me leave."

The Viking's jaw stiffened, and he snarled, "I would kill you on the beach, throw you into the water, and let the fish devour your flesh."

Matthew smiled, saying, "When you are stronger, we can fight. We will see which God is stronger, yours, or mine. If mine is stronger, will you worship my God, and join me?"

A vicious grin covered the Viking's face. "And if I kill you, then what?"

The Viking had swallowed Matthew's bait, so he set the hook. "Then my troops will let you and your sailors leave with as much of this treasure as you can carry in your arms. But I ask you again, when I win, will you serve my God?"

The Viking looked at the huge pile of silver armbands by the cavern's entrance, and with a hearty laugh, agreed. He had bested many warriors larger and fiercer than this one. Kele placed two dry furs beside the Viking, who immediately grabbed them, rolled over, and went to sleep, most likely to dream of his hot meal and the piles of gold he would soon possess.

Matthew's warriors entered the cave carrying five more Vikings. After these men were fed and given furs, Matthew informed them of the coming fight and the conditions their captain had agreed to when — not if — Matthew won. He was not sure if they would understand him, but apparently they did, for they gazed on their sleeping giant of a captain with his rippling muscles, and laughter exploded from them. Confident their god would win, they nodded in agreement to Matthew's terms. Matthew got up to confer with Kele as the Vikings, now with full bellies, covered themselves with their new soft furs and fell into a sound sleep.

Kele led Matthew into the treasure room, where small and orderly piles of treasure now dotted the floor. Matthew went to the pile of daggers and ordered Kele to gather all the warriors with one or more sons in front of this pile. After they assembled, Matthew allowed them their choice of one dagger for each of their sons. The Pict warriors filed very solemnly past Matthew to the pile of daggers, and chose the daggers for their sons. Never had they had a leader who actually cared not only for them, but for their families! They thought back to their youth, and what it would have been like to have their fathers come home from a battle and give them such a precious prize. Smiles began to penetrate hardened faces, like a plant bursting from stony ground, as they envisioned returning home with daggers for their boys.

One warrior told Matthew that he had one son and five daughters, and asked the leader for a gift for his daughters. Matthew was feeling generous, and asked Kele if there was a pile of women's wrist bracelets. There was, indeed, a small pile of silver wrist bracelets, and Matthew ordered each warrior with daughters to take one bracelet for each daughter, and a silver necklace for his wife. Matthew assured Robert that he would replace each silver necklace taken with a gold one from his own treasury.

The warriors, to a man, smiled from ear to ear, and contemplated how this new God had blessed them with such riches. No raid in the history of the Picts had produced such presents for a warrior's family. Each warrior envisioned his wife wearing her silver necklace to bed, and the nights of passion that would follow such a gift. Kial's Pict clan envisioned themselves the richest clan in all of Scotland, and all the warriors clutched their treasures to their chests as they fell asleep that night.

They had earned that treasure, and they would earn it again, and yet again, in the brutal confrontations that were still to come.

The Ultimate Dragon

CHAPTER 16

The next morning Matthew ordered wagons filled with treasure and sent to Loch Ness. Scouts were dispatched north along the coastline, ahead of the army, to search for fleeing dragon worshippers. The army followed behind, eager to complete their task and turn west, to return to Loch Ness and their families.

The scouts returned at midday, and reported to Matthew that a small town at the end of the Dee River was overrun with dragon worshippers, all desperately seeking passage on any ship heading south. Many had already fled to Normandy, and word of a new leader in Scotland who proclaimed freedom and slew dragons now spread across Europe. Matthew issued plans for a dawn attack upon the town, and his army envisioned an opportunity for wealth and revenge for the horrors they had suffered for the past thousand years.

Dawn broke, and Matthew's army stormed the town, his warriors attacking with such ferocity that within a short time, the streets of the town were covered with the bodies of dead dragon worshippers, and pools of their blood congealed in every pit and wallow along the stone and dirt pathways. The dragon worshippers fled right up to the water's edge, only to find death snapping at their heels. On land, the Scottish army took no prisoners, in retaliation for the cruelty inflicted by dragon sacrifices.

There were three ships anchored in the harbor, which Matthew and his scouts seized. Terrified, the crews and dragon worshippers on board offered no resistance, but cowered in fear. Matthew's army had quickly stripped the dead dragon worshippers of all valuables, and assembled on the docks by the three ships. Matthew halted his army from boarding the ships, and summoned Kial on board, directing him to deliver the prisoners below Hadrian's Wall with one-tenth of the treasure they carried. Kial's smile turned sour as he contemplated the long trip south.

Sensing what was in the Pict's mind, Matthew ordered Kial, "Before you do anything else, first separate your silver armbands from the dragon worshippers' treasures." Kial jumped on this order like a starving gorilla on a bunch of ripe yellow bananas, and started throwing passengers off the ships on to the docks. Suddenly the trip south didn't seem so bad.

Kial's clan immediately joined in, and began searching the dragon worshippers for valuables. All the valuables, except silver armbands, were placed in front of them. The silver armbands were placed at Kial's feet, until a stack of two hundred of them lay in a large pile in front of Kial. Kial's eyes shone with lust as he looked upon the shimmering pile, his face beaming with a Cheshire-cat smile. Matthew feared the man might actually make love to the treasure in front of the whole army.

He said, "Kial, choose your most trusted warrior, and have him commandeer a wagon from this town to deliver these armbands to your home at Loch Ness. Your daughter Brigit and her husband will guard your treasure until your return from Hadrian's Wall.

"And now, don't you think that, with all your new wealth, you need to take a wife to help you guard it? Inspect every unmarried woman in the Pict camps, from Hadrian's wall to Loch Ness, and invite the most beautiful ones to Loch Ness to view your wealth. In fact, invite them to bring their clans, so that they may view the wealth of the clan of Kial the dragon slayer. Many in your clan are without a mate. Since you may only have one wife, let the other females find mates in your clan. Only choose the most beautiful Pict women to come to Loch Ness. Can you do this?"

Kial nodded excitedly, and ordered the bags of Scottish Crosses that Matthew had entrusted to him brought forward. He took ten Scottish Crosses and gave them to a warrior to pay for one wagon from the town. He did the same with nine other warriors, and within an hour, ten wagons appeared on the shore. Matthew was pleased that Kial had paid for the wagons, and the townspeople relaxed, relieved to know that these warriors were not out to steal from them or kill them. After this trade, many of the people began to emerge from their huts.

Matthew had Kele separate all the silver necklaces and place them aside for Robert Roybridge. Then the surviving dragon worshippers were allowed to pick one-tenth of their remaining valuables. Matthew instructed Kial that, if one of his warriors stole the prisoners' wealth on the trip south, Kial must personally cut off the warrior's right hand. The prisoners relaxed when they heard this, but grouped closer together.

Matthew shouted, "Only one in ten of the Scottish army can go with Kial to Hadrian's Wall!" So Kial commandeered four of Matthew's ten scouts, and selected those one in ten to march south with him. As he headed south, leading his band, Kial turned once to gaze upon his wagon, brimming with silver armbands. Matthew waved, knowing Kial would make the trip to Hadrian's Wall in record time, and swiftly return to his beloved armbands.

* * *

The townspeople watched as the Scottish army departed, and Matthew told them, "They will return with an even greater army in the future, to slay any remaining dragon worshippers. Now, should a dragon worshipper request passage below Hadrian's Wall on a ship, you must charge him half of the treasure he carries. Be sure to post guards night and day on the ship, to insure that the dragon worshippers do not kill you in your sleep. To reduce the chance of murder by the dragon worshippers, I suggest that the captain's payment be left in port."

The people of the town swore, by Matthew's God, to follow his instructions. Matthew knew that word would quickly spread that the price for safe passage below Hadrian's Wall was half of one's wealth. He felt pleased with himself as his army headed for Loch Ness.

It took the army a week to return to Loch Ness, but to these weary warriors it seemed much longer. They were joking, laughing, and singing as they finally crested the hill north of Matthew's castle, with the sun's rays sparkling off their silver armbands. Matthew entered his castle, climbing the stone stairs to the parapet above the castle gates. He faced his army, now spread out in front of his castle, proud of their swelling numbers and obvious unity.

"The Scottish army serves its leader and its God with courage and honor," he called out. "When you return to your village, tell of your bravery in the battles with the dragons. Wear your silver armbands as a badge of your courage. You are Scotland's liberators from the fear of the dragons. Give your beautiful wives silver necklaces, that they may give you much pleasure tonight! Give your sons their daggers, and your daughters their silver wristbands, to keep them quiet while you make love tonight! Come when I send for you, and God bless you all. Now go to your families!"

The army roared back, "God bless Matthew Wolverine and a free Scotland!"

A smiling Matthew gave the signal for his army to disperse, then felt something brushing against his leg. It was Yellow Rose, and he picked her up, tickling her tummy, and noticing that she had put on three or four pounds. "It is nice that someone appreciates that I am home, but you need to gain some weight. Why, you are just fur and bones!" Yellow Rose's purrs increased to a roar. She definitely agreed that she was underfed. One could almost hear the reasoning, in her cat-mind, that the bigger the cat, the more of her beauty there was for others to behold. As a matter of fact, Matthew had yet to met a cat that felt it was overweight. The word simply didn't exist in a cat's vocabulary.

Raquelle waited for her father to descend the stairs into the courtyard, then ran to him, throwing herself upon him in an exuberant embrace. "Father, I really missed you, and the wolves missed you too. They have really grown." Then she sniffed the air and scrunched her nose. "Father, you need to swim with Alanna. I will get our swimsuits, the heating towel, and the other children. Shalee will have supper for us when we return."

Matthew suddenly noticed all the children milling around the courtyard, and not a warrior or female in sight. Even the wolves wandered in the courtyard. Then, he heard the sounds of rising moans and panting that escaped from the windows. He sighed. If there was any time that he had ever needed a wife, it was now; instead, here he was, babysitting all the children and the wolves.

The moans and gasps intensified, filling the courtyard, but before any real outcry could start, Matthew hustled the children and wolves out of earshot, and on to the beach. This was not to say that he had any particular difficulty in doing so, because the children were all more than eager to play, especially with the great guardian of the loch. They ran giddily toward the water, plunging in, still wearing their clothes, and even the wolves joined them in the water.

Matthew shepherded the children close to him, and they were merrily splashing, laughing, and engaging in heroic water battles when up from the depths emerged the three lake guardians, causing a tremendous splash and wake that sent the children somersaulting in all directions. At this sudden commotion, Matthew would have sworn that his wolves actually ran across the water's surface to get to the beach. Once the pups had reached the safety of the beach, they turned to growl and snarl at Alanna, Elizabeth, and Eric. Raquelle got out of the water to settle the wolves, which was all the more difficult, since she could scarcely contain her own laughter at the spectacle.

Matthew smiled at Alanna, and suddenly realized how badly he had missed her and her children. His thoughts formed a question that only she could hear: *Did the castle guards make sure to share their food with you?*

Alanna's thoughts responded, her sadness unmistakable: *Aye, but they fear us, and keep their distance. Not one of them hugged me or swam with me. I cannot even talk to them, and I really tried. I have grown to love having the children ride on my back, but the guards put a stop to that as soon as you left.*

And those noisy creatures on the shore are cloud killers. I see them kill clouds day after day. The clouds really need someone to care for them, because they are stupid, although the males can be brave when pressed to it. Sometimes, they fight the cloud killers and drive them away. Once, I swallowed a whole male cloud, but his big head hurt my throat, then, oh, how my stomach hurt. Now, I only eat ones with small heads when they come to the loch for a drink, but they are hard to catch.*

Matthew was confused by these thoughts of eating clouds, and asked Alanna if the clouds she spoke of were animals the color of the sky. He pointed to a cloud overhead to make his point clear.

It frustrated Alanna that Matthew thought that she ate the sky. She bid him ride upon her back, so that she could show him the "clouds."

Matthew shouted to Raquelle, "Watch the other children and the wolves. Alanna is taking me to see clouds. You stay here, and await my return."

Alanna cut through the water with smooth, powerful strokes. Matthew clutched tightly to the base of her neck, riding her like a quarter horse, but the cold wind quickly began to cut through him. He could feel his grip faltering as the first stages of hypothermia set in. He asked Alanna if it was much farther, but her only response was to quicken the pace of her strokes. Soon, she was skimming along like a water jet at better than twenty knots, and the wind whipped across Matthew's body, chilling him even more.

After what seemed like hours, Alanna rounded a bend and entered a cove. On the hillside jutting up from the water's edge, Matthew saw hundreds of white dots, moving slowly about the grasses that covered the hill. *See what I mean?* Alanna conveyed to him. *Clouds!*

Matthew blinked and rubbed his eyes in disbelief. He had never seen so many sheep in his life. After he had looked upon the great flock for a few moments, Matthew's thoughts turned again to his body, which was, by now, chilled to the bone. He thought to Alanna, as his lips chattered involuntarily, *I am about to freeze; take me home.* Alanna made a sharp U-turn, tossing Matthew into the water. She then wheeled about and swam up to him, but he was too weak to climb on her back. Alanna submerged, centered Matthew on her back, and headed for shore, this time more slowly, so Matthew wouldn't fall off.

The later it got, the more worried Raquelle became. She looked around toward the castle at the six Vikings standing on the hill overlooking the beach, and she shuddered, wishing her father would hurry back. Then she spotted Alanna, racing toward the shore. Alanna plowed onto the beach, and Matthew slid off. He lay there, wincing with pain from violent cramps in his calf muscles, and Raquelle wrapped him in the heating towel.

The six Vikings descended the hill, approaching him, as Matthew struggled to draw his sword. They came closer, swords drawn, their eyes

163

set for combat. Matthew thought the Vikings had slipped away after the battle in the town on the North Sea, as there had been no sign of them on the return trip. He tried to fight the cramps in his legs as he said to them, "You look no worse for your ordeals, but why the drawn swords?"

Their captain with a red beard boasted, "It is time for our fight, to see whose god is stronger."

Matthew, standing there shaking from the cold, thought that God must indeed have a sense of humor. At once, both of Matthew's hamstrings cramped, sending him to the ground. Thinking to seize the opportunity, several Vikings rushed from behind their captain to kill the fallen Matthew. At that moment, Alanna bellowed out a deafening roar that sent the Vikings scurrying back behind their leader. Before long, they recovered their bravado, challenging Matthew to stop hiding behind this monster and come out to fight.

Matthew used his sword to push himself up to a standing position. "This contest is between only your captain and me, so you other men keep your distance. Alanna, if this man kills me fairly in combat do not hurt him. Are you ready to fight now, Viking?"

The red-bearded Viking nodded silently, then the two of them began to circle each other. The children and Vikings formed a large circle around the combatants, as Alanna and her babies looked over the top of the crowd. Matthew was shaking so badly from the cold that his sword trembled in his hand; his opponent took this as a sign of fear, and launched a brutal attack. This Viking captain had Herculean strength, and his upward thrust sent Matthew flailing backwards, into the air.

As Matthew landed, his right calf began to cramp so badly that he couldn't move his leg. The Viking continued to rain blows down on Matthew, attempting, it appeared, to literally beat him into the ground. Matthew repelled each blow, but his back muscles eventually betrayed him and began to spasm in a painful cramp. The Viking's next blow flung Matthew hard to the ground. The Viking raised his sword high above his head, preparing to plunge it through Matthew's body; to Matthew, the sword seemed to hang in mid-air as the huge man stared at him. The Viking could feel Alanna's hot breath upon the back of his neck, but paid little heed. He was focused now upon his impending kill, and nothing else existed.

At the last moment, Matthew rolled to his right, and the Viking's blow fell wide of its mark, striking the stony ground. As Matthew rolled, he swung his sword upward in a swift arc, coming to rest touching lightly upon the Viking's neck. The wound he inflicted was a minor one, a warning that, should Matthew's hand twitch even slightly, the Viking's jugular vein would be severed. As Matthew rose to his feet, he ordered the Viking to yield, or die.

The man swallowed hard, and Matthew could see the struggle in his face. Matthew could almost hear the thoughts that raced through his opponent's mind, and the critical choices he was being forced to make: to die and gain Valhalla, or live with Matthew's God, who showed mercy to shipwrecked sailors.

The Viking averted his eyes to look at the children and Alanna. These Pict children fearlessly rode this monster, so their God must be strong, and must wish to protect them. His eyes turned back to Matthew, and his thoughts were transparent. *Here is a man who leads an army that ferociously kills their enemies, yet he shows mercy to helpless sailors, stranded on a beach.*

At that, the Viking released his sword and knelt, saying in his broken Gaelic, "Your God gives to you a strength that is greater than the might of my arm, which has never before been bested. I yield to you and your God." As he rose to his feet, Alanna, whose head was only inches away, slathered a fishy lick across his back. Then she turned to go back into the water. But as she passed, she shot Matthew a thought, *If he had killed you, I would have bitten him in half, no matter what I promised Saint Columba so long ago, and you but moments before.*

Matthew extended his hand, and asked the Viking's name.

"My name is Eric the Red." Matthew had only a moment to wonder if this was *the* Eric the Red, father of Leif Ericson. But there was no time for questions, because Eric broke in with an urgent appeal.

"Before we speak further, I have a request. Please, don't let the monster go. I want to ride on her back!" This prompted a belly laugh from Matthew, and he was laughing so hard that he could barely tell the Viking that Alanna would gladly bear him. Alanna, pleased to feel her friend's jubilation, turned back to the shore to await her rider. Eric stripped his clothes off so fast that the children and Matthew got an eye full, as the grinning, naked Viking plunged into the icy water and climbed swiftly upon Alanna's back. Alanna was off like a shot, and they rushed forward through the water at breakneck speed. Eric's men could only stand and gawk as their leader clung giddily to Alanna's back, his delighted howls echoing back to the shore. Then, another cramp hit Matthew, and Raquelle and the children helped him toward the castle.

As they entered the castle, Matthew's body began to shake violently, and he fell to the ground, taking a few of the children with him. Kele saw the fall, and quickly summoned a warrior to help him bear their leader. The two men hoisted Matthew straight up, and carried him, his feet dragging the ground, to his bed. To Kele, carrying Matthew felt like carrying a block of ice.

When they reached Matthew's bed, Kele ripped off Matthew's wet garments, and placed him naked under the furs. Yellow Rose jumped on the bed to see what was wrong. Violent convulsions seized Matthew, flipping the cat off the bed and onto the floor, where she scampered away. A few moments later, Shalee entered the room, just as Matthew's convulsions were ending. She touched Matthew's face, and was stunned by how cold his skin was beneath her hand.

Turning to Kele, Shalee ordered him to clear the room except for Raquelle. "Then stand guard outside the door, allowing none, save the animals, from entering or even looking in," she commanded. The room cleared, and Kele slammed the door. Shalee ripped off her clothes and crawled under the covers to press her own body against Matthew's. His body was like ice, and Shalee winced from the shock. The cold assailed her flesh, and she had to fight the urge to pull away.

Raquelle stood gawking open-mouthed at Shalee's actions. Was Shalee trying to rape her father?

Shalee's eyes narrowed, and she growled, "Take your clothes off and get in here beside him to warm him. Do you not realize that your father is dying? If we don't warm him soon, we will bury him this day."

Raquelle snapped out of her stupor, swiftly removing her clothes, and climbed into the bed. The coldness of her father's body, and the memories of Damian's big body against her, repulsed the child, and she jerked away. Shalee grabbed her shoulder, pulling her back. "We must transfer our heat into his body, or he will die. If you love him, hug him with all your might and give him your warmth."

The door cracked open, and in streaked Yellow Rose, leading her kittens and the wolves. Yellow Rose jumped on the bed and scurried to Matthew's face, then slid under the furs to curl up across his chest. Shalee and Raquelle moved their arms over the big cat to hold her body close to Matthew's chest. With only her head protruding from the furs, the cat began to meow loudly.

At the sound, the kittens and wolves leapt upon the bed, curling up on the furs, and completely covering Matthew's body with their warmth. The unconscious Matthew had no awareness of this action taking place, but his body drank in their warmth.

After three long hours had passed, Matthew began to stir. Shalee and Raquelle slipped out of the bed, dressed, and quietly went out the door. Shalee instructed Kele that, when Matthew awakened, Kele was to help him dress, and accompany him to the dinner table. Then Shalee and Raquelle turned to go to the kitchens to help the cooks prepare dinner. As they walked, Shalee ordered Raquelle never to tell her father what went on in that room. Raquelle's reply echoed her embarrassment. "You need not worry about me telling him of my shame."

Shalee abruptly turned to face the girl. "See here, Raquelle. We did what we had to do to keep him alive. Matthew is so righteous that he would denounce us for our actions, but I feel in my heart that my God is more merciful than my leader. Nevertheless, you must swear never to tell him of our action. He can be so strong in battle, but he cannot take the cold that is Scotland. This winter will be hard on him, so we will have to watch him closely. But now, let us make him hot delicious stew to feast on when he awakens."

Raquelle nodded, her shame replaced by gratitude that this woman so loved her new father.

* * *

Matthew lay there, dreaming uneasily of giant weights, crushing him. The weights pinned his legs, and he found it hard to breathe. He tried to move his arms, but found that they, too, were pinned. Then his eyes flicked open, and he found himself staring into the face of a huge feline, who greeted his return to the living with a cat-kiss upon his nose. "Yellow Rose, thank you for keeping me warm," he whispered. "I was so very cold, and still feel the chill in my bones. But I am all right now, so all you animals can get off my bed." The animals hopped down, and Matthew rose, staggering slightly, and began to dress.

Kele, hearing the noises within Matthew's chamber, opened the door and entered. "My leader, you really had us worried. We thought you sure for the grave. Do you feel strong enough to walk to dinner?"

Matthew's eyes sparkled as he tried to separate what had been real from that within his dreaming. "I remember fighting the Viking, Eric the Red, and winning. Then, the children were helping me stagger toward the castle. I was so cold. Then I remember falling, and blackness. I dreamed I was encased in ice, when two blazing fires mystically appeared, one on each side of me, and they melted the ice. I was never so cold in all my life. The animals must have warmed me. Kele, go to the beach, and bring the six Vikings to join us in our meal. They are now our allies and accept our God."

Kele pondered whether to tell his leader what had really happened. For a second, he watched Matthew reach out for the wall, to keep himself from falling. The cold had almost killed his leader, and Shalee and Raquelle had done whatever they did to keep him alive. *Better to leave him with his* dream. Shalee will speak of this, or not, as she sees fit, but I shall keep silent." Kele turned to leave as Matthew proceeded towards the dinner table.

Shalee was relieved to see him up and walking. "You had us so frightened. You must be careful of the cold. It almost killed you."

Matthew agreed, and told Shalee of his strange dream. All talking in the room ceased, and the people hung on every word. Shalee listened intently, agreeing that the animals must have warmed him, and telling him that she and Raquelle had stayed in the room until the danger had passed. Which was certainly not a falsehood, she thought to herself. Matthew thanked her, and silently gave thanks for her caring heart. Then, Kele appeared, leading the six Vikings, and they took their places at the table to await their food.

Matthew sat with Raquelle at his right, Shalee to his left. He grabbed a cup, then rose and turned to Shalee to offer a toast, "Shalee, you have a caring heart. Beauty may blossom and wither, but a caring heart is a treasure that lasts a lifetime. Thank you for saving me today."

Shalee's gaze bored into Raquelle, who gently shook her head to assure Shalee that, true to her word, she hadn't told her father anything. Shalee's shoulders relaxed, and she smiled and gazed up at Matthew. Looking deep into those lovely emerald eyes, Matthew momentarily lost his train of thought, until Eric the Red shouted a question…something to do with ship building…that brought Matthew back to earth.

Matthew turned to the Viking and said, "I want to commission the construction of four ships, to be built simultaneously, each stronger than any ship that now sails the seas. Payment for building the four ships will be one ship, of my choice, given to you, and ten gold necklaces for each of your crew. But you must teach other Scotsmen your way of building these ships."

Eric, who fancied himself quite an astute trader, countered, "I will build the ships, but I will require everything you have offered, plus twenty gold necklaces for each of my men, and a sword with jeweled hilt for myself."

Matthew said, "I will give to each of your men five gold necklaces, and to you a jeweled dagger."

Eric mulled the offer in his mind before he agreed. "Very well, Matthew Wolverine. You are a wily trader, and I fear that, were I to continue in this barter, I would end up paying *you* for the honor of building your ships!" When the laughter around the table had died down, he continued, "I will start tomorrow, selecting trees to be felled for the wood I will need."

Their business concluded, all returned their attentions to the delicious meal before them. There was a smattering of conversation, about ships and dragons, mostly, but Matthew's mind kept returning to the image of Shalee's beautiful eyes, and to the even more pleasurable, if unsettling, images that lingered from his dreams, but of which he had spoken not a word.

* * *

During the next month, Matthew's focus was upon increasing trade with nearby residents, supplying labor to his farmers, constructing a large building to house the dragon treasure, and swimming with Alanna. Shalee continued to manage the trading at the castle. The traders who came learned very quickly that her word on trades was final, and that trading was only done from ten in the morning until time for the noon meal. Matthew held himself aloof from the trading, but inspected his storage rooms nightly to view the fruits of Shalee's bartering. As Shalee traded the fish from Alanna for lambs and calves, Matthew could see his herds expand daily.

The changes that Matthew had instilled continued to work their magic on the people under his control. They saw the expanding herds, the daily fish from Alanna, the nightly feasts of delicious food, and the bountiful crops in the fields, and became increasingly optimistic about their lives. For the first time, they knew what it meant to be happy.

Shalee designated one room in the castle as the treasure trading room. After the noon meal, all the women of the castle gathered in that room, without their children, to try on jewelry and to chatter amongst themselves. Shalee read Matthew's book on how things were made, but was most fascinated with glass and mirrors. She eventually talked Matthew into casting a full length mirror for her, which was placed in the trading room, where it was highly prized by the women. Gold and silver jewelry had become a common sight in Matthew's castle, and the wives of traders from afar were invited to attend the daily two-hour gathering of women.

After the first few days of this, the warriors and castle guards found themselves watching the children during the women's trading time. Soon the warriors found tasks that would take them outside the castle walls from breakfast until supper, leaving only the castle guards to watch the children. Some of the guards complained about this to Matthew, and he made the mistake of going into the trading room during the women's meeting.

As Matthew entered the room, he could almost feel the temperature drop, from the women's icy stares. In a low, but altogether commanding voice, Shalee informed Matthew that men were not welcome in the treasure room during this time. "Haven't you noticed that there is less fighting and shouting at night since these sessions were started?" she asked. Matthew looked to Raquelle for support, but she was as stone-faced as Shalee, so Matthew had little choice but to quickly state the problem.

Shalee listened calmly, then nodded and told him that the problem would be corrected within the week. "But in the future, please tell me of any problems in the morning, outside the treasure room."

Matthew exited quickly, and all the women's eyes turned to Shalee, worried that this time would be taken from them. Shalee called all the castle guards' wives into a circle around her. "The success of my plan rests squarely on your shoulders. I want each of you to return to your homes as soon as you leave here, and immediately bathe and wash your hair. The other women will gather scents from the forest for you to wear. You are each to choose one item of jewelry from this room, which I will give to you as payment for the tasks you will perform for the next seven days, and which you are to wear tonight.

"Make sure the children are asleep as soon as possible after the evening meal. Remove your husband's clothes, and have him lie on his stomach on the bed. Gently rub his entire body, starting at his neck, and working your way down to his feet. Take your time doing this. Whisper softly to him that, because he is such a good husband to watch the children during that short period in the day, you have the energy to please him at night. Rub and knead him until your arms ache, then tenderly roll him over, and slowly make love to him. After you are done, cuddle him, and tell him again how much you appreciate him watching the children. This must be done for seven days in a row." The women left the treasure room, giggling and chatting amongst themselves, eager to put Shalee's plan into action.

During the next several days, Matthew marveled that all the castle guards were smiling, where they had been scowling and surly before. He could not find a frown among them. Some were even singing. They now even seemed eager to watch their children. Matthew asked them the reason for the change, but got only broader smiles in response. He wasn't quite sure what was going on, but he had an idea, and the level of his respect for Shalee grew even higher.

* * *

Meanwhile, Eric the Red was busily crafting ships of exceptional quality. He had now assumed the habit of joking with Matthew at the dinner table. He was becoming a real friend, but the other Vikings avoided

Matthew and his people, preferring to keep to themselves. Matthew trusted Eric, but not the other Vikings, and would never turn his back to them.

This summer in Scotland felt cold to Matthew, but the rest of the people assured him that the weather this year was actually very warm. His swims with Alanna did get longer, but Raquelle secretly kept a close eye on him. When she noticed her father's body shivering, even mildly, she knew that he was too cold, and would tell him that she needed to get back to the castle immediately, knowing that he would not allow her to make the journey alone.

Each day, Shalee would prepare a large cauldron of hot vegetable soup over a fire by the front gate. As Matthew would enter the gate with Raquelle, Shalee would hand him a hot bowl, on the pretext of seeing if it was to his liking. Raquelle would make sure he finished the entire bowl. Shalee and Raquelle were deft in their conspiracy to insure that Matthew never again suffered from hypothermia. Matthew, like the castle guards, had no idea of Shalee's subtle plots to keep a healthy and happy castle. It went right over his head, without singeing a single hair.

The month that followed was magic. Matthew courted Shalee sweetly, bringing her flowers, sharing his thoughts with her in frequent talks, and taking long walks together in the surrounding lands. Matthew learned that Shalee still dreaded the return of the dragons. She told him that she would rather die than live under their rule again. Matthew assured her that this would not happen as long as he was alive and able to function as a warrior. Over time, her dread seemed to diminish, and their talks turned to happier matters.

Among the things they talked about were Matthew's idea that his people needed a larger castle, one with great kitchens to simplify the preparation of the ever-grander feasts they held, and with quarters befitting the many guests they received. As Matthew began the process of drawing up plans for building the new castle, Raquelle and Shalee both became increasingly excited at the thought of their new home. Each day after breakfast, Matthew would share his thoughts on the new castle with artists, who would work at the task of drawing up plans until around noon. Then, Shalee would take the plans into the treasure trading room to discuss them with the other women. Invariably the women would come up with more changes. The artists would then redraw their work, to present to Matthew before the evening meal.

Matthew found that the castle plans would change dramatically from day to day, but he didn't mind, because he was falling in love with Shalee, and was glad of the opportunity to please her. This was to be her castle too, and he wanted her to have a say in its design. He vowed to himself that after Kial returned, and the Scottish army had marched to Antoninus's Wall and back, he would return to Loch Ness to marry Shalee. Matthew chose to keep his intentions silent, however, thinking to surprise Shalee.

It was a decision he would ultimately regret.

Chapter 17

As the month ended, Kial returned at last, reporting that some dragons had fled below Hadrian's Wall, but that many remained, along with their worshippers. He assured Matthew that the Pict camps to the south would join with Matthew in his fight against the dragons when the Scottish army marched south. Kial, Robert, and Matthew drafted plans for the march to Antoninus's Wall, and Matthew dispatched scouts to all the Pict camps, rallying the Scottish army to assemble in three days. Once mustered, they would join together for training before marching south to whatever destiny the fates had prepared for them.

Three days passed quickly, with Matthew preoccupied with preparations, and Shalee feeling the weight of his impending departure. As the sun rose on the third day, Matthew finished an early breakfast and pushed his chair from the table. He began to speculate on the battle ahead, wondering how many warriors would answer his call. Lost in deep thought, he didn't see a streak of fur shoot across the floor from his right and leap upon his empty lap. It was only when he felt the sudden weight and the sharp claws that he was jolted from his reverie.

His visitor was an agitated Yellow Rose. She sat on Matthew's lap for a few moments, then stood up and circled several times, as if trying to get comfortable. She seemed to weigh a ton in his lap; indeed, she had gained at least five pounds since he had last seen her. After a few restless circles, interspersed with clumsy efforts to push her hind end in Matthew's face, Yellow Rose jumped down onto the floor and began rolling around frantically, emitting a throaty yowling sound that was quite different from her everyday voice. Then she hopped back up onto her master's lap, rubbing against his chest and purring loudly. Finally, she plopped her ample self down again and stared up at him intently. Matthew was puzzled by her actions, until it dawned on him that this was the behavior of a cat with one thing on her mind.

173

Matthew picked her up under her front legs and, with more effort than had once been necessary, lifted her into the air. Smiling, he said, "Why, with all this beautiful weight, I bet the tomcats are fighting to get to you. I must order more castle guards to patrol our gates, just to keep all those pesky toms from getting inside our castle."

Yellow Rose flinched and gave Matthew a look as if to say, "Bite your tongue!"

Matthew chuckled. "Only kidding, Yellow Rose. As a matter of fact, I will issue orders to our castle guards to open the gates to any tomcat that happens to wander by and wants a — shall we say — conjugal visitation." Even held in the air, Yellow Rose's body began to dance, as if she understood every word Matthew was saying. He gave her a hug and put her down, with the admonition that the castle still had too few cats. "You need to correct that situation immediately," he told her. So, with her tail and head held high, Yellow Rose scampered off, now a cat on a mission.

Matthew left the table for the castle gate. At that moment, Kele was approaching in the courtyard, and Matthew ordered him to tell the castle guards to open the castle gates to any tomcats that showed up, and allow the toms to visit Yellow Rose.

Kele gave him a funny look, shaking his head and wondering to himself if he would ever get used to this leader's eccentric ways. Nevertheless, he had an order to carry out, so he duly climbed the stairs to inform the guards. It wasn't long before one of the guards looked over the wall and spotted an enormous tan cat slinking just outside the gate. The cat emitted a loud and lusty howl, leaving little doubt, to anyone who understood cat language, of his intentions. He began clawing at the castle gate, trying to get inside. Yellow Rose, meanwhile, was engaging in her frantic rolling display, answering the tom's lusty cries with her own song. The young wolves, who had gathered around her with the intention of playing, stood back looking quizzical as one of the guards opened the castle gate, and a tan blur shot inside, heading straight towards Yellow Rose.

At the sight of this large male cat streaking in their direction, the wolves instinctively formed a protective wall in front of Yellow Rose. She was their leader, and they would fight to the death for her. Yellow Rose, however, immediately made it clear that that this was not at all a wise idea. One hiss from her, and the wolves scattered, whereupon the two felines made a bee-line to the stables, and the placid silence of morning was broken by a cacophonous love duet that was to last into the night. Matthew smiled as he headed towards the front gate and whatever surprises waited beyond the gate on this tense morning. He had the cat deficit problem well in hand; if only all of his problems could be solved so easily.

* * *

The guards opened the gate, and Matthew strode through. Emerging into the open, he stopped short at the sight of hundreds upon hundreds of men and boys, sitting quietly on the grass in front of his castle. Kial came to his side, boasting, "Behold your Scottish army! All are willing to serve your God and die for you. My silver armbands have convinced many Picts that you are more than fair with all those who serve you and your God. All you need do is treat these warriors as you treat me, and your army will know only victory."

Matthew nodded, and then his eyes turned towards a row of large jugs standing against the castle wall. "What are those?" he asked Kial.

"I have had my women prepare a deadly poison to coat our spears and arrows before every battle. The jugs you see are all filled with this poison."

Matthew nodded his approval, then began scanning the vast field of men and boys, looking for warriors. Some of the boys were not more than ten years old. His first task, therefore, was to weed out the boys from the men.

He addressed his prospective warriors. "All who want to fight beside me, go into the forest and gather several fallen branches no wider than your hand can enfold with finger and thumb touching, and no taller than you stand. Also, gather several stones no larger than the size of your head. At the edge of the forest, there are wagons, upon which you must load these branches and stones. Now go quickly. We have much work to do." At that, the candidates spread out in all directions on their noisy quest, and before long the wagons were filled.

Wagons and warriors then proceeded to a level clearing just south of the castle, where, as Matthew had instructed, each warrior unloaded five branches and six stones.

Meanwhile, Matthew and Kial were busy making preparations inside his castle. Matthew informed Shalee that food must be prepared for five hundred warriors for the evening meal. "Three wagons stand ready in the courtyard to carry the cooking pots and food to the south field," he said. "Roast all the fish from Alanna, and have cauldrons of soup and stew boiling for supper. And your trading time will have to be suspended for three days. There will be many injured warriors to tend to, so have the women prepare bandages for their injuries in advance. I shall dispatch scouts to all of the farm families, inviting them to assemble at our castle for the next three nights before sunset, for a great feast." Shalee nodded, then hurried away to begin her preparations.

***

The troops were now assembled, and Matthew began the drill. In a booming voice he instructed, "You must be able to kill swiftly, but expend as little energy as possible. I will demonstrate. Kele, draw your sword and aim for my chest; then slowly charge me." Kele did so. "Now watch carefully," Matthew continued. "I shall use my own sword to deflect his, as I turn my left foot perpendicular to his body. Now I shift my weight to my left foot, and raise my right leg just above the enemy's left knee… then, with power, my right foot descends to hit above his left knee. This blow should cripple any enemy."

The crowd watched intently as Matthew went on. "And now… with your sword hilt behind your left ear, slash horizontally to remove your enemy's head. If your first blow does not completely sever the enemy's head, make an instantaneous second slash. The enemy's head must roll away from his body. This will demoralize our enemy and give the troops behind you encouragement. Has anyone here ever fought an enemy who has no head?"

Matthew remained silent to let this question sink into their brains. It took a few minutes, but Kial was the first to catch on, breaking into a robust laugh. What started as ripple built to a mighty wave, the laughter swelling until some of the warriors held their sides and rolled on the ground.

Matthew waited until the laughter subsided, then raised his hands above his head, "I have never fought a warrior who had no head, and neither have you. Remember that without a head, the man is dead. Now repeat that: 'Without a head, the man is dead.'" As they began to chant, Matthew marched between the rows to inspect each warrior. He bellowed, "I can't hear you! Do I hear little children whispering? Because warriors shout much louder than these whispers." The sound soon echoed through the fields and reverberated inside the castle. "WITHOUT A HEAD, THE MAN IS DEAD!"

The booming sound drew the women from within the castle, to crowd atop the castle wall. Matthew turned to the women and bellowed, "Some of the warriors before you will be coming to you this day with wounds, not from battle, but from the preparation for battle. Be ready for them!"

He turned again to address his troops. "Warriors, take leather or cloth, and tie it from your right ankle to your knee. Drive two branches into the ground, an arm's-length apart, then pile stones behind each branch. Watch as I show you." Matthew's sword, gripped in both his hands, stuck straight up over his left shoulder. He planted his left foot perpendicular to the first standing branch, raised his right foot to a height just above a man's knee, and made a loud grunting sound as he smashed his foot through the branch. With one motion, his sword arced as his left foot swung forward. Matthew's sword slashed through the second branch, sending the top of the severed branch flying into the ranks of his warriors. "Now," he said, "are there any questions?"

Kele sheepishly asked, "Is that strange noise you made important?"

Matthew thought for a second, then said, "Deep inside each warrior lies extra strength, that he is not aware of. The grunt releases that strength." Matthew then commanded each warrior to plant two branches in the ground, with three stones behind each branch. Matthew, Kial, and Kele observed as a warrior in the front row attempted the kick and slash. His kick broke the first branch, but his slash at the second branch was poorly aimed, striking with the flat of his blade, rather than the edge. The sword ricocheted off the branch, slamming the man in the head, and he fell unconscious at Matthew's feet. Matthew realized that this was going to be a long afternoon, and shouted for a medic. His warriors just stared blankly at him, which reminded Matthew that he was not back in his recon unit. He turned to Kele, and told him to help the unconscious warrior into the castle.

All that afternoon, the women in the castle were kept quite busy with the stream of injuries suffered as the clumsy warriors learned Matthew's lessons. As the training proceeded, Shalee supervised the cooks. Per Matthew's orders, the food preparation was done outside the castle, where the smells of simmering cauldrons of fish stew and vegetable soup, along with the roasting rabbits, fish, mutton, and game birds would carry their enticing aromas into Matthew's training area. When the food was ready, Shalee set up wooden planks, upon which she placed the roasted foods.

When he saw that the meal was prepared, and the tables set out, Matthew stopped the training, telling the men, "Each of you warriors must go to the stream and wash your hands before you take any food." Matthew set the example by going to the stream first, and washing his hands, arms, upper body, and face. The hungry troops rushed to obey this, the only task that stood between their famished bellies and the feast that was laid out for them. Soon, the freshly-washed troops lined up by the planks of food, more than ready to eat.

Seeing the eagerness on their faces, Matthew knew that he needed to instill a sense of frugality in the men. "The Scottish army eats well, but wastes nothing. Eat only until you are full. Those of you who have bowls, get in line first for stew or soup. Those of you who are without bowls, get your wife to make you a large bowl. And, before we eat, we shall bow our heads and thank our God for this meal and a free Scotland. Now, go!"

As the warriors began their assault upon the laden tables, a line of farm families came cresting the hills, heading straight for the feast. Matthew called for them to halt, and then he shouted, "Before you eat, look upon the splintered branches, lying in the open field. This is a present for you, your firewood for winter, if you can collect it in wagons before the sun sets." The farmers looked at the food, then at the firewood and empty wagons. They ordered their families to gather the branches as they drove the wagons. The wagons were filled with such speed that some warriors were still standing in line for their first serving when the farm families joined at the end of the line. Matthew ordered his scouts to drive the wagons to the farmers' land, unload, and return the wagons to the front of his castle that night.

Finally, all sat down at Matthew's table to give thanks to his God, and then to enjoy the feast.

* * *

Raquelle finished her meal quickly, then asked her father to walk with her. She had recently turned twelve, a milestone birthday, and she was beginning to take very seriously the responsibilities she had as the daughter of the leader. As they walked into the training field and made their way among the stones that littered the ground, Raquelle asked Matthew, "Why did you give the firewood to the farmers? I feel you must have had a reason, beyond the goodness of your heart."

Matthew had to smile, pleased that his daughter was so quick to see through his actions. "The farmers feed us. If they die, then we follow quickly. By supplying them with firewood, it gives them more time to tend to their crops. The wives rest easy at night because, in front of their homes, are stacks of wood that they see as warmth for this winter. However, most important, look around you. Do you see even one branch? The field is picked clean and ready for my troops to train tomorrow."

Raquelle sighed and looked down. "When you explain your actions, they are so logical. Why can't I see them before you explain them to me?"

Matthew stopped Raquelle and knelt to hug her. "The fact that you question my actions and understand when I explain my reasons makes me very proud. Wisdom does not come all at once; it grows day by day. Now, that you are twelve summers, I must ask you to accept more responsibility. In two more days, I leave to liberate Scotland as far as Antoninus's Wall. I need you to supervise the castle and protect Shalee."

Raquelle shook her head in disbelief. "You want me to run the castle and watch over Shalee? Why don't you leave Shalee in charge?"

Matthew was hard pressed to explain this in terms she would understand. "Well, you are my first born, and will be leader when I die. So you are the most logical choice to rule the castle in my absence. Don't be afraid of making mistakes, for that is how a person learns and grows in wisdom. At twelve summers, you are no longer a child, and I need your help to rule Scotland. Will you help your father?"

Raquelle frowned as she considered her father's words. Then, the veil of childhood lifted from her eyes, and her duty became clear to her. "Aye, I will protect your castle — and your woman."

As Eric the Red approached, he saw that Matthew had a stunned look, apparently brought on by Raquelle's last comment. Nevertheless he strode boldly forward to state his need. "Scottish leader, I need more men to complete the ships I build before winter."

Matthew turned to face Eric and said, "My daughter is in charge of my castle until I return from our liberation of southern Scotland. Make your requests to her." Matthew then walked away, leaving Eric to face Raquelle.

Eric was, at first, reluctant to ask a female so young for help, but he reasoned that it was the only way he could complete his ships and return home before winter. So he swallowed hard and blurted out, "I still need twenty men to complete the four ships before winter."

Hoping her voice didn't reveal her nervousness, Raquelle, in her deepest voice, responded, "I will have forty men from Robert's and my father's castle dispatched to you in two days. Now, follow me into the castle, and I will have the women sew you a fur coat, so you will not freeze on your journey home. Choose from our best furs in the trading room."

Raquelle led Eric into Shalee's fur storage room, which was filled with separate piles of bear, fox, wolf, and rabbit. Eric the Red, true to his name, chose red fox furs. As he carefully selected matching furs, Raquelle gathered the seamstresses to make his coat. "Have the coat finished by tomorrow night," she ordered. "Eric the Red must wear his new coat when he sees his leader, Matthew Wolverine, off on his liberation crusade." There was now a sharpness and authority in Raquelle's voice that caused the women to cower and nod, assuring her that it would be done. Raquelle left Eric with the women, feeling quite surprised, and quite pleased, at how easily she had donned the mantle of command.

The next day at sunrise, Eric was at the castle, pestering the women to finish his new coat. Matthew stopped in the fur room to see why Eric was not working on the ships, only to find Eric trying on his new coat, strutting around like a peacock. Matthew saw only a gigantic red bear,

179

for the coat was sewn so expertly, one would think it was one solid fur from a mammoth red fox. Eric was stroking the fur, exclaiming that he had never seen anything so beautiful.

Raquelle happened into the room just then, and exclaimed, "Oh, Eric that coat is so beautiful. There is not a Viking on earth who has a coat as lustrous as yours."

Eric jutted his chin and nodded his head as he strutted about the room. With a sly look and a tilt of her head, Raquelle asked Eric if his wife would like a matching coat. Eric stopped in his tracks, as if he had hit an invisible wall. "You would have one made for my wife?"

Raquelle looked at the Viking with an expression so innocent, one would never suspect the wiliness that lay behind it. "Eric, I need you to protect this castle while my father is away. Pick from our finest furs, and give your wife a present that will fill all other Viking women with envy. We appreciate you in Scotland, and hope that your wife will return with you, to visit us and perhaps even settle in Scotland."

Eric picked Raquelle straight up, telling her that he would not only protect the castle, but would lay down his own life to protect her from any harm. Matthew smiled, then quietly left, comforted with the assurance that his daughter now understood how to wield power. She would one day be a formidable leader.

* * *

Matthew's thoughts were interrupted by the sounds of a commotion at the front gate, where Shalee was conducting her trading. Matthew rushed toward the noise to see if Shalee needed help. A tall, handsome Irishman was kissing Shalee's hand as Matthew drew near, and Shalee and the Irishman stared into each other's eyes as she introduced him to Matthew. "This is Shawn O'Conner from Ireland. He and his men came to trade and to see Alanna. They request permission to stay with us. He offers this gift of a silver chain and one gold bar. I gave them permission, my leader."

Matthew folded his arms, scowling as he replied, "I have not given permission, or am I no longer leader of my own castle?"

This broke the Irishman's spell, and Shawn and Shalee turned simultaneously to face a stern looking Matthew. Shawn quickly apologized. "Your wife conducts her trading so skillfully that I thought this her castle. I did not mean to offend you by asking her for permission to stay, but coming here, we heard that Matthew Wolverine is hospitable, but that he had left to liberate the south of Scotland. It was thus that I assumed she commanded the castle in your absence."

Matthew could see that this Irishman was a charmer. Shawn had a warm and friendly smile, with straight, white teeth. His shoulder-length jet black hair was clean and shiny. He carried himself with decorum, and had polished manners and an air of authority. Matthew judged him to be Irish nobility — a nobleman who was smitten, nonetheless, by the beautiful Shalee.

Matthew smiled broadly. "No harm done, but to clear up matters, Shawn, my daughter, Raquelle, commands the castle while I liberate the south to Antoninus's Wall. Shalee is not yet my wife. How long is your stay?"

Shalee took note of the phrase, *not yet my wife*. Matthew had not even asked her to marry him, but, apparently, assumed she would agree. Then she recalled the incident in the kitchen with the black robes, and she rubbed her arm, remembering the Matthew she had seen that day. It was at this point that Shalee decided Matthew Wolverine needed to be taught a lesson.

She scrutinized every feature of the Irishman who stood before her, figuring he would serve well to that purpose. He was, after all, extremely handsome, and she could use that to keep Matthew on his toes. She said, "Shawn, you will stay at our castle until Matthew returns from his crusade. It will be a short crusade, only two months, at most. Is that not correct, Matthew?"

Matthew felt suddenly boxed in. To himself he thought, *This Irishman may control troops in Ireland that could be helpful next spring in liberating the land between Antoninus's Wall and Hadrian's Wall.* And yet… he saw the look Shalee was giving Shawn, and the look the Irishman gave her in return. In the end, however, he found himself agreeing, though reluctantly, that Shawn could stay until he returned. An uneasy feeling settled over him as the words of welcome came out of his mouth.

Shalee was all smiles as she took Shawn's arm in hers to escort him into the castle. Matthew burned with anger at this sight, but managed to subdue it as he busied himself with the preparation for tomorrow's march to the south.

As Shalee fussed over Shawn's bed and filled his room with luxurious furs, the Irishman informed her that he had five men out hunting, and if there was a place in the stables where they could sleep, he would be further in her debt. "I am sure that something can be worked out," Shalee said, looking at him with her intense green eyes.

"And I've one final favor to ask you," Shawn said. "Your reputation as a cook has spread all over Scotland. Could you prepare for my evening meal the bounty my hunters bring from the forest?"

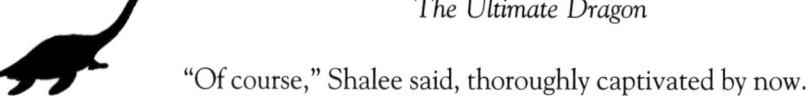

"Of course," Shalee said, thoroughly captivated by now.

At that instant, the five Irish hunters approached the castle gates, carrying a large, freshly killed boar. The castle guards were reluctant to admit them, knowing full well their leader's loathing of all pork. Robert Roybridge had driven that point home to them on Matthew's first day at the castle. So they sent for Shalee to deal with the matter.

Shalee climbed the stairs to the castle wall and looked down upon the dead boar. She was torn by inner conflict. Shalee was more than aware of Matthew's revulsion for pork; he had even shared the reason with her during one of their long talks together. And certainly, no boar had defiled Matthew's castle since he had become leader.

But here was Shawn now at Shalee's side, reminding her of her promise, and looking ever so appealing with his dark twinkling eyes. Shalee's forehead furrowed. She had an obligation to Matthew, but she also had a duty, and she considered it a sacred one, as a host. Surely Matthew would understand. Hesitantly, she ordered the gates opened and the boar roasted for the night's meal.

***

The rest of the day passed quickly, and Matthew gladly took his seat at the evening meal. Raquelle sat at his right, and they talked of his coming crusade. Then Shawn entered, talking with Shalee, and sat at Matthew's left, with Shalee sitting at his left. At that moment, the roasted boar was brought in by five Irishmen and deposited on the table. Memories of that loathsome Russian boar and its pursuit of Matthew came flooding back, and Matthew stood up, glaring at Shalee as he shouted, "Who dares to desecrate my table with pork?"

Shalee began to shake as she stood. "I promised Shawn that I would cook whatever his huntsmen killed. Then I learned they had killed this boar, but I had already promised. I could not break my promise to a guest of this castle."

Shawn rose between Shalee and Matthew, and smiled as he spoke. "I did not know you despise pork, but since it is here, cooked and delicious, please allow those of your people who wish to enjoy my present to eat their fill."

Matthew fought to control his rage. "You Irishmen will remove this beast from my castle. If you wish to eat the flesh of swine, you will do it outside my castle walls. Don't ever think of carrying a swine into my castle again. Castle guards, if any man bearing a swine tries to enter my castle, you are to fill his body with your arrows before he can enter." The Irishmen hustled to lift the boar and carry it outside the castle gates. Matthew had everyone move from the table, then ordered Kele to have his warriors carry the table outside the castle walls and burn it. "Tomorrow, you will build a new table. Tonight, have the cooks bring clean food to my chambers." Then, without further word or a farewell to his guests, Matthew and Raquelle left the dining hall and walked to their chambers.

Shalee was thunderstruck by this turn of events. Shawn asked her to join him outside the castle to enjoy his feast of pork, but Shalee shook her head and rushed to her room. She had miscalculated how violently Matthew would react to swine in his castle. Only against dragons had she ever seen such hate displayed by Matthew Wolverine. With head hung down, Shalee went to her bed. Matthew could hear her crying as he tried to fall asleep, but he made no move to get up and go to her chambers to comfort her.

* * *

The next morning, Matthew and his troops began their march south. As Matthew turned to look back, he saw Shawn standing beside Shalee. He turned away, trying not to let his shoulders slump. Then he set off southward, and did not look back again.

The first day was uneventful; they encountered neither dragons nor dragon worshippers. That night found Matthew lonely and restless in sleep.

At the castle, meanwhile, Shawn set to work in earnest, romancing Shalee with ballads and stories. When he had heard Matthew say, "Shalee is not yet my wife," he had heard everything except the word *yet*. As far as he was concerned, and Shalee gave him no reason to think differently, he had as good a shot as Matthew at winning her hand. And so he was constantly around her, causing Raquelle no end of worry.

It wasn't just Shawn's presence that worried Raquelle; it was also the change that had come over Shalee. Shalee relaxed her supervision of the cooking, and the meals soon became more disorganized. Eager to keep her father's castle according to his desires, Raquelle assumed the task of organizing the castle — rearranging the trading goods, food supply, and the treasure — and Shalee was so preoccupied with Shawn that she didn't even notice.

As the weeks passed, a steady stream of wagons appeared at the front gate, each wagon overflowing with dragon treasure. Raquelle stored the treasure in every possible space in the castle, but soon there was no more room, so she improvised. All the cats now wore gold and silver wristbands around their necks. Raquelle considered them portable treasure storehouses.

More weeks passed, and Raquelle observed that Shalee was spending every waking minute with Shawn. Raquelle was now doing all of Shalee's work — supervising the meals, handling the trading of Alanna's fish, and

183

managing every aspect of running the castle. And she began each new day in dread of hearing Shalee announce that she would marry Shawn.

* * *

Eric the Red came to the castle one morning to announce that the four ships were finished, but that he needed ballast. Just then, two wagons full of dragon treasure crested the hill and proceeded toward the castle gate. Raquelle told Eric, "Take the dragon treasure to your four ships and use it for ballast, at least for a short while." Eric grinned.

Approaching Raquelle, the wagon drivers announced that her father would be back the next day, and that Matthew Wolverine now controlled all of Scotland to Antoninus's Wall. Eric said to Raquelle, "Well, that is grand news! I will have the ship made ready, so that Matthew may take the first voyage." Raquelle nodded her approval, and Eric turned to leave.

Just as he walked away, Shalee came toward her. Apparently, she had been searching for Raquelle, and upon finding her, Shalee blurted out, "Shawn has asked me to marry him."

Raquelle's worst fear had come to pass. But her face and voice betrayed no emotion as she said coldly, "My father will be returning home tomorrow, so it will be better if you married Shawn today and left immediately for Ireland."

Shalee was surprised at Raquelle's response, and looked closely at the dispassionate girl. "Can you offer me no congratulations, or wishes for a happy life? Or is it, 'Just get out of here before my father returns'?" Shalee was hurt, and her words were barbed. "I have not accepted Shawn's proposal, but it is my first marriage proposal, and I am not as young as you. Matthew did not even bother to ask me before he left. He just assumed we would marry."

Raquelle struggled, but was able to remain detached as she replied, "Aye, he loves you and assumes you love him. Men tend to take such things as understood between lovers. You know how he has suffered because his first wife, his daughter, and his unborn son were torn from him. That left him with a sadness that brought him near the grave. It would crush his spirit to see you marry Shawn. This is why it would be better for him if you were to marry Shawn today and immediately leave for Ireland. I will be here to comfort my father and keep Death at bay!"

Raquelle's words were so matter of fact that Shalee was taken aback. This was not the same little girl Shalee had known. This person weighed the options, and made her decision without the influence of her heart.

"It would seem that my father has taught you well," Shalee murmured.

"Aye," said Raquelle. "One thing he taught me is that to be a leader means to make decisions that may hurt, but must be made for the good of Scotland. Go now."

Shalee stammered, "But I have not told Shawn I would marry him. I love your father, but he has not asked me to marry. I am twenty-one summers, and this is my first proposal of marriage!" Shalee began to cry then, but Raquelle stood like a statute. She gave Shalee a few moments to cry, and then she said, in a voice even colder than before, "You still have a choice. But you must make your decision to marry Shawn or not, and you must do it quickly."

As it happened, one of Shawn's men was eavesdropping by the door and, fearing his master would lose this beautiful woman, he formed a malicious plan in his mind. He swiftly left the castle to search out Matthew Wolverine. The Irishman headed south, and it took him the rest of the day to find Matthew's camp. The sun was setting as he was escorted to Matthew with important news from the castle.

Matthew was excited about hearing news from his castle, but the first words he heard were of Shawn's proposal to Shalee, and her probable acceptance. His face drained of all emotion as he sat motionless upon the ground. He thanked the Irishman for his news, and sent him away without rising.

Kele noticed his leader's gloomy attitude, and dared to press him to speak his mind. Matthew told him the news of Shalee's proposal, and ordered Kele to go to the castle and inform Raquelle that Matthew would not be returning right away but instead would go to the north to see the progress on Eric's ships. If Shalee was going to marry the next day, Matthew did not want to attend the ceremony.

He told Kele to come for him with a wagon to Eric's camp after the ceremony, but only after Shalee and Shawn had left the castle for Ireland. Matthew made it clear to Kele: "I do not want to look upon Shalee at all after she has married that Irishman."

Kele shook his head in disbelief that Shalee would marry anyone but his leader. Hesitantly he asked, "Did you not ask Shalee to marry you before we left?"

Matthew merely slumped farther forward and shook his head, blurting out, "I had assumed she would just wait for me!" Kele could not think of a response that would make things any better, so he left his leader to his dark thoughts. He knew that he must attempt to put things right.

The Ultimate Dragon

Long after Kele left his presence, Matthew remained where he sat, unmoving upon the ground, and consumed by an emptiness he had not known since another night, a lifetime ago.

※ ※ ※

Kele rode with all the swiftness his steed could muster, streaking through the night, driven onward by the image of his once-proud leader, now reduced to a shadow by his grief. He arrived at Matthew's castle while it was still dark, and was immediately granted entry by the guards at the front gate. He went at once to Raquelle's room, and pounded the stone of the open doorway to awaken her. Raquelle rose from her bed, dagger in hand. Kele kept his distance until Raquelle, recognizing his voice, put down the dagger and bid him enter.

Without even greeting Raquelle, Kele blurted out, "My leader heard from an Irishman who came to our camp that Shalee is to marry Shawn. He does not wish to attend the ceremony, so tomorrow he passes our castle and goes to Eric's camp to see his ships. I am to follow him with news of when the marriage will take place. My leader wishes to wait until Shawn and Shalee leave before he returns to his castle."

Raquelle missed her father, and had been looking forward to seeing him the next day. Shalee awakened and, hearing the whispering, she rose to light a candle and hastened to Raquelle's room. Upon seeing Kele, Shalee feared that Matthew might be dead or hurt, and asked Kele if he was all right.

"Oh, he is fine," Kele assured her, "at least in his body. But his heart is a different matter. The news of your impending marriage reached our camp, and has greatly unsettled him. Though he had been planning to return to the castle tomorrow, he has changed his plans and will go to Eric's camp until you and Shawn have left for Ireland."

Shalee asked, "How was it that the news of Shawn's marriage proposal reached your camp?"

Kele replied, "One of his men arrived suddenly to give us the news. I must say, my lady, that this news quenched all joy of our leader's victory in the south."

Shalee's eyes flashed green fire. She ordered Kele and Raquelle to follow her to Shawn's room, which she entered, screaming, "You son of a dragon! How could you send word of your proposal to my leader before I accept or reject it?"

It took Shawn a few moments to recognize that Shalee was screaming at him. The sun was just rising, and its light began to pour into the room. Shawn yawned, then rubbed the sleep from his eyes. Ignoring her angry words, as well as the presence of Kele and Raquelle, he smiled at Shalee and asked, "Well, my little one, will our wedding be today?"

Shalee glared at him, her emotions turned to steel. "I will not marry you, you cur. Now pack your belongings and leave this castle. I will see that the cooks feed you before you go, only because it is the wish of my leader that none leave these walls hungry. Were it left to me, I would have you fight with the carrion-birds over the bones of some dead thing upon the road. I shall go to be with my beloved, to beg his forgiveness for the hurt that he has suffered. My future husband lies not here, grinning stupidly from his bed, but at the camp of Eric the Red."

Kele saw to it that the Irishman's preparations went smoothly — and quickly — and Raquelle supervised the preparation of the meal, which, to be truthful, was far less delicious than any served in the castle since Matthew's arrival. With the coming of the sun, full upon the faces of the travelers, they climbed upon their steeds and plodded through the castle gates and to the valleys beyond.

"But I'll be back for you!" Shawn cried as he left. "Mark my words: Shawn O'Conner always gets what he wants, and even the great Matthew Wolverine will not be keeping me from possessing you for my own, Shalee!"

The Ultimate Dragon

Chapter 18

Raquelle, now bearing the mantle of authority as if she had been born to it, sought out the castle guards to inform them that Matthew's army would return to the castle that day. "Shalee, Kele and I will take a wagon to Eric's camp to meet our leader," she said. "Send a messenger to all of the neighboring farms to announce that Matthew Wolverine is expected home before evening. And if Shawn O'Conner and his men should try to return to the castle while we are gone, do not let them through the gates. Send them away, with force if necessary."

With these orders issued, Raquelle finished her preparations. Soon thereafter, her wagon was brought up, and the three climbed aboard and urged the horses onward. As the wagon passed through the front gate, Raquelle thought how glad she was that they did not have to walk to Eric's camp. There were misunderstandings that needed mending quickly, and she was anxious to see her father again, and to have him back to set things aright in the castle.

* * *

Matthew rose before sunrise and ordered Kial to take the Scottish army to his castle, and then release them from his service. "Tell them that they have served Scotland, and our God, well, and to keep an ear to the winds, for we may need to call upon them again soon." As soon as Kial had left to carry out his commands, Matthew fetched his horse and rode swiftly to Eric's camp. The coolness of the morning breeze, and the warmth of the sun upon his face, felt refreshing, yet could not lift the shadow on his heart. He pushed his horse to its limits, as if by spurring the beast to greater speed, he would somehow escape the sadness that filled him. He did not know that he was riding swiftly from one betrayal to yet another.

As the sun rose, Eric busied himself preparing his ship for the journey home. His men were especially rowdy that morning, letting their captain know, in no uncertain terms, that they were anxious to leave this land and return home with the dragon treasure. After listening to their grumbling for as long as he was willing, Eric finally stopped his work and ordered his crew to gather round.

"All this morning, I've listened to you moan like old women, and I've heard enough. I remind you that I have given my word to serve Matthew Wolverine and his God, and I will keep my word. Any of you who isn't willing to accept my orders can step forward and face me now!" The sailors grumbled, but their fear of their captain was great, and none stepped forward. They would obey him for now, but their eyes revealed the treachery that each of them held in their hearts. The remainder of their tasks were performed amid a silence that was thick with their malice.

After a time, Matthew rode up to the beach and dismounted. As the two men greeted each other, Matthew's gaze fell on the ship. "Eric, your ship looks magnificent, but can she sail?"

Eric laughed and waved him aboard. "See for yourself! We are just about to take her on her maiden voyage."

Matthew scanned the ship with wary eyes. Except for Eric, this vessel was manned by men he didn't trust. He said, "Eric, why not take off your coat, and untie your wife's coat from the ship? My warriors will guard these until you return." Eric complied, and when the coats were safely in the hands of the warriors, he said, "So, Matthew, you will be sailing with us, yes?"

Matthew's warrior instinct told him that this was a voyage best not taken. But the events of the past few days had worn him down, and he found himself increasingly reluctant to listen to that warrior's voice of reason. Another wave of sadness washed over him as he stood looking at the ship. He wondered, was Shalee now on a ship, bound for Ireland with her new husband? Suddenly her betrayal overshadowed everything else. Why not throw caution to the sea; what did he have to lose anymore?

Without another moment's hesitation, he climbed on board.

* * *

The first thing Matthew noticed was the dragon treasure that had been tied down all over the ship. "What is the meaning of this?" he asked. Eric told him that Raquelle had given it to him to use for ballast. "I needed the ballast, and she needed a place to store the surplus treasure," he chuckled. Even through the cloak of his despair, Matthew could not help feeling a surge of pride at his daughter's resourcefulness. Raquelle! He felt a lump in his throat. Shalee might be gone, but he still had a life — a daughter — back on shore.

"Well, Matthew, are you ready?" Eric asked.

"Yes, but let us take only a short voyage on the North Sea," Matthew answered. "I must be back before night fall." Eric nodded.

As they launched the ship, Matthew decided he was in a frame of mind to make small talk with Eric. "Tell me about your family, Eric."

Eric grinned and replied, "I've a wonderful wife, and she bore me a son, Leif Ericson, who is ten summers old. He will be a great sailor like his father, Eric the Red."

So this was, indeed, *the* Eric the Red. Matthew said, "I have been wondering about this since we met. I am honored to know Eric the Red, father of Leif Ericson! Your name, and his, are in the history books of my own time. When we return to my castle I have maps I want to give you, but they are for your son's eyes only. He will discover my homeland, far to the west, in the future."

Eric grunted his thanks, but seemed surprisingly uncurious to know more. Well, maybe it wasn't so surprising after all, Matthew thought. Eric's eyes had lost focus; he looked to be immersed in a daydream. And indeed he was, dreaming about his wife and child, wondering about their welfare, and longing to get back home.

Matthew looked west back to Scotland, over the gray and choppy North Sea. Eric's life was happy, crude and simple as it might seem by twentieth-century standards. Why couldn't Matthew's life be happy in *any* century? He thought about all the fairy tales and fantasies he had heard and read. In these past few months he had actually lived many of the events in those tales. He had, by some miracle or quirk or terrible cosmic joke, traveled back in time one thousand years, had become lord of a splendid castle, had slain dragons, had even tamed the monsters that swam in the deep inland waters of this wild land. But the happy ending had eluded him. The princess had run off with someone else. It wasn't supposed to happen this way.

Matthew perceived vague movement on the distant beach, but assumed it was Kele. His thoughts continued on their morose track. Unbidden, a vision of Shalee came to his mind, and he let out a deep involuntary groan. He regretted not having made love to her, not taking advantage of the opportunities that would never come again.

With a force of will he turned his mind away from his lost love, and to a fantasy about a sumptuous Viking maiden. He envisioned cotton-soft flaxen hair, draping down over a sleek back and shapely bottom. He thought of crystalline blue eyes, and a voluptuous body tightly wrapped in doeskin, or, perhaps, not wrapped at all…

Eric, pulling himself away from his own daydreams, noticed the rapturous expression on Matthew's face. "That is definitely the look of a man whose mind is on a woman!" Eric roared. "Tell us about her!" This

Matthew did, and in great detail. It was exactly the wrong conversation to share on a shipload of lustful, woman-deprived Vikings. As Matthew finished his lyrical description, the Vikings began clamoring to sail to the Viking lands and buy themselves some willing maidens with the dragon treasure. They tried to entice Matthew to join them. "A Viking maiden would make a good wife!" one of them said, and the others shouted in agreement. Matthew smiled and shook his head. "It is sorely tempting, but I must get back to my own home," he said. To himself he thought, *even though much of what had made it feel like home is now headed for Ireland.*

Suddenly Matthew's attention was drawn to an area near the hatch, where a securely fastened jug had been placed. It looked like one of the jugs of poison prepared by Kial's women for use in battle. A long spear lay near the jug, also securely tied. Matthew walked over, pointed to the jug and spear, and demanded, "Eric, what need do you have for poison on board this ship?"

At that, the mood of Eric and his crew instantly changed from boisterous to somber.

"We fear the *Kraken* may attack us again," Eric explained. "But if that happens — thank the heavens you are here now! — all you have to do is take this long spear and plunge the tip into this jug of poison. Then you throw the spear through the *Kraken*'s eye. If your God blesses us, then you will kill the *Kraken*, but if He forsakes us, then the *Kraken* drags us into the water to drown us and eat us one by one. Oh, and that large blade you wear on your leg may be needed."

Without thinking, Matthew reached his right hand down to enfold the hilt of his Bowie knife and extract it. He always kept the knife razor-sharp, and he now raised it to his face, forcibly steadying his hand despite his growing alarm. He began casually scraping off his whiskers. This, of course, was for the benefit of the Vikings, and they did not fail to notice the sharpness of his blade. They moved to the front of the ship to whisper among themselves. Matthew was grateful for his knife but wished he had his .44 Magnum with him. Of course, he also wished that he hadn't run out of bullets. But the point was moot anyway, for at this moment, the gun was hanging over his bed at his castle, a useless relic. And only God knew if Matthew Wolverine would ever see bed, gun or castle again. Perhaps that .44 would be a mystery for his descendants to ponder over the next thousand years.

For now, Matthew had his own mystery to ponder. What in the name of creation was this terrible *Kraken* that had the Vikings so frightened? He searched his memory for any reference to the term, but came up with nothing. As the waves ascended higher and the troughs grew deeper, Matthew's mind dredged up all the sea monster movies of his childhood. He shivered. The sea upon which he now found himself spawned all the ancient terrors in his mind: visions of slimy, cold, slithering tentacles that shot up from the depths to wrap around his body and drag him ever downward into blackness. It was every child's nightmare. It most certainly had been the stuff of his own nightmares as a child, and at some deep level he carried the fear within him to this day. Yet he didn't even know exactly what he was afraid of.

Matthew did not want to betray his ignorance and certainly not his fear; he must not do anything that could compromise his precarious authority over these brutal men. But he had to find out the nature of the enemy he might be called upon to fight. It wasn't that he didn't trust his God; of trust he had plenty, but he had long ago learned the truth of the old saying that the Lord helps those who help themselves. Maybe if he asked the right questions of Eric, he could solve the puzzle from the context of Eric's words.

Forcing himself to assume a casual manner, Matthew asked, "So, Eric, have you ever fought a *Kraken?*"

Matthew's heart sank as he observed, for the first time, terror enter Eric's eyes. "It was more running than fighting," Eric began slowly. "The *Kraken* attacked us in these very waters. We were on our way to raid Scotland and we'd already counted and spent the wealth we knew we would bring back. We went to sleep happy men.

"Only one man was awake, steering our ship. I myself was awakened when I heard a splash, and saw that he had just disappeared. I thought maybe he leaned over the side to relieve himself, and a wave had knocked him overboard.

"So I awoke the others, and we circled and called his name, but to no avail. We had lost him. That frightened us mightily. So the second night we only half slept. In the middle of the night, a blood-stopping scream awoke us; we helplessly watched a thrashing sailor be pulled from our ship into the dark waters, by something shiny and black that was wrapped tightly around his chest. The air was filled with a foul smell. My blood ran cold. It was the first time in my life I felt real terror. There and then, I vowed not to sleep until we reached Scotland.

"The third night we were on guard there came again that foul smell to our noses."

"What sort of smell?" Matthew interjected, thinking this might provide the clue he was looking for.

"Sharp and strong… a smell that put me in mind of a cave of bats," Eric replied, wrinkling his nose at the memory.

193

Matthew remembered the time he and Cate had gone hiking in a beautiful area called Lost Maples, in the heart of the Texas Hill Country. They'd ventured a little way into a bat cave, and had nearly been overwhelmed by the stench of... ammonia, the result of generations of bat urine. What sea kind of sea creature emitted an odor that smelled like ammonia?

"Continue with your story," he urged Eric, trying not to focus on the fear on his friend's face.

"The smell grew stronger, then we heard a loud scraping along the side of our ship. It sent chills up our backs. I stood in the middle of my ship and called on my gods for help. With my spear at the ready, and my men behind me, I watched as two slimy black tentacles snaked over the stern of our ship toward us."

Tentacles. Ammonia. So... in this murky sea of a thousand years ago, there really had been such creatures as giant squid. Matthew remembered Alanna's horrified description of the "many-legged death" that dwelt in the great waters. He shuddered involuntarily as Eric continued his tale.

"Mightily I threw my spear. It entered the right tentacle, whereupon the monster reared back like a whip and launched that tentacle upon my side so hard, I thought I was going through the bottom of my ship. An arching left tentacle grabbed a sailor just behind me. My men's swords slashed at the tentacle, but the *Kraken* held fast. I sprang from the ship's bottom and sliced off the tip of the tentacle. That must have hurt, because the creature raised the man straight up. Loud clicking assailed our ears, freezing us within this nightmare. Helplessly we stared at our shipmate suspended over the water as our ship gradually edged away. And, still frozen, we gawked at the *Kraken's* beak snapping open and closed as it leisurely lowered him, still screaming and kicking, into its shredder.

"His final death scream aroused us to action. We hoisted all sail, then we rowed like men possessed. We prayed to our gods for deliverance. Then a violent storm appeared from nowhere, and drove us to the shores of Scotland, and we cheered! As if the *Kraken* heard us, it rose to lash its tentacles out of the water, like mighty fists taunting us with a slimy death.

"Every time we thought the storm had driven the monster away, we heard violent scraping on the bottom of our ship. It toyed with us and dissolved all hope of escape. Raw terror began to fill every portion of our hearts. My crew became edgy, and daggers became an extension of every hand.

"Then a lull in the storm unleashed an even more intense scraping on the bottom of our ship. My first mate, Olaf, exploded in fury, vowing to kill this putrid *Kraken*. Before we could stop him, he leapt into the sea. For a few minutes nothing happened, but then Olaf came to his senses. He dropped his dagger and turned to swim to the ship. When he was only an oar's-length from the side of the ship, I reached out to help him.

"All at once, tentacles flashed out of the water and the slimy thing touched me. The tentacles pushed on the side of our ship, and then retracted around Olaf. Our ship drifted farther away, and then the *Kraken*, like an arrow, jetted back toward us, towing a screaming Olaf behind. Then, just as we feared it would hit our ship, it submerged. Only the slimy thing didn't take Olaf below the water, and his head hit the side of our ship with the force of a thunderbolt. The sickening thud and the blood caused two of my sailors to heave over the side.

"I ordered my men to the oars, and we rowed like demons. I swear I saw Death sitting on the bow of my ship, licking its lips for me. We rowed so hard our arms and backs cramped under the strain. We all lay slumped over the oars, awaiting the vile stench of the *Kraken*. Then the sky poured rain upon us, and the waves grew to mountains. I prayed the *Kraken* couldn't follow us through all of that.

"We were so drained we all fell asleep. Suddenly we found ourselves in the water, fighting to stay on the surface. Then, as the waves tossed me into the air, blackness came as I entered the water. I awoke to your stare. Often I wonder why you didn't just kill me."

Eric paused then, and the silence hung heavily around them. Then he concluded, "I have reasoned that if this poison can kill a dragon, it can kill a *Kraken*. The spear will open the wound to make a way for the poison to enter the beast." Eric's words were brave, but his shoulders sagged as he continued to steer the ship through the dark and choppy waters.

Matthew swallowed hard, but struggled to maintain his brave front. "Well, Eric, I certainly hope we don't meet that *Kraken*, but I will keep my Bowie knife handy just in case. But now, because I had Robert mold me a fishing hook, I believe I will do some fishing."

All of the Vikings except Eric snickered at these words, but within an hour Matthew had caught several small fish, which the sailors instantly devoured raw. Matthew, who in his old life had never been one to frequent sushi bars, knew that eventually he was going to have to learn to eat raw fish — just not today. When he saw that the sailors had eaten their fill for now, he pulled in his fishing hook. He patted the jug of poison, as if that act would give him the reassurance he so desperately sought.

* * *

As the afternoon waned, Matthew decided it was time to turn around and head for home. The ship had proven herself seaworthy, and with luck, they would be back in Scotland by nightfall, as planned, without encountering the *Kraken* or any other deep-sea monstrosity. Eric was still at the rudder, traveling due east. Matthew turned to his friend and said, "It is time now to head back to Scotland."

The other Vikings stiffened, and slowly moved their hands around their daggers. Eric, as if he had not heard Matthew, continued eastward, staring straight ahead and refusing to meet Matthew's glance. A scarfaced Viking named Roland turned to face Matthew and jeered, "Do you think you can kill all of us if we rush you?"

Mustering all of his bravado, Matthew snickered. "The first three will definitely die. Say, do you detect that terrible stench that smells like a cave of bats?"

Roland beamed a vicious smile. "That trick won't work! I'll tell you what I'm going to do, Matthew Wolverine. I am going to take your knife, cut open your belly, tie your arms, then throw you overboard to drag you behind our ship until the sharks tear your body to pieces. There won't be anything left of you for the *Kraken* when it comes."

Matthew flashed a silent prayer, *Well, God, there are only six of them against just you and me… so I know the victory is ours.*

Then suddenly, an ammonia-like odor really was in the air. As the acrid fumes assaulted Matthew's nostrils, he realized that his worst childhood nightmare had begun to come true. The first visual sign was a slimy tentacle, rising high above the rudder and deliberately creeping inside the ship. The tentacle brushed Eric's back, as if sadistically teasing him about the agony to come. Eric catapulted from his seat like a pilot ejecting from a crashing jet. He leapt high into the air and landed on his crew. The terrified men fell into a noisy pile.

Eric was up in a heartbeat, struggling to untie the spear. The squid surfaced to Matthew's right, shooting a look that could only be described as malevolent at Eric's red hair. Rarely in his life had Matthew seen such a stare of utter hatred, and it penetrated to the depths of his soul. This was an enemy that could not be reasoned with or scared off. Pure and simple, this was evil that must be obliterated.

Eric finally had the spear untied. Matthew tried to unfasten the cover on the jar, but it was tightly sealed. The *Kraken* fastened numerous tentacles to the ship and began dragging it through the water. Eric slipped and dropped the spear, but fortunately Matthew was quick. He retrieved the spear and drove it fiercely through the cover of the jug of poison. The jar shattered.

Frustrated, Matthew yelled a few expletives into the air. He muttered, "Great. I have a monster in front of me that is eager to eat my flesh raw and in stripes, six Vikings at my back who want to cut open my belly for a shark feast, and now I stand in a puddle of deadly poison. The odds don't look too good. Well, *Kraken*, I will send you to hell first!"

With this thought, Matthew launched his spear, aiming straight for the monster's right eye. Then Matthew entered into an all-too-familiar state of detachment from this scene of horror. Time slowed to a crawl. Once he had released the spear, Matthew just stood there with hands at his side, watching the spear move, seemingly at a leisurely pace, towards the *Kraken's* right eye. The creature blinked, and Matthew feared it would submerge before the spear hit its mark. But the squid remained above the surface, its eyes shooting their pure evil in Eric's direction.

Eric sensed the hatred directed at his body, and he rose to return his own loathing to the *Kraken*. From Matthew's perspective, events were still moving with the pace of a snail crossing a two-lane highway. Would his spear ever get to the *Kraken?* Matthew longed to run on the water, pushing the back of his spear through the *Kraken's* eye until it exploded out the top of that repugnant head. Then the *Kraken* blinked, began to submerge… and Matthew's spear finally found its mark. The point entered the creature's eye and continued to bore deeper into its target. In triumph Matthew raised his arms straight up, like the referee in a football game announcing the winning touchdown.

But the game wasn't over yet. The *Kraken,* though now submerged, wasn't about to capitulate, not without taking the enemy down with it. Within seconds, a single tentacle erupted from the water, found its way to Eric, wrapped itself tightly around his waist, and hauled him over the side.

With his Bowie in his right hand, Matthew leapt for that tentacle, sawing at it before he even hit the icy water. The beast plunged toward the depths, taking his unwilling riders with him. Every second plummeted them deeper into the abyss. Cutting the *Kraken's* tentacle was like cutting a wire cable with a butter knife. *I have definitely lost my appetite for calamari*, Matthew thought as he worked. His lungs burned for air, the salt water stung his eyes terribly, but still he kept on cutting, cutting, cutting. He half-expected another tentacle to wrap around him any second, crushing his crest. Before long a tentacle brushed his back with that dreadful, malevolently teasing, touch. Matthew stopped sawing for a moment, but the tentacle didn't wrap around him. So he continued sawing;

only a strand of flesh remained now. He tried to remember what he had learned in his high school biology class about the nervous system of cephalopods...They felt pain, didn't they? He fervently hoped so. His one wish right now, besides rescuing Eric and himself, was that he was sending the *Kraken* to hell in agony. At last his knife surged through, and Matthew grabbed the tentacle, praying that Eric was still attached to it, and still alive.

At this point, Matthew was disoriented, not knowing which way was up. He let out a breath and followed the bubbles upward, kicking his legs to gain speed to the surface. How far down had the *Kraken* towed them? Matthew broke the surface of the water, still dragging the severed tentacle, which, he was relieved to see, was still wrapped around Eric. Matthew swam to the ship, where the sailors hauled him on board. Gasping for breath, he shouted an order for them to hoist the tentacle and Eric onto the ship.

Matthew tried to remove the tentacle, but it was like removing a surgical glove. The claws in the tentacle clung fast to chunks of Eric's flesh. And Eric was not breathing.

Matthew tried his best to remember CPR. He pinched Eric's nose, cleared Eric's mouth, and breathed air into his lungs.... one, two, three. Then Matthew checked for a pulse, but there was none. Trying not to let desperation get the best of him, Matthew placed his palm down over Eric's heart, with his other hand on top, and he pumped ten times. Still no pulse. Matthew heard himself screaming, "Don't you die on me, Eric! Not after I killed a *Kraken* to save you!" He looked heavenward. "God, why don't you just heal him? I could use some help here, you know!"

Hearing his frenzied prayer, the other sailors began backing away from Matthew. They had always considered him a little crazy, but talking and breathing into the dead was a whole lot crazy. Matthew feared he was doing the CPR all wrong, and fervidly wished he had taken that CPR refresher course with Cate and Rachel last summer. Still he continued the pumping motion, leaning down at intervals to breathe into Eric's mouth. At last...praise God!... a rumble emerged from Eric's chest, and he gushed water all over Matthew's face. Opening his eyes and looking up at Matthew, Eric coughed out, "Are we dead?" Matthew hugged him, assuring him that they both were very much alive.

As the feeling returned to Eric's body, he winced in pain. He ran his hands over his body and then looked at them, seeing they were covered with blood. "What are these?" he asked Matthew in bewilderment. "Are they stab wounds?"

Matthew pulled the tentacle over for Eric to see. "These are the claws of the *Kraken*." Eric shuddered and lay back. Matthew turned to the crew and barked, "Sailors! Begin cutting out the black beaks from this tentacle, and head this ship for Scotland." This time there was no question that Matthew's order would be obeyed; even scar-faced Roland had been subdued. The experience with the *Kraken* — not to mention the sight of Matthew raising Eric from the dead — had removed any thought of mutiny. This sea was deadly dangerous, and it seemed obviously now that Matthew, and his God, were all that lay between the sailors and the fate that had befallen several of their mates.

* * *

Matthew continued to tend to Eric. He found a small jug of salt and poured it gently into Eric's wounds. He was fearful of the spilled poison in the bottom of the boat, however, and bade Eric to sit up in the ship. He ordered one of the sailors to use an empty jug to bail out the water and, hopefully, the poison as well. At last Eric slept peacefully, the worst of the crisis over.

Night had fallen, and the ship continued towards Scotland. Regrettably, most of the provisions, including the furs, had been washed overboard. Matthew looked for something to wrap in to sleep, but found nothing. He wished that the coat Eric had picked for his wife was still on board, for the wind was turning downright icy now. Still, Matthew pulled his legs to his chest and tried to sleep. Exhaustion finally took its toll, and sleep did come, but it brought no peace. It brought only fevered dreams in which the *Kraken*'s tentacle grabbed Matthew's back, inflicting the most excruciating pain he had ever felt. He moaned in his sleep. Then suddenly he was screaming, and he awakened to find Eric standing over him, shaking his head.

Eric lamented, "The coldness lives in his body and is tearing it asunder. Only Helga can make him whole."

Matthew wondered fleetingly who Helga might be, but his fevered brain was unable to hold any thought for long, and he quickly forgot Eric's remark. He struggled to stand up, but could not. "Eric," he gasped, "is there an iceberg on my back?"

Eric's face had turned pale. "It is the coldness that enters your bones from the *Kraken*. You killed him, but his coldness enters your body as his final revenge. Only Helga can drive it out. We land in Scotland at dawn. You saved me from a horrible death, and I shall repay in kind. Know that I will not let you remain like this for long." Now it was Eric's turn to bark out commands. "Sailors, get to the oars and row like a *Kraken* is behind us!"

Matthew's back muscles went into spasms, and then his upper leg muscles followed suit. Matthew rolled around the ship in agony as he endured one muscle cramp after another. At last the sun rose, and Matthew, through bloodshot eyes, beheld the shores of Scotland, and a waiting wagon. At Eric's behest, four Vikings carried Matthew from the ship to the beach and put him down. Raquelle, Kele, and Shalee rushed from beside the wagon to see how badly Matthew had been hurt.

Shalee?!? The last thought Matthew had before he lost consciousness was that surely he must be hallucinating. If so, what a cruelly beautiful hallucination it was: Shalee looked even more stunning than he had remembered. Or was she really here, bearing the radiant glow of a new bride? If so, what was she doing still in Scotland? Someone was going to have to answer to Matthew Wolverine… Then everything went dark.

Trying to remain calm, Raquelle asked Eric, "What happened?" Eric spit out, "*Kraken!*" He seemed to be recovering well enough from his own wounds, and was in a hurry to get back on his ship. He grabbed his coat, and the coat for his wife, from the warrior whose duty it had been to watch over the garments. Meanwhile, Shalee and Raquelle helped Matthew into the bed of the wagon. As Eric headed back towards his ship, Kele followed, pumping the Viking for the whole story. Eric made it brief, and then he and his crew climbed back aboard their ship and shoved off.

Kele sprinted to the wagon, where he saw that Matthew was coming to again. He whispered into Matthew's ear, "The Vikings are stealing the ship and dragon treasure." Matthew shook his head vehemently, struggled to his elbows and, as loudly as he could manage, he said, "Eric is my friend, and I trust him with all my heart. I will hear no more of this nonsense. He has gone to get help for me, and, mark my words, he will return." Then Matthew fell back, and he thought he saw another glimpse of Shalee's lovely face before he descended into blackness once more.

Kele raced the wagon home as Shalee nestled Matthew's head in her lap. No warrior ever likes to come home in a wagon, and those around him hoped that Matthew would remain unconscious for awhile longer so he would not have to experience this less than heroic entrance. As they entered the front gates, however, Matthew awakened long enough to complain that he was freezing. "Kele," he ordered, "Build me a watertight tub so I can take a hot bath in my bedroom."

He closed his eyes against the pain, and slipped into a deep sleep. Dreams of Shalee were interspersed with nightmarish vignettes of the murky North Sea, and somewhere in all of this he heard Eric's voice talking about someone named Helga.

***

How much later it was he couldn't say, but Matthew lay in his bed, cold and in pain and still somewhat feverish, waiting for the tub to be finished. He stared up at the empty .44 Magnum pistol hanging on the wall, feeling that he was as useless as that weapon on the wall. Hours seemed to pass, and depression began to grip Matthew's mind. He was stiff and sore all over…and so profoundly cold!… and his limbs felt worse than useless. If the hot water from his bath did not cure him, what would he do?

Raquelle entered the room and noticed her father wince in pain as he tried to sit up in the bed. She struggled to think of something pleasant to cheer him up. "The building that holds your large cross is completed," she finally said, brightly.

Matthew just hung his head lower. "I would have to crawl out there to pray. It really doesn't matter, though, because I do not feel much like praying."

"Father, will you still worship your God if your condition doesn't improve?"

Feeling too depressed to give her a lecture right now, Matthew got right to the point. "Aye, because our choices here and now, in this place and time, are to serve either the dragons or our God. Since I can't serve the dragons, my God wins by default. No matter what happens to me, I serve my God."

Raquelle ventured further than she ever had on this topic. "Who says we have to serve anyone or anything at all?" This was the kind of question that in some times and places might have landed the questioner in a lot of trouble, particularly if such insolence came from a female child. But Matthew, despite his pain and depression, was secretly pleased that his daughter had the temerity to ask. This child never failed to amaze him.

"Many people before you have asked that question, and many will ask it after you and I are long gone," he said. "And some have chosen, and will choose, to go their own way, serving nothing, believing in nothing. But I don't know of any case where such a choice has led to happiness. We seem to be made to serve, and, lacking God, we must serve something or someone. Otherwise there is a void, and we can't bear that void, something has to fill it. We can't help it. Well, I've explored some of the alternatives, and I would rather cast my lot with a God who has never led me wrong."

Raquelle, being Raquelle, had to push the point. "But Eric, the ship, and the dragon treasure inside the ship are all gone. Why did you jump into the water to save him? All that has resulted is that your God has left you crippled. Doesn't that make you doubt your God, even in the slightest?"

Matthew struggled up on one elbow. "First of all, I still have faith that Eric will return. He is my friend. Second, even if he does not return and he has truly betrayed me, know that I saved Eric because I had no choice. I could not stand by while the *Kraken* dragged him to a horrible death. If that had been me in his place, and I had cried out for help, I would expect my God to send me a savior.

"But to be a savior requires a great sacrifice. I didn't want to jump in that water, Raquelle, believe me. As a child my worst fear was being grabbed by a giant squid, and slowly dragged into the black waters of the abyss to be eaten. I would wake up screaming at night, sure that the monster had me! My parents would rush into my bedroom to find me thrashing in my tangled covers. They would comfort me for a long time before I could go back to sleep. I became Eric's savior in that fight by confronting my worst fear.

"The fact that Eric sailed away — and that he may, for one reason or another, not return — and the fact that my God may leave me crippled… these things cause me sadness. But I took the actions I had to take, and I do not regret taking them. My God may or may not be the source of some of my greatest pain — I could drive myself mad trying to figure out why things do or do not happen, and what hand God had in it. But no matter how terrible my pain, I can almost always see the hand of grace as well, and I have to choose to keep looking to the source of that grace." Matthew lay back, weary, smiling at Raquelle. "I'm sorry, daughter, I did not intend to preach a sermon."

Now Raquelle was the one looking sad. "Father, I don't know if I have the courage to stand up to my worst fear." Then she fell silent, making it clear she did not want to talk anymore about this subject, but she was still visibly distressed.

Even in his pain Matthew wanted to comfort his daughter. Raquelle lay down on top of the animal skin that covered her father, and leaned her head gingerly on his chest. They lay there for a long while in silence, a measure of peace finally descending upon both.

***

Their peace was broken when Shalee — Shalee! — entered Matthew's bedroom, large as life, as lovely as he had remembered. Behind her came a brigade of workmen bearing a large tub. So she really *was* here. Matthew's heart was pounding, his throat dry, his emotions reeling, but he said nothing, and Shalee would not look at him as she directed the workmen to place the tub close to his bed. A stream of women followed, carrying buckets of very hot water to fill the tub. Then the women, including Shalee, left. Raquelle kissed Matthew lightly on the cheek and said, "Father, I hope the hot water heals you completely. I will be right outside your room if you need me." Then she too was gone, and there was only Kele and Matthew.

Kele helped Matthew undress and get into the tub. The hot water permeated every sore muscle in his body. The healing liquid loosened his tight muscles. An hour drifted by as Matthew sat, engulfed in this glorious heat, glad to get his mind off of Shalee for awhile by telling an eager Kele the whole story of the *Kraken* fight. Matthew left out nothing, and by the time the story was over, Kele's admiration of Matthew had reached a whole new level.

At last Matthew stood up in the tub, extending his arms at shoulder height from his sides, and he began swinging one arm in front of his body as the other swung behind his back. Then he reversed directions. Kele was startled at the sound that filled the room. It was much like the sound of walnuts cracking. When Kele realized the noise was coming from Matthew's back, he asked, "What is it in your body that makes such a sound?"

Without ceasing his repetitive motions, Matthew said, "That is the sound of my vertebrae returning to their proper alignment."

"Your what, doing what?" Kele asked, more puzzled than ever.

"The sections of my backbone, getting back into the position they were in before the *Kraken* knocked the living daylights out of me!"

Matthew bent over to touch his toes, but his back muscles were still very sore, and he could only touch his knees without excruciating pain. "I need a deep sports massage," he said. "But, like so many other things I'd like, that is one thousand years in the future. Perhaps Raquelle can give me a deep massage. Bring her to me." Matthew flopped on to the bed and covered the lower half of his body with the animal skin.

Raquelle entered the bedroom to see her father lying face down on his bed. "You wanted me, Father?"

203

"Aye, I want you to take one thumb on each side of my backbone, and press both thumbs down very hard for a short while, then let up."

Raquelle did as she was told, pressing very hard. The resulting pain caused Matthew to let out a long groan, and Raquelle pulled back in dismay. "It's all right, Raquelle," he insisted. But she couldn't understand why her father would want her to cause him pain. Flustered, she told him she could not continue, and she fled the room in tears.

Matthew still needed that deep massage. He could ask Kele, but he had never been comfortable with a man giving him a massage. Matthew lay on his bed for several minutes, debating what to do next. And then Shalee entered the room, trailed by Kele and another warrior, carrying an all-white lambskin bed covering. This startling pure whiteness blinded Matthew for a second and he couldn't move.

Shalee looked at him, and then looked quickly away.

Matthew's heart was in his throat.

Chapter 19

Mustering all of the decorum he could manage under such circumstances, Matthew jumped up, wincing only slightly, clutching the animal skin around him while Shalee and the warriors placed the lovely lambskin on his bed. Matthew tried not to think of how Shalee might look, stretched languidly upon the covering, her shimmering black hair an astounding contrast to all that soft whiteness. The image was disquieting; Matthew struggled to shake it away. This was neither the time nor the place, and besides, Shalee had a whole lot of explaining to do.

Shalee could not help noticing that Matthew was now moving more easily, apparently only in slight pain. He stood up to his full stature, and she looked up at him, allowing her eyes to really meet his for the first time. Kele and the other warrior took their leave, and then suddenly Matthew was alone with Shalee. He saw fear in her eyes, but a measure of defiance as well, and she would not allow her gaze to leave his. Matthew opened his mouth to speak, and when he did he thought he saw her flinch, ever so slightly.

"Shalee," he began, "Can I ask a favor of you?"

This was not what she'd expected. Shalee relaxed visibly. "Anything, Matthew," she murmured.

"I need a very deep massage to get the poisons out of my back muscles. I tried to get Raquelle to do this, but she was afraid of causing me pain. But there must be pain first in order for the healing. You must go very deep to heal my body. Can you do it?" He then proceeded with the same instructions he had previously given Raquelle.

With a look of determination on her face, and no small measure of relief, Shalee assured him that she could indeed give a deep massage. She bid him lay down, and she began, her thumbs working with exacting pressure down Matthew's backbone. Then she worked his shoulder muscles and his lower back. The pain was terrible, but Matthew withheld his groans, on the off chance that Shalee might turn out to be as squeamish as Raquelle. After a time, Shalee relaxed the pressure and gently slid her hands up and down Matthew's back. Matthew sank into a state approaching bliss; at least it was as close to bliss as he had been in a long, long time. There is something profoundly therapeutic about the strokes of a beautiful woman's hands caressing your body. The touch of Shalee's fingertips dispelled all of Matthew's tension. As she loosened his hurt muscles, he was overwhelmed with a sense of inner peace that bordered on the spiritual.

He could not help but notice that there was no ring on her left hand. This didn't necessarily mean anything; admittedly, he didn't know much about the wedding customs of this time and place, but it could be a hopeful sign. Besides, Shawn seemed to be nowhere in evidence.

Relaxing, Matthew finally began to talk, but he was not yet ready to talk about the matter closest to his heart. So he chose a somewhat safer topic. "That *Kraken* really scared me."

At first Shalee thought Matthew was teasing her, so she teased back. "My leader was scared! I don't believe it." The intensity of her caresses deepened then, and she quickly switched back to a light touch as she glided her fingernails over Matthew's back. She moved to a position at the head of the bed and placed her knees around Matthew's head, stretching his arms behind her back.

He was growing dizzy, and he could scarcely breathe, and it wasn't from pain and sickness anymore.

Shalee, as if unaware of the exquisite tension she was creating, casually released Matthew's arms, and let his hands slide down her back to lightly rest upon her bottom. Matthew sank deeper into the lambskin bedspread, and began to tell Shalee about his childhood fear of the giant squid.

Shalee listened intently, and when Matthew had finished, she said, "But I talked to Kele after your bath. He told me the whole story. It was Eric who was being drawn into the abyss. How could you be so afraid, and yet jump to certain death to fight the *Kraken* — when you weren't the one in danger?"

Matthew shrugged his shoulders as his hands unconsciously pulled Shalee's body a little closer. "I couldn't stand idly by watching Eric slip to such a horrible death. Then I was in the water, cutting at that tentacle as the monster descended. When I thought I was about to die, all I could think of was you! I deeply regretted never making love to you. Shalee, you have to know that I adored you from the first moment I saw you. But I figured that you, like the women in my time, probably dreamt of a white knight in shining armor, with blonde hair, blue eyes, a baby face, and smooth skin, unmarked by the scars of battle. But a true warrior has many scars — some on the body where they can be seen, and some hidden in the depths of his soul. The death of my wife and children left me with such scars. Now, marriage scares me more than a *Kraken,* but less than the thought of losing you."

Matthew rose to his knees to face Shalee. She cocked her head and studied this curious man, then said, "I know that your scars run deep. I waited for you to ask me to heal them, but you constantly rejected me."

Matthew face showed his bewilderment. "How did I ever reject you?"

Shalee wondered if Matthew could really be that dim-witted. "How many times did I come to your bed at night? — and never once did you make love to me! We serve the same God, or so I thought, but you have to be so righteous. You have to be married! So, I waited for you to ask me, but you never did. Then Shawn came, and he did ask me to marry him.

"Do you think I am made of stone? I want to feel your kisses, and the thought of descending upon you in the middle of the night is constantly upon my mind. Some nights, I stood in the doorway and wanted to jump into your bed, to rip your clothes off and give you pleasure beyond your wildest dreams. Not very ladylike, is it, Matthew? And certainly not very righteous! Do you think you are the only one who has desires that need to be met? My insides burn for you, but you don't quench the fire. Night after night, I cry myself to sleep, because you ignore my hunger. If I am not beautiful to you, tell me, because I am tired of sleeping alone. Either take me now, or release me, so that I may leave for Ireland."

Shalee got up from Matthew's bed, then turned to face him. She took two steps backward, and loosened the sash at her left shoulder. Once again, Matthew watched as time seemed to slow to an agonizing halt. The simple shift that she had worn drifted slowly, as if borne upon wings, toward the stone of his chamber floor.

When the cloth finally settled in a heap about her ankles, he allowed his eyes to wander where his dreams had often trod. He beheld the litheness of her legs, the gentle curve of her hips as they flowed inward to the narrowness of her waist. As his eyes drank in every inch of her, they came at last to the suppleness of her breasts, now rising and falling with the rage of her own desire. Just as Matthew thought he would dissolve within the exquisite rapture of the vision before him, Shalee spit out a challenge: "If you want this body, take it now — or never."

Her brazenness made Matthew's desire even more powerful. Without conscious thought, he rose from the bed, leaving the sheet to fall to the stone beneath his feet. Stepping toward Shalee, he reached behind her head, gently drawing her hair over her shoulders to drape her breasts, shielding them from his gaze. As hot as his desire burned within him, he knew that he should hold his passion in check. Finally, the war between his hunger and his honor grew too intense to be kept silent, and he struggled to speak. "Do you swear by our God to take me as your husband, to love me, and to never hurt our children?"

Shalee's eyes twinkled as she stepped forward and whispered, "Aye." Her arms rose to enfold Matthew's neck, drawing him only close enough for her breasts to entice his chest with their nearness. Matthew realized that the shimmer of her hair as it rested upon her breasts enhanced rather than diminished his craving for her. Knowing that he had reached the limits of his self-control, Matthew cried out, "I take you now, before my God, as my wife. Tomorrow, we will have a public ceremony, but as of this moment, you are my wife!"

Shalee squeezed Matthew tighter, raising his passion to a fever pitch. At that moment, Raquelle entered the room, and froze in her tracks at the scene before her: her father standing with his back to her, quite obviously naked. Then she saw Shalee's dress on the floor, and gasped. Shalee, startled by the sound, responded swiftly as a cat, hissing, "Leave us, child! My husband and I consecrate our marriage this night. You shall sleep in my room tonight. Now, leave us!"

Raquelle was dumbfounded, caught between shock and joy. "Your husband? Then that makes you my mother! Oh, my mother, let me embrace you!"

Shalee's voice screeched with the passion that would not be denied or delayed any longer. "Not now! Leave us!"

Matthew heard Raquelle's footsteps as she turned, then slowly walked down the hall. He kissed Shalee deeply as he lifted her body off the ground. So great was his focus upon his hunger for her that he thought her light as a feather as he carried her to the bed, where he gently laid her down upon the lambskin bed covering. Shalee sank deep into the lambskin, and Matthew looked in awe as it framed her body, softness upon smooth skin. He slid onto the lambskin next to her, and she turned to meet his gaze. As he looked into her emerald eyes, he was drawn ever deeper into the ecstasy of the love he felt for her.

With his left hand, he reached up, touching her face, his fingertips following the curve of her cheek and her neck, then moving downward to brush away the strands of hair that still concealed her right breast. He lightly cupped her breast, holding it as one would caress some priceless treasure, and allowing his fingertips to drink in its firmness. Her body responded of its own volition, and she rose up to kiss him, but he pushed her back down on the bed. "Relax and enjoy the pleasure I give to you. When your cup is full then you may pleasure me, but first allow your body to listen, as my own body speaks its love for you."

Shalee let her body go limp as Matthew gently kissed her, first upon her forehead, then moving slowly down to her lips. His own lips were lost in their worship, savoring the silken moistness of her mouth as it opened slightly, beckoning his tongue to the sweet paradise within. His tongue gently circled her lips, bidding them open more. As her mouth yielded, their tongues found each other, joining in sweet dance to music heard only to the two of them, cadence drummed by the pounding of their hearts.

Matthew realized that, at this pace, he could not long restrain himself. He released Shalee's breast, moving his left hand up over her shoulder and behind her neck. His left forearm gently pressed her right shoulder back into the cushion of the furs. Breaking his kiss, he whispered in her ear. "My beautiful Shalee, I love you so very much. Drink in my caresses, and let your mind wander freely to whatever place your passion takes it. Let my caresses unlock your body's deepest desires. I pray that you may cherish my every kiss, my every touch, and my every loving glance. As my body speaks, let your own body listen and understand."

His words faded into movement as his lips found their way to the side of her neck. He nibbled, then lightly bit at her soft skin. From deep within her rose a soft moan, wordless testament to the fire that had long smoldered, but was now burning hotly. The sound inflamed his own desire, and threatened to shatter his deliberate movements, driving him into his own animal frenzy. But he was determined to go slowly, to give to this, his dearest love, a pleasure beyond any she had known even in her most wanton dreams. His journey was deliberately slow, with each kiss and caress raising her to a higher level of pleasure. Even his slightest movement against the soft lambskin stimulated his body, but he struggled to ignore the sensations, wishing to give her ecstasy before tasting its sweetness himself.

Slowly, he traced downward, following the line of her body with his lips, while his hands paid their own gentle tribute to the glory that was her skin. With his left hand, he caressed her body from her breast to her knee, his slow, rhythmic strokes hesitating to cup the fullness of her bottom. Turning his head to the side, he placed his ear over her heart, listening to its rapid beating, and delighting in the soft moans and sighs that told him she was truly afloat upon the pleasure he was giving her. With each quickening of her heartbeat, each soft cry of pleasure, Matthew found himself filled with a sense of peace that was as powerful as his hunger.

As he recommenced his kisses, placed softly down her chest, his left hand drifted across her knee, moving lightly upward, along the inside of her thigh, to brush the moistness of her womanhood with a feather touch, then across her stomach to softly enfold her right breast. His cheeks softly nuzzled between her breasts, gently caressing each in turn, his lips following the swell toward, but not quite touching her sensitive nipples. With each pass, the circle he drew with his lips grew smaller, until, as his hands enfolded her breasts with a gentle squeeze, his lips found their way to her nipples and sucked them, each in turn, into his hungry mouth. He slowly drew in most of her breast, then succulently, dreamily, released it until only the nipple remained, stiffening against the flicking of his tongue. Shalee's breath was quickening, as her sensual awareness approached its crest.

Then, Matthew's kisses drifted down her ribs to her navel. With a few tender kisses around her navel, Matthew brushed his cheek across Shalee's stomach, entranced by the contrast of his own roughness against the smoothness of her skin. Shalee spasmed slightly, whispering, "That tickles!" Matthew grinned to himself, knowing that every muscle in Shalee's body was like a taut violin string, quivering at his slightest touch. Raising his head, he slowly slid his body over Shalee, until his eyes locked with hers. "I am sorry, my beloved, but you are so delicious, I could eat all of you, and I think I will."

Matthew issued a low growl and descended upon Shalee's neck. The passionate kiss left a mark, but she eagerly rose to receive another. It occurred to Shalee that every time Matthew came back to her neck, the slow, voluptuous process of his ascent began again, and she snuggled deeper into the bed in anticipation. Then Matthew slid his body off hers, to lie at her left side. Her lustful panting rose, as Matthew's left hand drifted across her right side, causing her to instinctively open her legs slightly to grant him greater access to the center of her passion. His hands danced so very close, almost touching that part of her that so ached for his caress, then moved away, drifting back to the summit of her knee — teasing her, threatening to drive her to the fleeting madness whose only cure is release.

Finally, as he cruelly, sweetly taunted her breast with his tongue, his hand descended, plummeting to rest ever so delicately in the folds of her womanhood. He could feel the warm moisture against his hand, and Matthew's passion flared almost beyond his ability to control. But, at least for this moment, Matthew's resolve was the stronger emotion, and he was able to wrestle his passion into submission. His moist kisses again tasted her lusciousness, and she responded by clutching her fingers deep into Matthew's back muscles. His muscles tightened beneath her touch, telling her of his struggle to retain control over his passion. She sensed that her slightest move would send him reeling, his passion out of control. She eased her pressure on his back then, content with her new sense of power. The slight relaxation in her body only increased Matthew's desire to bring her passion to its crescendo. His left hand writhed within the soft folds of her now steamy wetness, stimulating an outpouring of her warmth. She was so very delicious, and so willing!

Her warmth enticed his kisses downward past her navel. Matthew's hands slid under Shalee's bottom to elevate her. Her panting now seemed to inflame the room, wave upon wave, cries answering themselves. As Matthew's tongue circled her opening, Shalee's juices began to flow unabated. Her deep gasps filled the room, then fled to echo down the outside halls. When the gasps and cries rose to the pitch of stifled screams, he knew that she was ready. His tongue plunged into the depths of her most private passion, matching the rhythm of her body as she arched upward to meet his embrace. With each stroke of Matthew's tongue, Shalee's sighs grew deeper and more throaty. She felt the pleasure inside her soaring beyond her most shameless fantasies until, in a searing peak of sweet agony, she screamed, and it was a scream that burst from deep within, from a place past thought or memory, a scream which, once released, caused the very stones of the ancient castle to ring out in celebration of her joy. Then, she gasped, her body sinking, contented beyond contentment, deeper into the lambskin. Matthew slid beside her, exhausted.

After a few moments, Shalee's eyes fluttered open, and she flashed him a smile. "This was incredible! Is every time of lovemaking like this?"

Matthew thought, *If it is, I won't last five years. Remember, show some bravado and, above all, evade that question.* But he said, "Did your loving cup overflow?"

A frolicsome Shalee laughed as she rose to straddle Matthew. As she let her warmth descend upon him, her hands circled his chest, cupping his muscles. She looked in his eyes, gloating, and she cried, "Aye, now my spring of warmth invites you in!" As Matthew touched that warmth, he reached up to cup her breasts to push her higher.

As she raised and lowered herself with sensual rhythm, Matthew lost himself, and finally gave in to the passion that had been burning for so very long. With a deep, guttural growl, he erupted into her, his entire body seeking to find ever deeper sanctuary within her, plunging into her with a rage that was, at the same time, the pinnacle of tenderness…and then he fell down, down, down to contented stillness within the sweetness of their shared embrace.

They both smiled as Shalee pressed herself down upon his chest, draping her legs over his. Matthew opened his legs to let Shalee's drop between them, then pulled the furs over both of them and enfolded her in his arms. This, he thought, made all the battles in the world worth fighting. Shalee snuggled deeper into Matthew's chest, and he buried his fingers in her hair. Then, filled with contentment, they closed their eyes, and wandered together into a deep sleep.

* * *

The sound of very loud footsteps awakened them. Without looking in, Raquelle called out, "Father, I bring food for you and mother. I am setting it just outside your door. But I must ask one question. Father, what took you so long to marry Shalee?" Without waiting for a reply, she added, "Well, it does not matter. Even though you are sometimes a bit slow, I love you anyway."

Matthew chuckled at his daughter's teasing. "Thank you for the food. And even though you are so much smarter than I am, I love you, too, my wise daughter."

Shalee stirred, then stretched her arms lazily over her head. "I feel so peaceful inside." She sat up, straddling Matthew, and playfully pounded on his chest. "After all those frustrating nights, I am finally satisfied. Were you serious that I am your wife, or was that merely your lust talking? Because even if it was only lust, I love you, Matthew, and I will share your bed whenever you want me."

A shocked look came across Matthew's face. "Do you think I lie before my God? Before Him, I took you as my wife, and you *are* my wife." Shalee grabbed Matthew so hard he thought she might crush his ribs. They were completely naked, but perfectly at ease, and Matthew thought to himself, *So this is what it is like to find your soul mate.* He had never had such a feeling, not even with Cate.

Shalee got out of the bed to get their food, and Matthew drank in the beauty of her strides as she crossed the room. Matthew thought to himself that God must be a male, because He made the female body so perfect. And then he issued a silent prayer that God would always give him the strength to show Shalee how deeply he loved her, while banishing his native fear of what other men might think of his actions.

Shalee returned to the bed with their food, paused at the edge, and spoke. "Matthew, when I dug my fingertips into your back muscles, and felt the power inside your body, it made me wonder, could our great Creator possibly be a female? Who else would make the male body so powerful and beautiful?"

They both burst out laughing. In that moment, they locked themselves in each other's arms. Matthew whispered in Shalee's ear, "I love your beauty, your strength, your passion, and your sense of humor. *You are why I traveled one thousand years back in time.*"

* * *

Suddenly, the sound of many warriors' footsteps filled the hallway outside their chambers. Instinctively, Matthew leapt out of the bed and grabbed his sword to defend his wife. In rushed Robert with his warriors, only to find a naked Matthew, with sword held high. Robert's eyes fell to the bed, as Shalee pulled up the furs to cover herself. Robert gave a disapproving look, then turned to Matthew.

Feeling a twinge of conscience, Matthew blurted out, "Before God, I took her as my wife. We will have the ceremony tomorrow."

Robert's face turned crimson, then he looked at the ground as he said, "That is all well and good, but we have real problems. Last night, a dragon flew over my castle. The dragon killed a lake guardian on a nearby beach, and left most of its carcass to rot in the sun. Alanna wails beside what is left of the body, and rumors arise that the southern kingdom amasses an army to invade us in the spring."

Matthew put down his sword, telling Robert and his warriors that he would meet them in the castle courtyard. After they left, Shalee jumped up and rushed into Matthew's arms. Matthew stroked her hair and whispered that he had wanted today to be special, but that he must now go and comfort Alanna.

Shalee hugged him tighter, and assured him, "It *was* special, my love, and tonight will be special as well." They looked again into each other's faces, each feeling that they must be the luckiest person alive. After a moment, Shalee released Matthew, and began to dress, so that she could go with him to console their friend.

The Ultimate Dragon

Chapter 20

Robert, Matthew, Shalee, and Raquelle walked solemnly to the beach, a squad of warriors close behind them. Their hearts were rent by the spine-chilling sound of Alanna's wails, which spoke, wordlessly, yet ever so clearly, of her deep agony. Alanna stood above a crumpled mass, which Matthew could not identify at first. As they approached, he could tell that it was the corpse of one of Alanna's babies, but still did not know if it was Elizabeth or Eric.

Then as he drew closer, he saw the purple spot on the creature's head.

When the procession was about thirty paces from Alanna, Elizabeth charged out of the water to block their approach. Matthew told Elizabeth that her mother needed his comforting, and that none among the group of humans would allow any harm to come to her. Elizabeth, however, stood fast, and would allow only Matthew to come near. As Matthew stood at Alanna's side, he saw that except for the flesh on the head, only Eric's bones remained. Alanna continued wailing at the sky.

Matthew touched Alanna gently, thinking, *I am deeply sorry for your loss. I know what it is like to lose a child.*

Alanna stopped her wailing, and Matthew heard the self-recrimination in her thoughts. *I told Eric not to go out feeding alone at night, but he felt he was so strong and brave that he could take on a dragon. I should have watched him more closely. A good mother would have done so. That dragon feasted all night on my son, until I came looking for him. When I rose from the water to look on the beach, the dragon stood glaring over his body, and warned me that next time, it would be my daughter. It was the female dragon...the one with the missing eye.*

Matthew could relate to her pain, and could well feel the despondency that filled her. *Just a short time ago, my own family died — my wife, my daughter, and my unborn son. At first, I wanted only to join them in death. Instead of granting my wishes, though, God sent me here, and now I have a wonderful daughter and a new wife, Shalee.*

Alanna lowered her head so close to Matthew's that he unconsciously took a step backward. Momentarily forgetting her own sorrows, she sent him a blunt question: *I have been wanting to ask you: what took you so long with Shalee? Are you just slow? Did Shawn cause you to finally move faster?*

Matthew was quite taken aback. *Alanna, how did you know of this?*

Shalee came down in the early mornings while you were away at war. We would talk, female to female. I told Shalee that when I was carrying Eric inside me, my mate took off through the tunnel with a herd of young females from the vast waters. When they did not return in a few days, first I, then Elizabeth tried to swim the tunnel to the vast waters to look for him. When we had come a long way through the tunnel, we found a boulder blocking our way.

I told Shalee that I suspect my mate pushed this boulder in after his new mates passed through. He loved the vast waters, and longed to be free of the Loch. Elizabeth swam over the boulder to the end of the tunnel, looking for her father, but as she entered the vast waters, she saw the many-legged death coming toward her, and she fled back to me for safety. She never tried again.

My hope had been that Eric and Elizabeth would became full grown, and the three of us together could move the boulder and swim in the vast waters. Now, with Eric dead, so dies my hope of finding another mate in those waters. I have only the hope of revenge to carry me onward. Someday, I will kill that dragon, and I will die happy. With that, Alanna gently lifted Eric's remains and dragged them into the water, with Elizabeth following close behind.

* * *

Matthew stood for several moments alone on the beach, staring out over the waters. Shalee was the first to approach him, and sat down beside him on the soft sand. For quite a while neither of them spoke, as Matthew simmered in the pain of lost loved ones. It was not only his own losses that moved him, but those suffered by Shalee, Kele, Robert, and now Alanna. He felt a wave of anguish for the many sorrows in Scotland, which ran as deep as the waters of Loch Ness, and just as cold.

Then it occurred to him that Alanna said she had talked with Shalee. Turning toward Shalee, he finally spoke. "Alanna told me that you talked to her. I know that she can read all our thoughts, but can you read hers, as well?"

Shalee continued to gaze out over the waters. "One morning, I rose before the sun came up, and I was drawn to the beach. I came here that day and prayed, asking God to guide me in my choice: whether to marry you, or Shawn. This was even before Shawn asked me. As I sat here, deep in prayer, Alanna came up on the beach, and she startled me. She said that she was sorry, and asked what was troubling me.

"I told her of my problem, and she told me how her mate had left, so long ago. We talked until the sun rose, and I walked back to the castle. It was not until after breakfast that I fully realized I had actually communicated with her. It seemed so natural while it was happening. For many mornings thereafter, we would sit together on the beach and talk. She is very lonely without her mate, and she missed you. That is one thing we had in common, but I was the lucky one, for I knew that you would return. And you did." With that Shalee wrapped her arm around Matthew's, and they rose together to walk back to the castle.

* * *

Shalee told Matthew that she thought it would be best to delay their wedding ceremony until the following day. Matthew agreed, for he did not want the memory of his most joyous day tainted with the memory of sadness. "In fact, we can delay it longer, if you think that would be more appropriate," he said. "We are wed in the eyes of God, so we do no harm by putting off the ceremony."

"No, even Alanna will understand that even in the midst of sorrow, ceremonies of happiness must go on," Shalee replied. "That is the way of things around here." Matthew had to agree with her logic. The two of them walked the rest of the way to the castle in silence, filled with the bittersweet thoughts of lives ended, and others just begun. And when they reached the gates, they each went their separate ways, for both had many tasks to accomplish before the morrow.

The next day, the sun rose bright upon a clear sky, as if to share in the celebration of the wedding. The ceremony was an island of solemnity, flanked on all sides with the jubilation that the people felt, seeing their leader pledge his love to Shalee. Tables were set up outside the castle, laden with the finest foods available, and no small measure of ales and other, stronger drink.

Kial was one of the first to arrive, bringing his whole camp to the feast. The minstrels from his clan joined in with those from Matthew's castle to fill the air with sweet melodies that stirred the souls of all who listened. As everyone knows, Pict music is always sensual, even at its most lively tempos.

Shalee and Matthew loosed their passions as they swirled and glided to the beat of this music, until Matthew could rein in his desire no longer. He whisked Shalee up in his arms and raced with her, inside the castle gates. Whether due to his mounting passion, or the exertion of carrying

Shalee in his arms as he ran, Matthew decided to detour to the stables. Since everyone was at the dance outside the castle, he figured that they were safe from being discovered. In an instant, all thought of the revelers outside the castle walls vanished, and soon they were making passionate love in the hay.

After the initial intensity of their passion was quenched, Matthew got the feeling that they were being watched, and began to look around. Across the barn, perched upon a great mound of hay, he spotted an enormous tan tomcat beside Yellow Rose. The cats both looked up at the roof, as if to say, "We didn't see a thing," then scampered off to another corner of the barn, beyond Matthew's sight. Moments later, the barn was filled with the loud cries of the cats' mating. And such was the way of it for several hours: a chorus of passion and merriment that filled the entire castle, spilling out into the fields beyond.

Matthew and Shalee made love again in the hay, and then dozed peacefully in each other's arms. In the late afternoon, with the party still going full force out by the castle, Shalee roused Matthew and said, "Well, my love, I suppose we should rejoin the merrymakers; they might think us rude if we stay away too long from our own festivities."

"You're right," Matthew said. "But why don't you go on ahead, and I'll join you presently. I have an errand to attend to."

"All right, darling, but don't be long," Shalee said, kissing him. She jumped up, straightened her clothes and hair, and ran back in the direction of the gathering.

Matthew headed straight for their room, where he found his knapsack. He picked it up and opened it, taking out the urn with Cate's ashes. Since his arrival in Scotland, he had been putting off the trip to Carn Mhic (and that was, in fact, its name in this time too, though Matthew had nicknamed it "Caitlin's Hill," and the people of the castle had taken to calling it by that name as well). Even though much of his time and energy since he'd gotten here had been devoted to dealing with "situations" — boy, was that an understatement — there had also been plenty of time for him to carry out the mission that had originally brought him to Scotland. Yet he had always found some excuse not to do it. Well, it was time now.

Taking the urn and Glenna's map, he walked out of the castle and into the soft peach glow of the waning day. He didn't really need the map; he had determined months ago that Carn Mhic was only a short walk from the castle. He could get there even faster by horseback, but he felt like walking; it was such a fine afternoon, and the sunset promised to be a glorious one. He slipped past the revelers, and over the path leading into the hills.

Carn Mhic — Caitlin's Hill — was not a very high hill, and he had no trouble scaling it. Once he reached the top, he sat down and breathed in the cool sweet air. Unlike many of the surrounding hills, there were no wildflowers on this one; even so, the place was haunting and lovely, a perfect playground, he thought, for the dreamy child that Cate must have been. He shut his eyes tight, trying to visualize the little dark-haired girl who had run and shouted on this hill, in that long-ago time that was still ten centuries away.

He opened his eyes and beheld a most amazing sunset, and then at last he stood, holding the urn up to the dying light. For a moment he thought he saw a reflection of Cate's face in its smooth surface. Then the image disappeared, and try as he might he could not summon her features again. Was it possible that he had forgotten how she looked? He said a brief prayer aloud in Gaelic, and there were tears in his eyes as he removed the lid from the urn and released its contents into the wind. "Goodbye, Caitlin," he whispered, as the ashes settled over the hillside. "Go with God, my love."

Taking the urn and the map with him, he turned then and descended the hill, walking back through the violet-blue dusk to the life that awaited him.

* * *

For the next two weeks, the farmers toiled at harvesting their crops. Because the yield was so great, Matthew dispatched warriors from the Scottish army to help in the harvest. Every farmer's barn was filled to bursting, and even the houses were used to store the abundance of food. Matthew had the excess stored at his and Robert's castles, and in the vacant dragon caves. The warriors from Kial's camp had never seen such bounty, and looked upon it with envy.

Matthew ordered tables set up at his castle, where the farmers could barter their crops for furs, sheep, cattle, and live and dead game birds. The Picts were truly in their element when it came to trading. The farmers were shrewd traders, and Matthew had to admonish them to be lenient with the Scottish army. The farm families expressed concerns regarding how much of this crop was theirs, and how much was Matthew's.

Matthew told them, "Ten percent of all crops are to be presented as an offering to God, to build churches and feed those who spread His word. The balance will be split evenly between the farmers and myself.

"In exchange for the duty I collect, I will have members of the Scottish army help you plant in the spring, and harvest in the fall. I will pay the Scottish army out of my half, but each farmer will be required to plant four times as much next year as he planted this year." Matthew made it clear that these terms were not negotiable.

At first thought, the farmers felt that their burden was too great, and the duty expected of them too high. As they gazed upon the piles of goods their abundant crops had acquired for them in trade, however, they realized that they were now wealthier than they had ever dreamed. They readily agreed with their leader's terms.

The people in the surrounding lands now looked upon the castle of Matthew Wolverine as a storehouse of plenty. Matthew's people grew bigger and stronger than other Scots, because food was abundant and always shared. Word had long since spread throughout Scotland that a stranger never left Loch Ness but with a full belly. And the smiles of the people let Matthew know that, in their minds, the future of Scotland looked bright, indeed.

So plentiful was the harvest, that all agreed another celebration was in order. Matthew encouraged this, knowing that, even in the hard times that might come in the future, memories of joy and plenty would lift the people's spirits. At his direction, Shalee prepared over one hundred roasted fish, forty sheep, and ten cattle for the feast.

As darkness fell on the night of the grand celebration, bonfires were lit, and the feasting and dancing began. Kial appeared, sporting ten silver armbands that shimmered and clanked merrily as he danced. Every family now owned a share of the dragon treasure, and they displayed it proudly.

As all about him were giving themselves up to the festivities, Robert approached Matthew, a grave look on his face. "There are rumors," he began, "that the southern kingdom is making preparations for an attack."

Matthew brushed him aside. "I appreciate your concern, Robert, and I know we must maintain vigilance against the king of the south. But I know they will not attack at least until spring, and probably not even till summer. Who knows, they may literally have the fear of God in them now, and decide not to attack at all!" He bid Robert not to fret about such things that night, but rather to dance and enjoy himself.

With some reservation at first, Robert joined in the dance. After a few dances — and a few more draughts of ale — he finally began to relax, and soon was laughing and dancing with the abandon of a child who had no cares in the world.

* * *

The merriment went on for many hours. Towards midnight, Shalee slid up beside Matthew and put her arm around his waist. "This is a miracle," she whispered in his ear. "I never thought I would live to see such abundance in this castle. Everyone stores enough food for two winters. Each day, furs stream to Loch Ness from the four corners of the land. I even made a new bedspread out of red fox for Raquelle. She has my old, cold room, but she will sleep very warm under this fine bedspread."

Matthew beamed a smile at her. "You are a good mother, my love."

Sighing mightily, Shalee said, "I hope to be… soon."

Matthew, catching her meaning, smiled even more broadly and replied, "Well, as far as I am concerned… the sooner the better!" Then he swept her up in his arms, and made haste with her to their chambers.

The Ultimate Dragon

Chapter 21

At breakfast the next morning, a castle guard rushed up to Matthew and announced that a group of thirteen Vikings had been sighted approaching the castle gates. What now? Matthew thought wearily. To the guard he said, "If they seek an audience with me, allow them to enter the castle. But they are to be escorted into the dining hall by no less than ten warriors."

The guard left to carry out his orders, leaving Matthew wondering what the visitors had in mind, and whether there might be some treachery afoot. Just as Matthew finished his breakfast, Eric the Red came striding into the dining room, his massive arms thrown wide, and his face filled with a smile that bore no deception. Matthew, enormously relieved, rose and gave Eric a bear hug, wincing when Eric returned the embrace. Eric noticed Matthew's pained grimace, but could also see, in Matthew's smile, that he was happy to see him. Matthew said a silent prayer of thanks that his faith in his friend had been vindicated. He knew the lesson would not be lost on Raquelle or anyone else who had doubted Eric's integrity.

Laughing, Eric said, "How I missed you, Matthew! And now, I want you to meet my son Leif, and Helga, the healer."

Matthew warmly welcomed Leif, and then he turned to the woman. At first glance, Matthew thought her quite fat, but upon closer inspection, saw that she was actually what he would have called "broad of beam," or big-boned. When she took his hand in greeting, he discovered that she was remarkably strong, as her handshake almost broke his hand. He thought to himself, *this is one woman I would not want to meet in a dark alley.* She didn't release his handshake, but reached up with her left hand to Matthew's right shoulder and squeezed. Matthew almost buckled with the pain. Seeing this, she nodded to Eric, as if to confirm some point they had discussed earlier, and released her grip on Matthew. Then, without saying a word, she turned to clear the table. After it was cleared, she turned back toward Matthew and boomed, "Eric the Red brought me

223

here because I am well known for my healing skills. If you will allow it, I can heal your pain. Will you take off your shirt and get up on the table?"

Even though she had phrased her request politely, Matthew could tell that this woman was accustomed to being obeyed, and figured that she had probably tempered her speech at Eric's suggestion. Even in her politeness, she still spoke with the authority of a medical doctor, and Matthew found himself instinctively obeying her. Stripped to the waist, he climbed stiffly up onto the table and lay down, crossing his arms under his chin. Helga immediately began to press her palms deeply into Matthew's back muscles, causing him to groan in pain. The castle guards looked curiously at each other, and reached for their swords. Matthew saw this, and raised his hand to stop them. As her fingers kneaded Matthew's shoulder muscles, Helga bellowed, "You hurt very much, I must go deeper to heal you."

Matthew grabbed the side of the table, his grip tightening until his knuckles turned white, and held his death-grip as Helga worked every muscle, from the top of his head to the soles of his feet, using not just her palms, but her beefy elbows as well. To Matthew, this felt like he imagined it would feel to be beaten for an hour with a baseball bat. By this time, everyone in the castle had come into the dining hall to witness their leader's trial. Helga finally slapped Matthew on his bottom and proclaimed that he was finished for the day.

Matthew slowly rose from the table, drew his sword, and began swinging it over his head. To his surprise and delight, he felt no pain, and his movements were as smooth as silk. He sheathed the sword and turned to Helga. "Woman, you truly have the gift of healing." Observing Kele unconsciously rubbing his back, Matthew said, "Kele, you have some back pain, as well. Come over here and have Helga work on you."

Kele turned pale, and looked for a quick escape, but Helga quickly grabbed him by the shirt, ordering him to take it off and get on the table. Reluctantly, Kele took off his shirt, and Helga went to work on him. Kele let out one very loud groan, and Helga let out a laugh. "I haven't even begun with you yet. Groan again, and I will really go deeper." Kele gripped the table so hard that both his hands turned white, as she continued to work on him. Helga may have lacked finesse, but she made up for it in skill, her powerful strokes driving the poisons out of Kele's muscles. After about twenty minutes of this knuckle-whitening torture, Kele got up, a broad smile on his face. Bending over to touch his toes, he laughed out loud, proclaiming that he was completely free of pain, and that she truly was a healer.

After that, Matthew had his castle guards line up for massages, and told Helga that he would pay her one Scottish Cross for every fifteen persons she massaged. He knew that his army must be healthy for the campaigns that would be waged in the spring, and figured that Helga's ministrations would be of great benefit to them.

"What is a Scottish Cross?" Helga asked, obviously not terribly impressed. Matthew took one from his pocket, handed it to her, and told her that this was her pay for this day. "And you will receive one Scottish Cross on each day that you work your healing magic on fifteen of my warriors." Helga looked lustfully at the shimmering coin, nodded her head, and then slipped the coin into the folds of her ample bosom. Her demeanor was as stern as ever, but it was obvious when she returned to her work that she did so with renewed enthusiasm, massaging even more deeply on the poor guard who had the misfortune of being on her table at that moment.

* * *

Out of the corner of his eye, Matthew noticed the other Vikings, standing quietly to the side in a straight row, cloaked in leather from head to toe. He quickly counted. Ten of them, and not one had uttered a word so far. They didn't seem to pose any threat, but it would be best to know who they were, and so far Eric had volunteered nothing. "Who are these warriors?" Matthew asked, pointing at the taciturn Vikings.

"Ah, I thought you'd never ask!" Eric replied, grinning, and he turned to them and motioned for them to uncloak. As each cloak dropped, it revealed a stunning Viking beauty with long lustrous blonde hair. The women were clothed, though only marginally so, in body-tight doeskin. And they were just as Matthew had fantasized and described on that ill-fated voyage with Eric — in other words, they were drop-dead gorgeous. Eric motioned for Matthew to inspect each of them, and Matthew prayed that he wouldn't slobber all over them. Eric boasted, "These are all virgins! I had Helga check them. It is not good for you to sleep alone, so choose one for your mate….or take them all."

Matthew swallowed hard, and from the corner of his eye he saw Shalee, her face flushed with anger, and her fists clenched. Matthew drank in their beauty, and his mind raced. *Where and how did Eric get these beauties? If it weren't for a watching God and the vows I made to Shalee, I would have an orgy with these women for months on end.* Then reason entered his mind. *If I don't turn this to my advantage, I can forget sleeping and making love with my wife.*

An idea flashed into his mind. "Eric, you have not heard that I have married the beautiful Shalee, who brings me both pleasure and wisdom. Your own wisdom in bringing these alluring Viking women to inspire our warriors to greater acts of valor is brilliant. Only our bravest warriors may court these women, but each woman shall have the right to say no to a marriage proposal." He did not even have to look in Shalee's direction; he could tell by the very feel in the air that her anger had dissipated.

Turning to the women, he continued, "You Viking women must treat my warriors with respect, but remember that you have a choice, and you must choose only the one warrior who you feel will make you happy for the rest of your life. But before you choose, you must accept my God as your God, and He will bless your union."

There was a moment of hesitation, and then the smallest woman in the group stepped forward. "Your God gives us the right to choose our own husband — and to be happy?"

Matthew chuckled. "Aye, so choose wisely. Now, shall I expect my brother in God to present these fetching women free of charge? No, each warrior who wins the hand of one of these Viking women must pay Eric one Scottish Cross, one silver necklace, and ten of his best sheep as payment for her transport to Scotland."

The ten women eagerly agreed to Matthew's proposal, and accepted his God. Eric was beaming. Then Helga stepped forward again. Addressing Eric, she said, "Please make these young women available as needed for the treatment of Matthew Wolverine's back. I am going to have my hands full tending to all of the warriors. All of these women are adept at the art of massage, as they have already proven by working on your back."

Helga then noticed Shalee's hateful stare, and looked back at Eric. "Matthew's wife can be present if she wishes, to insure no mating takes place."

Shalee could take no more, and bolted for the bedroom. Matthew excused himself and hurried after her. He found her sobbing on the lambskin bedspread. If there is one scene every man hates, it is to enter his bedroom to discover his wife, in tears, on the bed. When Matthew silently entered the room, Shalee sat up in the bed and shouted, "If you want those beauties, take them!"

Matthew sat down on the side of the bed and smiled at Shalee. "It is good to have such an understanding wife. They are very beautiful. They could offer me incredible pleasure."

Like a cobra rising to strike, Shalee shot up. "So you *are* planning to mate with them?"

A broad smile crossed Matthew's face as he reviewed the facts. "You offer them to me! Do you think I would not accept such an offer? They possess enticing, seductively clothed bodies, lustrous blonde hair, and velvety skin that would be heaven to touch. I admit, all this does ignite my amorous nature. I have only one problem."

Shalee's head fell to her chest as tears streamed down her face. "You have no problem, Matthew. I will still love you after you mate with them, and I will share your bed when you want me. Do you wish me to find another bedroom for myself?"

Matthew reached his hands behind Shalee's head to gently clasp two handfuls of her hair. "No, my problem is one you fail to recognize. Yours is the only body I want to caress at night. When I waken in the mornings, I want to look into only your eyes. Last, but hardly least, yours is the only womb I want my sons and daughters to spring from. I am a man, and will, perhaps, be tempted, because I love to look at beautiful women. But know for a certainty that you are my one true mate. Never will I let another woman come between us."

Shalee wiped away her tears, and asked Matthew if all men from his own time were like him. Matthew shook his head. "Too many are like I once was, too busy chasing wealth to realize what is really important until it is lost to us. God gave me a second chance, and I will not lose you, because you are my real treasure."

Shalee buried her head in Matthew's chest, her tears still streaming, but now from relief and joy. "Please, my love, just hold me for awhile." And they sat in silence for a long while, Matthew tenderly holding Shalee, caressing her hair with his fingertips, filled with adoration for this beautiful woman who was so strong, and yet so fragile. Their shared passion in those moments was expressed in stillness, and in their mere presence with each other. When they finally made love, they did so on a level that reached far beyond their bodies.

* * *

After several hours had passed, Raquelle appeared at her father's and mother's bedroom door. From the hallway, she called out, "I am placing hot food beside the door. With all your lovemaking, I will have at least twelve brothers and sisters. Mother, thank you for the fox bedspread. I showed it to the Viking women, and they consider you a wonderful woman to give such a luxurious gift to a daughter. They cannot wait to talk to you at the evening meal. I love you both." Matthew and Shalee called out their thanks and their love, and Raquelle turned and went out into the courtyard.

Matthew rose to fetch the food Raquelle had brought, and he and Shalee took the light meal at their leisure, talking aimlessly about things both important and nonsensical. It did not matter to them what they spoke of, but only that they were there, together, with no walls of doubt between them. Between their words flowed a love and a trust that filled them more completely than any meal. Long after the food was gone, and all the words that needed saying had been spoken, they finally rose to dress for the evening meal. With laughter in their hearts, they emerged from their chambers and found their way to the dining hall.

A grand new table with many new chairs had finally been finished, and nearly filled the hall. Raquelle had busied herself with the task of rearranging the dining room and making the seating arrangements for all the guests. Matthew was seated in the middle of the table with Eric, Leif, and Helga sitting directly across from him. Shalee sat on Matthew's right, and Raquelle on his left. The young Viking women sat five to the right of Eric, and five to the left of Helga. After Matthew blessed the food, the meal began.

Matthew first directed his attention to Leif, asking him how he liked sailing on the North Sea. It was obvious from the boy's animated response that he was passionate about sailing. He went on to thank Matthew for saving his father from the *Kraken*. Leif pulled at a chain he wore around his neck, drawing it outside of his shirt. Dangling from the chain was a *Kraken's* claw. Leif's chest swelled as he said, "These claws have made my father a legend among our people. He traded most of these claws at our village for ten ships. The treasure he brought home is being spent constructing a very large castle for us. Father bragged on the piles of dragon treasure stored by Matthew Wolverine, and lamented that such a great man had no wife to keep him warm at night. Word spread quickly, and we had hoards of pretty ladies descending on our village to sail to Scotland and warm Matthew Wolverine's bed at night. My father picked the prettiest, and dressed them in our finest doeskins. He said it was to get the attention of Matthew Wolverine. Tell me truly, did they get your attention?"

Matthew liked this child's artlessness and straightforwardness, but felt, in light of his earlier exchanges with his wife, that this was a subject best not pursued. He hesitatingly acknowledged that they did, indeed, get his attention, looking out of the corner of his eye all the while to see Shalee's reaction. But she was smiling placidly, and hers was the smile of a woman who knows, beyond all doubt, that she is truly cherished. Matthew said another silent prayer of thanks.

* * *

The next morning Matthew rose before sunrise, slipped out of bed, and headed for the beach. He had seen precious little of Alanna since Eric's death, and it worried him. He knew that grief can kill. Grief unbridled can rob the bereaved of all will to live — didn't he know that firsthand! — and it did not limit its insidious work to the human heart. Hadn't he read a newspaper article, back in his own time, about a zoo elephant who had literally lain down and succumbed to sorrow after its cellmate had died?

As he walked along the beach, he turned a bend and saw Elizabeth, Alanna's surviving child, in the shallows. She had been waiting for him.

Elizabeth wasted no time on greetings or small talk; instead she blurted out — inasmuch as a thought could be considered "blurting" — that her mother was miserable.

Matthew's thoughts and sympathy went out to her. *I can understand that*, he communicated. *Your mother has suffered a terrible, terrible loss. I have been worried about her, because I've not seen her around here since Eric's death. Where has she been hiding herself?*

Elizabeth's thoughts shot back to him: *She spends most of her time in that tunnel that leads to the North Sea, still trying to move that giant boulder that is blocking the way. That boulder, and revenge on the dragon that killed my brother, are all my mother ever talks about! I am so lonely, and I'm bored too. She acts like she's forgotten all about me. It isn't fair!*

Elizabeth lowered her face to the ground, and Matthew communicated, *She hasn't forgotten you. She still loves you very much, and so do I.* He stroked her head and neck as he sent his thoughts to her. The touch of another is important to all of us, and Elizabeth was obviously starving for touch. She drank in all of the affection that Matthew offered. Without even thinking, he began to massage her head and neck. After about a half hour of this, his hands were truly beginning to ache, and he had new respect for Helga and her Viking-virgin assistants. Still he kept on caressing her.

Leif Ericson emerged from around the bend and stood for awhile in hushed amazement at the sight of Matthew massaging this odd-looking beast. All of his life Leif had heard tell of Scotland's loch monsters, and, of course, he had heard about how Matthew had tamed the monsters. And how here was proof. It was obvious this creature was just a baby, but even so, she was huge and fearsome looking. Matthew looked up and motioned the boy to come over and take a turn at massaging Elizabeth. Leif hesitated but a moment, then raced over and began to massage with gusto.

Leif spoke aloud to Elizabeth, telling her how beautiful her skin looked. "And I hear that you can fly through the water," he said. "I wish I could do that."

Suddenly Leif grew silent. "It's like she's talking to me and I can hear her... but I am not hearing it with my ears!" he exclaimed. "She's *thinking* at me. She is telling me that after she and her mother chase the fish ashore today, I can go for a ride on her back. Do you hear her, Matthew?"

Matthew said, "Yes, Elizabeth and I have learned to read each other's thoughts. That is how we communicate, and that's how I communicate with her mother too. Not just anybody can communicate with the lake guardians. This makes you very special."

Ecstatic, Leif rubbed harder, and he and Elizabeth continued their silent exchange for several minutes. Matthew sent his thoughts to Elizabeth: *How did you know you could make him understand you?* She thought back, *I just knew I could, and so I did. And I was right, wasn't I?* Matthew sensed that some of Elizabeth's playful spirit was returning, and he was grateful for Leif's presence. *Kids will be kids*, Matthew thought, *and they have a way of understanding each other, even if one of them is human and the other happens to weigh several hundred pounds and has an advanced case of fish-breath.*

Finally Elizabeth told them, somewhat reluctantly, that she had to get back to her mother. *Go with God, Elizabeth*, Matthew thought to her. *And please tell your mother we love her and miss her.* Elizabeth said she would do so, and into the water she disappeared.

* * *

Matthew and Leif talked as they walked back to the castle. "I plan on visiting with Elizabeth every morning, Leif, and you are welcome to join us," he said.

"I'll be there!" Leif said enthusiastically.

Then Matthew changed the subject. "Leif, tell me, are you brave enough to sail into unknown waters?"

"Brave? I am the son of Eric the Red, and I will be as brave as my father someday!"

"Then I want to tell you about a land that even your father hasn't seen, nor have any of your people yet seen it. It lies far to the west, and has an abundance of food and water. There are lakes and rivers and pure streams, green valleys and enormous mountains and vast deep forests, wild beasts of every description, and birds that when they fly they blot out the sun. Would you someday like to discover such a land?"

Leif laughed. "This is every Viking's dream!"

"Well, then, come with me," Matthew said as they entered the castle. He took the boy to a tiny room just off the courtyard. Inside was a small table and two chairs. Matthew took a book that was hidden in the wall, and placed it in the middle of the table. Leif sat down and gazed in awe at the brightly colored book.

"Before you look at this book," Matthew said, "you must take an oath."

Leif cocked his head. "What type of oath?"

"Do you remember that land I was just describing?" Matthew asked, and Leif nodded. "It is a land that has been truly touched by God with plenty. But there are people there already — a noble people who roam this vast land, and never take more than they need from it. If you will take an oath not to cheat, lie, or conquer these people, but to show them only kindness and fairly trade with them, I will show you how to sail to their land."

Without a moment's hesitation, Leif agreed, his eyes shining with eagerness. Matthew opened the book and pointed to the northern United States. "You must sail west, past Scotland, and then southwest to reach this land," said Matthew.

Bewilderment covered Leif's face as he began to comprehend the vastness of the lands to the west. Matthew continued, "I give you my permission to study this book any time you wish, but remember this: if you share this information with other Vikings, then they will go to this land before you. So if you want to be the first Viking to see it, you must guard this secret." Leif, being a true Viking, vowed to keep this information secret even from his father. "I will be the first Viking to set foot in this new land," he declared. Matthew closed the book, and off they went to breakfast.

Matthew had mixed emotions as he ate breakfast. He had not done anything that would change history, though in a way he wished he could. Not many years hence, Leif would land on the North American coast, and, as far as Matthew knew, he would be fair with the native people. Those who were to come after Leif were the ones that Matthew worried about. But there wasn't much he could do about them. *I suppose if God had really wanted me to change history, He might have sent me back to 1492,* Matthew mused to himself. This thought was followed by another, and there was no getting around it: without the European explorers — or exploiters, depending upon your point of view — there never would have been a United States of America. *No matter what the time or place, tradeoffs are hell*, Matthew thought. *Somebody always has to lose.*

* * *

The weeks passed, the days grew shorter, and the air took on a bitter chilly edge. It was time to make preparations for Christmas. This was not, however, a season of unadulterated joy for Matthew and Shalee. Shalee was not herself these days. She was terribly tired much of the time, and frequently nauseated. She was throwing up every morning, and was often "not in the mood" for lovemaking. At first Matthew thought it might be the food... but of course it wasn't.

"I am with child," Shalee finally told him one evening, a fortnight before Christmas. Matthew was ecstatic, no doubt about it. Perhaps this child would be the longed-for son. There was still one big problem, though: he hungered for Shalee, whereas it seemed that sex was the last thing on her mind lately. It didn't help that the place was overrun with those stunning blonde Viking women, any of whom would have gladly lavished her therapeutic skills on the lord of the castle.

Christmas finally arrived, and many gifts were exchanged. Music, parties, and lavish feasts blossomed every weekend in Matthew's and Shalee's castle. The winter was a mild one, or so everybody kept saying, but to Matthew it was anything but mild. He was continually cold, and still suffered residual aches and pains from the *Kraken* attack. Helga kept urging him to take advantage of the therapy offered by her young blonde accomplices, but Matthew didn't think that was such a good idea. The last thing he needed was more temptation, especially given his present state of sexual deprivation.

Life has a way of offering up compensations, however, and during this time of diminished sexual activity Matthew's friendship with Shalee became even deeper and sweeter. In fact, the dark winter months worked their subtle magic on everyone in the castle. The deep snows and confinement caused everyone to become closer, and the relationships among Matthew, Shalee, Raquelle, Leif and Eric evolved into solid bonds of friendship.

The New Year came and went; they were two weeks into the year 1000 before someone mentioned that the millennium had turned with no sign of the end of the world, or the Second Coming, or anything remotely apocalyptic. By now most of the inhabitants of the castle were longing passionately for the end — of winter, that is, which, from their perspective, seemed endless.

Spring finally arrived, as it eventually always does, and nobody was happier than Matthew. Shalee now looked as if she had swallowed a basketball. It had not been an easy pregnancy; she was still sick much of the time. Matthew was climbing the walls, but hoped he was playing the part of the patient and understanding husband well enough. Despite all of his hard-learned lessons, he still found patience a challenge.

On the first reasonably warm morning, Matthew, in a burst of spring fever, raced to the beach with his heating towel in hand. Elizabeth was waiting for him, but there was still no Alanna in sight. Dropping the towel, Matthew dove into the water. It was liquid ice. *Nothing like a cold shower to get my mind off Shalee*, Matthew thought grimly. Elizabeth immediately plunged into the water after him, and Matthew climbed on her back, grabbing two handfuls of flesh. One flex of his knees sent her jetting through the water. After a few moments, the spring sunlight began to warm his winter-weary bones, and before long he was able to relax and truly enjoy the ride. Suddenly he found himself nearly overwhelmed by…everything!…the beauty of this splendid morning, the thrill of flying through the water on the back of this magnificent beast, the joy of knowing that the love of his life was a few weeks away from bearing his child. Clenching his legs tighter around Elizabeth's sides, he let go of his death-grip around her neck, raising his arms to the heavens in praise and thanks.

But his mother had always taught him to share, and there were others waiting for their turn. After a few minutes, Matthew leaned to the left — Elizabeth's signal to turn and head back to shore. Their arrival found Raquelle and Leif arguing about who would get the next ride. *Typical kids*, Matthew thought to himself, smiling, still giddy with the wonder that his life had become.

Matthew dismounted and gave Elizabeth a big hug and a kiss. Her tongue shot out in a joyful return of that kiss. *Fish-breath, indeed!* Matthew thought, before he remembered that Elizabeth could read his thoughts. But there was no problem; she took it as a compliment. Matthew turned and pointed to Leif, and said, "Your turn, my boy. Hit it!" Overjoyed, Leif catapulted himself upon Elizabeth's back, and off they jetted.

Raquelle, bringing her father his towel, asked why Leif got to go first. "Leif is our guest," Matthew explained. "Besides, he is still a child, while you are transforming into a woman." At that Raquelle blushed. She was, indeed, becoming a woman. Her chest had begun to develop, and she had recently experienced her first time of bleeding. That was not something she felt comfortable discussing with her father, even though they had always been able to speak candidly about nearly anything. Thank God that she now had Shalee to confide in as well.

These days there were many subjects that gave Raquelle pause when it came to her father. But something had been weighing heavily on her mind. She felt the growing tension between her father and mother as Shalee's birthing time grew nearer, and she sensed how the presence of the Viking women somehow exacerbated that tension. Standing on the beach now, shifting uncomfortably from one foot to the other, Raquelle finally could stand it no more, and she blurted out, "Father, if you had not already been married to Shalee, would you have married a Viking beauty? They all… well, they all have larger chests then Shalee."

Alas, neither father nor daughter heard Shalee approaching. Shalee froze at Raquelle's words. She gazed down at her own relatively modest chest and enormous belly, overcome with the fear that had been welling up inside her the past few weeks. Would she never again be attractive in the eyes of her husband? Tears blurred her eyes, and she wanted to run away, but she had to hear Matthew's reply to their daughter's blunt question.

For his part, Matthew was taken aback only momentarily by Raquelle's forthrightness. She really was becoming a woman, and she missed nothing. "First of all," he began, knowing he was treading in that place where fathers fear to go, "there is more to a woman than the size of her chest. Don't ever let any man convince you otherwise. Shalee has — and is — everything I have ever wanted in a woman. She has beauty and grace and a caring heart. And she loves me with all her heart. The Viking beauties are pleasing to the eye, but they do not stir my soul. Shalee is my soul mate, Raquelle, and she is worth more to me than all the dragon treasure in Scotland. My prayer for you is that you will someday find a man who treasures you the way I do Shalee."

If it had been a thousand-odd years in the future, and Matthew had been a contestant on the game show known as "Family Feud," his teammates would have rallied around him and said, "Good answer!" That was, indeed, the best answer he could possibly have given, particularly since he didn't know that Shalee was listening in. Her tears came in earnest now, but they were happy tears. She cried a lot these days, it seemed. Hastily wiping her eyes, she stepped forward and made her presence known to her husband and daughter, and the three of them put their arms around each other, watching in contented silence as Leif and Elizabeth cavorted in the distance.

Suddenly Leif slid off Elizabeth's back, landing in the icy loch with a loud splash and disappearing beneath the surface. Matthew and Raquelle were up like a shot, plunging into the water to rescue Leif. But as they swam toward Elizabeth, a large wave pushed them off course. In the midst of their struggle to re-orient themselves, they saw Elizabeth speeding to shore with Leif on her back, apparently none the worse for wear. As Elizabeth beached herself, Leif slid off, turning to point and laugh at his would-be rescuers.

"I really gave all of you a fright, didn't I?" he shouted exuberantly to Shalee as she grabbed the boy and enfolded the heating towel around his shoulders. She shook her head in mingled exasperation and relief as Matthew and Raquelle angrily swam to shore. Shalee knew that her husband and daughter would not be nearly as gentle with Leif as she. Emerging from the water, Raquelle verbally tore into Leif for his foolish prank. Matthew held back, knowing he needed to get the whole story before he dealt with the boy.

What happened? he asked Elizabeth.

I don't know, she communicated back. *One minute we were gliding along, and then Leif just seemed to release his grip, and he plunged off my back. I was frightened. I feared he would drown or freeze in that icy water. I immediately turned and went under to find him. Then Leif suddenly surfaced, laughing, and climbed back on my back and told me to go back to shore.*

Matthew turned to Leif. "Explain your actions," he said sternly.

Leif shrugged and said, "I thought it would be fun to have you and Raquelle swim out to save me, like you did for my father. I did not mean any harm; it was only a game!"

"Do I need to remind you, Leif, that your father was being towed to his death by a *Kraken*? That was no game; he and I very nearly lost our lives, and I almost became crippled as a result. I certainly didn't enjoy fighting the *Kraken*, but your father needed my help. You, on the other hand, did not need help. This act was not funny. Now go back to the castle, and tell your father what you have done." Then Matthew turned to Elizabeth and loudly proclaimed to her, "Leif is not to ride on you ever again." Leif dropped his eyes to the ground and set off in the direction of the castle, completely subdued. His joke was not very funny any more.

* * *

Shalee had said nothing throughout this exchange, and Matthew turned to her now. "How are you this morning, my love?" he asked. "I notice the color is back in your cheeks. Were you not sick this morning?" A glimmer of hope arose within him...maybe they could make love today!

Shalee shook her head. "No, for the first morning in a long time, I was not sick. I am feeling a little better. Even so…" and her voice trailed off as she looked at her protruding stomach. Then she looked up at him. "Matthew, I overheard Raquelle's question about the Viking women… and I heard your answer to her. Your words made my heart glad. I had been so fearful that you would no longer find me beautiful."

"Shalee, you have never looked more beautiful to me!" Matthew whispered fiercely, drawing her closer to him. Raquelle was standing a short distance away now, pretending to be absorbed in something out on the loch, when in fact she was listening intently to her parents' conversation. A big grin spread across her face.

Shalee said, "I haven't really said good morning to Raquelle yet. Let me go do so, and I will be right back." She wandered off towards the edge of the shore to join Raquelle, and Matthew turned back to Elizabeth. Elizabeth conveyed to him, *Why is Shalee's stomach so big?* Matthew was glad Shalee couldn't hear that question.

Shalee bears my child, he conveyed, *and before long a baby will be born.*

Elizabeth's large awkward body began shaking from side to side, and it struck Matthew that she was doing a little dance right there on the beach. She was obviously very pleased and excited.

Then Elizabeth asked, *May I listen the baby's heart, please?*

Well, why don't we ask Shalee? Matthew replied.

He summoned Shalee over to them, relaying Elizabeth's request. Shalee was delighted. Elizabeth lowered her huge head against Shalee's belly, and Shalee pulled her closer, gently clutching the beast's skin. Elizabeth closed her eyes and seemed to smile as the sound of the strong heartbeat traveled through her entire being. Her sensitive ears detected a gentle whooshing sound as the baby moved about in its warm interior ocean, and she conveyed to Matthew her wonderment that humans had water inside so their babies could swim. *That is very wise,* she thought to him. Just then the baby kicked violently, startling Elizabeth into abruptly raising her head. Shalee was carried off the ground with her, and Matthew quickly grabbed her legs so she didn't fall. Shalee released her grip on Elizabeth's head and Matthew set her down.

Elizabeth's thoughts shot out to Matthew: *You have a strong male child in there, and he has a powerful kick!*

How do you know it is a male? Matthew asked.

Elizabeth conveyed, *I just know. I am not sure how I know, but I feel it very strongly. Will you name this male child Eric, after my dead brother? I miss him so much.*

Aloud, Matthew asked Shalee and Raquelle, "What do the two of you think about the name 'Eric' if this child be male?" Looking at Elizabeth and then back at Matthew, Shalee and Raquelle nodded enthusiastically. Then all three of them — Matthew, Shalee and Raquelle — turned to Elizabeth and began to stroke her, soothing her in her loneliness.

After a while Elizabeth communicated to Matthew that she needed to get back into the water. As she slid below the surface, Matthew placed an arm around the waists of his two women, and the three slowly walked to the castle. The child in Shalee's womb shifted and then settled peacefully, as if secure that all was well in the vast world beyond its tranquil sea.

* * *

But all is never well in a world where there are dragons and those who worship dragons. Indeed, for the past several months, even the most peaceful and happy moments at the castle had been marked by a menacing undertone that seemed to grow stronger as the snows began to melt. A tempest was brewing among the remaining enclaves of dragon worshippers — men who had grown restive and more dangerous from months of confinement — and that tempest was nurtured within the dank caverns where the dragons themselves were stirring from their long winter sleep. True, there were not many dragons left in Scotland; the efforts of Matthew and his warriors had thinned the population down to only about fifty of the beasts — but these were the biggest and fiercest of the lot, and, whether through instinct or intelligence, they were well aware of who was behind the movement to eradicate them. None of this bode well for Matthew and his entourage. With the first quickening of spring there came a renewed energy among the forces that sought revenge on the interloper who seemed so bent on destroying them in the name of his God and a free Scotland.

Eric was standing at the castle gate as Matthew and his family strolled up after their morning on the shore. Matthew expected a confrontation over Leif, but that was not what was on Eric's mind. As they entered the gate, Eric wasted no time.

"I want to build ships to sail in Loch Ness," he said to Matthew. "It is time. With ships, we can transport troops swiftly to the south when needed, and after a battle we can transport them back to your castle."

Matthew was impressed with Eric's plan. Not only was it good strategy, but his intuition told him that his friend's sudden urge to build more ships was particularly prescient. "I will dispatch one hundred warriors to cut trees and help on the building of these ships," he assured Eric. He immediately summoned some of his swiftest messengers and sent them on their way to begin the recruitment. Then he turned back to Eric. "And now, we eat! I have worked up quite an appetite out there on the loch."

Eric nodded and said, "I am sorry that my son gave you such grief. He told me what he did, and you have my word, as well as his, that he will never pull such a trick again."

The Ultimate Dragon

After a full breakfast, Matthew and Eric conferred about the ships, and then Matthew sent the latter off to get the project underway. There was tension in the air now, no mistaking it. Something big was coming, and he needed to be ready. It was high time he met with Robert Roybridge and Kial. He sent messengers, ordering the two warriors immediately to his castle.

But Robert arrived soon after the messengers had been dispatched — too soon for them to have reached him. It was obvious he had come of his own volition. Matthew took him to a small room and closed the door. With a grim expression on his face, Robert said to Matthew, "I have heard word that the king of the south will invade at the beginning of July. A breach is now being cut in Hadrian's Wall for the army of the south to march into Scotland. Many dragons have massed to the south as well, and it is rumored that the king of the south has a pact with them."

"And what is the nature of this pact?" Matthew asked, fearing that he knew the answer.

"To destroy you, my lord, and to occupy Scotland. The word from the south is that the day Matthew Wolverine dies is the day that Scotland falls forever under the rule of the dragons and their worshippers."

CHAPTER 22

Matthew dropped his face into his hands when he heard Robert's words. The news was hardly surprising — in fact, it was inevitable, wasn't it? — but that didn't make it any less disturbing. Now the inevitability had a time and a place attached to it, making it all the more real. Well, at least now Matthew had a better basis for planning his strategy. When he looked up, he said, "Robert, are you positive about this invasion?"

Robert was adamant. "Yes, as certain as ever I've been about anything."

"Well, thank the Lord we already have a plan underway," Matthew said. He told Robert about Eric's shipbuilding project. "I also have plans for Kial to take most of the Scottish army north on a secret mission," he added. "I have sent for him, and will explain this mission to him when he arrives.

"Here is what I need you to do, Robert. A whole new army must be raised from the people to the south, from Ireland, and from the Vikings," Matthew said. "As people come to trade at Loch Ness, we will use the dragon treasure to entice them to join the Scottish army. We will ask that they remain with us only until harvest. Robert, I want you to travel east to the North Sea, and recruit warriors. Then return here before the end of May and prepare to march south."

Robert said only, "I understand. It will be done." He rose to leave, and Matthew said softly, "Go with God, my friend."

Kial arrived as Robert was leaving, and Matthew took him into the same small room. First he gave him the bad news about the planned invasion in July. Kial instinctively reached to touch the handle of his sword, and he said with gritted teeth, "They do not stand a chance against us! What would you have me do?"

Matthew said, "Kial, yours is a very crucial role. I want you to herd all of the swine in Scotland — wild and domestic alike — and, when the time comes, you must drive them through the breach in Hadrian's wall and into the southern hinterlands. You are to use the Scottish army to help you."

Kial immediately became very distressed. "But you are asking me to give up what I love most! Must I sacrifice all of my own pigs as well? Even that sow that you presented to me as a gift when you first took control of Damian's castle?"

"Kial, you must listen to me. Your cooperation is very important to my plan. And the plan is, in turn, very important not only to me, but to Scotland." What he didn't elaborate upon was the fact that if Kial and all of the other allies did not embrace the plan with all their hearts, eventually the dragons and dragon worshippers would prevail, and Matthew, as the main target of their wrath, would certainly die. And now that his life had been blessed with a beautiful wife and a loving daughter — and another child on the way — Matthew wanted passionately to live. Kial's face, however, still wore a look of belligerence. Matthew thought fast. He decided it was time for the hard sell.

Without missing a beat, he said, "Kial, I know that I am asking you to sacrifice much, but my God knows that you are the only man in Scotland who could accomplish such a feat. He has commanded me to reward you with five armloads of silver armbands. A wagon awaits you in the courtyard to carry you and your treasure back to your camp. Now we go to my treasure room, where a large pile of silver armbands awaits you."

Kial thought a moment, then grabbed Matthew's hand and began to shake it exuberantly. "God is so wise. All right, you have my word on it: this task will be accomplished. You did say five armfuls, did you not?"

Matthew nodded his head and headed towards the treasure room, with Kial rushing ahead of him. They entered the room and Kial's eyes lit up as he spied a large pile of silver. He instantly placed eight armbands on each arm, and then grabbed such a large load that Matthew feared he would rupture a disc in his back. But Kial staggered to the wagon that, as promised, awaited him. He dropped the load into the wagon, removed the armbands on his arms, and bolted back to the treasure room. Matthew grinned as he watched. When Kial, sweaty and exhausted, had finally deposited the fifth armload, he crawled in among the silver armbands as if upon a soft bed. Then he looked up at Matthew, standing beside the wagon, and he laughed and shouted, "Swear to me that you will bury me among a bed of my silver armbands!"

"If I still live when that time comes, it shall be done," Matthew said amiably. "Now go make good on your promise. Go with God, Kial." The driver shouted to the horses and the wagon made its slow, lumbering way out of the castle toward Kial's camp. Passersby shook their heads or stopped to gawk at the spectacle of a rapturous Kial, rolling in a wagon bed full of silver armbands. Matthew was amused, but even more than that, he was relieved. A very tricky part of his master plan had been put into play.

Matthew next walked to the area where Eric's men had begun hauling wood to build the ships. Dozens of men had already been recruited for the task, and word was spreading fast. Eric stopped work when he saw Matthew approaching. Wasting no time on small talk, Matthew informed him of the coming invasion of the south kingdom. "Your shipbuilding campaign began not a moment too soon," Matthew told Eric. "Robert has just told me that when July begins the army of the south will invade, with the dragons as their allies. I need these ships completed before then." Placing his right hand on Eric's shoulder, Matthew continued, "My life, not to mention the freedom of Scotland, depend upon your actions. And if you succeed, then not only I, but all of Scotland, will always hold a warm place for you within our hearts. After these ships are built, I want you to return to the Viking lands for your ten ships, and fill them with all of the ferocious fighting Vikings you can find. Then unite with me at Hadrian's Wall by the end of June."

Eric's eyes narrowed and he looked off in the distance, lost in thought for a few moments. Then he asked, "Will you fill my ship with dragon treasure that I can use to recruit this army?" Matthew nodded and replied, "Of course." That was all Eric needed to hear, and he returned to his work, all smiles.

* * *

Somewhat reassured but still deeply troubled, Matthew turned to walk back to the castle. Far ahead at the castle gate he spied Shalee and Raquelle, supervising the daily fish trading. Even in her advanced state of pregnancy, Shalee handled more than her share of trading each day. Matthew was very proud of her, but also quite worried. Looking at his pregnant wife, he silently implored his God.

Lord, my son is due in July. And I wish more than anything to be home for the birth. I was not there for Rachel's birth — I just had to close that deal in Hong Kong — and Cate never forgave me. I have never forgiven myself. Please let me be by Shalee's side to see my son come into the world.

And Lord, I pray that this is to be my last war. You above all know that I have never enjoyed killing, and You also know how profoundly I regret that carnage seems to be the inevitable price of freedom.

Please protect my beloved Shalee, Raquelle, my soldiers, and me through the battle to come, and may we be able to welcome my son into a world of peace.

As Matthew was walking toward the castle deep in prayerful thought, a group of warriors crested the hill. They headed straight for the castle, and Matthew, spotting them, quickened his steps. The warriors reached the outside of the castle before he did, however, and one of them approached Shalee and engaged her in conversation. Drawing near, Matthew saw that the audacious one was Shawn O'Conner, and there were angry words coming from the Irishman's mouth. Matthew heard most of them, for Shawn did not bother to keep his voice down.

"I told you I would be back for you, Shalee! I heard some nonsense about you marrying Matthew Wolverine, but I did not believe it. Even as I speak, my stonemasons are constructing a new castle for you and me. I have an army now of five hundred warriors, and they are prepared to march on this castle and take you by force. I have only to give the order."

The old Matthew would have been ready to punch his erstwhile rival's lights out at these words. Things were different now. It would be worse than foolish for Matthew to pass up the opportunity to form an alliance with a man who had an army of five hundred. As he made his final approach to the castle gate, he vowed to turn this situation to his advantage, and assuage Shawn's anger in the bargain.

With a wide grin on his face, he shouted out, "Shawn, it is good to see you had a safe journey from Ireland! As you've no doubt heard by now, Shalee is my wife, and as you can no doubt see, she bears my child. Married life is good, Shawn, it is very good. Being such a handsome man, you need to be married yourself, wouldn't you say? Well, if you're looking for a wife, you've come to the right place! Raquelle, gather the virgin Viking women and have them take the children to the beach." Raquelle, smiling at her father's cleverness, raced toward the guest quarters to fetch the young women. Matthew turned to Shawn and asked pleasantly, "And Shawn, would you and your men please guard those women and children for the afternoon? I know that they will feel much safer under the protection of mighty Irish warriors."

Shawn's wrath had dissipated, and his face betrayed his sudden confusion. Matthew had thrown so much information at him that his thoughts were muddled. As he stood before Shalee and Matthew, struggling to focus his thoughts back on anger, the first Viking woman emerged from the front gate, breathtaking in her tight doeskin garment. She strolled up to Matthew, with three children close behind. "My leader, may I borrow your heating towel? The water is too cold for some of the children."

Matthew nodded and then, ever so casually, introduced her to Shawn. The maiden, whose name was Freya, took stock of Shawn's strong shoulders and his chiseled features, and the fine texture of his clothes. She asked, "Are you Irish?" Shawn grinned and said, "Aye." Freya sensed this man was of noble blood, but it soon became apparent that she was not one to fuss over protocol.

Looking boldly at Shawn with her clear blue eyes, she said, "I would like you to settle a matter that the other Viking ladies and I were discussing last night. In fact, this matter kept us up talking for most of the night!"

"And what would that be?" Shawn asked, his own eyes twinkling.

"It is this. All our lives we have heard rumors that Irishmen are great lovers. This we do not doubt, though we've yet to find out for ourselves, of course, as we are all virgins. But tell me, is it the Irishman's technique, his ability to talk so sweetly of love that he completely enchants a woman — as some of my sisters maintain — or is it, as I myself believe, the size of the Irishman's member that gives a woman such satisfaction?" All the time she was talking, Freya's eyes never left Shawn's face.

Shalee, meanwhile, had almost swallowed her tongue in embarrassment at the boldness of this young woman. Matthew held his breath too, but Shawn's eyes twinkled even more merrily as he made his reply not in words, but by gently grasping Freya's hand and raising it for a tender kiss. For the past thousand years, the art of charming a woman had been distilled in Ireland. This art was inbred in the Irish nobility, and it rose inside Shawn now, illuminating his every feature, pouring from his lips and radiating into the very being of the woman whose hand he now kissed. Like a cat enraptured by a catnip mouse, so Freya was completely spellbound by the charm of the Irishman. Matthew knew she didn't stand a chance.

By now the other Viking women and the rest of the children had gathered. As Shawn and his men headed towards the beach with the women and children in tow, Matthew turned to Shalee. Again he found himself pondering the heart of this woman whom he loved so completely and had so very nearly lost. Shalee had withstood the considerable charm of the Irishman. She'd had every opportunity, and more than one good reason, to flee from Scotland to a life of luxury and relative safety on the Emerald Isle. Yet she had chosen Matthew Wolverine. Matthew took both of Shalee's hands and raised them to delicately kiss each one. Then he told her, with his eyes as well as his lips, how beautiful and desirable he found her. Perhaps a bit of the charm of Ireland still lingered in the air, because Shalee felt to the core of her being that in Matthew's eyes, she was the most beautiful and desirable woman in the whole world — bulging belly and all. They slipped away to their bedroom.

* * *

The evening found Shawn still romancing the maiden Freya. Matthew had sent for Eric to eat with them tonight, and as they entered the dining hall, Eric was quick to discover what was going on between the Irishman and his own countrywoman. He pulled Freya aside, reminding her of the terms of his payment for her passage. She nodded, and then took her place at the table beside Shawn.

The talk was merry among the diners at the great table, and when there was a lull in the conversation, Freya turned to Shawn and said sweetly, "Shawn, I find you to be a man of great charm, and your words are as charming as you are. But we Vikings like a man who backs his words with action. What would you do if I asked you to win a battle for me?"

Shawn was by now completely taken with this young woman. He was enamored of her beauty, and he liked her directness too. Truly, she was a jewel that he should be proud for all of Ireland to behold on his arm. His response to her question was simple: "When and where?"

Matthew jumped in with both feet. "Well, as a matter of fact, Shawn, there is to be a battle against the south kingdom this summer. We have word that they are planning to invade, and the dragons will be fighting with them. They want to destroy me and all who would accept my God, and then their intent is to enslave Scotland. This will not be an easy battle for us to win, but with you and your army fighting with me, our victory is assured."

Before Shawn could get a word in edgewise, Matthew continued, "I see you have become quite smitten with the young woman who sits beside you. Indeed, you and Freya make a handsome pair. But know that she and the other young Viking women are here by Eric's good graces. Upon their arrival in Scotland, an agreement was made that each of these women could choose one of our warriors for her husband, and the lucky man would pay Eric one Scottish Cross, one silver necklace, and ten of his best sheep as payment for her transport to Scotland. But if you will agree to fight with me, I will pay Eric's price of passage myself! Freya has to accept your proposal of marriage, of course, but what maiden could turn down the charm of a noble son of Ireland?"

Freya gave Shawn a shyly seductive smile, and then sat up a little straighter, tossing her long blonde hair away from her face, and displaying to full advantage the voluptuous roundness of her bosom. She ran one hand casually through her hair, then let that hand slide down across her breasts and lightly onto Shawn's thigh, all in one smooth, seemingly unconscious, movement. Then she reached her other hand to Shawn's face in an intimate caress, turning his head towards her as she lightly kissed him on the mouth. A less cocksure man would have been a tad embarrassed at such a public display of affection. But this was Shawn, who had been further emboldened by the look and the movement and the wild sweet scent of this woman. Sitting so close to her, breathing in a heady blend of leather and aromatic oils and her own subtle musk, he was completely intoxicated. In such a state, any man would have agreed to nearly anything, and Shawn quickly said yes to Matthew's terms.

Matthew eyed Eric, and saw a cunning smile emerge on the face of his friend. Eric's mind was already envisioning a budding trade in seductive Viking maidens. If all ten of the maidens found husbands here, why, that meant Eric would be paid a total of one hundred sheep. And that was just the beginning! There would be many dozens more, perhaps hundreds more, eligible young Viking women who would be only too eager to come to Scotland under the same terms as the first ten. No telling how big a herd of sheep Eric would end up with as a result. The animals would supply him with food and wool… yes, a fine livelihood would be his in these highlands. Of course, he would need land to gaze his herds. He knew there was a small village to the north; Eric thought it was called Inverness. Not only was there good grazing land, but there would be a harbor for his ships…

"Penny for your thoughts, Eric," Matthew whispered. Eric, jolted from his reverie, told Matthew about his vision of vast herds, and asked Matthew for lands around that northern village to graze his sheep. Matthew said, "Of course I will grant you the lands you request, and I'll even help you build your castle after the battle with the south has been won, but I ask you to remember that there is no slavery in Scotland. Every maiden has the right of refusal to a marriage proposal, and she must come with you willingly from the Viking lands."

Eric thought a moment. "I can live with those conditions!"

After the meal, Matthew told Shawn and Eric he wished to meet with each man separately the next morning, to go over battle plans.

* * *

Matthew and Shalee retired to their bedroom, but sleep eluded Matthew. Usually he found it calming to cuddle with Shalee just before sleep, placing his hand gently upon her belly to feel their child moving within her. This did not help him tonight. Matthew tossed and turned for most of the night. Finally, at about three in the morning, he dozed off. But his sleep was invaded by a terrible dream — or a vision? — he couldn't tell. All he knew was that while it was happening, it seemed very real. He was sailing over dark and choppy waters, when suddenly and without warning, a flying dragon dive-bombed his ship. Matthew sank arrow after arrow into the dragon's flesh, but the creature attacked again and again. The whole ship was ablaze, fire spreading upon the surrounding waters, and Matthew saw no escape. The fire licked his flesh, and the heat was intense. Matthew saw his flesh beginning to burn. He watched his skin blister and peel. He jumped into the water, but there was no escaping the horrible pain. Then he was on land, with someone squeezing his hand, but he felt his life slipping away. Excruciating pain covered his body, and he let out a blood-curdling scream — for real. He sat up in bed.

Shalee sprang up as well, asking Matthew what was wrong. He could only gasp, "A dream!" He lay back down, and Shalee lay down beside him, trying to rest her head and hand gently upon his chest, but she could not get a grip on his slippery, sweat-covered body. Matthew was shaking violently; she had never seen him in such a state. Raquelle rushed into the room with a candle, and Kele and several warriors appeared with swords drawn at the bedroom door. Matthew sat up, crying, "It was nothing but a nightmare! Go back to bed!"

The men left but Raquelle remained, taking a seat at the foot of the bed and asking her father what had scared him so. Reluctantly, Matthew shared the details of the dream. "What if this is a premonition of the outcome of the battle in July?" he asked. "I have to look at the possibility that Scotland could lose and be enslaved by the south."

"No!" cried Shalee and Raquelle as one. Shalee continued, "You yourself are convinced that your God — *our* God — brought you here to crush the dragons' power. And our God will not let you fail."

"Shalee is right!" Raquelle chimed in. "So the dream must have another meaning. Or maybe it has no meaning at all. Sometimes I have the most nonsensical dreams."

"Perhaps you're right," Matthew replied. "There is a part of me that fears the battle may not go well, and maybe my dream was just reflecting that fear. Sometimes our dreams are simply a way for our minds and bodies to express the feelings we don't want to talk or think about when we are awake." To himself he thought how remarkable it was that he felt so at ease talking about his fears in the presence of these two women. The old Matthew would never have admitted to being afraid of anything. Even now, Matthew knew it was not wise to talk freely about such matters in front of his men. But his wife and daughter were a different story. He knew this talk would not go beyond the bedroom door.

Still, he couldn't get the thought out of his mind that his terrible dream might be more than just a synaptic letting-off of steam. Well, he would deal with the matter tomorrow. Now he needed to sleep, and so did everyone else.

Matthew said, "I feel better now, and I thank both of you. Now let's all try to get some sleep. And Raquelle, after breakfast this morning I want you to accompany me to the beach to talk to Elizabeth." Without questioning the reason, Raquelle agreed, and said good night to her mother and father. When they were alone again, Matthew lay down, holding Shalee very tight to his chest. He finally fell into a deep, and thankfully dreamless, sleep.

* * *

Matthew had his strategy meeting with Shawn before breakfast. He shared his battle plan with the Irishman, and Shawn's eyes shone as Matthew spoke. When Matthew told him of Kial's task to drive the pigs through Hadrian's Wall, he became downright ecstatic. "Since you do not want any part of those filthy creatures," he said to Matthew, "will you allow me to take possession of them? If you give me that prize, I will gladly commit my five hundred warriors to the battle!"

Matthew said, "Take them, take them. My only demand, where the pigs are concerned, is that not one of the loathsome beasts shall remain in Scotland." On this, Shawn was in complete agreement.

"I have one more request," Shawn added. "I would like to try an experiment, and I ask for the right to the use of ten of your sheep." Without even pressing him for details, Matthew agreed — he was in a very agreeable mood by now, thinking of a pig-free Scotland — and then Shawn took his leave, too excited to eat breakfast.

Next Matthew met with Eric. They discussed Eric's mission to take a shipload of dragon treasure immediately back to the Viking lands, recruiting as many Viking warriors as could fit into his ten ships. "When you return to Scotland," Matthew said, "you will dock your eleven ships at Inverness, and then complete the building of the ten ships begun on Loch Ness.

"When you return to Inverness with all of your Viking warriors," he continued, "you will sail your ships north around the tip of Scotland, and then south to Hadrian's Wall. The king of the south has workers cutting a hole in Hadrian's Wall on the very western end, through which he will march his army. That is where he will invade Scotland. Your army, Shawn's army, and the Scottish army will meet just above Hadrian's Wall and wait for the southern army to appear. I have already sent warriors to the south to secure the opening once it is complete." He had dispatched his recon team within hours of hearing Robert's news about the pending invasion.

Eric nodded, and then with Matthew's permission he left for the treasure room to gather the gold and silver and jewels with which he would lure his army.

It had been a busy morning for Matthew, and he had not even had breakfast yet. After a hasty meal he and Raquelle walked to the beach, where Elizabeth was waiting for them. Matthew related his dream to her.

Elizabeth responded, *Why does this dream burden you? It was just a dream, after all. I have scary dreams sometimes, and nothing has ever come of them.*

Matthew conveyed to her, *I've thought about the dream and the reason I had it. I think this dream was a reflection of the things that have been troubling me lately.*

And what would those things be? Elizabeth asked.

I am very worried over the safety of my family, but I am also worried about you and your mother. In fact, I think I am more worried about the two of you. If the dragons and the dragon worshippers should prevail, my family and I could escape to Ireland. But that would leave you and Alanna alone in Loch Ness.

Oh, you need not worry about us! Elizabeth communicated. *My mother is still completely obsessed with escaping through the tunnel. She works day and night trying to move that boulder from its opening. She has gotten it to budge a little, at least that's what she thinks, and she is not going to give up until she gets the tunnel open. And she has decided that when she does, then we will go to the river that leads to the land of Atlantis. We will be safe there. And it is there that she will find a new mate, and she will even pick one out for me when I'm old enough. I wonder what my mate will be like...?*

At Elizabeth's mention of Atlantis, who should appear but Alanna herself! Matthew saw a furious motion just under the water off shore, and suddenly his old friend bolted out onto the beach, thundering towards them so that the very earth seemed to shake with trepidation. There was a huge scowl on Alanna's face, and murder in her eyes. This was not the Alanna Matthew remembered. This was a dark and bitter creature whose menacing demeanor prompted Matthew to shield Raquelle behind him.

Towering over Elizabeth, Alanna scolded her daughter for revealing their mystical mating grounds. Sternly she ordered her child into the water, and Elizabeth obeyed without hesitation. Hatred filled Alanna's face as she turned to Matthew. There was no joyful greeting, no mention of their long months away from each other, no inquiry about his and Shalee's and Raquelle's welfare. No, Alanna had but one thought for Matthew: *Have you seen the dragon with one eye?*

Matthew shook his head, and tried to reach out his hand to calm his friend. But Alanna would have none of it. She vowed that she would kill that dragon one day, then she descended into the water and was gone.

Raquelle emerged from behind Matthew and asked, "Was that really Alanna?"

"Yes, I'm afraid it was," her father replied. "Alanna is living proof that anger and hatred are more destructive to the one who hates than to the one who is hated. Hate unchecked will annihilate you. Alanna can't release her hatred for the one-eyed dragon, and that loathing has changed her."

"Aye, and what a terrible change it is," Raquelle said.

"Yes, it is. I love Alanna, but I fear I am losing a good friend to hatred. I only hope Alanna doesn't take out her hatred on Elizabeth…. Raquelle, I want you to remember what you have seen here today. I have seen warriors consumed with hatred of an enemy, and they were bitter men. I make a practice of never letting the sun go down on my anger or hatred, and I never dwell on it."

"Yes, but you hate the dragons and their worshippers, don't you? You're going to war because of your hatred of them."

"I hate the dragons, it is true, because of the harm they do — and I will kill them and defeat their worshippers, as well as the king of the south, because that is what must be done for a free Scotland. But what drives me is not hatred; rather, it is my love for my God, my love of freedom… and my love for you and Shalee."

Raquelle was quiet after that, and she put her arm around Matthew's waist as they walked back towards the castle. She was still stunned by the change in Alanna. She listened intently to her father's words, for this was another lesson she knew she must not forget.

* * *

As they approached the castle, a strange spectacle met their eyes. Shawn and his men were standing over ten sprawled-out, and apparently dead, sheep. Matthew charged over to them, yelling that Shawn must pay for those dead sheep.

"Say, wait a minute!" Shawn said, grinning. "First of all, you told me I could have these sheep, did you not?"

249

"Yes, but I did not give you permission to kill them," Matthew growled. "I should have asked you what you were planning to do before I gave you *carte blanche* to waste perfectly good livestock."

Shawn's grin was wider than ever. "Cart *what?* Well, never you mind. You will see in a moment what it is I've been up to." Still snarling, Matthew watched, and within a few moments, one sheep staggered to its feet. A pungent odor, somewhat like ether, assailed Matthew's sensibilities. His anger faded, but now his head was spinning. What in the world…? Matthew quickly moved away as the rest of the sheep began to stagger to their feet. Shawn clapped Matthew on the shoulder and said triumphantly, "My experiment works! Now I shall leave for Ireland, and we will meet on the designated day at Hadrian's Wall. Matthew, you may have your sheep back, and I thank you kindly for their use. They'll be good as new in no time… oh, perhaps they shall have an aching head for a time, but they'll be their old selves by the morning."

Shawn and his warriors said their farewells then, and took their leave, with Matthew shaking his head. The men thought he, Matthew, was crazy, but he had nothing on this out-of-control Irishman.

Matthew was pleased that several of Shawn's men had new Viking brides in tow, and while all were joyful, surely the most joyous among them was Shawn, who had wed his lovely Freya just a few days earlier. And when Eric the Red returned, he would be happily counting sheep, and it would not be because he had insomnia.

The next weeks were filled with the preparations for the coming battle. Eric returned as promised with eleven ships full of Viking warriors, and he had plenty of help completing the ten ships that were to sail on Loch Ness. As these ships transported supplies south, Eric's original eleven ships sailed north, and then turned south toward Hadrian's Wall. Meanwhile, the Scottish army assembled, and on a bright, clear morning in late June, Matthew finally began to lead them south.

There was no turning back now.

Chapter 23

The march south was long and hard, but the men's spirits were high, and they gathered many volunteers as they marched south. When the army arrived at Hadrian's Wall, they saw the opening that had been created by the southern army. As planned, Matthew's recon troop was in full control of this breach. Now there was little to do but wait. Eric's army, and Shawn's, were due to arrive soon.

Eric's army was the first to appear, hale and hearty and ready to kill dragons. They set up camp at the base of Hadrian's Wall on the north side, and Eric posted Viking sentries on top of the wall. Now when Matthew turned in for the night, he felt very secure.

The next morning, Shawn's army arrived. The first thing Matthew noticed was that there were only about a hundred men. "Where are the other four hundred?" Matthew demanded.

"Not to worry, my lord," Shawn boasted. "My army of one hundred archers is worth five hundred ordinary warriors!"

Matthew was furious. He had counted on five hundred warriors. But he had little time to waste on reproach; he must make do with what was there now, so he posted Shawn and his entire Irish army of archers as sentries on Hadrian's Wall.

Other worries plagued Matthew now. The scouts that he had sent south had not yet returned; they should have been here days ago. As night fell, a worried Matthew fell into a fitful sleep. Then just as dawn broke, an Irish sentry screamed, "Dragon attack!"

At least fifty dragons — which, according to all reports and observations, made up the whole of the remaining dragon population in Scotland — were flying in a V formation at treetop height. As the dragons approached Hadrian's Wall, they began spewing a sea of flames at the bottom of the wall. They rose as if in slow motion to clear the wall, while Shawn rallied his men to the crest of the hill to witness the dragons and their fire rising up the hill. With one mind, the dragons concentrated

251

their fire on any bush or warrior they happened to spot on the south side of the hill. As they crested the hill, they flapped their wings furiously, shooting straight up to about one thousand feet, and then circling south to regroup into a V formation for their next attack. The smoke from the fires on the south side of Hadrian's Wall blocked the archers' vision of any approaching dragons from the south. Shawn rallied his archers just over the ridge on the north side of the wall. The smoke was now so thick that by the time one of his men could spot a dragon, it was almost on top of him. "You have not a moment to waste!" Shawn shouted. "Fire as soon as you see a dragon's head." His men fought valiantly, but over a quarter of them were lost in this first attack.

Fortunately, help was on its way. Immediately upon hearing of the dragon attack, the Vikings at the base camp had grabbed their battle axes and rushed up the wall. They were primed to kill, and they climbed this wall like a starving spider climbs its web to feast on a big juicy fly. Before the dragons could regroup into their V formation to launch their second assault, the Vikings were there at the side of the Irish archers. Eric saw the thick smoke as a great advantage. He ordered his Vikings to grab small rocks and hurl them into the smoke with all their might, but to keep their battle axes handy.

Still in V formation, the dragons flew into the dense smoke, perceiving victory. Instead they were met with the pelting of rocks, and their formation began to disintegrate, their flaming involuntarily ceasing. As the smoke dissipated, so went their cover, and as they tried to escape they were assaulted with a sensation much like that of gigantic bee stings. Now the Irish archers were in their glory; whether it was from fear or from courage or a little of both, these Irishmen had suddenly developed superhuman strength. Their arrows penetrated deeply into the dragons, plunging past scales and into the thick flesh.

Eric was among the first to notice that the dragons were no longer shooting flames, and he rose to slice his ax through the lead dragon's wing, totally severing it. The dragon spun around in midair and crashed headfirst into the advancing wave of his fellows. It was like a chain reaction in an automobile pileup, as one beast after another slammed into the rapidly rising wall of dragon flesh.

Intrepid Vikings continued to climb this growing hill of wriggling dragons, standing like conquering heroes upon the squirming pile of flesh. There was flesh aplenty in which to bury their axes to the hilt. But the battle was far from over, for most of the dragons were only stunned or, at the most, slightly wounded, and one by one they took off from the pile. Still hacking away, the furious Vikings slipped and slid on the dragons' backs. One dragon took off with a Viking still clinging to its back. Filled with rage, the dragon landed, and then immediately rolled over to crush the hapless man. As it screeched in victory, its fellows landed around it, rallying to ensure that the antagonist had indeed breathed his last.

Matthew's army took this opportunity to swarm on these temporarily grounded dragons like an army of ants on a dying butterfly. Within moments, Scottish warriors covered the dragons so completely that all Matthew could see were the bloody daggers of his men, pumping again and again into dragon flesh.

The battle with the dragons raged for over an hour. Matthew fully expected the southern army to come pouring through the opening in Hadrian's Wall, but they didn't. Then suddenly all was silent. Matthew looked around at fifty dead dragons. He counted, and then counted again to make sure. There were no more live dragons in sight, not anywhere — not even a hint of a living fire-breather. Could it be true, then? Could it be that the cancer that had eaten away at Scotland for over three millennia had finally been excised?

Could he even hope?

Of course, there was still the southern army to deal with…and that was a whole other battle…but Matthew could not deny the feeling of joy that was rising within him. The dragons were all dead! As far as he knew, all of the surviving dragons in Scotland showed up for this battle, knowing it was to be to the death. And to the death it was, for all of them: not one had fled.

"Praise God!" Matthew shouted out loud. And then he set to work. There would be plenty of time to celebrate later.

Matthew issued a command for all the dragon corpses to be placed in two rows perpendicular to the opening in Hadrian's Wall, with the beasts' heads touching nose to nose. This would extend about 600 feet, creating a funnel for the enemy troops.

"Then sever each dragon's head," he ordered, "starting with the dragons closest to the breach. The warrior whose axe or sword severs the head will possess the teeth. The severed heads and necks will be placed in two rows on the south side of the wall, as a warning to any dragon worshipper who even thinks of coming back to Scotland. Their gods are dead, and they are not welcome in Scotland!"

At that a mighty shout arose from the men. "The dragons are dead! Long live Matthew Wolverine!" Matthew motioned for them to cease. "We celebrate later," he admonished. "Now we must get to work."

Vikings descended upon the dragon necks closest to the wall…*just like a pit bull demolishing turkey necks*, Matthew thought, and he couldn't help but grin at this expression that had popped into his head. His Uncle Edgar, a good ol' boy from East Texas, used to say that. It was an apt illustration of the spectacle before him. The Irish archers scurried to the end of each row and began to decapitate dragons, while the Vikings were busily slicing off dragons' necks at the front of the rows. The Vikings had beheaded forty dragons before they began to come across dragons that had already been beheaded. The Irish worked energetically, dragging the severed heads to a pile at the end of the rows. As a result, many Viking warriors did not get a dragon head, and they were incensed. They first went to Eric, then turned to belligerently march to Shawn.

Fortunately Matthew reached Shawn first, turning his back to the approaching Vikings. "Shawn, listen!" he shouted. "The Vikings got forty dragon heads. They are swifter than the Irish!" In a lower voice he said, "Shawn, give me your word that there will be no fighting with the Vikings over these forty dragon heads." Then once again in a loud voice, he announced, "The Irish only get ten dragon heads to the Vikings' forty. Do you know that some of these courageous Vikings rode a dragon from the top of Hadrian's Wall to the ground? Shawn, do I have your word that the Irish will not complain upon only receiving ten dragon heads?" Matthew extended his hand to the Irishman as he said this.

Shawn's eyes were twinkling, and he returned the handshake with gusto. He knew Matthew had just saved some Irish lives. It was time to solidify his gentleman's agreement with some good old-fashioned Irish charm. "Ireland will be satisfied with only ten dragon heads on one condition, and one condition only!" he roared. "And that is if the courageous, fearless, heroic Viking warriors who rode on those ferocious, bloodthirsty dragons will share their stories here and now!" Shawn crossed his arms and he winked at Eric. Matthew thought, *Shawn really can put the blarney on thick, but then again… if you ask a warrior to tell you a war story he will move heaven and hell to get to you.*

The Vikings who had ridden the dragons jumped up when they heard Shawn's request, and shoved through the other Vikings, even bumping Eric aside in their haste to reach Shawn. They all began telling their story at once, pointing to the ridge in emphasis. Everyone knows that the Irish can never resist a good tale, and these Irishmen all immediately sat down to listen. Matthew tried to bring the crowd to some kind of order. He commanded the biggest Viking to tell his story first, and then the others would relate their stories in turn, one at a time. Matthew and Shawn sat down with everyone else, settling in to listen to the saga. The huge Viking cleared his throat and shouted so all could hear.

Matthew knew he should post guards on the ridge, and later he would berate himself over and over again. But the peace between the Vikings and the Irishmen was a fragile one, and the situation could still turn into a riot at any moment. Besides, all was quiet on the southern front. He could afford to take a few moments of R-and-R, couldn't he?

Everyone makes mistakes, and this was a major blunder for Matthew. While the Vikings were regaling the crowd with their tales of daring-do, the king of the south and his entire army were approaching the breach in Hadrian's Wall. They intentionally advanced at an angle to the breach to avoid detection by the Scottish army. The king, seeing his advantage, commanded his army to proceed on foot, and silently. His army reached Hadrian's Wall undetected. The sight of the dead dragons, far from shocking or angering the king, gave him great relief. He had struck bargains with the dragons and their worshippers for half their treasure in Scotland. With the dragons dead, all of Scotland's treasure would be his! If the dragon worshippers objected, he would bury them. Now, however, he needed them.

As expected, the dragon worshippers were enraged at the sight of their dead gods. Before the king could even give orders, they had rushed through the breach and were upon the backs of the seated warriors who were listening to the Viking tales.

Matthew and Shawn rose simultaneously and charged head-on into the midst of the dragon worshippers. Many Scottish warriors were to die in the charge of these fanatics. The entire southern army now occupied the corridor between the rows of dragons, extending all the way up to the twentieth dragon. And the dragon worshippers fought like badgers. Matthew knew he must keep them from getting to the twenty-fifth dragon, for if that happened, the southern army could spill out and surround the Scottish army.

But it was an arduous battle. The incredible mass of the southern army pushed Matthew back, step by step. They passed three dragon bodies, and Matthew ordered Vikings to the front. The axe wielders spearheaded the offensive, which invigorated the Scottish and Irish warriors, and finally the southern army retreated one step. Then the south dug in, and blow after blow was exchanged, but no one advanced. Matthew pulled back to let fresh troops fight in the front for awhile.

As he reached the back line of his warriors, he was suddenly smacked in the rear with such force that he tumbled head over heels to the ground. Matthew looked up at the enormous hind end of a gigantic boar. The boar sliced through the Scottish army and cut a hole through the southern army. Its massive head smashed warrior after warrior, cutting a wide hole straight down the middle of the corridor. Matthew heard thundering hooves, and he rose just in time to get out of the way of a veritable tidal wave of boars, all stampeding towards the opening in Hadrian's Wall.

Matthew shouted for his warriors to fall back and climb up the dragons. He himself scurried up the nearest dragon, helping other warriors ascend to safety. All at once the southern army was faced with an onslaught of angry boars with one goal in their brutish brains. That goal was to plow through the southern army and straight into what looked to them like freedom.

Meanwhile, Matthew dispersed his troops along all the dragons that reached to Hadrian's Wall. He would allow no enemy to climb upon a dragon for safety. The back of the southern army pushed forward as the boars hit the front warriors with such force that warriors were driven through other warriors. Like the pressure of lava exploding from a volcano, tens of thousands of infuriated boars surged upon the southern army. The beasts climbed the southerners' backs and trotted on their heads in their headlong rush to get through to the breach in Hadrian's Wall.

What the boars didn't realize was that warriors and boars could not occupy the narrow corridor at the same time. It was a simple law of physics, but physics was not the pigs' strong suit, apparently. Boars were climbing over other boars to jump on the packed-in warriors. The sheer weight of the pigs upon these warriors crushed the unlucky men to the ground…and the next wave of boars climbed over these downed boars to leap on new warriors…and so on. This leapfrog technique quickly produced a red carpet through the passage.

Matthew turned north to see Kial riding hard, whirling a whip and shouting like some ancient Scottish cowpoke. Kial smacked the whip on the rear of the slower moving boars, and they sped up. Other warriors with whips followed Kial on foot. The boars in the rear, feeling the sting of the whips, sped up to pass other boars. Now they were all fleeing the whips. Just as cars, in the movies, fly off a speed ramp into the air, so the boars raced up the backs of their fellows to catapult themselves into the air. They landed smack on the southern troops, causing the red carpet to become a red wave.

Shawn pointed and shouted, "Pigs flying, pigs flying!" Next, of course, Hell would freeze over, Matthew thought, with a huge grin on his face. It was worth being in the presence of this much repulsive pork to witness such a spectacle. At Shawn's words, the Irish all ceased fighting just for a moment, only long enough to cross themselves, and then they returned to fighting. The first boar broke through the end of the southern army, packed like sardines in the corridor, and with a loud victorious squeal, the beast raced for freedom. Other boars followed, hurdling over the southern army towards freedom.

And that was it for the army of the southern kingdom. Their spirits broken, they and their king turned to flee in the direction from which they had come.

As Kial reached the rows of dead dragons, he stopped at the sight of the sea of blood. The boars had crushed more than half of the southern army. Matthew rallied his army, and they ran over the dead dragons to scale Hadrian's Wall, and then leapt down to exit the opening. An Irish rider approached Shawn with a horse in tow.

Shawn mounted the horse, and he commanded his army to turn the herd of boars to the west. As they began to carry out his command, Shawn turned to Matthew and said amiably, "Mission accomplished, Matthew. Now to take my prize of boars to God's greatest island! You drove the boars out of Scotland and right into the waiting arms of hungry Irishmen. Every ship on the east coast of Ireland now swears allegiance to me. They await this prize in the west bay. My army will run these boars to exhaustion by the bay — and then my sleeping potion, which I tested on your sheep, and I thank you again, will let Irish ships transport them to Ireland. Praise our God that you hate pork, and we Irish love it. The blessings of Ireland be upon you. Freya and I shall name our first male child after you!" With that, Shawn turned and headed west with his men.

Kial dismounted and sat on the ground, and Matthew and the whole army followed suit. No one felt like pursing the southern army. They were sick of blood, death, and war. Scotland was free, and it was time to pause and savor this miracle.

Eric suddenly realized that the Irish had left the ten dragon heads with their teeth intact. He ordered his Vikings to pull all the teeth of these dragons — and quickly, before the Irish returned. "Return the teeth of the ten dragons to me," he told his men, "and I will make sure that every one of you receives at least one dragon tooth to remember this great victory." In no time at all, the teeth were pulled and returned to Eric. True to his word, Eric presented one dragon tooth to each of his warriors, and they were ecstatic. Matthew knew what gave them such joy about this simple act. It was the fact that this story would be told and retold around camp fires for hundreds of years to come. A dragon tooth was proof, for those who might doubt, that the tale was true.

* * *

By evening, Kial was already complaining that he missed pork. "Ah, well, if the desire gets too great, then I suppose I can always sail to Ireland," he mused. He turned to Eric and asked, "Will you be keeping a fleet of ships on the west coast of Scotland for trade with the Irish?" Eric considered a moment, and said, "That is a very wise idea!"

It was, as Matthew inevitably used to say at some point during the cutthroat negotiations that were so much a part of his old life, a win-win situation. Only this really *was* a win-win deal. With Shawn returning to Ireland in possession of all those swine, his influence over the east coast of Ireland would be considerable. Eric liked Shawn a great deal, and vowed to trade with Ireland through Scotland. So a fleet on the west coast of Scotland was a brilliant plan. Matthew was glad Kial had suggested this idea. He wanted to lure Eric the Red into staying, for Viking allies could only strengthen Scotland.

Celebration was rampant that night, and the air was filled with the warriors' shouts. "The dragons are dead! Long live Matthew Wolverine! God bless us, Scotland is free!" Their cries rang out through the trees and into the high hills, and in their elation not one among them, not even Matthew, heard the menacing whisper in the wind. As Matthew sat before the campfire that night, the future shimmered before him like ripe sweet fruit. It was understandable that he would see it that way, and understandable too that in the blind joy of victory, even Matthew Wolverine was capable of forgetting that even the sweetest fruit can be deadly poisonous.

CHAPTER 24

At Matthew's command, the Scottish army began filling the breach in Hadrian's Wall. He decided that Kial would supervise until the task was complete, then lead the army north to Loch Ness. Matthew wanted Kial to stop at every Pict camp along his northward journey, and tell them of the victories of the true God over the dragons and the king of the south. "I want you to make it clear that the dragons are gone, and that Scotland is finally free!" he said.

As Kial and the army closed the breach in Hadrian's Wall, Eric the Red and Matthew led the Viking warriors west to board their ships. Eric sailed west, then northeast into the Firth of Lorne. When they had reached the end of the bay, they landed, and Eric ordered the Vikings to build shelters. This was to be his new base for trade with Ireland. Matthew, Eric, and ten warriors then headed northeast. Two days' hard march found them just a mile from the southernmost tip of Loch Ness.

They set up camp but were on the move again at the crack of dawn, for Matthew wanted to get home as quickly as possible. The future looked very bright as they boarded a ship on Loch Ness to head north. Eric stood upon the deck, his eyes closed, savoring the feel of the breeze as it pushed them along. He said, "Our God gives us favorable winds, Matthew. We are almost to your castle." Matthew nodded. After several minutes of comfortable silence, Eric said, "What are your plans for the future?"

Matthew was enjoying the calmness of this voyage. "Peace has come to Scotland. I plan to help you build great fleets that will sail north and west to catch schools of fish that are huge beyond even your imaginings. You and I will be partners, and our fish will be traded in all of Scotland. Your herd of sheep will grow. My iron plows will spread throughout Scotland, and our food supply will thrive and swell. We will trade with the Viking lands and the rest of Europe. Scotland will be the trade center of this age." Matthew smiled as he considered the prospects, and Eric imagined fleets of ships under his command. Contentment filled the two sailors.

The Ultimate Dragon

Amid his dreams of great things for Scotland, Matthew found himself wondering about Shalee. She had been so close to her time when he left, and he had heard no word from home. He still half-hoped she had not yet given birth, so he could be there to hear his son's first cry. Yet a part of him hoped she had already given birth and had recovered. Though it might be selfish, he needed to make love to her... tonight, if possible! That thought sent him on an entire new reverie.

As Matthew was dreaming of making love to his bride, a shadow crossed the deck at his feet. When he noticed it, his first thought was that it might be about to rain. But as the shadow loomed over him he looked up, and was startled to see that the sun was blotted out by blackness. The shadow now covered his face and Eric's, and both men realized at the same instant that this was not a cloud... but a dragon.

A dragon?

There was no mistaking it. Like a bomb dropping, the beast plummeted straight for the ship. The dragon had them at her mercy, and she was fresh out of mercy. Fire streaked from her mouth, hurling down upon the ship. Eric hurled his spear, but it only skimmed the dragon's belly. Matthew froze in disbelief. He could not believe that, after all the battles, a dragon still lived in Scotland.

Then he looked more closely at the dragon, and a chill raced through him as the dragon looked back. The hatred in her single eye penetrated Matthew's brain and sent ice into his soul.

Matthew barely had time to hurl his own spear, and it landed just below the dragon's chest, slightly to the right, penetrating her liver. At first this seemed to do nothing but enrage her, and the men were blinded by another burst of dragon fire. If she was going out, she was going to take Matthew Wolverine with her.

Eric lunged at Matthew, trying to grab him and dive over the side of the ship, but his grip faltered, and Matthew fell overboard as Eric went under the water. Matthew looked upward as he fell, and saw the flames coming down to envelop his body. The searing pain spurred his brain into action. Matthew's hands, arms, and chest were charred. The pain was so intense that he couldn't swim; he could only thrash about in the water. Three other Vikings dove into the water and swam for shore.

The dragon, bleeding profusely, weakening rapidly, but still full of wrath, made sure the other seven Vikings on the ship had plenty of fire to keep them warm. As she pulled out of her dive, she gave them a Viking funeral, sending them to their deaths in a fiery ship. Now she circled the ship, spewing her liquid fire on the water. Matthew and Eric were under the water as the surface glowed orange with the dragon's fire.

At last Eric spotted a clearing in the fire, and grabbed Matthew, dragging him to the surface to gulp air. He noticed that Matthew was blistering and in terrible pain. The dragon continued to circle, watching the men struggle. Eric spied the shore not too far away, so he dragged Matthew under the water and began swimming in that direction, towing Matthew behind him.

When Eric's lungs could last no longer without air, he surfaced, and saw people standing upon the beach. But, alas, they might as well have been a continent away, for there was nothing they could do to help him. The dragon made another dive, turning her flaming rage upon the three Viking sailors bobbing in the water. After she transformed the last of them into screaming cinder, she returned her attention to Eric and Matthew. Eric wrenched Matthew under the water, and they held their breath. As the seconds passed, Matthew struggled to free himself from Eric's grip and return to the surface, but Eric held fast.

Matthew's lungs were about to burst when he finally broke free, swimming madly upward to the air he so desperately needed. The dragon hung in the air overhead, filled with her malevolent resolve to capture Matthew and Eric in her teeth, and then to carry them, screaming, high into the air, where she would release them to their deaths.

As Matthew struggled to surface, a storm of bubbles engulfed him, pushing him upward. Like a geyser, the swirling waters shot up toward the dragon, carrying Matthew and Eric toward her jaws of death. With her mouth wide open, the dragon swooped to snatch Matthew from the water.

And then suddenly, out of the geyser burst Alanna, like a guided missile streaking directly toward the dragon's throat. This seemed to give the latter a new burst of energy. Though stunned, the dragon sank her teeth into Alanna's neck. Both now held each other in a death grip, as blood flowed from each of their necks. The dragon was already weakened from the wound to her liver, which poured out a river of black blood. Still she struggled to rise higher, but the pair remained suspended in midair. Then, as if a massive steel beam had been suspended on cables that suddenly snapped, Alanna's weight plunged them into the water. And that was the last Matthew saw of Alanna and the one-eyed dragon: two grieving mothers locked in a death grip, both willing to pay the ultimate price to have revenge. The water turned red and black with their blood as they sank deeper into the abyss.

* * *

Eric struggled to get Matthew to shore. Upon reaching the shore, he pulled Matthew out of the water. Matthew was so badly burned and blistered that Eric's eyes saw only one possibility: death. He hoped it would be quick and merciful. "Do not worry about your family; I will protect them," Eric whispered in his friend's ear. "May God bless you and keep you."

Shalee and Raquelle rushed to Matthew's side, and Shalee gasped in horror as she looked at her husband's charred body. Even her gentle touch on Matthew's hand made him wince with pain. Raquelle fell to her knees to plead with God to heal her father. Through the fog of his pain Matthew saw a stout red-haired woman whom he thought he recognized…her name was Shanna, he believed; he and Shalee had talked about retaining her services as a nanny after the baby was born. In Shanna's arms was a small bundle, wrapped in a blanket of the palest and softest blue. Matthew could barely speak now, but he looked at her and said, "Is that…?"

The woman stepped forward and said, "Aye, this is your son: Master Eric Matthew Wolverine, and a fine strapping laird he will be!"

"He has your eyes, Matthew," Shalee said in a broken voice.

Matthew smiled weakly. He knew there was something else he had to tell them. He struggled, and it came out as a faint whisper, "I love all of you. And… Scotland… is… free!"

His eyes closed then, and waves of blackness flooded his mind. A distant light appeared, and Matthew was sure he knew what it was, and he knew he had to muster all of his power to fight going into that light. The strength was gone from his body, but his will was still fiercely strong, and he was able to pull back from the light for awhile. But then, like the jerk of a fishing line, it reeled him back in. He could not stop it.

Unlike that first journey he had taken, the one that had spirited him back through the centuries to Loch Ness, this flight did not thrill him. He was moving much too fast, and the light hurt… not his eyes so much as his heart and his soul. He had always heard about this astonishing light, how its all-embracing luminescence gave comfort and hope on the final journey, and he had even experienced something like it on that first strange flight through time, but now!… there was no comfort here. He thought of Shalee and his heart cried out to God, *What is the point of finding my heart's desire, just to lose it?* There was no answer, and the light only grew brighter, but Matthew still kept his eyes shut tight and tried to turn away. He wished with all of his might to return to his family… and then he became confused. Which family? Cate and Rachel? Shalee and Raquelle and his new son Eric? Who was Matthew Wolverine, and where did he belong? *When* did he belong? And then all was truly black. The pain was gone, everything was gone, and Matthew's thoughts and hopes and longings were no more.

*　*　*

Someone was shaking his body.

His body. A body of solid flesh and bone and muscle... and the searing pain was gone.

Matthew Wolverine slowly opened his eyes. The first thing he saw was a massive stone cross, softly glowing, with a strange dinosaur-head symbol in its center. He realized with a start that he was in the old church where he had begun his bizarre journey. A worried old man and his wife hovered over Matthew, asking if he was all right. Though the old man spoke in a thick Scottish brogue, he spoke English — modern English — and not Gaelic. He and his wife were dressed in modern clothing, and as Matthew's eyes came more into focus he saw that their clothes were dotted with political buttons heralding the new Scottish parliament.

"Are you all right, m'boy?" the man asked again.

"Should we be summonin' a medic for ye?" his wife asked.

Matthew sat up gingerly, amazed that he was in no pain. There wasn't so much as a blister on his body. And then he looked down and saw that he, too, was dressed in modern garb, wearing a button identical to one of those that the old man wore.

"No, no, I'm all right," he said slowly. "I... I came in here to..."

"Ah, I see," the man said, winking, and his wife smiled broadly. "Sleeping off a big one, eh? Well, there's been plenty of that, I'll say that much, what with all of Scotland celebrating...I tell ye, it's been one non-stop party since the New Year, and no sign of lettin' up for a long time to come!"

Matthew smiled lamely. Better that the old couple think that he was sleeping off a hangover than that he was suffering from some mad delusion about a near-death experience brought on by dragon fire.

"Well, lad, if ye think ye will be all right, the missus and I'll be gettin' back to Loch Ness. They say there was another Nessie sighting this morning, and the news media are all out there in force. Maybe ol' Nessie is finally going to show her face once and for all, and help us celebrate our freedom!" Matthew thanked the old couple and waved them off, and they left, laughing and singing a merry song about the Guardian of the Loch.

So, what the...? Matthew stood up slowly. His mind raced with questions. Where was Shalee? Had this all been a grotesque nightmare? Sooner or later everybody, even the most faithful among us, experiences that dark instant of wondering if God even cares. At this moment in his life, Matthew truly had his doubts. He felt as if God had looked down upon the turbulence that was Matthew Wolverine's life, and responded with a shrug.

Well, finally and forever, Matthew didn't care, either. He walked out of the church, emerging into what looked and felt like as fine a Scottish summer day as ever he'd seen. But he had no heart to appreciate the beauty of the day. Despondently, he turned and headed towards Loch Ness. It was a long walk, but he knew the way so well he probably could have found the place in his sleep. At this point, he had no proof that he *wasn't* sleepwalking. When he got there, he saw the beach was very crowded, and there were swimmers in the loch. The old couple he'd spoken with spotted him from a distance, and waved. He waved back, smiling half-heartedly.

Matthew searched the sea of faces, hoping against hope that he would spot Shalee… or anyone that he knew. But with the exception of the merry old couple, whose names he didn't even know, he was alone. Utterly, completely alone.

Worse, he had no notion, really, of who he was, or *why* he was. Maybe a swim would clear his head… or… something. He had no idea what he expected. But the day was warm, and the water looked inviting, and he had to do something, because if he continued to stand here in this crowd of strangers he felt he would go berserk. Somewhat surprised to realize he was wearing a bathing suit under his clothing, he stripped down to the suit, dropped his clothes on the beach, and plunged into the water.

And then Matthew just began to swim. He swam without purpose and without joy. Hope, faith, and even the urge to survive died a little with each stoke. He was emotionally drained, and an awful coldness enfolded his body, a coldness that went beyond the chill of the water.

It was as if everything were shutting down; even Matthew's military mind resigned itself to embrace nothingness. His swimming became mechanical, without direction. He let his mind wander back to Shalee, and the sublime pleasure of her body. For once in his life, he had been truly happy. Was it a dream? Maybe, but if so, then real life was a brutal assault, and he was tired of being assaulted. Matthew continued to swim, but each stroke became more difficult.

At last his strokes ceased… and he floated for a moment… and then he sank. Down, down, down he went, and he didn't even care… As the water covered his head, he thought fleetingly of the times he had ridden on Alanna's back, and then later Elizabeth's, jetting through the water. Or maybe that had never happened.

It seemed real enough, though…

Suddenly something touched Matthew's legs. His first thought was, *a Kraken!* Inwardly he screamed, "God, let me die in peace!" Fear shot through his body, but he had no strength anymore to struggle. The *Kraken*, or whatever it was, would just have to take him. No creature in the flesh could be worse than the dragon of despair that consumed him.

264

Then he felt his body rising toward the surface. When he surfaced, Matthew involuntarily gasped for air and tried to find his bearings. His first impulse was to plunge back into the water, but something was not letting him do that. Then he realized that the "something" was a smooth and oily surface, upon which his body rested…but what in the world could it be? Matthew turned 180 degrees, and there, smiling at him, was the gentle face of Elizabeth, Alanna's daughter, fully grown. *Boy, this is some hallucination,* he thought.

And then he heard Elizabeth's thoughts. *Hello, Matthew,* she communicated. *You're shivering! I think I need to take you back to the beach.* And she was off like a missile towards the shore. Matthew was dimly aware that the crowd on the beach was growing rapidly larger and louder as he and Elizabeth drew nearer. Now they were shouting something… what was it? Then they were screaming, and finally he understood. They were screaming, "Nessie! Nessie! Nessie!"

Elizabeth plowed right up to the beach, ignoring the crowd, which had gotten dangerously close to being a mob. Yet when Elizabeth actually climbed onto the beach, lumbering into the people's midst in all of her oversized glory, a sudden hush fell over them. There was nary a word as Matthew slid off of her back, grabbed her head, and gave her a huge kiss.

Elizabeth's thoughts came in a rush now. *I missed you, Matthew. Where have you been all this time? I finally got the tunnel open, and I visited the river in Atlantis. My mother was gone, so I had to find a mate myself. We live in Atlantis most of the time. And I have a family! I named one of my sons after you, and one after my dead brother, Eric. But when I return to Loch Ness now, people try to catch me in nets and in things that swim under the water. I never hurt them; why are they doing this? And where were you all this time, Matthew? I waited for you and waited for you. I must have waited hundreds of years!*

Matthew was elated that he had found Elizabeth, and that she was, judging from all the evidence at hand, very real — all eight thousand or so pounds of her. At least he was not completely alone, and that was a start, anyway. The crowd surrounded Matthew and Elizabeth as they continued to converse. The people were still silent, as if they knew that something wonderful was going on, and feared they might ruin it if they made a sound. Matthew sent his thoughts to his friend, *I can't explain it, Elizabeth, but we are together now, and I will protect you.*

The silence was suddenly broken by two shrill, childish voices, and at that same moment, Matthew felt something latching onto his waist and his left leg. He looked down to see a small boy and girl looking up at him and tugging at his swim trunks. The boy had blonde hair and aquamarine eyes, much like Matthew's, and the girl had piercing green eyes and the most lovely head of black hair he had seen since… and then his heart caught in his throat as he realized that the children were talking to him, and they were calling him, "Daddy!"

The girl spouted off, "Daddy, Daddy, I knew we would see the lake guardian! And it let you ride it! Now it's our turn, but can I ride it first? Please? Don't let Eric ride it first. Please, father, you always said 'ladies before gentlemen,' and besides, I *am* the oldest!"

The little boy zealously argued his side. "Raquelle always gets to do everything first, and it's not fair! Come on, Daddy, I'm your only son! Let *me* ride the lake guardian first!"

Matthew reached down to tightly grasp these children — his children! — and he silently thanked God. Aloud he said, "I love you both."

Raquelle squirmed and said, "Yeah, yeah, we love you too, Dad, but right now we want to ride the lake guardian."

Both of them squirmed out of Matthew's grip and pulled away. Matthew couldn't help himself anymore. He had to know. He burst out, "Is Shalee… is your mother… around?"

Eric looked off into the distance… were those tears welling up in his eyes? A puzzled look came over Raquelle's face, and then she stated, matter of factly, "You know she is gone."

The words cut deep, especially that last word; it was a stake through Matthew's heart. Gone. There was such a finality about it.

Gone.

Then Matthew looked at his two shining children, and he forced a smile. "Let me introduce you both to Elizabeth. Elizabeth, this is my daughter, Raquelle, and my son, Eric. Now you take them for a ride, but not too deeply, and bring them back when you see they are cold." Matthew placed Eric closest to Elizabeth's neck, and then Raquelle wrapped her arms around Eric's waist. "Hang on tight, kids!" Matthew urged. Elizabeth backed into the water, then jetted out a short distance to swim in circles close to shore. The crowd on shore stared in awe at this exhibition, and then turned to Matthew.

Then they were on him like vultures, everyone asking questions at once. Cameras were flashing. Microphones were in his face. The din was uproarious. Matthew finally said, in his most friendly Texas drawl, "Look, folks, I don't know much more than y'all do. I was just swimming, and suddenly this creature came up under me and just lifted me out of the water. I saw that she was friendly, thought it might be fun for the kids to take a ride… and that's it! Guess I've always had a way with animals." He smiled weakly and shrugged his shoulders. "And now, if y'all don't mind, I would like a little breathing space. I'll talk to y'all some more later on, if you want."

The crowd fell back; miraculously, even the news hounds let up on their pursuit, allowing Matthew to take a solitary walk up the beach a ways. He stopped and stood on the shore, watching his children and thankful that his life still, apparently, had meaning. Eventually he would figure everything out — maybe — little details such as how he'd gotten here, and why — but for now, he had a little boy and girl to look after.

Then he began to contemplate raising two children alone. It would be hard, but he would be a good father. They really needed a mother, and he could sure use a wife… Which made him think of Shalee again, and tears welled up as he thought, *Gone*. He wondered how she had died. Somehow he would have to find out.

Well, he knew one thing: if he ever had the great good fortune to get married again, he would know how to treat his wife. This time, he would appreciate her, and he would make her know he appreciated her every day of her life.

From behind him, he heard a soft, sweet voice, "I cannot get over it! You have such control over that beast, even trusting your children to ride it!"

Matthew cautiously turned to see who had spoken, and he beheld a gorgeous blonde in a very tight bathing suit that looked as if it were made of doeskin. Her beauty surpassed even that of Eric's Viking virgins. But there was one big difference now: Matthew was a free man.

Matthew hoped he was not drooling as he smiled and asked, "Is that a Swedish accent I detect?"

Her blonde hair bounded up and down as she nodded and said, as if she were making an observation about the weather, "You are very handsome." Then she laughed. "You know, you look much like the gentleman on this beer label!"

Matthew noticed for the first time that she was holding a bottle of beer, some dark brew called Saint Something-or-Other. Geez, must be that the micro-breweries had invaded Scotland too. The girl held the label up so he could look at it more closely, and he saw with a start that the painting on the bottle did, indeed, look as if it could have been a likeness of him, dressed in highland garb. Even more surprisingly, the beer was called "Saint Matthew's."

"Surely that is not intended to be the biblical Matthew," he mused aloud.

"Oh, no," the girl said, laughing and fixing her clear blue eyes on him. "This is Saint Matthew of Loch Ness, known around here as the man who killed all of the dragons in Scotland. They say it happened one thousand years ago." Her eyes would not leave him.

"Do you believe such tales?" Matthew asked, returning her stare with an equally flirtatious one of his own.

"Well, look around you!" she said. "There are no dragons at Loch Ness, and I hear tell there are no dragons in all of Scotland." Then she reached over and touched him lightly on the shoulder, and her touch felt electric to Matthew, who had not had a woman since... well, he honestly couldn't say since when. He realized she was speaking to him again, asking him, "Shall we have dinner together tonight... about eight? There is going to be a magnificent display of fireworks right here on the beach. We can watch them together. I would like that very much, would you not?"

Matthew stared intently at the blonde's body and thought, *Yes! There is a God in heaven!* Little by little he was starting to come back to life, and he was relieved to know that his appreciation for beautiful women had survived intact. He was just about to accept the invitation when suddenly, from his right, there came a sweet, sharp, and oh-so-familiar voice. The voice said, "Back off, Blondie, this one is taken."

The blonde shrugged, looked at Matthew, and retreated. And then Matthew turned to face Shalee in a skin-tight bathing suit, made of a soft material that was the tawny shade of a lioness. Her words were stern, but her eyes were smiling as she said, "I swear, Matthew, you attract blondes like a magnet."

Matthew could only blurt out, "Shalee! Raquelle said you were... gone!"

Shalee looked at him as if he had momentarily lost his mind. "Of course I was gone, silly. But the conference ended early, so now I'm back. I thought we could take a swim, have an early dinner together and go watch the fireworks afterward. And then, who knows... maybe make a few fireworks of our own."

Matthew looked at Shalee's long black hair, shimmering with that glorious tinge of blue as it flowed in the breeze. She was even more beautiful than he remembered. He swept her off her feet — literally — and onto the beach, covering her with kisses. Between kisses Matthew said, over and over, "You are my wife!"

Shalee could only giggle. She finally gasped, "You act like you haven't see me in a thousand years. Uh... before we get too involved here, where are the kids?"

With great force of will, Matthew drew away from her and, still staring into her green eyes, pointed in the general direction of the Loch. "They're out there riding..." And then he realized he probably had some explaining to do about Elizabeth. At that moment, however, both children came running up, flushed and happy from their ride, and Matthew looked toward the Loch just in time to see the movement in the water as Elizabeth submerged and disappeared.

"Oh, gee, Mom and Dad are at it again," Raquelle said to her brother, at the same time that Eric shouted, "Mom! You'll never guess what we just did!" Matthew and Shalee had sat up by now, trying to compose themselves, and before Shalee could reply to Eric, Raquelle burst out, "We just took a ride on the lake guardian… on Nessie! But her name isn't Nessie, it's Elizabeth!"

"That's nice, dear," Shalee said, giving each child a hug and winking at Matthew as if to say, *Kids and their imaginations…* "Now, why don't you two go find Shanna, and see if she will take you to lunch. Oh, there's Shanna now."

As the children ran off towards the young red-haired woman who was smiling and waving at them, Shalee turned back to Matthew and said, "Now, where were we?" Matthew pushed her back gently onto the sand, kissing her deeply on the mouth, and then turning his attention to her creamy neck and shoulders. "Oh, I do love the feel of your mouth on me," she whispered, "and I want to feel it all over me. If you don't stop, we may end up doing it right here on the beach. Is that what you really want?"

Matthew's eyes looked into hers, and then he said, in his most perfect Scottish brogue, "If I say, aye, lass, what would be your answer?"

Shalee replied, in an equally perfect Scottish accent, "I love ye to your bones, Matthew Wolverine. So… do as your heart desires, my soul mate."

*　*　*

It was after midnight, and Shalee slept peacefully beside him in the huge bed, worn out from their lovemaking, but sleep would not come to Matthew. He lay awake in the hotel room, listening to the boom and crackle of the fireworks that still lit up the sky to welcome the new era of Scottish independence. But the fireworks were not what kept him from sleep. His thoughts were racing.

A man could drive himself crazy pondering the imponderable, but Matthew could not stop his mind from going over and over the mystery of how he had ended up here, with this raven-haired woman who appeared to love him passionately, and had borne him the two gorgeous little children who slept in the next room.

Talking to Shalee and subtly digging for details throughout the day, he had established the particulars of his life. He was still a very successful businessman — though apparently quite the philanthropic, pillar-of-the-community type, and not at all the cutthroat hardball player he remembered himself being. He still lived in Texas, still in Houston, as a matter of fact, and he and Shalee and the kids, along with Shanna, their Scottish *au pair*, were here on summer vacation to celebrate their heritage and help the Scots rejoice in the commencement of a truly independent Scotland. Shalee had also attended a writers' conference in Edinburgh — it seemed she was a successful author and illustrator of children's books, and her latest, *A Ride on Nessie*, was an international bestseller. This book had been inspired by Raquelle's and Eric's obsession with the Loch Ness monster; both children had eagerly anticipated this trip because there had been many more "Nessie sightings" since the beginning of the new millennium.

A new era, a new millennium. Everything felt new and splendid and alive with promise.

And yet, and yet…

For the hundredth time Matthew mulled over the possibilities. Maybe, by making that journey back in time to Loch Ness and befriending the lake guardians and killing the dragons, he had created some ripple in the scheme of things and had somehow changed the course of his own history. Or perhaps that distant life with Cate and Rachel had been nothing but a prolonged dream with a very bad ending. He had no tangible proof of that life, in any case; there was no sign anywhere of that old knapsack of his. And probably it was just an interesting coincidence that the hill he knew as Carn Mhic was known to the locals as Caitlin's Hill, which, legend had it, was given that name by the lord of a castle that had stood in this area around the turn of the last millennium, or so most folks thought.

Matthew had picked up *that* little tidbit from the bartender as he and Shalee sipped wine while waiting for their table in the restaurant that evening. He had spotted a picture over the bar, a beautiful photograph of what he could have sworn were Texas bluebonnets in early spring. But no, said the bartender, this photo had been taken on a hill not too far from Loch Ness — the Gaelic name was Carn Mhic, but people around here had always called it Caitlin's Hill. The castle lord of old had given it this name in honor of his young wife, lost in some tragedy that had been forgotten over the centuries. Supposedly she was buried on the hill, though no remains had ever been found. What was known was that this hill was home to many species of wildflowers, including some that did not bloom in any other part of Scotland. "They sure do look like Texas bluebonnets," Matthew murmured.

What was real, and what wasn't? Maybe that whole Scottish interlude a thousand years ago had been a dream as well. Maybe he'd had a mild stroke or was suffering from amnesia or some rare sort of delusion or… But what about Shalee? She was very real — praise God! — and she looked exactly like the beautiful black-haired woman he had known in ancient Scotland, though the Shalee of here and now was in her late thirties. And how was it that Elizabeth knew him? Elizabeth was definitely for real too, and so were the crowds of gawking tourists and the hordes of news media types that had descended upon him and wouldn't even leave him alone while he and Shalee tried to share a romantic dinner. Matthew was the hero of the day; everybody wanted to interview and photograph this affable Texan who had not only brought Nessie into the clear light of the public eye, but had ridden on her back.

The more he wondered, the more confused Matthew became. The only thing that seemed clear was that he had been given a second chance. Or a third, depending upon what was real…and what wasn't.

So maybe he should just chalk it up to grace, and let it go at that.

With this thought, a wave of peace washed over him, and he knew sleep wasn't far behind. Probably he would never know what had happened to him, or why. In that respect, he wasn't so much different from all of the other sentient creatures that have been thrown "into the Universe and why, not knowing," as the poet Omar Khayyam once wrote. But despite all of the answers that eluded him, there were three things Matthew Wolverine did know for certain, on that fragrant night, in that fine old hotel room in Scotland, on the threshold of peaceful slumber. One, he was lying in bed next to the most beautiful woman he had ever seen, in any era. Two, the Loch Ness "monster" was for real. And three, if that blonde had been correct, and he had no reason to doubt her, there were no more dragons in Scotland.

The End

still to come...

Matthew Wolverine just can't stay in one place (and time)! Be sure to join him for his next adventure, which takes place on the presently-lost continent of Atlantis. For more information, write to:

    TimeDancer Press
    14625 Greenville Street
    Houston, Texas 77015-4711

    Call toll free: 877-396-1308
          or 713-455-1073
    Or send an e-mail to scifiwriterforever@hotmail.com

Visit us on the web at www.TimeDancerPress.com

Want to share the adventure, but don't want to lose your copy? Then order more copies of

The Ultimate Dragon!

Copy the handy order form below, and mail orders to:
TimeDancer Press - U.S.A.
14625 Greenville St. • Houston, TX 77015-4711
or call 877-396-1308

Name: _____
Street Address: _____
AptNo.: _____
City: _____
State: _____
Zip: _____

Please send me _____ copies, at $14.95, plus $3.00 shipping & handling per book (US customers only. Foreign orders include $6.00 US per book). Enclosed is my check or money order in the amount of $_____

Please allow 1 ~ 2 weeks for delivery